Instead of Doing Nothing

A novel by Leigh Foley

ISBN-13: 978-0-9967897-8-3

To those who fight evil,
you have my infinite gratitude

Instead of Doing Nothing, 2025

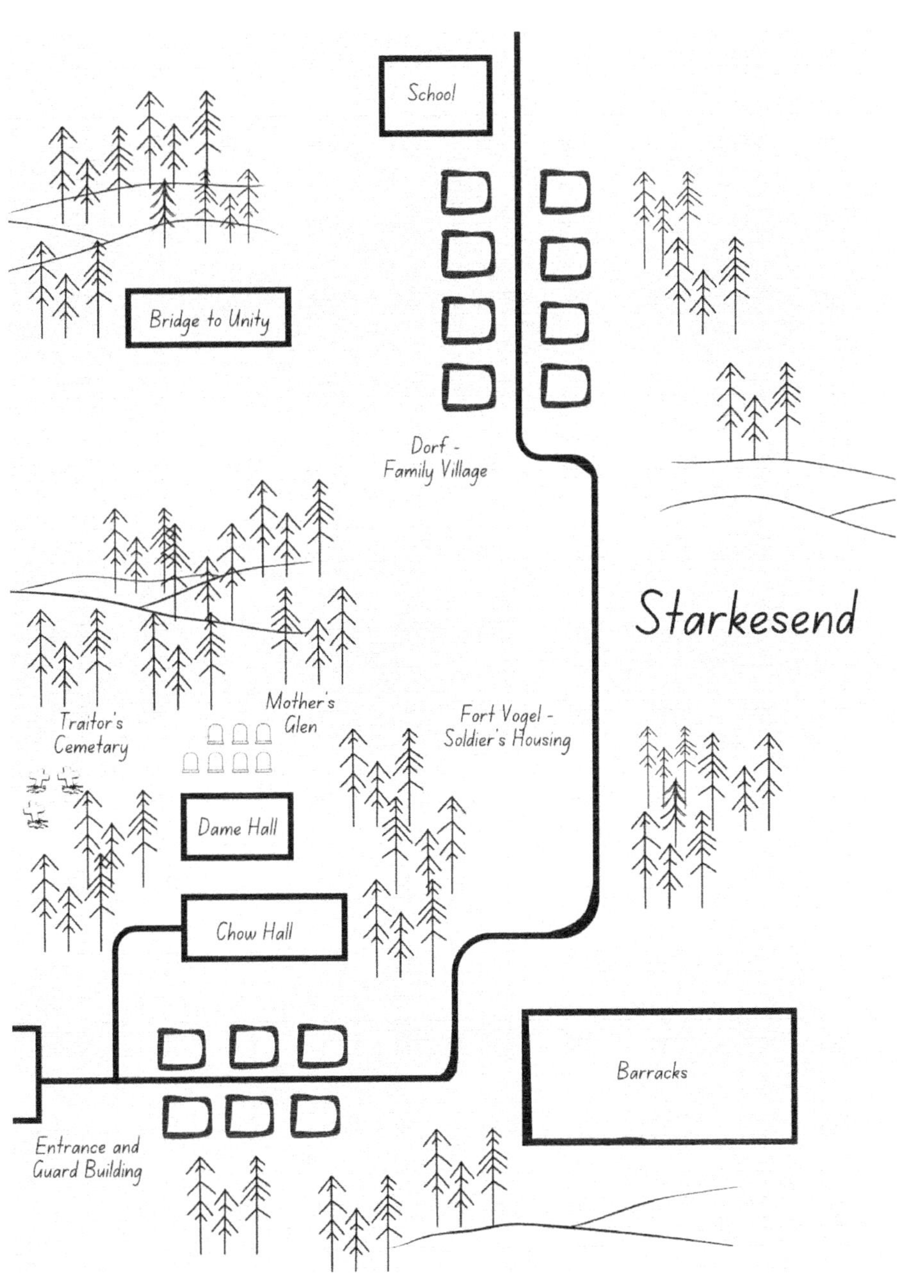

School
Bridge to Unity
Dorf -
Family Village
Starkesend
Traitor's
Cemetary
Mother's
Glen
Fort Vogel -
Soldier's Housing
Dame Hall
Chow Hall
Barracks
Entrance and
Guard Building

Lizbeth, 1936

Chapter 1 – Lizbeth

Oak leaves concealed my body as I withdrew the paper hidden inside my pocket. Last month, I'd written myself a message, scrawling the small rebellion while crouching behind my bed. Since then, I'd unfolded it hundreds of times. Always in private. Always with a mixture of fear and hope racing through my body. Getting caught with the note meant exile or worse—I knew this—but I kept the dangerous message.

The thrill was worth the risk.

I pushed thoughts of punishment from my mind and opened the note. Despite the paper's creases and smudges, the words were clear.

Eighteen-year-olds don't marry soldiers. You're almost there, Lizbeth. You can make it.

My lips stretched into a smile, and I read the message again. And again. Each time I cycled through the phrases, flutters of happiness expanded in my chest until I was weightless. Unburdened. The promising warmth pleased me, and I didn't want it to end, but I knew that it must. People noticed missing girls. Too much longer and the others would start searching.

I tucked the paper back into my pocket and peered between two branches. The tree grew in a blind spot, but I always checked for observers before emerging. It was safer that way. I kept my eyes open and my head clear. I also listened to gossip and paid attention to whispered words that might hint at a girl with a secret. So far, I've avoided any trouble.

A cold breeze slid over my skin as I stared through the leaves. I fought off a shiver, but there was no stopping my teeth from chattering. Thankfully, wind gusts masked the sound, and I scanned the area, making sure no one heard my body's reaction to the chill. After ten quiet seconds, I slipped from the oak's cover and merged onto the dirt lane that cut through Dorf, the village half of Starkesend. My leafy sanctuary was on the path's only curve. The rest of the road ran straight.

As I strolled, the sentences from my note replayed in my head. I got the most hope from seeing the paper—there was something reassuring about feeling the sheet between my fingers or tracing the handwritten letters—but even recalling the words provided comfort. I'd take any glimmer of positivity. It made the days easier to bear.

I strode toward the schoolhouse, keeping my face neutral, unsuspecting. When the dull brown building came into view, I picked up the pace, knowing the morning bell would soon ring. I didn't want to join the Sixteens and Seventeens standing outside the upper-grade hall, but I did. Because it was expected. My classmates huddled together, seeking heat to ward off the autumn weather. There was a small break at the back of the group, and I nudged my way inside. The warmth from twenty bodies welcomed me.

In moments like this, I almost forgot how little we had in common. My eyes closed and I lowered my head. I spent the last minutes before class nestled between two Sixteens, listening to them chatter about their future. A future involving a dashing soldier and a flock of children, of course.

The morning bell interrupted their conversation. Like clockwork, the group filed into the building, saluting the Nazi flag hanging just inside the door. We marched past the boys' quarters, where they've been studying since dawn, to the Matrimonial Classroom, our home away from home for the last six months. Today's course would complete our marital education. Then we'd be done with learning. In Starkesend, girls didn't need higher-level academics. Knowing about cooking, cleaning, and coupling was enough for our soft brains and overemotional moods.

The unfairness made my stomach turn.

Our teacher, a Pair Maker named Etta, stood in front of the room, smiling in welcome. For an adult, she wasn't so bad. Etta never hit us, and she used the blackboard frequently as she lectured, which I enjoyed. The smooth whoosh of chalk gliding across the enameled surface soothed me. The sound provided relief from the nauseating content of her sessions.

Etta's voice was also a comfort, her tone warm and measured. Exactly the opposite of the material she conveyed. I was glad she'd been selected as the instructor. The other Pair Makers spoke in a fiery style, making every phrase they uttered a call to action. I couldn't have handled a spirited sermon every day. At least Etta's communication made the past months tolerable.

I tuned in to her voice as she began the final lesson. "Good morning, girls. I'm very proud of you. You've shown up eager to learn and I'm pleased to say that after today, you'll be ready to run a successful household." Etta picked up a piece of chalk. "If you remember one item from our time together, I hope it is this."

The hem of her yellow frock swayed while she wrote on the board. The end of her chestnut braid followed suit. They danced together until she stepped back from the board, revealing words in a swirling script—*Fertility for the Fatherland.*

I cringed, instinctively loathing the phrase. The classmates in front of me leaned closer to the Pair Maker, rapt in their attention. In a blink, I copied their actions, trying my best to blend in.

"There are four letters in wife, and four in frau," Etta said. "Tell me, ladies, what else do these words have in common?" Hands shot into the air, waving around. I raised mine to match, hoping I wasn't picked.

Etta scanned the room before settling her gaze on me. "Lizbeth," she said.

I smiled demurely. The expected reaction. "Yes, ma'am. Wife and frau share definitions, and both contain an F."

The Pair Maker nodded. "Correct. For your final lesson, we will focus on the letter F and learn that it signifies your most precious asset. If you ever doubt the Starkesend mission, recall the phrase you see on the board." She pointed to the chalky script. "Fertility for the Fatherland. These words start with F, and they highlight your primary purpose. It's a purpose so vital, that without it, our community, and our Fatherland across the ocean, would crumble."

Etta was asking a group of teenagers to populate Starkesend and beyond. It was a heavy burden. Were my classmates as wary as me? I glanced at the nearest girls, and noticed their eyes glued to our teacher, hanging on her every word. While I wasn't ready to relinquish the little freedom I possessed, my classmates appeared keen to start the next phase of their lives. To begin their journey as bride and mother. To become another's possession.

My goals differed. For the past six months, throughout the lessons on wifely duty, I plotted a life far away. A life that offered more choice, more adventures, and more variety, items I would never experience if I stayed where I was. These factors grew in appeal the longer I listened to the expectations awaiting me. Marriage and motherhood were potential roles, but not until the future, when I was older. Now, I wanted to taste what the outside had to offer.

The biggest obstacle was fear. I didn't have the courage to speak with my parents yet, to convince them to pack up our family and flee the place we'd lived for over a decade. This level of bravery might take weeks or months to reach since the thought of leaving Starkesend still caused tremors to ripple through my body. It's startling what ten years of indoctrination does to a person. Paralyzing, really.

But once I turned eighteen, a mere nine days away, I'd be clear of marriage's immediate threat. Then I'd focus on building my nerve and nurturing my grit. Soon I'd be ready to discuss my dreams with my parents and pray they'd listen to me. I knew I'd have to leave on my own if not, a terrifying future. Until then, I planned to lie low, willing time to move faster, pushing me closer to my birthday and freedom from a forced marriage.

I wished time would fly in the matrimonial class, too. Etta lectured and the minutes dragged, so I filled them by visualizing the places I'd visit across America. Maybe even the world. The more you breathe life into a dream, the higher the likelihood it will happen, and inside my head, I was huffing and puffing as hard as I could.

The dismissal bell brought me back to the present. Etta motioned for us to remain seated, and when everyone quieted, she addressed the room. "Thank you for staying. I wanted to leave you with some thoughts. I'll speak quickly, since I know there are after-school chores waiting." She flashed a smile and began weaving between desks, touching each girl's shoulder as she passed. "I enjoy teaching this class. There's something special about the Sixteens and Seventeens, and it's not your youth or beauty. It's your attitude. Your excitement. You can't wait to grow up and have a family of your own. It's an admirable goal, and all we've discussed for the past several months. But let me give you one piece of advice."

Etta stopped at my desk, resting her palm on my shoulder. "Take care of yourselves. Pay attention to your mind and body. And if you need something, don't be afraid to reach out."

She removed her hand, returning to the front of the classroom. "I wish you health, happiness, and abundance." She curtsied, her back knee almost touching the ground. It meant we had her blessing. It meant we were women.

Etta spoke when she righted herself. "Go now. May only good line your path."

One by one, we returned her curtsy and filed from the room, raising our arm in the Nazi salute on the way out. Excitement buzzed around the schoolhouse, following us down the hallway, and outside into the yard. I allowed it to settle on my skin but not into my heart. It was fine to look happy. In fact, it was necessary. A shiny appearance discouraged prying, and I used that to my advantage. But absorbing the information was too much. I refused to conform.

With a wave, I left my classmates talking in groups. Their siblings were close in age, but I had a six-year-old brother I walked home every day, a favorite task of mine. The sun warmed my cheeks as I strolled, and a pair of thrushes chirped from their nest. The melodic notes lightened my mood, and a genuine smile snuck onto my lips.

When I reached the primary school, my brother bolted from the gray building and into my arms. I squeezed him tight, adoring the energy he emitted. Ellis possessed a contagious vibrancy, and I enjoyed the hours we spent together, playing hide-and-seek or tag. But our games took place behind closed doors, not outside, which meant now wasn't the time to indulge in Ellis' after-school exuberance. There were too many eyes, too many potential busybodies out in the open. It was best to wait until we got home to let loose.

I scanned the grounds, confirming we were alone. There was little danger of an observer reporting Ellis' enthusiastic exit, but still, I reminded my brother of his place. "Remember yourself, half-pint. Running is reserved for recess, not the halls. You don't want another markup."

His grin faded. "I'm sorry, Lizbeth. I saw you through the window, and it made me happy, so I ran out."

"I'm happy to see you too, buddy." I held out my arm. "Let's head home."

He took my hand, and we strolled down the dirt road that led to our house, passing twelve brown and tan one-storied rectangles before we reached our front door. I turned the handle, and Ellis rushed in. "No one can see me run here," he said, and circled the dining table twice.

"Have you gotten faster?" I asked.

"You really think so?" His eyes gleamed.

"I do. Not a doubt in my mind." I swung my gaze toward the sink. "Ready to wash the dishes? There's a sink-full waiting for us."

"Can I scrub today? I'll be careful. Promise."

I held my chin and considered his question, making a show of deliberating. "Ellis, now that you're the fastest person in the house, I think you're ready to scrub instead of dry. You've earned it."

He rushed to the pantry and grabbed his stepstool, dragging it to the sink. When he got settled on top, he patted the counter next to him. "Come on, Lizbeth."

I joined and helped fill the basin with soap and water. Ellis was serious about his new duty through half the stack of dishes. After that, he blew palmfuls of suds into the air, shrieking with delight as the bubbles floated around the kitchen. When I grabbed a handful and sent it drifting toward his face, Ellis doubled over with laughter.

That's when we heard the knock—a precise tap, tap, tap that cut through our merriment. Ellis stopped laughing and asked, "Race you to the door?" He flashed a gap-toothed smile before wiping at the soap on his chin.

I reached over, brushing the remaining suds away. "Is that a challenge, half-pint?" His eyes gleamed as he nodded. "All right, let's have a race. But take it easy on me." I squinted at the ground. "Oh. And watch out for the puddle on the floor. You wouldn't want to slip." I ran off while my brother looked down. It took him a few seconds to register my joke, and by then, I had reached the door.

"No fair," he said, but I could see his grin across the room.

"It might not be fair, but you fell for it," I laughed and waved him over. "Hurry up, silly, and I'll let you open the door. We don't want to keep our guest waiting."

Ellis loped toward the entry. After some giggles, he cleared the amusement from his face, fixing his features into a serious expression. My brother swung the heavy wood open, bowing deeply as he spoke. "Welcome to Dietrich Manor."

Silence was the only response to his polite words.

We peered down, noticing an object at our feet. A parcel rested on the wooden porch, the sole memento of the visitor who'd left in a hurry. Parchment was attached to the package with a ribbon, and a swirly font spelled out my name—*Lizbeth,* it screamed in looping letters. I picked up the small square, and although it couldn't have weighed more than a few ounces, it felt heavy as I brought it close.

I swallowed hard, knowing what this box and paper signified. Together they meant my childhood had ended.

To make sure, I opened the parcel with my thumbnail and found three pieces of chocolate resting on a bed of pink tissue. Normally, I would have delighted at receiving the confections, but this delivery represented something horrendously wrong.

"What's that?" a voice piped up.

I'd forgotten my brother was on the porch. I turned his way. "Oh Ellis, it's nothing. Just a little treat. Why don't you go inside, and I'll join you soon."

"Okay," he hesitated, "but you look funny. Not like I do when I get a treat."

I reassured him with a smile. "Go ahead. I'll be right behind you." He ambled, glancing over his shoulder every few steps. I kept the encouraging grin on my face until he was out of view, then my worry reemerged.

Before I was sure of my fate, I needed to verify one more item. The box's ribbon untied easily, and I grabbed the letter that fell loose. I unfolded the thick paper and read with growing horror, the words on the sheet confirming my fears.

Dearest Lizbeth,

We request the honor of your presence at the exciting Frau Rennen, which begins at sunrise on August 26th. As a Seventeen, you have the opportunity to cheer on our triumphant warriors as they race to the finish line. This event will mark the beginning of your glorious future.

Warmest regards,
Your Pair Makers

Tomorrow I would become a wife. Tomorrow I would lose myself. Tomorrow would destroy my dream of leaving Starkesend.

"It's not fair," I choked out. Misery pulsed through my veins, matching the rhythm of my heart. The staccato beats were like pinpricks, and they jabbed me from the inside. Why me? Why now? I would have escaped this cruel fate in nine days, when I turned eighteen. Instead, my world had receded. A scream rose in my throat, but I clenched my jaws, stifling it. I didn't want anyone else knowing about my pain.

The door creaked behind me. "Lizbeth?" Ellis asked, his voice unsure.

I closed my eyes, gathering strength. There was no use upsetting my brother. He'd be sad enough in the morning when his big sister left. I turned and forced a grin. "You're just the person I wanted to see."

Ellis' worried expression faded. "Are you coming inside?"

"You bet." I stepped forward and scooped him into my arms, holding tight to his little body. "I'll miss you, Ellis," I whispered, the words escaping before I could stop them.

He squirmed out of my grip, fixing me with a curious gaze. "Where are you going?"

His sweet voice pushed me over the edge, and tears slid down my cheeks. I rested my head on his chin, hiding my sorrow before he noticed. "Don't worry about it, half-pint. Let's finish the dishes before Mom and Dad get home." When I released our hug, he ran to the sink, distracted by the chore. I wiped at my eyes, then called out, "I need to freshen up. Why don't you work on the bowls, and I'll be back before you know it."

"Okay." He grabbed a dish, singing under his breath as he worked. "A is for ant, a tiny little guy. B is for bat, who flies so very high. C is for cat, who goes meow purr. D is for dog, who chases after her."

The joyful verse followed me as I picked up my mail and brought it to the bathroom. A quick splash of water calmed the redness on my face. Ripping the unwanted invitation eased my anxiety. Flushing the chocolates quieted my fury. My family didn't need to deal with these symbols of dread and destroying them gave me a small measure of control. A minute of breathing steadied me enough to return to the kitchen, assuming my place beside a beaming Ellis.

"Do you want to learn the alphabet song, Lizbeth?" he asked.

"Is that what you were singing?"

"Yep. We learned it in school." He flapped his arms. "My favorite part is about the sparrow. I bet you'll like the bouncy, flouncy rabbit."

"You know me well." I tousled his hair, happy for the distraction. "Teach me the song, and we can give Mom and Dad a concert."

Excitement filled his eyes. "Good idea. You start with A, just like the real alphabet."

For the next thirty minutes, Ellis guided me through twenty-six animals and their adventures. By the time our parents walked in the door, we could recite the song as a duet, switching back and forth between the letters. We'd moved to the sofa, and Mom and Dad came right over.

"Hey, you two. It sounds like you're having a good time. Can we join in?" my father asked.

"Right here, Dad." Ellis moved over, patting the spot next to him. I scooted over too, and when everyone settled, we launched into our tune.

After we finished to a round of applause, I turned to my brother. "Half-pint, would you give me a minute to talk privately? I'll come get you when I'm done."

He nodded. "Sure, Lizbeth. Is this about your package?"

I nudged him toward his room. "It's nothing for you to worry about. Just boring adult stuff."

He trudged down the hall, drawing out each step, but eventually, I heard his door close. Before I could say anything, my mother wrapped her arms around me. "We heard about the Frau Rennen. How are you feeling?"

I lost my composure at her words. "Mom, what can I do? I don't want to get married, especially to a soldier. Especially after what happened to Klara."

Almost two years ago, at the first wife race, my sister Klara was paired with a man whose exposure to death and destruction had tainted his soul with violence. After less than a year of marriage, her husband's wrath slipped out one night and tiptoed to my sleeping sister. He interrupted her peaceful slumber with rough hands that no longer differentiated between love and war.

In death, they said Klara had a smile on her face, like she was pleased to have perished while serving the aims of her community. Like she was delighted to have died at the hands of her husband, the man she matched with at the Frau Rennen.

I didn't want to end up like her.

Mom pulled me close, and Dad joined the embrace. They held me for a moment before my father spoke up. "Lizbeth, everything will be okay. Trust the process. There's nothing we can do besides that."

I clenched my fists, furious at their indifference. They were supposed to be my protectors, and instead, they were letting go without a fight. "May I be excused?"

"Of course, sweetheart. We're here if you need to talk," Mom said.

My tears waited to fall until I was in my room. I wiped the drops with my hem. The misery darkened the fabric, leaving blotches of emerald on the spring green. I stared at the stitches along the bottom of my dress. They were precise and uniform, resembling the rigid structure Starkesend praised.

I couldn't stand looking at them.

In a flash, I rummaged through the trunk at the end of my bed. My sewing kit was at the bottom, and I threw it on the mattress. Spools of thread rolled out and needles sparkled on the blanket, but the item I wanted remained inside the burlap pouch.

I reached inside, freeing the scissors. The steel would cut through my cotton frock without issue. No more precision. No more uniformity. Only shreds.

I hacked through the fabric, cutting through the stitches that mocked me with their exactness. Not satisfied, I reached into my pocket and brought out the note that had given me hope earlier this morning. I sliced through the paper, knowing my wish to escape marriage would never become reality.

Pieces of paper fell to the floor. So did the broken fragments of my heart.

After I finished cutting, a thought came to mind. I abandoned the shears, and instead overturned the sewing kit, spilling what remained in the pouch, hoping my mother hadn't borrowed what I sought.

But they were there. The embroidery scissors gleamed against the bedspread, seeming to agree with my plan. I tucked them into my slip's bodice, careful to avoid the point. The cool steel rested against my skin, chilling me.

My weapon wasn't the biggest or sharpest, and I might not be brave enough to use it when the time came, but for now, I had something. The scissors were my only form of defense.

Chapter 2 - Lizbeth

At sunrise, I reported to the Frau Rennen. The marathon ended in a wooded expanse, and a ribbon strung between two firs marked the finish line. The peach fabric sliced through the air, its only job to wait for impact. When the winning soldier passed through, it would flutter to the ground, having served its purpose. It may be plucked from the grass and thrown away, but it would never be used again.

How many of my classmates would meet the same end—given a run through, then discarded? The thought stopped my breath and caused a hollowness in my chest. We were merely prizes to be won, objects to be owned. It hurt to realize, to really, truly understand our insignificance. The kernel of hope I nurtured while planning a life outside Starkesend shrunk to a pinhead, and I could feel it retracting further. My dream was in danger of disappearing.

I brought a hand up, and touched the steel nestled against my heart, tracing its outline through my bodice. My secret grounded me. It gave me strength. I pushed the scissors into my skin, enjoying the pressure and cold density of the metal. The sensation reminded me that I was composed of flesh, and not just a thing.

After a second more, I dropped my arm and continued into the field. Workers had decorated the surrounding trees with slender pieces of tulle. The material swayed gently in the breeze, beckoning passersby. Arrangements of rose and hydrangea dotted the grassy field, bursting with brightness, releasing their perfume.

To me, the frills were a mask, an attempt to beautify a terrible reality by hiding the evil simmering below the surface. Who could be suspicious when flowers and gauzy fabric were strewn about? Starkesend's leaders knew they could disguise the ugly truth with a little sparkle.

And it was working. I glanced around, taking in the other girls. Not a single person appeared bothered. If anything, my classmates were the happiest I'd ever seen them. Each maiden wore a frock in spring green, the shade of a budding bloom. Like their dresses, my classmates' expressions coordinated as well. Dazzling smiles and ringing laughter rounded out their ensembles. There was no questioning their joy. They were looking forward to marrying a soldier. I was alone in my dismay.

Besides the Sixteens and Seventeens, Pair Makers were the only others present. The yellow they wore complimented the pale green of their charges, a purposeful choice. Where the brides-to-be were flowering beauties, the Makers were their nourishing sun.

In addition to teaching us, the group of four women oversaw the Frau Rennen by coordinating matches between a soldier and lovely lass. To do this they collected stats, dimensions, and pedigrees. They also compiled each man's wish list. Since there were only twenty girls and over fifty men, final matches were conducted after the winners finished the race. At this point, Pair Makers inserted everything into a complex formula that guaranteed marital bliss for years to come, according to our lessons.

Because of the contrast in numbers, some participants met their demise during this all-out quest for a mate. The marathon's steep climbs and treacherous swims became the final battles they fought. To have survived the atrocities of war only to be killed by the thirst for young flesh was a tragedy of a different sort, one I had no sympathy for.

But it was best not to focus on these things. Dark thoughts at such a grim event would only pull me further down. My mind needed a boost, so I forced myself to walk around, move my body, and try to enjoy the remaining moments of my childhood. Activity wouldn't start until racers reached the final bend, leaving plenty of time to calm my mind and prepare for what was to come.

I heard familiar voices from a circle of maidens and smiled when I recognized my neighbors. Talking with them might alleviate my growing panic or at least lower its level. I headed over, and when I neared, they enlarged their ring to let me in. There was barely a pause in the lively conversation.

Marta, another Seventeen, giggled. "I'm sure they'll match me with Aren. He's so handsome, and I know he likes blondes."

A second voice chimed in. "I hope the Makers pick Nicholas for me. He wants a large family, and it's my fertile time right now." She scanned the eager faces. "Can you imagine? Me, a mother? I'm lightheaded with anticipation."

Marta responded. "Don't faint now. You'll have plenty of time for that in the bed chamber tonight." She gave a coy smile, attempting to convey the knowledge she clearly lacked. "And anyway, I don't care who I'm matched with. If it's Aren, swell. If it's Wilmer"—she paused and grimaced—"I'll make do. Honestly, getting a husband is the only thing that matters to me. I'm happy to do my part and support our warriors."

Without warning, Marta's attention turned to me. "Lizbeth, what about you? I bet you'll get placed with a general or something. Your father knows people."

Her suggestion made me nauseous, but I knew how to respond. "Yes, that would be lovely." Thankfully my answer was enough to satisfy. The girls swung their attention to a new topic and began discussing which baby names were the most patriotic.

I had approached the group to relieve my anxiety, but their chatter worsened everything. These were no longer the girls I'd grown up with, they were citizens through and through. The years of brainwashing had worked. Groupthink had replaced individual thoughts and desires, making events like the Frau Rennen a cause for celebration rather than alarm. This was a glee-filled party brimming with beauty. The colorful decorations and promise of marriage were alluring to everyone. Everyone but me. I knew this day didn't guarantee a happy ending. Klara's murder proved it.

A shout rang out from the finish line, breaking my reverie. "I see them! Soldiers are rounding the bend."

Marta turned to the commotion, then back to the group. "Let's hurry over and welcome the winners." Everyone around me disbanded, running toward the action with eager smiles. Marta hesitated, "Are you coming, Lizbeth? The view's better up there." I shook my head, and she flashed a grin. "I'll save you a spot in case you change your mind." She left and joined the crowd, raising her arms and clapping like the rest of the girls.

I turned away from the noise, relishing my final minutes of peace. The shouting gradually died down, and after twenty men finished, the Pair Makers assembled to complete their calculations. Every few minutes, squeals of happiness cut through the air. Matches were announced, and the duos were ushered off.

After some time, I heard my name. "Lizbeth, come this way, dear. We're ready for you," a Pair Maker called out. My stomach dropped, but I made no move to acknowledge her. "All right then," she sighed. I heard footsteps approach, and when they reached me, the Maker laid a gentle hand on my shoulder. I walked with her to the coupling area, keeping my eyes on the ground.

"Here we are. It's time to meet your soldier. You're very lucky, dear. He placed first in the race." The Maker retreated, and another person took her place. When a muscular arm brushed against mine, I raised my head to peer at the man who would soon be my husband.

Screams burst from my throat when I saw Gunnar Cruse staring back.

The Makers had matched me with Klara's murderer.

Chapter 3 - Lizbeth

A calloused hand cut off my screams. I scanned the coupling area, desperate for help, but no one was nearby. Gunnar and I were by ourselves. I was alone with my sister's killer. My heart pounded and a shudder passed through my body. Would he hurt me like he'd hurt Klara?

I tried to step back, but Gunnar leaned in and whispered, "Relax, Lizbeth. I didn't mean to startle you."

The softly spoken phrase did more startling than the hand over my mouth. In my imagination, Gunnar possessed a raspy voice, and the words he uttered would sound like a snake's hiss. This wasn't the case. Gunnar's voice wasn't coarse or gruff. If anything, his words were comforting. I stopped struggling to free myself and focused on his eyes. Concern and curiosity were the only emotions I noticed.

Now I was more confused than ever. This was the man who had murdered my sister a year ago. After her death, he had returned to war, and tales of his bravery and unquenchable patriotism were repeated in every household. To have praise given with such reverence was only reserved for those who would do anything for their society. This included killing innocents and plundering their lands. The voice that flowed from Gunnar belied this. He sounded trustworthy and kind, but I knew better.

I snapped to attention, pushing him away. "Don't put your hands on me. I'm not a baby who needs hushing."

"I was only trying to help. The way you were screaming…well, I thought you might topple over. Stopping you from falling was the only thing on my mind. I'm sorry I've angered you." His words sounded genuine.

This was all wrong. Gunnar wasn't supposed to be polite or helpful. I knew corruption was buried inside him, but it should have been showing more clearly on his face and through his mannerisms. His misdeeds should taint everything about him, and evil should seep from his pores. That wasn't the case, and I didn't know what to make of it.

"Can we please leave? It's been a long day, and I'd like to rest," I said.

"Yes, we can go as soon as everything's complete. We still need to be Joined as husband and wife to make our commitment official. Your yelling stopped the ceremony, so we'll need to tell the Makers we're ready." He tilted his head. "Should we let them know?"

The ceremony. I had forgotten about it in my panic. For the union between Gunnar and me to be recognized, we had to recite our vows in an event called the Joining. The last six months of my training involved learning the vows I would say during this ceremony. I had honed them to perfection and could recite them with no hesitation. Although I had doubts about society and its practices, learning lessons was an entrenched part of my habits. While I had memorized the Joining's ceremonial aspects, I hoped I would never have to use them, but that is not how my life unfolded. In only a short while, I would speak the words that would bond me to my husband. That is, if I went through with the wedding.

Thoughts of my older sister's death and Gunnar's calming voice conflicted in my head. I was terrified of him, but I was intrigued at the same time. Maybe I could discover details about Klara's life with this man. When a Sixteen or Seventeen is matched at the Frau Rennen, they leave their childhood home and never return. Klara lived with Gunnar for a year before her murder. What had she done while she was with him? I'm not sure why the question hadn't occurred to me before, but now that it was in my head, I couldn't let it go.

If I Joined with Gunnar, maybe I could learn more about my sister's final days. The person who would have the most insight was staring at me, waiting for an answer. I hated him, it's true, but he didn't look dangerous. He didn't sound dangerous. Perhaps there was more to Klara's death than I was told.

I pressed a hand against my chest, locating my steely secret before replying. "Yes. Let's tell them we're ready."

I approached Gunnar with trepidation, and he linked his arm with mine. We made our way to the white tent where our union would occur. The ceremonial structure was quite splendid, like everything related to the Frau Rennen. Painted roses, hydrangea, and lilac decorated the outside walls, their silver color so similar to the tent's white that they appeared to shimmer in the sun. Light beams danced and reflected off the lustrous shapes, twinkling at everyone who passed.

The tent was called the Bridge to Unity, and I was about to partake in a ritual created by the settlers of our state. My people enjoyed customs, especially ones that touched on the beautiful aspects of our world, and the Joining of a soldier and his new bride was about as wonderful as anything could get, at least in the eyes of most.

Gunnar's grip was light, but he led us to the Bridge to Unity with determination. After parting the front flaps, we stepped inside and waited for our eyes to adjust to the difference in lighting.

When my vision cleared, a gasp escaped my throat.

A dim, flickering glow provided the only illumination in the vast space. The tent appeared sizable from the outside, about as big as four houses put together. The internal perspective was infinitely greater.

Candles were lined up in precise rows that stretched until they reached the same point at the end of the room. A towering altar is where the lines of waxen light-givers coalesced and more melted on the surface of this structure. The orange-yellow light from the totality of flames was shocking when you compared it to the inky shadows that dominated most of the Bridge to Unity. The combination of absolute darkness with the ever-moving light from the candles made the tent appear to continue forever. Where no light reached, the rich ebony of shadows created an almost tangible blackness. It was like gazing into the night sky. You never noticed a starting or an ending point to the vastness.

The illusion shattered when someone came through the entry. Dazzling sunlight shot through the gap in the tent flaps. This beam brightened the entire area for a few moments. That brief snippet of time was enough for me to locate the corners of my surroundings and know there were boundaries to its size.

I saw the Bridge to Unity for what it was—a large room. An ordinary space. Knowing that I wasn't standing in an unending passage of gloom lent the situation a sense of normalcy. I'd take whatever amount of ordinary I could get.

A Pair Maker spoke up. "Lizbeth, Gunnar, I saw you headed this way and came to offer my assistance. Welcome to the Bridge to Unity." She nodded at me. "Lizbeth, follow me, and we'll get you ready for the ceremony. Gunnar, someone will be along shortly to guide you in your preparation."

My vision was clouded by the burst of light, but I recognized Etta's voice. I remembered the first day she stepped in front of my class. Excitement had rippled through the rows of desks when she'd walked to the lectern to begin her lessons. Girls learned about the Frau Rennen from older siblings and mothers, but seeing a Pair Maker meant that becoming a soldier's bride was a possibility and not just a bedtime story.

Not every Sixteen or Seventeen married a warrior. Since the wife race only happened when the military completed a mission, the chance to become bonded with a hero only happened every so often, and the race today was only the second event.

When Etta began her lessons, I was seven months away from turning eighteen. I hoped my birthday would come before the soldiers returned home, but nine days had forced me into a role I wanted nothing to do with.

Unlike my classmates, being linked with a warrior was something I had nightmares about. In these dreams, my sister would warn me about the dangers of having a war-tainted husband. When she was alive, Klara had been as indoctrinated as my classmates were. Her pleasure at getting her Frau Rennen invitation was the opposite of my dread. I can still picture her beaming smile when we sat on her bed, talking about what her future mate would be like.

In death, her attitude had changed. Gone was the smile that decorated her lips the last time I saw her. Instead, her mouth twisted in horror, and each word she spoke was heavy with sorrow. Now in a direct dishonoring of everything she'd warned me against, I was being coupled with the man who was responsible for ending her life.

A nudge from Etta pulled me out of my thoughts. She offered her hand, and I took her fingers, allowing her to navigate us through the tent that had returned to shadows and candlelight. She moved with confidence through the darkness, so I trusted her guidance.

I tried to ignore the light-bending sensations because all they did was distort reality.

Paying attention to my surroundings was the best way to combat my fate. To defeat Gunnar and Starkesend, I must learn how each operated. Hypervigilance needed to become my new best friend because the more I learned, the better the outcome. The attentiveness would also help me discover clues about my sister.

I shook my head to clear it and felt my pulse return to its usual speed.

At the same moment, Etta stopped walking. I wasn't prepared, and almost tumbled away from her, into the darkness. Etta gripped my arm and helped me straighten. "This is where you'll put on your robes. Once you enter, there's no more speaking until you face Gunnar on the altar. Do you understand?" I nodded. "Good. Our time together ends here. You're a special one, Lizbeth, and I wish you nothing but happiness. If you ever need anything, let me know." She flashed a smile, then disappeared into the darkness.

In Starkesend, adults and children maintained aloof relationships, but I sensed sincerity in Etta's voice. For the first time, I felt connected to a high-ranking society member. I stored her words in my memory and hurried in the direction she'd pointed, careful to avoid the candles lining the path.

Chapter 4 - Lizbeth

As I neared the entrance of the bridal suite, a figure approached. It was another Pair Maker, and they motioned for me to follow. As we walked, the flickering light added grace to her movements. The Maker appeared to glide, and I wondered if my stride looked the same. The warm glow of the candles added a dreamy element to the experience, and it was a struggle to remain grounded, to stay immune to the otherworldly vibe.

I pinched the inside of my wrist, the pain clearing the languid haze from my vision.

When we entered the changing room, two girls were dressing for their Joining. A Maker assisted each almost-woman in getting the pieces of her garb exactly right. Ember, the closest to me, was adjusting her auburn hair in a silver-rimmed mirror.

The marital robe's golden fabric hung from her body like a flowing stream. A delicate lacy veil covered her face, and ornately stitched slippers peeked from beneath her hem.

The effect of the whole outfit was enchanting. Ember was usually a homely lass, but now she radiated beauty. Each piece of her silken attire complimented the flush on her cheeks and the thrill in her eyes. The veil could do nothing to mask her joy. It beamed through the airy material. Ember nodded at her reflection, then turned and floated toward the altar, where her groom awaited.

She must feel elated. I was terrified.

Was not fighting this marriage a mistake? It's true that my efforts would be immediately crushed, but maybe a failed rebellion was better than no rebellion at all. Perhaps my actions would reach the hearts of those in charge, and they would reconsider their oppressive ways. But cruelty had likely demolished their empathy. My resistance would be something they laughed at and rallied against, not something that opened their mind.

I inhaled sharply. Now, wasn't the time for defiance. My lack of power dictated that I accept my fate, at least for the present. I needed to remain passive and focus on learning about Klara, a task I would conceal. In a world where girls were given few choices, it was nice to keep something to myself, and I nurtured the spark of defiance as I walked across the changing room.

A Pair Maker waited next to the wooden chest that held my regalia. She waved me over, and at this point, training overtook my actions. While I had never been inside the Bridge to Unity, I had been over the ceremonial steps numerous times. When each girl turned sixteen, seamstresses made a robe for her to wear should she ever need it. Measurements were taken, and the garment created, but a girl did not see the finished product unless she received an invitation to the Frau Rennen. If her sixteenth and seventeenth years passed without a call to the event, her robe was recycled, and the material used for the next round of potential brides. Starkesend was as frugal with its supplies as it was with its compassion.

I moved toward the trunk, stopping in front of the Maker. She smiled and gestured to my clothing, reminding me it was time to undress. I did so slowly, careful not to upset the scissors in my slip. Mercifully, the cold weight stayed in place as I handed over my frock. It was the last time I'd see the green dress. The materials would be reused on a younger girl, one just entering her sixteenth year.

The Pair Maker held up my robe, unfolding it in rippling waves. She passed me the garment, and I took it, sliding the silk between my fingers before I put it on. The fabric slipped over my body without a hitch. The Maker held up a finger and circled it in the air. I turned around, and she tied the garment at the small of my back before nudging me toward the right, where slippers and a veil waited.

By now, I was the only person dressing. The silence became heavier after everyone departed, and I felt its weight from all directions. I rushed to pull on my shoes and place the veil on my head. Speeding up this process meant I would get to the alter sooner, something I was loath to do, but the room's quiet loneliness was disturbing. Almost maddening.

In less than a minute, my attire was in place. Several mirrors were placed throughout the dressing room, and I approached the closest one. A gasp escaped my lips.

The reflection staring back was the embodiment of brideliness, the model for how a girl was supposed to look during the most important day of her life. My honey-colored hair shone in the candlelight. The gown's champagne- fabric and lacy veil combined to create an aura of beautiful innocence. No wonder soldiers coveted the Sixteens and Seventeens. Possessing something this lovely was like winning the prize of a lifetime. Even through my unease, I saw the allure.

I turned away from the glass when I felt a light tap on my arm. The Maker who helped with my robe beckoned. Meeting Gunnar at the Matrimonial Altar was the next step in the Joining ceremony. She was here to lead me past the flickering rows of candles and up the steps that would take me to my betrothed.

The thoughts racing through my mind were more tumultuous than ever. I knew that Gunnar was a murderer, but this conflicted with how he'd treated me after the race. Either he was a cunning actor, or there was more to my sister's doom. Learning the truth about Klara's death suddenly became the most crucial thing in my life. Fulfilling my destiny and becoming a bride seemed like the only way that I would be able to untangle the mystery. After that, I could escape Starkesend. I was only pushing my plan back, not abandoning it.

I took a deep breath and followed the Maker into the main chamber. Gunnar was waiting at the altar. His crisp colonel's uniform glinted with medals, and his eyes gleamed with an eagerness that alarmed me. This marriage would happen, and he seemed as excited as I was nervous. His anticipation wasn't a surprise, but it was unsettling to see it in person. I was being confronted with a desire that I wanted no part of, and it made my stomach turn.

I ignored the queasiness and focused on my mission. Gunnar's knowledge would bring me clarity and finally answer my questions about Klara. It was enough to balance the distaste and keep me moving toward the altar's stairs.

A deep voice interrupted my timid ascent. "Come now, Lizbeth. There's nothing to be afraid of." The gray-haired officiant gazed at me expectantly.

I bowed my head. "Yes, dear Elder. I'm very sorry."

He chuckled. "There's no need to be sorry, child. Or worried." He turned to Gunnar, smiling. "You've got yourself a shy one here. Take care not to rush her."

Gunnar returned the grin. "Don't worry, dear Elder. I don't plan on rushing anyone. Lizbeth can take all the time she needs."

I didn't know what to make of his words, but I could think about them later. Now was the time to advance toward my future, to continue moving before unease overcame me.

Both men stared as I ascended the steps. Their gazes unnerved me, but I made sure not to show reluctance. It was better for them to see a bashful girl who needed a little encouragement, not someone sickened by what was happening. I made it to Gunnar's side and curtsied. He responded to the greeting with a salute.

Instead of returning his hands to his sides, Gunnar reached over and grasped my fingers. He gently maneuvered my body until I was facing him. We regarded each other in the candlelight, his gaze curious and mine guarded. His smartly creased uniform complemented my flowing gown. Our attire was designed with masculine and feminine in mind—he projected strength, while I projected softness.

Our society embraced these characteristics and highlighted them whenever it could. Men who were intense and brutal rose through the military ranks. Women who were nurturing and soft-spoken matched with high-ranking men. It paid to conform to these expectations.

For as long as I could remember, I'd concealed my true feelings, and from the outside, I appeared compliant. This was probably why I was matched with an officer.

The officiant began the ritual by recognizing family ties. "Gunnar of the Cruse line and Lizbeth of the Dietrich branch, I am here to join you as one. This power has been granted to me after many years of service to society, and I undertake this duty with the most believing of hearts. I, Elder Lang, am blessed to oversee the beginning of this divine coupling."

He paused and considered Gunnar. "Such a brave man deserves to be honored with beauty, for it is only when valor is tempered by grace that you will find true meaning. Your wife is the embodiment of feminine, and she will soothe your battle-weary soul."

Now it was my turn. He swung his gaze to me. "A timid girl needs a bit of brashness to fire up her hearth. You will grow more confident in your ability to ease troubled waters as time goes on. Your husband is the embodiment of masculine, and he will provide you with purpose and passion."

Elder Lang walked toward us and placed his hand atop our entwined fingers. "Gunnar, Lizbeth, when you leave the Bridge to Unity, you shall no longer be singular beings. Your bond will lift you and take you to heights you would not have reached alone. Together you will flourish."

He nodded at Gunnar. "You may now make your pledge."

"I, Gunnar of the Cruse family, pledge my loyalty and life to you, Lizbeth Dietrich. I will protect our union at all costs and fight off any harm that comes your way. Together we will serve Starkesend." Gunnar's voice was quiet but filled with determination.

I tried to match his resolve. "I accept your pledge and make my own in return. I, Lizbeth of the Dietrich family, pledge my loyalty and life to you, Gunnar Cruse. I will cherish your spirit and nurture our union in any way possible. Together we will serve Starkesend."

I added a separate pledge in my mind. *I vow to honor my sister. I will find out what happened to Klara.*

The Elder stepped back and lifted his hands. He gazed skyward and proclaimed the ceremony's final phrase. "Through unity, our society prospers. Blessed be the pair before me."

Although those were the last words spoken, our Joining was not complete. I'd been dreading this part, but there was no way to avoid it. With my eyes closed, I removed my fingers from Gunnar's grasp. It was time to finalize our match. I forced my breathing to slow and my hands to steady. Hot anxiety rolled through my body, but I pushed it down and found the strength to continue.

For my sister.

The lacy veil had gained the weight of my captivity since the Maker had pinned it on. Lifting it would feel freeing, but I would immediately become ensnared again, this time in the bindings of marriage—one burden in exchange for another. I pushed back the lace and leaned toward the man I knew so little about. His mouth met mine timidly, without force. We sealed our bond with the most fleeting of kisses. I was grateful for the brevity.

Elder Lang opened the curtain behind him, and Gunnar and I exited into the fading sunshine. The remaining daylight was welcome after the dim flickering inside the tent, although my eyes were grateful for the late hour. They adjusted to the purples and reds from the sinking sun, and I took one last glimpse of the Bridge to Unity before Gunnar led us away.

His grip on my hand was firmer than before, more controlling. From this point forward, I would remain under the watchful eye of my husband.

My husband. That would take getting used to. The label felt unnatural, forced, much like our union. My life had taken an abrupt turn—from washing dishes and laughing with Ellis to becoming the possession of the man who had killed my sister. Everything had changed in the span of a day, a heartbreaking, infuriating twenty-four hours. I knew there would be further shifts, and we headed toward them at a rapid pace.

Gunnar walked us to the north with brisk strides, along the roads of my village. We went past the market, the town square, and the schoolyard. I knew this area well. If we kept heading straight, we would pass my family's home.

My heart lurched at the thought. Everyone would be settling around the dinner table, talking about their days.

Most parents in Starkesend had a formal relationship with their children, but my mother and father were different. They spoke with Ellis and me and wanted to know our thoughts. I missed our conversations. Being listened to was rare in a place where children were seen only as tools to boost the population.

We continued, and I felt my excitement build. There were only six more houses to pass, and we would be at my childhood home. Maybe I would get to see my family one last time. Maybe I would get a final hug.

When we reached the familiar brown structure, Gunnar stopped. My pulse raced as I noticed light shining through the living room windows. That meant dinner was over, and leisure hour had started. My family cherished their time doing needlework or playing chess, but they would happily interrupt their fun to welcome me. I strode up the drive, anticipating their surprise.

Panicked words halted my steps. "Lizbeth, stop." I turned Gunnar's way, my face full of questions. His eyes were wide with panic. "You know the rules. I just…" He trailed off.

"You just what? Brought me here to torture me? To remind me of what I'll never have again?" The words burst out before I could stop them, but they were the truth. Visiting my childhood home had exhausted the resolve I'd built up over the course of the day. Now, the only thing I wanted was a hug from Ellis and my parents.

"Why did you bring me here, Gunnar?" Tears rolled down my cheeks, and a pleading tone marred my words.

He bowed his head. "I'm sorry I upset you, Klara. I thought you would be pleased to see your home one last time, but now I know it was the wrong idea." He peered up, tears shimmering on his face. "Can you ever forgive me?"

I froze at his mistake and struggled to find my voice. "What did you call me?" The question came out as a sob.

He blinked hard and shook his head, sounding more in control when he spoke. "What do you mean, Lizbeth? I was apologizing for my thoughtlessness." He smiled, wiping the moisture from the corner of his eyes. "Are you ready to start our life together?"

When I matched with Gunnar, I was frightened of his murderous rage. Now I was afraid he was losing his mind.

I stared at him, gauging his condition. His haunted expression had faded, and he appeared alert, lucid. While he waited for my answer, Gunnar scanned the perimeter, and I used the opportunity to find my weapon, to make sure it was still in place. The cold metal reassured me, and the faintest confidence flashed through my body. I could do this. I could handle whatever he threw my way. And it was only for a little bit, until I discovered more about Klara, and closed that chapter of my life.

"I'm ready to go," I said, and when Gunnar beckoned, I followed. Ever cautious. Ever observant.

Chapter 5 - Lizbeth

The journey to my new home passed in silence. Under normal circumstances, I was fine with quiet. In fact, I enjoyed the absence of conversation. It was wonderful to just observe the surroundings, rather than filling it with chatter.

But *this* quiet? This wasn't a comfortable silence—it felt uneasy, restless. So, rather than focus solely on the environment, I switched my attention back and forth between the passing scenery and Gunnar.

Although, I wanted to speak with my husband and gauge his level of sanity, I sensed he wasn't open to discussion. Gunnar resembled a well-regulated machine. His steps were rigid and measured, almost like he was marching. His breathing was in time with his pace—an inhale on the right foot, followed by an exhale on the left. Asking questions would throw off the rhythm he'd established, and I didn't know how he would handle an interruption. I remained hushed but attentive, noting every detail I could.

Growing up, I had remained inside the village's confines, having little reason to wander from Dorf's familiarity. Tonight, we journeyed outside the area I knew. While I wasn't sure how far we traveled, I did notice that the trees had grown thicker and the paths narrower the further along we moved. This observation wouldn't pinpoint my location but recognizing the changes gave me a small measure of comfort. The more I perceived, the better prepared I felt.

After hiking a while, Gunnar stopped at a hilltop, pointing to his left. I followed his finger and spotted a thick wall several yards away. There was a gate built into the barricade, with a lean-to situated near the entrance. "That's where we're going, Lizbeth. We're almost home."

I wondered about the purpose of the barricade. The village wasn't surrounded by a wall, and the precaution here seemed excessive. The forest enveloped Starkesend, and the natural cover prevented outsiders from stumbling upon the isolated community. Was the barrier designed to keep intruders out or residents in? Neither option was favorable.

As we approached the structure, I noticed shadows moving inside. Gunnar barked instructions into the night air. "Open up. It's Colonel Cruse. Don't keep me waiting." The shadows materialized into two uniformed men.

Both guards must have recognized the Colonel because they saluted in sync. Once Gunnar returned the gesture, they started the process of granting us entrance. Each man grasped a chain on opposite sides of the metal gate, and they pulled in tandem, groaning with the weight as the barrier lifted inch by inch.

When the gate was raised, the guards, approached with a clipboard in hand. "Good evening, sir, ma'am. May we have your paperwork?" the man closest to me asked in a curious, but firm tone.

Gunnar reached into his pocket and pulled out a thick envelope. "Everything is here, Conroy." He nodded in my direction. "This is Lizbeth. Make sure to add her to the bridal roster. We wouldn't want her missing out on anything."

Conroy opened the envelope and gave the contents a cursory glance. He passed it to his partner then turned back to us. "Yes, sir. We'll certainly add her to the list." He notated something on the documents he was holding. "Looks like you two are the last pair we needed to check in. Everyone made it here safely."

Gunnar appeared pleased with the information. "Good. Now excuse us, it's been a long day."

Conroy took a step back, giving us room to pass. "Have a nice night, Colonel."

Gunnar grunted a reply and walked past without pausing.

"Thank you for letting us in, sir." I nodded at the guard.

He smiled my way. "No need to call me sir quite yet. I still have a few more battles to win before that's necessary." He raked his eyes up and down my body. "But I'll fight anything for a prize like you." I froze in place, not knowing how to react. He winked. "Welcome to Fort Vogel, ma'am. We'll take good care of you here."

I picked up the hem of my robes and moved away from the lewd soldier, trying to put distance between us. When I felt safe, I dared a glance back and found Conroy staring my way with lust in his eyes. Like his wink, the unprovoked desire unnerved me. My cheeks burned with shame.

I checked to see if Gunnar had witnessed our exchange, but he was well ahead of me. Since we'd passed through Fort Vogel's gate, my husband seemed less interested in providing protection. The walls around us did inspire a sense of security, but I knew disturbing things could still happen behind barricades—Conroy's vulgar behavior was the perfect example of this. For now, it was best to stay with Gunnar. It was safer.

I caught up with him, before I let my guard down enough to observe our surroundings. Trees and wildflowers provided pockets of nature, but the overall feeling of the base was orderliness. Like Dorf, the buildings in Fort Vogel were bland but neatly kept. Houses only appeared in two colors— brown or beige—and no design features separated one from the next. Each rectangular home had the same number of windows facing the street, and the small front stoops all matched. Everything blended. Nothing was jarring. My new home was perfectly dull, something I was quite thankful for.

Too many pivots transpired today, and I was having difficulty maintaining equilibrium.

The Frau Rennen. *Pivot.*

Matching with Gunnar. *Pivot.*

Our Joining. *Pivot.*

And now, Fort Vogel. *Pivot, once again.* I wasn't sure I could handle much more.

This bland row of houses was an antidote to the chaos. I saw the structures and knew what was ahead. No surprises or shocks awaited me on the next street, only identical, drab rectangles bordered by the same greenery. Simplicity is the cure for commotion. It stilled my weary brain. It calmed my frayed nerves.

I trail Gunnar, basking in the consistency. When he stopped in front of a brown dwelling, I knew our journey had ended. He turned my way. "This is our home, Lizbeth. I hope you enjoy it."

He was relaxed and far different from the man who had marched me to this faraway place. I knew what to expect from the paint scheme in Fort Vogel, but I still didn't have a handle on Gunnar's mood. It changes rapidly, without warning. I'd have to stay on guard.

"Will you show me?" I asked.

"Of course, sweet wife. I'd like nothing better than to show you inside." He took my hand, gently this time, and walked us up the drive and onto the front porch. "Would you like to do the honors?" A small silver key rested on his upturned palm. He gestured toward the front door, willing me to say yes.

Before I could stop them, memories of my brother flooded through me— his smile, his laugh, the soap bubbles on his chin. *Did he miss me yet?* Thinking of Ellis threatened to destroy the tiny threads of acceptance I'd weaved, so I tucked the flashback away. If I were to survive, I had to exist in the here and the now. This door was not the same one Ellis opened yesterday. This door was the entrance to my new life.

I reached over, plucking the key from Gunnar's hand. The metal twisted smoothly in the lock, and the knob turned without protest. I took a step toward the entrance, but Gunnar stopped me.

"Not like that, Lizbeth. Let me help you." He lifted me and carried me inside. After he settled me on my feet, he bowed. "Welcome to Cruse Manor."

We entered through the kitchen. Everything around me gleamed with the shine of unuse. No decorations or personalization adorned the countertops or walls. The space was clean—too clean—and it appeared untouched.

From where I was standing, I could see most of the interior. A table, two chairs, and a cot are the only articles of furniture in the living and dining rooms. The space contrasted sharply with the warm and colorful atmosphere I'd grown up in. Maybe I'd be allowed to cozy up the space. I hoped so because the sterility was off putting.

Gunnar seemed to read my thoughts. "I know it doesn't look like much, but I was hoping you could make it feel more welcoming." He gestured to the cot. "It's rare that I spend a night at home. When I do, I sleep out here." His voice took on a somber tone. "The past year has been difficult. I'm glad that you're here now."

A year had passed since my sister's death, and it sounded like it had been a rough period for us both. But his melancholy didn't make sense when you considered that he was the reason for the turbulent interval. If it weren't for Gunnar's murderous actions, he wouldn't be feeling so awful. I could empathize with his hurt because I also felt the loss of Klara, but I couldn't sympathize. He would never have my understanding. He was a killer.

I moved past the painful topic. "Is there anywhere I can wash up? I'm tired, and a splash of cool water would feel nice."

He pointed to a closed door. "That's where you'll be staying, Lizbeth. We share the main washroom, but I set up a sink in your room. Extra blankets and towels are on the shelf in the corner, and some clothes are in the trunk near the bed. I think you'll find the room more than adequate."

"That's very kind. Thank you, Gunnar." I was confused. He made it sound like I would have the space to myself. That's not what I'd anticipated.

"Go ahead and get settled. I'll say goodnight shortly." He walked toward the room he'd pointed out but turned before reaching it.

I could hear him in the back of the house, the ordinary sounds of his bedtime routine slipping down the hallway. Perhaps the events of the day were finally coming to a close. The thought buoyed me as I walked into my room. The clean bed and bath were a welcome sight, and I locked the door before removing the marital apparel from my body. Despite the fabric weighing very little, it felt like I had shed a thousand pounds. I folded the robe and placed it in the chest, smiling as I distanced myself from the silken burden.

I searched the trunk, combing through garments I assumed were my sister's. Instead of bothering me, using Klara's clothes was a comfort. The mundane fragments of her existence were beautiful, and memories of home and family danced through my head while I rummaged around.

There weren't many items, so I located nightclothes quickly. The floor-length nightshirt was scratchy, but it had a pocket. After I slipped it on, I tucked my scissors inside, relived to keep them close in this unfamiliar environment.

A knock on the door interrupted my bedtime preparations. "Lizbeth? Would you please come out?" Gunnar asked in an odd voice.

My words were shaky. "One moment, please." Trickles of ice ran through my veins, freezing every inch of my body. This was it. It was time to become one.

The Pair Makers had told us about this part, describing it in a way more suitable to small children than the teenage girls they were talking to. They had explained that the most sacred role in society was that of mother. The wives with the most children received better rations and held higher ranks than their less fertile counterparts. Each year, ceremonies were held to celebrate the births that occurred. New mothers constantly beamed at these events, holding their babies smugly, proud of their elevated role.

My mom had three children, an ordinary number, but our neighbor, Lina, was the proud mother of nine. I saw the favoritism she was given. She got more choices with goods and was given six free hours a week, as opposed to my mom's two. Of course, being the perfect nurturer, Lina spent her leisure time helping the teachers at the primary school or knitting blankets to swaddle newborns.

I'd witnessed first-hand the benefit of having children. The Makers bolstered this idea when they explained the needs of our future husbands and how meeting those needs put us one step closer to motherhood. My classmates discussed how wonderful it would be if their wedding night was successful, and they became mothers right away.

I feigned agreement to blend in, yet I hoped I'd never have to satisfy the needs of a soldier. Or have a child with someone I was forced to marry.

But now, it was real. A spouse with expectations waited on the other side of my new bedroom door. I needed to maintain a charade to learn more about Klara, and my only option was stepping into my wifely duties.

Or I could craft an excuse to avoid Gunnar's attention. I plodded toward the door, gathering courage while scheming for options. My mind raced with pleas and justifications, but nothing seemed urgent enough. I closed my eyes and gripped my scissors. The courage they bestowed propelled me forward, and I swung open the door, expecting to see my husband on the other side.

Instead, he was sitting in the dining room, head in his hands. I approached timidly, clearing my throat when I reached him. "Gunnar, you called for me?"

He peered up, wiping tears from his cheeks. "Lizbeth. Thank you for coming out. I'm sorry if I've interrupted your evening preparations."

His sadness caught me off guard. "Gunnar, I didn't expect an apology. Of course, I came out. It *is* our wedding night." I hesitated. "But I do have something to tell you." I still wasn't sure of my excuse, but perhaps my mouth was more cunning than my brain, and it would come up with a reason on the spot.

Red creeped into his cheeks. "Lizbeth, there's something I need to tell you first. That's why I asked you out here." He took a deep breath before continuing. "I have to sleep alone." His voice quickened as he continued. "It's not what you think. I get angry if anyone gets close when I'm trying to relax." He lowered his eyes. "It's not always anger. Sometimes I'm sad. Sometimes I'm scared. I can't explain why. I just know I feel terrible every time another person tries to lie in bed with me."

I wondered if he'd warned Klara or if she was one of the people who had invoked his nighttime rage. "Gunnar, I don't understand. Why…why would you want a wife if you can't stand being close to people?"

"Because it's my right as a soldier." Steeliness replaced the shame in his voice. "There aren't many rewards for the time and dedication I've put into this life, and when I'm allowed to earn one, you can bet I take it."

A reward. That's all I would ever be. Not a person with their own thoughts, but a token of Gunnar's devotion to Starkesend. Adapting to this idea was tough, especially since I come from a family where I was valued. But if I were going to blend in and earn my husband's trust, I would have to play the expected role.

"You're right. I forget my place sometimes." I bowed my head. "Is there anything I can do to help?"

I heard Gunnar stand and walk toward me. I peered up when he clutched my shoulder. "There is something you can do, Lizbeth. Lock your door at night." His grip tightened. "And if you hear screaming, stay in bed."

Gunnar turned away and I took it as a signal to leave. I sped to my room, ensuring the lock was secure before lying down. My breathing had quickened, but it calmed as I stared at the ceiling. Despite the uneasiness his words caused, the eventful day caught up to me, and sleep quickly came.

∞∞∞

Screams didn't wake me that night. It was moaning. Gunnar's volume rose in crescendo after crescendo, and I sat up in bed. I strained my ears when I noticed a few words, but they were too muffled to recognize. One thing I heard clearly was the rattling of a metal object. It clanged loudly whenever Gunnar made a sound. I couldn't pinpoint its source from my room, so I would have to investigate in the morning.

Thankfully, it wasn't too long before both noises quieted. I dropped my head to the pillow, and the day's exhaustion caught up with me again, and I fell asleep with little effort, comforted by the locked door and the scissors hidden under my pillow.

Chapter 6 - Lizbeth

Life at Fort Vogel started early. I heard Gunnar rustling before five, and he was fully awake by 5:30. The warm aroma of coffee slipped under my door, beckoning me into the kitchen. My interrupted sleep hadn't refreshed me, but some caffeine would clear the grogginess from my head.

I dressed in a navy frock and braided my hair before emerging. In the kitchen, a smiling Gunnar held out a steaming mug. "Morning, Lizbeth. Glad to see you're an early riser. Ms. Granth will be happy with that too."

A name—one small clue to my future. School had been part of my before-life, but I knew it would no longer be on my schedule. I was curious to learn what an officer's wife did with her time, and it sounded like someone named Ms. Granth would be a part of those hours.

I gratefully accepted the coffee. "Thank you for this. I need it after last night."

Gunnar frowned. "I hope I didn't keep you up. When a lot is going on, my nights can get rough."

"It wasn't the yelling you warned me about, but I did hear tossing and turning. And a strange noise. There was some sort of clanking happening. Do you know what it could have been?"

When I'd left my bedroom, I scanned Gunnar's sleeping area for a hint of what could have produced the metallic rattling. The blanket on his cot was folded with military precision, and there were no stray items on the bed or the floor. Whatever had made the clanking was not in sight.

Gunnar grinned at my question. He entered the living room and grabbed something from the end table drawer. "I should have mentioned it last night.

This is what was making the noise." He held out his hand. A thick pair of handcuffs rested on his palm. "I use them for safety." His forehead wrinkled in thought. "Maybe I can put something on the cot railing, so it doesn't wake you. Something to deaden the sound it makes when I'm having a nightmare." He nodded. "I'll do that when I get home from work."

I was taken aback by his nonchalance. To Gunnar, it might be normal to use handcuffs overnight, but to me, it was not. It was odd. And a bit frightening. "I'm sorry, but I don't understand. Why do you have to restrain yourself?" Before he answered, it hit me. *Klara.* She'd been sleeping when she died, but what if Gunnar had been sleeping too?

"Does this have to do with my sister?" I needed to know.

"I started sleepwalking after her death. Handcuffs keep me in bed instead of roaming around base." He frowned. "I had no control over it before I used restraints. I'm not sure if I was ever dangerous, but how can you be sure of your intentions when you're in a dream-state? I lock myself up for safety. For mine, and for yours now, too."

"Thank you for protecting me." I offered a hesitant smile.

The grin he returned was full of relief. "And thank *you* for understanding. I haven't confessed my nocturnal wanderings to anyone else. I'm glad you didn't go running in terror."

We finished our coffee in silence. After Gunnar washed the mugs, he left to get dressed. I used the alone time to explore the kitchen, opening cabinets and drawers, searching for hints of his personality. His actions and words painted a strange picture, one moment calm and friendly, the next defensive and short. But the bland cutlery and cookware conformed to the same simplicity that dominated the rest of the house. It seemed there would be no revelations from the décor. I'd have to hunt elsewhere.

I sat down, waiting for Gunnar to return. He was in a dark olive uniform, holding a hat and briefcase when he did. His blond hair had been combed back, and he'd shaved his stubble. The polished look made him seem older, more mature. Or maybe it was the commanding presence he'd assumed. "Lizbeth, I'm off. I'm usually back around 1900, but sometimes later. Do you need anything before I go?" He spoke in a staccato tempo. Gunnar was all business now.

I still had no idea what I'd do while he was working. My mind went to the name he'd brought up. "If it's not too much to ask, would you tell me where I can find Ms. Granth? You mentioned her earlier, and I thought it would be nice to get to know someone."

Gunnar's booming laughter rang out. "Oh, don't worry, Ms. Granth will find *you*." Before I could ask what that meant, he tipped a salute with his fingers and left for work.

And just like that, I was by myself in a new place. I wasn't sure where the closest infirmary was, when the mail came, or who my neighbors were. I knew nothing.

It felt safer to stay inside, but I knew that would keep my world small. Learning about my new surroundings would help pass the time, plus give me insight into what life had been like for Klara when she lived here. I decided a stroll down the street would be an excellent place to start.

I searched my room and found Klara's shoes, thankfully close to my size. Her boots appeared new and sturdy, and perfect for exploring. As I slipped them on, I heard words from the front porch.

"Yoo-hoo, anyone home?" A bright, cheerful voice asked. An older woman peered through the front window. She wore a periwinkle dress with a yellow hat, and she beamed a smile as vibrant as the colors she wore. When she saw me peering her way, she waved. "Oh, hello, dear. I'm Ms. Granth, the ladies' coordinator. Colonel Cruse let me know that you'd be here this morning. Would you mind letting me in so I can stop yelling?"

I hurriedly opened the door and Ms. Granth bounded in, hugging me as soon as she crossed the threshold. At first, I resisted her embrace, but after a moment I relaxed my body and inhaled her apple scent. It reminded me of the pies my mother baked for the holidays. I closed my eyes, clinging to the memory.

When she stepped back, she took me in, moving her gaze from head to toe. "My, my, my, you're certainly a beauty." She fingered my long braid gently. "Your hair has the shine of youth. And those blue eyes. They're a different shade than Klara's, but they're as piercing. I can see why the Colonel wanted you as his bride."

What luck. I wouldn't have to bring up my sister, Ms. Granth had done it for me. "You knew Klara?"

She nodded. "I did, dear. She was a sweet, pretty thing who did all she could to make this a happy home." Her gaze shifted to the floor. "But unfortunately, she wasn't strong enough." Her head snapped up, and her smile returned. "Look at me, blabbing away about something I have no business discussing. I came here to bring you to morning duty, and instead, I'm prattling on." The coordinator stepped toward me and put her arm around my shoulder. "Let's be off to Dame Hall, dear, before we miss roll call."

I wasn't ready for the abrupt shift in our conversation, but Mrs. Granth pulled us toward the door, giving me only a moment to close it before we headed off at a pace slightly slower than a trot. She filled our walk with chatter. "Would you look at that? Sergeant Helmstedt's leaving a bit late today. I wonder what happened."

She tsked in disapproval. "Lizbeth, dear, we take promptness very seriously here. You can't run a base if people treat time all willy-nilly. Who would guard the perimeter, train new soldiers, or prepare rations if everyone decided to be tardy?"

Ms. Granth's words and movements mirrored this perception of timeliness. She walked with precision toward our target. And while she talked the whole time, she kept a swift pace and wasn't slowed by anything happening. Reaching our destination was her goal, and we were succinctly achieving it.

I tried to duplicate her single-minded focus, but it was difficult when everything was new. Although the houses and the streets were similar, there was a lot to take in. When we arrived at Fort Vogel, it had been evening and quiet. Now people were bustling about. Men in uniforms labored on menial tasks while clusters of women strolled the same direction the coordinator and I headed. Members of each group nodded as they passed each other, all seemingly happy with the way their lives were moving. Did they feel at ease with society's demands? Judging by their jolly expressions, I'd say yes. As always, I was the odd one out.

Ms. Granth interrupted my observations. "We're almost to Dame Hall, Lizbeth. Let's pick up the pace so we can be the first to arrive."

I'm not sure how we managed it, but we started walking faster. The other groups of women fell behind us as we approached a squat red building. A wall of windows gleamed around a tall metal door. It was there that we headed. Ms. Granth glanced over, looking pleased with our progress. "I think we did it. Thank you for hustling, dear."

As we approached the meeting hall, I noticed a flower-covered field hidden in the shadow of the building. Neat rows of stones were nestled between the red, yellow, purple, and blue blooms. The exactness that guided life in Fort Vogel also carried over into how the dead were arranged.

I left the coordinator's side and moved toward the arched gate surrounding the cemetery. A small plaque announced the field's title— Mother's Glen. Was Klara buried here? I walked up and down each lane, searching the headstones for her name. Mia, Hannah, Petra, Anna, Ilse, but no Klara. I turned when I heard footsteps approaching.

"I see you found the cemetery. Beautiful, isn't it?" Ms. Granth's face was red, like she'd run to catch up with me. Her words came between breaths.

"It is. But I was searching for my sister's stone, and I didn't see it. Do you know where it is? I'd like to come visit her whenever I can."

Ms. Granth paused a moment before responding. "Lizbeth, dear, I'm afraid Klara isn't buried here." She gestured around her. "Mother's Glen is only for those who died honorably. We celebrate them by letting them become one with the Earth. They give back and nurture, even in death."

"What do you mean honorably?" I asked. Klara had died in her sleep. It was hard to think of a more virtuous passing than that.

"Well, there is another field. It's behind the brambles back there. If you look hard enough, you can see the entrance." She pointed to a shadowy area I hadn't seen.

I squinted and could make out a break in the bushes. Ms. Granth swung around, her face lined with sadness. "That's where we lay the traitors to rest. I'm sorry, Lizbeth, I didn't want you to find out this way, but that's where you'll find your sister's grave."

Gunnar, 1933

Chapter 7 - Gunnar

My first experience with loneliness was a shock. When I felt the ache for companionship, the panicked realization that I would die alone, I knew something was off. These thoughts were completely unfamiliar, so it took time to recognize what was happening. A week passed, seven days of sadness and desperation, before I admitted something was wrong. As time continued moving, I grappled with my feelings of longing.

When I was a child, I never needed to be with people. There were always friends or family around, but I saw them as parts of life that just *were*. They were the background to my environment, the low hum of machinery you adapt to over time.

I never shared my deepest thoughts with another person. It wasn't necessary. Working on a farm or going to school didn't require exploring my desires or dreams. Doing chores and completing homework was enough to get by, and when I had questions, books gave me the answers. The texts were easier to understand than the ramblings or lectures I would surely get from an adult. Plus, I read faster than a person could talk. Conversations weren't an efficient way to spend time.

That changed when I pledged myself to Starkesend and began fighting for our cause. But not in the beginning. The initial months in my new community were filled with training and triumph. There was no time to think about relationships when the mechanics of war occupied your days and nights. After the newness wore off, I experienced tremors of emotional pain.

I knew about physical pain and had learned to relish and conquer it. This was part of the reason I swiftly rose through the military ranks. In my commanding officers' eyes, nothing beats a soldier who can finish a mission, even with broken bones. They knew I would persevere through any ailment and saw me as a man who would deliver much-needed wins. During each promotional ceremony, my commitment to Starkesend was reaffirmed by the pride I felt after each handshake or pat on the shoulder. I was doing the right thing.

But it wasn't enough. While my battle skills flourished, my internal regulators were beginning to fail. I noticed the deterioration when I returned from an important assignment. After nine months in Starkesend, I was rewarded for a successful mission. I had earned separate quarters and no longer lived in the barracks with the other troops. The quiet that came with this upgrade was initially a blessing. Although I had grown used to the sounds twenty men can make—the laughing, yelling, snoring, and coughing—their absence was a balm for my mind.

When you're with a group, it's not easy to wind down. I remained primed for duty long after the last night owl turned in for the evening. I expected interruptions and was always ready to offer my assistance during middle of the night emergencies. This restlessness affected my sleep. I was getting under three hours an evening, and the edges of my vision had grown fuzzy. No one had noticed my diminished capacity, but I knew it was only a matter of time.

When I left the barracks for my own small home, adjusting to the new environment took a week. The silence inside the house soothed my tired brain, but my nervous system hadn't received the stand-down message. I was edgy and ready to react to any provocation, and the first night in my home tested this vigilance. Shortly after midnight, a thump sounded against my bedroom window.

After that, my reflexes took over. I rolled out of bed and withdrew a knife from the bedside table, aiming for the intruder I knew was close by. My command voice boomed out. "Whoever you are, know that you're in my sights. Announce yourself."

And announce himself he did.

A loud ribbit cut through the room and caused the breath I was holding to burst out as a laugh. I walked to the window and pulled back the curtain. The intruder I'd been about to stab was a slimy green frog. It clung to the glass, oblivious to the human on the other side. My guest stayed for a few more ribbits. After it hopped away, I lowered myself into bed, smiling instead of clenching my jaw.

After the amphibian visit, my alert level receded. By the second week in my home, I was indulging in six hours of sleep a night. The luxury of it felt wrong. I knew the other men were getting less shuteye than me, the purple shadows under their eyes reminded me daily. But when I discussed these thoughts with my general, he put me at ease.

"Gunnar, it's admirable that you're thinking of your fellow soldiers. That makes you a good leader."

"It's the least I can do."

General Stillwell leaned over his desk, closing the distance between us. "Do you know what else makes you a good leader?" I shook my head. "Getting enough sleep." He raised his eyebrows questioningly. "Don't you think I noticed you barely making it through the days?"

While the men in my platoon hadn't recognized the signs of my weariness, my commander had. I felt my face heat up. "Sir, I don't know what to say. I thought I was doing a good job, but it sounds like I wasn't. Why didn't you call me out?"

He smiled. "Gunnar, even when you were worn out, you did better work than any other soldier. You're tough. You made it through every task we threw your way, even on less than three hours of shut eye."

"Thank you, sir."

"I take care of my men. When I notice that one of them needs something, I do my damnedest to make it happen. What good would you be to me…hell, what good would you be to the cause if we drove you past the brink of exhaustion?" He let the question hang in the air for a few seconds before he continued. "When you adapt to something difficult, earning a reprieve can feel like cheating. You were so used to fatigue that it became your normal. And now that you're getting rest, you feel like you're doing something wrong."

His insight shocked me. I'd adjusted to my poor conditions with little conscious thought. Even though I knew the amount of rest I got in the barracks was affecting my performance, I accepted it as a challenge that needed overcoming. Before long, it became another aspect of life, another part of the grueling training that made me a better soldier. When my circumstances changed, when my days were made more manageable through extra downtime, I decided that I wasn't working hard enough. The men in the barracks were still suffering through sleepless nights. How was it fair that I no longer shared this burden?

"You're thinking about the unfairness of it all. Am I right?" His question hit right on my worry.

I nodded. "I am, sir. How can I look anyone in the eyes when I know their nights are more stressful than mine? Isn't a good leader supposed to set an example?"

"You're the best example they will ever have, Gunnar."

"Thank you, General. But I don't understand how that's true."

"They see it in everything you do. You give your all to Starkesend and then some. You mentor the soldiers around you by lifting them when they need it and correcting them when it's warranted." He smiled. "And now the rest of the guys will see the reward for exemplary service. You gave blood, sweat, and tears. We've given you a purpose, plus a little extra freedom.

Won't everyone want to fight just as hard if there's some light at the end of the tunnel?"

I considered his words. While I wasn't motivated by the promise of living quarters and free time, I knew that some were. If my dedication weren't enough to inspire the other men, the added benefits that came with obtaining rank would be. "I feel much better, sir. Thanks for sharing your wisdom and helping me see the bigger picture." I pushed my chair back and stood. "If you don't mind, it's time for PT, and I think some running might do me good."

He chuckled. "Get out there, Cruse. I have a feeling you'll run laps around everyone."

General Stillwell was right. I lapped the other men in no time. My speed might have been due to the sleep I was getting, but I think it had more to do with the weightlessness I felt after our conversation. When we finished exercising, we got into formation, then made our way to the barracks.

We welcomed two recruits that day. Their initial hours were chaotic. The joiners ran around with panic in their eyes, responding to yells and demands for pushups. Sometimes recruits broke during this initial experience. We've had people walk out of the squad bay and continue for miles until they reached the edge of the compound. A few newcomers collapsed on the floor, refusing to respond to commands. They remained there sobbing until they were escorted from the building.

The men today, Augustin and Clatch, survived the initial hazing. The brutality would continue for weeks, until they had proven their loyalty to Starkesend, but the end of their initiation day ushered in a breath of calm. I spoke with each of them before I left for the evening. "What brings you fellas here? It's a long way to travel from Tulsa, and…was it St. Louis you hailed from, Clatch?"

He thrust his chest out. "That's right, Sergeant. It took me some time to get here from Missouri, but I made it."

"We welcome you with open arms and are grateful for the support." I took a step closer to the men. "But I am curious, and I always ask joiners, what made you leave your homes to enlist?"

Clatch answered the way most did. "I couldn't sit back and let the Jew scum overrun our country. I had to fight back" His nostrils flared. "And I ain't backing down."

"Well, you'll find ample support for those thoughts here." I turned to Augustin. "Do you feel the same way, recruit?"

"I do, Sergeant, but for me, there's more to it than that." His tone got solemn. "See, I got married last summer, and we have a little one on the way. My wife encouraged me to come here, even though she'd be alone with the baby."

Clatch chimed in. "That's a mighty fine woman you've got there, Augustin."

 "Thank you, soldier. She sure has been good to me." Augustin flashed a quick smile before furrowing his brow. "What pushed me to come all this way was something Ruthanne said last month, something that's stuck with me ever since." He narrowed his eyes, then recounted his wife's words in a prideful voice. "What it boiled down to was this: doing nothing allows the takeover to happen. Refusing to fight sends an invitation right to the Jews, welcoming them into our homes. If family is our most important asset, protecting them against the enemy is the only answer." He set his jaw, and determination filled his eyes "I had to come, Sergeant. Ruthanne and our baby mean everything to me. And I'd do anything for them."

I released both men to the chow hall and made my way home. As I walked, Augustin's words played over and over in my head. The buoyancy

I'd felt after talking with General Stillwell had been replaced with a deep ache. Instead of being fulfilled, a family-sized hole throbbed in my chest.

Chapter 8 - Gunnar

I missed the background rumble of the barracks that night. Without it, I couldn't ignore the troubling thoughts I kept having. Why was I concerned with Augustin's ideas about family? My role at Starkesend was more than enough for me. I had companionship, food, shelter, and purpose. A man needed nothing beyond that, yet I was lamenting that I hadn't yet registered for the upcoming Frau Rennen, when having a wife wasn't a priority of mine. Observing my parents throughout childhood showed me the downfalls of marriage.

My mother was a handsome, proud woman, who smiled with ease. There were two activities that made her the happiest. The first was baking flaky pastries for holidays and birthdays, and the second was playing piano. I benefited from her confections, but I was forever a fan of her musical abilities. When Ma played, the most beautiful sounds resonated through the house. She called me her muse. Mom would ask me for a key, and after I picked A major or F sharp, she would create haunting melodies I hum to this day.

Memories of my father are very different. Pa was a reluctant farmer who showed it by involving himself in everything but our land. His biggest point of pride was the militia he and a neighbor founded. They named it Freikorps, a word my father heard on the radio. He put out the call for memberships, and slowly, local workers trickled in.

There were meetings every month and family picnics once a year. The annual gatherings were a chance for surrounding factions to unite and celebrate their way of life. I would run around with the other children, playing tag and barely noticing the gunshots coming from the adult area. Ma stayed on the outskirts of the crowd. She didn't join the groups of women passing around babies or setting up the midday meal. Her apple cobbler would have won the baking prize, but she never entered the contests. Ma was present only in body, not spirit.

While my mother was not committed to my father's endeavors, she was supportive of her husband for most of my youth. As Pa gained more responsibility at Freikorps, Ma worked harder on the farm without complaint. She also taught piano lessons and took in washing when we needed extra spending money. Despite these obligations, her Saturday evening music continued. Ma would be bone-weary from a day of chores, yet her eyes would come alive when she sat down to play.

As time went on, tension blossomed between my parents. They tried to hide it from me, but their arguments cut through the thin walls of their bedroom.

"Henry, can't you stay? We need you here tonight." Ma's voice was quiet but firm.

"You know I can't stay. Stop torturing yourself by asking, Jo." Pa sighed. "You and the boy can take care of things. This won't be the first foal you'll deliver, and it won't be the last."

"That's not the damn point, and you know it." The floorboards creaked. I imagined Ma pacing, formulating what she'd say next. "If you asked me what I thought, I'd say this militia means more to you than your family. You forgot about me long ago, but now you're abandoning Gunnar. He's just a boy, Henry, a smart, sweet boy who still looks up to his father. Do you want to destroy that relationship too?"

The sound of flesh striking flesh rang out. Pa hadn't liked what he heard, and he made sure my mother knew it. "Josephine Cruse, I don't know what demon put such words in your mouth, but I never want to hear them again. I do everything for this family, *everything*, and if you're too blind to see it, I can't help you. I started Freikorps for you and Gunnar, to protect you from the impure influences out there. If I sit here and do nothing about it, aren't I welcoming them in?"

The slamming of the front door almost obscured Ma's reply. "I'd rather sit here and do nothing than run around spreading hate."

The years before I left home were filled with more of the same. Their fights increased in number until they were happening daily, and Ma and Pa no longer attempted to hide their animosity for each other. I kept my head down until I was old enough to enlist in the military. I also made a promise to myself—I vowed to stay a bachelor. Chasing girls wasn't worth it, especially if it ended in the type of relationship my parents had. I didn't want to go steady or take a wife. It was better to avoid the disagreements and cries for attention that seemed to fill romantic partnerships.

I held firm to my promise through trainings, deployments, and tours of duty. I directed my efforts at becoming an elite soldier, and commendations and promotions marked my progress toward that goal. When my enlistment ended, I opened an electrical company that kept me busy and away from the speakeasies people my age frequented. In my shop, I kept working relationships cordial. It was enough to know that my employees were hard workers, anything beyond this information was unnecessary. My business expanded as the years passed, but my social circle did not, a fact I was perfectly content with. But as time went on, I grew restless. I'd rocketed through the ranks in the military and developed a successful business from the ground up. I'd attained numerous achievements, yet something was missing.

Over the past few years, I noticed that life was different for others around me. The Depression had crushed many people, leaving them destitute and forlorn. They waited for hours in bread lines to get enough nourishment to make it through the day. Each morning the cycle was repeated, back and forth, from shanty to line. People couldn't think beyond their hunger. They operated in a world where their only goal was attaining the barest semblance of survival.

I observed these hardships quietly and resisted the pressure to judge the unemployed. My peers, the other shop owners who kept their businesses through the downturn, were more callous. They labeled broken men as lazy, and their families as burdens in need of disposal. When people knocked on their doors inquiring about work, they shooed them off with insults and threats. I'd reach out to the fleeing men and offer them a small wage for a few hours of labor. They were always grateful for the opportunity.

It was from one of these workers that I first learned about Starkesend. Johnny Blaylock was capable and determined. As soon as he accepted my offer of employment, he got to work sweeping the warehouse. He moved like a man possessed, so I wasn't surprised to find that he finished the job quicker than any laborer I'd hired in the past. Since there was still time before the church opened its evening soup kitchen, I thought he might be willing to take on more duties.

"I know we just met today, Johnny, but I have to say that you've already impressed me." I gestured around the building. "There's a lot of space in here, but you've managed to clean it up in half the time most guys take. I got more tasks if you're still looking for work. Simple things. For extra pay, of course."

"Mr. Cruse, you made this old veteran's day. I'll take whatever work you've got." He smiled. "I'm trying to get out to Starkesend, and every dollar gets me closer. I've made it this far, from Shreveport to Casper, and I ain't giving up yet."

"That's the spirit." I clapped his back. "Albert is back there putting outlets together. Why don't you give him a hand." I pointed to the rear of the shop, and Johnny headed that way.

Hours passed before I saw him again. As he walked past me, on the way out the door, I stopped him. "Johnny, it's past time for the free church meal. How about I treat you to some supper? The inn down the road has meatloaf on Tuesdays. I haven't had company in a good while, and it'd be nice to talk to a fellow veteran."

"You got it, boss. I'm not one to pass up a free meal."

We didn't talk much on our way to the inn, but Johnny opened up once we were inside and seated. Conversation was not a strength of mine, so I was happy to sit back and listen, nodding and agreeing when it was called for. I heard about Johnny's upbringing and his years in the service. He vented about the difficulties he'd had staying employed since the war.

"You'd think I was a second-class citizen. Just 'cause I'm a little rough around the edges doesn't mean I'm a layabout. You saw that, Mr. Cruse. But when other people stare at me, they see a man who's not polished, and they write me off." He shook his head and banged his fist o the table. "To make matters worse, the government's been delaying my benefits. How do they expect me to survive? I served this country, and I've gotten jack in return." He leaned closer and lowered his voice. "That's why I'm going to Starkesend. At least I'll be appreciated there."

I didn't ask about Starkesend that night, but the conviction in Johnny's voice stayed with me. When you're down and out, not many things seem inspiring. Men chased women, drank booze, or gambled away their earnings, trying to fulfill their sense of purpose. And while they ended up with nothing at the end of the night, the spark they felt when they were twisting in the sheets or shooting whiskey was enough to keep them going until the next day. Johnny found his spark in a physical place, one he put up on a pedestal.

His fervor for something different was refreshing. I hoped he made it there soon.

I didn't think about Johnny for a month. When the Starkesend recruiters showed up at my shop on a chilly morning, his leathery features and quick-to-smile face flickered through my mind. I thought he had sent the two representatives my way, but they later told me an impressed client had given them my name. I wasn't normally chatty on jobs, but I'd been lured into a conversation about the terrible treatment veterans were receiving. My client passed this information on, and the recruiters sought me out, hoping to bring me into their fold.

They knocked with a clipped beat, short and businesslike. I opened the door and found two well-dressed men on my stoop, appearing serious, but not in an off-putting way. They seemed like they had something important to share. Their brown suits and polished shoes matched, but their heights were quite opposite. The shorter of the two spoke first. "Mr. Cruse? We were hoping for some of your time." He nodded at his partner.

"Yes. If we could speak with you for a few minutes, I think you would like what we have to say."

"Hello, gentlemen. Good morning." I stepped outside, closing the door behind me. "It's a bit brisk out, and my coat is inside. I hope this won't take long."

"We won't be long unless you want to keep talking. It's completely up to you." The taller man stuck out his hand. "I'm General Stillwell, and this is Sargent Roccio. We're here from Starkesend."

After we shook, the men told me about their base, which was hidden deep in a forest, and their cause, which was eradicating the Jewish threat. These characteristics weren't what prompted me to sell my business and trek across the country to join them.

What caught my interest and altered my life path was something General Stillwell said. "We came here because we know you're a man of action, Gunnar. That's what we need—we need someone who doesn't just sit around, letting the enemy take over. If you don't do something, you're just welcoming the crooks with open arms. You're allowing them to take over." He fixed his gaze on me, imploring me with his sureness. "Come with us. Take your country back from the enemy."

∞∞∞∞

Doing nothing allowed terrible things to happen.

The phrase seemed to haunt me. The words first emerged in childhood and followed me to Starkesend. Maybe it wasn't the expression itself but its reoccurring quality. Whenever I heard it, I altered my life course. When Pa yelled it at Ma, I decided to join the military and avoid marriage. I dropped everything to pursue a new purpose when General Stillwell said the sentiment. Now, after hearing it from Augustin in the barracks this evening, I was questioning the vow of bachelorhood I'd made long ago.

When the recruit spoke with unabashed pride about his kin, something inside me responded. Was I really yearning for a family, or was I just seeking another change? The question kept me up for hours, and when I finally fell asleep, I still wasn't sure of the answer.

Lizbeth, 1936

Chapter 9 - Lizbeth

"I need another volunteer for the cafeteria. Which of you ladies will it be?" Ms. Granth's eyes darted around the room, imploring the seated women to raise their hands.

My attention wandered in and out of the discussion. I kept thinking about what I'd learned about Klara in the cemetery. My sister had been cast out from society. It was hard to comprehend, and once Ms. Granth revealed this news, she refused to explain further. While we finished our trek to Dame Hall, I asked questions—*What happened? Why was Klara considered a traitor? Are you sure there wasn't a misunderstanding?*—but my inquiries were met with silence. After we entered the building, Ms. Granth hurried away.

"I must be off, dear. Find a seat and get ready for your first morning meeting. You'll learn what it means to be a wife at Fort Vogel."

I chose a spot near the back of the room. It was the perfect place for observing arrivals and losing myself in thought. There were thirty chairs in total, and it wasn't long before they were filled with girls and women not much older than me. Almost all my newlywed classmates were in attendance. It was both comforting and surreal to see them in this new environment.

Roll call was mundane, but it gave me a chance to learn the names of everyone in the room. Each woman stood and curtsied when her name was read. I was glad to see the pattern before Ms. Granth reached me. My curtsy was stiff, but I made it through the movement without drawing attention my way. A former classmate wasn't so lucky.

"Marta Elridge." Ms. Granth paused for a moment, expecting the young wife to stand for acknowledgment.

As the pause stretched on, heads began to swivel. I joined them, searching for Marta, hoping to save her some embarrassment. A movement to the left caught my eye. Someone was nudging a slumped-over body. Their prods got more frantic as the seconds ticked by.

Ms. Granth descended the stairs on the side of the stage, rushing toward the disturbance. When she almost reached it, she yelled, "Marta Elridge, if you don't wake up this instant, there *will* be consequences."

The hunched over girl sprung up, toppling her chair in the process. Her eyes were bulging as she scanned the room in panicked confusion. I heard a low moaning intermingled with sobs. Marta was crying and making no attempt to hide her tears. Ms. Granth spoke softer now. "Oh, sweetheart, it's okay. Whatever's the matter, we'll fix it right up. Come with me, and I'll take care of everything." She gently placed her hand in Marta's, and the two headed toward the door at the front of the room.

The base's older residents stood and patted Marta's shoulder as she passed. The rest of us stared in shock. I bet we were all remembering the smart, vivacious person our classmate had been just a few days before. That version of Marta no longer existed. I let my mind wander to Klara. Did this happen to her? Did Starkesend break her, and that's why she was considered a traitor? The possibility chilled me.

My thoughts were interrupted by Ms. Granth's return. She made her way to the stage with a smile plastered on her face. "Ladies, thank you for your patience during our little interruption. I'm sure the poor dear will be in tip-top shape by supper." She dove back into roll call with no further mention of Marta.

Even though we avoided the subject, it caused a change in the room—curtsies were more hesitant, eyes were cast downward, hands twisted in laps.

Seeing raw pain on display tore at the heart, and we all felt the residue of Marta's anguish.

Except for Ms. Granth. She chirped along, ignoring our subdued mood and powering through roll call, volunteer assignments, and dress pattern handouts. She even increased her enthusiasm when it was time for pair matching. She explained the importance of this custom in an animated tone. "It's an exciting time here at Fort Vogel. We had fifteen brides join us last night! Most of you know what that means, but I'll explain it for the new folks."

Ms. Granth left the stage. She walked up and down the rows of chairs while she talked. "A soldier's wife is an important person. She takes care of her husband, raises any children she bears, and ensures that her household is in pristine condition. In other words, a soldier's wife is her family's foundation. Without her, chaos would ensue. You'll notice that we are treated respectfully by the men on base. They appreciate all that we do for the good of our cause."

Ms. Granth stopped pacing, and her voice became electric. "There are duties a wife performs outside her home. These assignments keep Starkesend running, and they are to be treated with the utmost respect. If you are given a task, make sure to arrive on time and stay until completion. This includes textiles, nursery, or cafeteria work, and the more crucial duties you'll learn about from your assigned guide. I know it can feel like a lot is resting on your shoulders. You may be thinking, how will there be enough time to take care of my family, plus serve our magnificent society?" Her voice swelled with pride. "But you *will* overcome these doubts. You will wake up every morning and put your all into the day because that's what Starkesend women do. We don't give up, we don't wear out, and we don't stand down. Each of us is responsible for defending our Aryan rights, and together we have the power to occupy our place in the world."

The concern in the room was replaced by a patriotic spark. Every woman sat on the edge of her chair, ready to spring into action if it was asked of her. I could see why Ms. Granth was in charge. She knew how to rouse a group. The women around me gave off an energy that could be tapped into. They would happily please their husband, raise their children, clean their houses, and then place their life on the line for Starkesend. They would do everything society demanded of them, and then some.

I never felt like the others. I sensed the magnetism of the speech, but it came from the speaker's emotions, not the content. Where others were pulled deeper into their devotion to our community by fiery words, I continued to exist along its fringes.

My parents gave up their possessions and joined the movement when I was six. I couldn't remember life before we came here. Starkesend was all I knew. Still, I wavered in my loyalty although I'd heard praise for the cause since I was a little girl. Some of it had to do with my mom and dad. They didn't speak about the Jewish threat or the fight for Aryan dominance. This differed from my classmate's households, where conversations centered on these beliefs. I was grateful to have spent our family time listening to operas or reading novels, rather than receiving lectures on Nazi ideals. The beauty in art was far more appealing than the dark underpinnings of our society, a thought I knew to keep hidden. As I grew up, I blended in well enough to avoid attention.

Now, I was on my own, with no way to avoid fanatical shows of devotion. I'd have to work harder to fit in, to mask the discontent that simmered in my heart. Eagerness was a good tactic. Concealing my true thoughts behind false passion would let me hide in the open. I raised my hand. Ms. Granth noticed and walked closer. When she addressed me, her voice had lost its intensity. It was back to being sugary sweet. "Yes, dear. Do you have a question?"

I smiled. "I do. I was wondering when we will find out who our guide is. It'll be nice getting to know her."

"Oh, silly me, I got carried away. You're right. It's time to announce guides and their trainees." She turned to the group. "Girls, take note. Lizbeth is an eager beaver, and we appreciate those here. I knew I made the right decision with her guide."

Ms. Granth pulled a slip of paper from her dress pocket. She announced pairs of names, one new Fort Vogel bride with one older resident. The more seasoned women would help their younger charges settle into their new reality. It was a way to ease the abrupt transition from child to soldier's wife. True to her orderly nature, Ms. Granth read the names in alphabetical order. When she passed C without calling my name, I became anxious. When she announced fourteen duos without mentioning me, the anxiety grew to worry. "There's just one more pair to announce, and then we can break for our noon meal. I saved the most exciting for last." Everyone's eyes were on me.

Ms. Granth continued in an upbeat tone. "After each Frau Rennen, we are blessed with new life. Some of the Sixteens and Seventeens go to our sister settlement in California. There were five who traveled there this year. Five dear girls who will take their Starkesend grit to their new home." She applauded at the news, and the rest of the wives followed suit. When the hall quieted, she returned to her announcement. "The bulk of the girls stay here, since our society has proven its fortitude. From this race, fifteen bright, lovely winners stayed with us, and found their new home at Fort Vogel. Of this fifteen, only one can be matched with the most senior ranking woman."

She paused before saying the words I was dreading. "Lizbeth Cruse, I am your guide. Together we will serve our glorious nation."

∞∞∞∞∞

My first week at Fort Vogel was busy. Morning meetings started the days, and afternoon shifts followed. Ms. Granth and I worked in the nursery, where we took care of the base's children, or served on textile duty, where we repaired uniforms and put together care packages for our allies abroad.

The investigation into Klara's demise had stalled. I asked questions whenever I had the opportunity, but the answers I received added no clarity. Ms. Granth was persistently cheerful, and she rebuffed my attempts to uncover the truth.

"Ms. Granth, do you know what type of work Klara favored?" I asked.

"My dear, we must serve faithfully and equally. I can't recall Klara's preferences, but I'm sure she completed all her chores without complaint." Her smile stretched from ear to ear.

I mirrored her cheeriness. "But I already enjoy working with the children, especially the ones close to my brother's age. I know I'm not supposed to pick favorites, but I find this duty much more pleasant than running the sewing machines. I'm sure my sister felt the same."

"Sweet Lizbeth, learning to appreciate the least enjoyable tasks will make you much happier. I'll make sure to sign up for extra textile shifts next week. You'll love stitching in no time!" She narrowed her eyes, fixing her gaze on my bodie. "Stop playing with your dress, dear. You'll wear a hole in the fabric if you keep rubbing it like that."

I dropped my hand, embarrassment warming my cheeks. "Yes, ma'am." I'd have to pay attention to my actions. Caressing the scissors had become a comfort, an almost unconscious one, but it was dangerous. Wives weren't allowed to have weapons, and if my disobedience were discovered, trouble awaited. Gaining negative attention was the last thing I wanted. Blending in was how I'd fight back.

The days went by, and whenever I mentioned Klara's name, Ms. Granth refused to provide the details I desperately sought. I hadn't grown close to any other wives, so my chipper guide was the only option for information. Unfortunately, my curiosity was no match for her evasive tactics. As the week ended, I realized I was no closer to learning what happened to my sister a year ago.

I did manage to visit her grave. The cemetery's weed-choked grounds were a far cry from the organized Mother's Glen. Plots weren't marked by carved stones. Instead, rotted wood signs jutted from the ground, labeling remains with just a first initial and last name. *K. Cruse*. The contrast between my beautiful sister and her decayed resting place couldn't have been starker. I wept at the unfairness. None of it was right.

Surprisingly, the easiest part of my new life was my relationship with Gunnar. We settled into a routine, and he asked nothing of me outside of it. Our morning coffee was accompanied by easy conversation. When we returned home in the evenings, supper was followed by a radio show or two. We skipped the news, where they only talked about the Depression or politics, and gravitated toward westerns or comedies. Gunnar's favorite was the Lone Ranger, while Fibber McGee and Molly always made me laugh. The exaggerated rescues and lighthearted jokes distracted me from the mystery I had yet to solve. When we went to bed each night, still in separate rooms, I was relaxed enough to fall asleep with ease.

Gunnar's terrors no longer interrupted the late hours. I hadn't heard moaning or clanking since my first night at Fort Vogel. He also seemed calmer during our time together. There were more smiles, and his military personality appeared less often. I think our partnership was working well for the both of us.

Our positive bond was reinforced early one morning. I woke to the smell of coffee, like usual, but noticed another scent in the air. It was a sweet aroma that reminded me of the cookies my mother would bake for special occasions. I followed my nose to the kitchen and found Gunnar peering into the oven. "Good morning." I breathed in deeply. "Something smells wonderful in here. I hope I get a chance to taste whatever you're making."

Gunnar turned toward me. "Happy birthday, Lizbeth."

"Oh, I forgot what day it was. How kind of you to remember." I gushed.

"And not only did I remember, but I've made you a surprise. My mother was the best baker. She'd create pastries and cakes for my birthdays that made any other sweet pale in comparison. My favorite recipe was her pineapple upside-down cake."

Gunnar peeked in the oven. "I think it needs a few more minutes. Would you like coffee while we wait?"

"Sounds like the perfect way to pass the time. Thank you, Gunnar."

He brought two steaming mugs to the table, and we sat sipping our drinks, enjoying the scents that filled the house. "You know, I haven't had anything sweet this year. Everything has been so scarce." I smiled. "This is really something. It'll be nice to have a treat."

"It's one of the perks of being an officer. I started searching for the ingredients the morning after you arrived and found the last one yesterday. Most times, you have to request items well in advance." He pointed to the radio. "It took me six weeks to get that, but it was worth the wait. In the barracks, we shared one radio. My men only wanted to listen to crime shows. Here, I pick the program."

The oven timer went off. Gunnar stood. "It's time to eat. How big of a piece do you want, Lizbeth?"

"That's a tough question for someone who hasn't eaten cake in ages. I'd like to say the whole thing, but I suppose I'll share." I spaced my hands apart, stopping myself from opening them too far. "How about something like this?"

"You got it. Something that big, coming up for the birthday girl."

The cake was perfect. I savored each bite, knowing it could be a while before I had another dessert. Gunnar showed the same restraint. We slowly worked our way to the last crumbs, lost in our thoughts. When I finished every morsel, I was shocked to see the hour. "I didn't realize it was so late." I picked up our plates and brought them to the sink. "I best be off to the morning meeting. Ms. Granth likes when I'm there before the other wives."

"I bet she does. I don't know where that woman gets her energy, but it seems limitless."

"You're telling me. I'm awfully glad she picked me as her trainee. There's nothing better than trying to live up to her expectations."

Gunnar sensed my sarcasm and chuckled. "It'll be okay. You'll be on your own soon enough." His tone got serious. "Just be careful today. Birthday celebrations can be overwhelming for first timers." Before I could respond, Gunnar headed out the door. "See you later, Lizbeth."

My happy mood evaporated. I was still grateful for Gunnar's thoughtfulness, but his abrupt parting tempered my appreciation. Why would he leave after such a cryptic message? I needed to calm down before I went to Dame Hall. I closed my eyes and took a deep breath, letting memories of my family flood my mind. My sixteenth birthday was perfect. Klara and Ellis had worked hard on my present, a portrait of the three of us laughing in the sun. My sister had drawn the figures, while my brother helped with the frame. It was beautiful. Klara's skill with charcoal captured the love we had for each other. Ellis painted the wood around the picture with the creative abandon of a small child. They'd known just what to get me.

My parents had as well. Novels were tough to come by in Starkesend. We had a fair collection in our home, but I had read the stories many times over. When I unwrapped two books, *The Good Earth* and *Brave New World*, I shed tears of joy. My father had managed to sneak these forbidden texts past our security forces. It was even more surprising that the books were unopened. The bindings showed no signs of use, so I would be the first to read them. In a world where most items were shared, it was a rarity to own something new. They were true treasures.

My birthday was the last family celebration. A short while later, Klara matched with Gunnar at the Frau Rennen and then moved to Fort Vogel. The remaining four of us acknowledged holidays and milestones, but we could never recreate the joy from that special day. It wasn't the same without my sister.

I focused on my happiness at the party, the feeling of all-encompassing love. Slowly, the anxiety caused by Gunnar's words faded, and I was ready to leave the house. Ms. Granth would be displeased with my tardiness, but I hoped she would let it slide this once. After all, it was my birthday.

I was the last to enter Dame Hall, and as soon as I sat, Ms. Granth brought the meeting to order. She ran through the day's business with a precision that bordered on rushed. There was only a moment's pause between each topic. It certainly kept her audience on their toes. We stayed alert in case we became the target of her focus. Luckily, everyone escaped scrutiny, and we were dismissed to our volunteer duties. As everyone was leaving, Ms. Granth's voice rang out. "Lizbeth, would you come up here, please?"

I'd been waiting for her to join me, which was our usual routine, but it seemed today would be different. I made my way to the front of the room, nodding to the others I passed. Everyone was cheerful, like always, and they returned my nods enthusiastically.

Most of the wives had departed when I reached the stage, but a few hovered about, lingering like they expected something to happen. I ignored their interest and spoke to Ms. Granth. "What do we have planned today? I'm ready for anything!"

"Well, dear, I hope that's true. Since today is your birthday, we have a special treat for you. Come with me." The remaining women kept their gaze on us while we walked through an exit on the left of the stage. Their knowing eyes frightened me. I wondered what I was heading toward.

When we reached the back of the building, Ms. Granth paused to open a set of doors on the floor. She motioned for me to follow her down the staircase that was revealed. I gripped the railing and trailed close behind. Our footsteps echoed as we descended, my rhythm slow and careful, Ms. Granth's rapid and precise. It was dark in the stairwell, but the light from below provided enough of a glow for guidance. I counted fifty steps before we reached the bottom. Like the stairs, the interior of the room we entered was made of stone. The gray ceilings were tall enough for me to stand upright, but the men in front of me had to crouch.

"Hello there, you must be Lizbeth. I'm General Stillwell, and this is Dr. Brandt. Welcome to our laboratory."

Gunnar, 1933

Chapter 10 - Gunnar

I told my parents about Starkesend separately. I wasn't sure what their reactions would be, but I knew they would differ. Causing strife between the pair, especially in their elderly years, was not something I wanted to do. Plus, these days, they were married only in name. After I left for the military, Pa transitioned to living full-time at Freikorps. Ma remained on the farm, paring the livestock and crops to a manageable level. Each was happier in their own environment, and they only interacted when taxes came due on the family plot. Their relationship was transactional, formal, but it worked to keep the peace between them.

The first stop was my father's bunker. When he answered the door, after a series of coded knocks, he blinked in the morning sun. "That you, boy? I recognize that block head of yours, even half-blind."

"It's me, Pa." I patted his arm. "You wouldn't have trouble seeing if you came outside more often."

He spat in disgust. "Outside? That's where they get ya. I've no interest in being out here." He scanned the dead grass, the empty fields, and shook his head. "I only come out for training. Not that there's much of it going on lately. Damn Depression's making everything harder to get, including ammo."

"You got electric out here?"

"Electric? Gunnar, you got spoiled working that big city job. I use candles for light, and wood for heat when I need it."

"Casper's a big city, sure, but I was on the outskirts, Pa. But you are right about one thing—I was definitely spoiled. That's what I came to talk to you about."

Even though his eyes had adjusted to the light, Pa squinted at me. "Oh yeah? You don't say. Come have a drink with your old man and tell me what's on your mind."

I laughed as I followed him inside. Of course, he had spirits. No oil or ammo, but plenty of alcohol. That was the way it was for a lot of men. They needed something to pass the time, and rotgut certainly helped. People could get booze from bootleggers, but many refused to pay a higher cost for whiskey when they knew how to make it themselves.

Pa grabbed his bottle and poured heavily into two glasses. He took a swig from his cup and refilled it before bringing our drinks over. He raised his glass. "To my son."

I raised my arm and gently tapped my cup against his. "To you, Pa. It's been a long time."

We drank but in opposite ways. Pa swallowed until he drained the last drop. I stopped after one sip. Much more, and I would never make it to see my mother.

Pa eyed my glass as he sat at the dining table. "Still not much of a drinker, I see. That's probably for the best. Too much of this stuff and…" He trailed off.

"How've you been, Pa? Sorry I haven't visited often. The shop took up most of my time, more than I'd like to admit. It's no excuse, just the truth."

He pulled out the chair next to him and gestured for me to sit. As I made my way over, he filled his glass, slopping liquid past the brim. His eyes were glassy, and I wondered if he'd started in on the whisky before I showed up. Not that it mattered. I wasn't seeking approval or understanding, I only wanted to make him aware of my plans. Whether or not he remembered them in the morning was his concern.

Before I could start talking, Pa spoke up. "Gunnar, a father wants to see his son go off into the world, so there's no need to say sorry about staying away. There ain't much in this town. Even less for a business-minded person like you. Hell, if I could take off, I would." He gestured around the room. "But who would take care of all this? I've put too much into Freikorps to let it go to waste."

I surveyed the bunker, noticing the sparsity. When I was a child, meetings took place within these rock-lined walls. Militia members kept the larder and armory stocked, staying prepared for an ever-threatening invasion. Now, the supplies only filled the corner of one shelf. My father was surviving on the barest means.

"Get any new blood lately?" I could guess the answer from the state of Pa's home but wanted to hear it from him.

"None. But there's trouble brewing across the ocean, and people are starting to talk about it in town. When there's trouble, that's when people come banging on my door, ready to join the fight."

Dedication showed through his drunkenness. My father might not look like much, but he would defend his beliefs to his last breath. I'd gained much of my personality from my mother, but this part, the stubborn loyalty, came from him. "I bet you're right, Pa. You'll have more members than you'll know what to do with soon."

"I'll drink to that." He raised his glass to his lips and threw back his head, gulping the caramel-colored liquid until it was gone.

I changed the direction of our conversation. It wouldn't be long before my father passed out, and I wanted to be done talking before that happened. "Pa, I've got a big change coming up. I'm moving north with a group of veterans, guys who can live off the land and defend it if necessary. They found me at my shop, explained what they were doing, and asked me to join them. I said yes." I paused. "They reminded me of you, said action is the only way to defeat the enemy."

I had his attention. "It's been almost fifteen years since I got out of the Army. Running the shop was fulfilling, but I miss that feeling, the one you get when you wake up in the morning, knowing you're making the world better. The trenches were…they were bad. Not all my men made it home, but everyone put their all into crushing the Central powers. Their dedication, my dedication, kept me going."

Pa nodded. "I hear you, boy. That's how I feel about Friekorps." His speech was measured, and there was no hint of a slur. He was either less drunk than he appeared, or something I was talking about sparked his interest.

"I know you love this place, Pa. I'm guessing you have an idea of how I'm feeling right now. It's time for me to move on from the comfortable life. Mostly, I came to let you know that I'm leaving. You might not see me for some time, maybe not ever again. But I also have this for you." I reached into my bag and brought out a stack of bills. "I sold the business and my house. Brought you and Ma some cash to help with the taxes."

"Thanks, son. This'll be a big help." He clutched the bills to his chest.

"Of course, Pa. Glad you can use it." I stood up, ready to move on to the next destination.

"Heading out?"

"The sun's starting to set. I better hurry if I want to get home before dark."

"Safe travels, Gunnar. Give my best to your Ma."

"Thanks, Pa. I will." As I walked out the door, I glanced back into the bunker, taking in my father one the last time. He was drinking straight from the whiskey bottle, gripping the money like his life depended on it.

∞∞∞

Ma was milking when I got to the farm. A soft lowing led me to the barn, and I smiled when I saw her talking to the cows in a soothing voice. "Okay, Frieda, that's enough for the night. Half a pail is better than none, and I know you'll have more in the morning." She patted Frieda's golden fur before moving to the next stall. "Buttercup, you're ready to burst. Let me give you a hand."

I stepped into the lantern light. "How 'bout I give you a hand, Ma?"

She turned and gasped. "Gunner Cruse! I can't believe it's you."

We hugged, and she stepped back to take me in. "It's been a long time, son. I see mostly a man in front of me, but there's still some boyish charm peeking out."

"And you look the same as always, Ma. You never change."

"Always the flatterer." She handed me the milking stool. "You offered to help your mother, so get to it. I'll head inside and rustle up some supper."

It felt good to use my hands. While electrical work involved labor, there was something about farm life that couldn't be replicated. The scents and the textures of the barn were earthy, basic, and they stirred a sense of connectedness inside you. Life's musky aromas captured your spirit and held it tight. After time, you couldn't fathom another way of existing, something separate from the dirt, the sun, and the living creatures. I'd left because of my parents but being here tonight reminded me of what I'd been missing. I took my time milking the last two cows, knowing it would be some time before I returned home.

After I finished in the barn, I made my way to the main house. The smell of supper put a quickness in my steps. I washed my hands in the pump and hurried inside. "Ma, it's been years since I've had a home-cooked meal." I breathed deeply. "Whatever you're making smells delicious."

"Years? You mean to tell me that you haven't been taking care of yourself, Gunnar?" Her eyes blazed with anger.

"That's not it. I ate plenty, but it was all from the hotel. Or cans. None of it was like your cooking, though. I'm can't wait until supper."

"You expect me to be so happy about your visit that I overlook your negligence? How can a mother feel good about her son when he isn't taking care of himself?" She started pacing. "Gunnar, this means you had no friends to eat with, no girls to cook for you. I imagine a lonely life, and it hurts my heart."

"Ma, I can't lie and say it wasn't lonely. There wasn't enough time to connect with anyone. I was in Casper to grow my business and nothing more." I caught her shoulder to stop the pacing. "But Ma, I'm going to be part of something bigger. That's why I came here, to talk to you about it."

The anger left her eyes and was replaced with concern. "My boy, there's always time to make connections. Don't end up like your Pa, all closed off from the world."

"I saw him earlier. Has he been drinking like that for long?"

She hung her head in sadness. Or maybe it was shame. "He has. When the last man left Friekorps, he locked himself in that hovel and stopped living. I'm surprised he let you in." She paused. "I'm more surprised he's lasted this long. My guess, is come winter, we'll find him alone and still, already food for the rats."

She said it with no emotion, announcing Pa's fate in the tone used for small talk. It seemed like she had made peace with her husband's demise, but it was fresh for me. I knew my father was not the kindest man. I knew he abandoned my mother in search of something better than farm life. I knew his love for me was not as strong as his love for his ideals. But still, he was my dad, and it hurt to know what awaited him. "Ma, can we talk about something else?"

"I'm sorry, Gunnar. I forget you see your Pa with different eyes." She went to the oven and brought out a bubbling casserole. "Let's eat. You can tell me about the something bigger you mentioned."

I filled Ma in on my plans. We talked about Starkesend and the role I would play there. Although she was sad that I'd be gone for so long, she supported my decision. Ma knew I couldn't sit idle and allow the enemies take over.

Chapter 11 - Gunnar

The trek to Starkesend was lengthy. We transferred trains until we reached the end of the line, then we used horses to navigate dense woods and increasingly steep hills. There were five of us in the group, all men. General Stillwell assumed the lead, followed by the three joiners close behind. Sergeant Roccio brought up the rear. None of us new members strayed from our guides. We followed the General in an evenly spaced line, plodding along at a consistent pace.

I wondered what would have happened if one of us had run. We weren't forced along, we'd all come freely, but I sensed an air of authority from our leaders. While they were courteous, their demeanor discouraged misconduct. They reminded me of the commanding officers in the Army—their presence made men want to obey. Their disposition, combined with the well-maintained firearms hanging across their backs, inspired compliance.

It had been years since I'd taken an order, but I fell back into the habit with ease. "Recruit Cruse, fold those blankets, and pack up the cookware. We're about to head out." General Stillwell's voice was raspy in the morning. It usually smoothed out after coffee, but we'd run out yesterday.

"Yes, sir." I cleaned up the campsite, enjoying the crisp air as I worked. There was a briskness to the morning, one that let you know fall was on its way.

I packed up the gear and tucked it into the general's rucksack. "Sir, I gather that we're near the end of our journey?"

"We are, indeed, Cruse. What made you ask?"

"Just an observation, sir. I'm a coffee-drinking man, and I noticed that we used the last of it with breakfast yesterday. I thought you might have packed just enough grounds to last through the trip, and it sounds like that's true."

The General chuckled. "Well, now, I can't put anything past you. It's too bad I guessed a little short. I sure could use some caffeine right now."

"I'm with you on that, sir."

He clapped my shoulder. "Saddle up, and let's get going. The quicker we finish this trek, the quicker we can get our hands on a cup."

We rode for three hours at a halting pace. The woods around our party grew denser, and General Stillwell stopped several times to hold branches while we passed. While it was earlier than noon, the darkness under the trees made it feel much later. I enjoyed the solitude of the forest. We didn't talk as we rode, and the silence gave me an opportunity to think about the direction my life was now headed. The unexpected change of course had kindled an excitement I hadn't felt in a long while. It felt good to be pursuing a new path. It felt right.

An abrupt stop brought me out of my thoughts. The General dismounted and walked toward a tall, stately tree. I noticed an S carved in its trunk, a swirling letter with flourishes on each end. "All right, men. We've reached the point of no return." He appraised each of us. "I know you joined Sergeant Roccio and me a'ways back, but now we need to hear you pledge allegiance to our way of life. Get off your mounts and come this way." We did as he asked and stood in front of General Stillwell, waiting for further instruction. "I'm going to call you forward. When I do, place your right palm on the S, the Starkesend boundary, and answer my questions with a true heart and mind. Recruit Miles, you're up first."

Ed Miles, a slender fellow with hard eyes, walked to the fir, and put his hand over the carving. General Stillwell did the same. "Edward Miles Jr., right now we're brothers, and our ranks mean nothing. I'm here to welcome you to Starkesend, to lead you to the place where history will be made. I'm a founding member of this community and my greatest source of pride is the high caliber of its newcomers. You see, not everyone is worthy of supporting our cause. It takes a lot to be selected by our recruiters, to stand out among the mediocre men who are all too common."

General Stillwell dropped his hand from the tree and began pacing. "We chose you for many reasons, Miles. Your valor during the Great War, your talent as an intelligence officer, and your experience in publication—this is what drew us to you. We know these skills will be put to good use in our fight against the rising Jewish tide."

During the evenings, after the day's ride was finished, we set up camp and cooked supper. These chores were completed efficiently, but mealtime was different. We relaxed while we ate. Around the fire, the five of us talked between bites and for hours afterward. We traded war stories, and I heard everyone's reasons for leaving their homes and joining Starkesend. I got to know the men I was traveling with. Except Miles. Miles hadn't revealed much about himself and wasn't interested in learning about his group mates. When he did enter the conversation, his clipped responses made it impossible to glean information. We eventually stopped trying to draw him into the banter. He obviously preferred privacy.

Now that I knew he'd been an officer, his attitude made sense. He must find subservience difficult. Being downgraded to a recruit was a blow to the ego, but only if you let it bother you. Humility was necessary when you were starting over. How could you ever learn, ever grow, if you didn't give yourself the opportunity to become a novice? I noted Miles' conceit and continued to observe his initiation.

"If you agree with my questions, answer aye after each one. Do you understand, Miles?"

He nodded. "Aye, sir."

"Very good. Do you agree to join Starkesend? To give this community your all, every day?"

"Aye, sir."

"Do you agree to use every weapon in your power to support your Aryan brothers and to stop our advancing enemies?"

"Aye, sir."

"Do you promise to lay your life on the line if it ever becomes necessary?"

"Aye, sir."

"Welcome to Starkesend, Recruit Miles. Thank you for your service." General Stillwell motioned for him to return to the rest of us. When he got back in place, the General called the next name. "Recruit Cruse, you're up."

I made my way to the boundary tree, and placed my hand over the S. We repeated the same back in forth, and then once more with Recruit Tanne. My electrical skills were praised, while Tanne's engineering traits were extolled. Starkesend attracted talented people, and I presumed there were more inside. The community I was joining was a strong coalition that operated on the fringes of society.

Once the ceremony was completed, General Stillwell dismissed us to our horses. When we were atop our mounts, he yelled out. "Okay, boys, let us in."

The dense wall of shrubs around the boundary tree parted. A narrow dirt trail became visible, and two uniformed men walked to the middle of the path. They saluted in sync. One man had red hair, freckles, and a boyish grin. The other had an olive complexion and serious brown eyes.

Freckles spoke up. "Morning General, Sergeant." He nodded at the men. "You brought us some new recruits. Welcome, fellas! I'm Corporal Cole.

You just follow this road to your new home, Fort Vogel." His smile broadened. "I think you'll like it here."

"Don't forget to check in and surrender your items." The second man spoke hurriedly while giving Cole an exasperated look.

General Stillwell waved them away. "Cole, Yarro, we'll take it from here. There should be no one else behind us. If you hear anything, sound the alarm."

"Yes, sir. Thank you for the update." Cole saluted again and stepped off the trail. Yarro joined him. They let the five of us pass before retreating to their vantage point. Much like the entrance to Starkesend, their watch station was hidden in the foliage. A great deal of care had gone into ensuring the secrecy of this place.

It didn't take long to reach Fort Vogel, the military portion of Starkesend. The path from the boundary tree had been cleared of undergrowth, but a canopy of leafy branches masked the trail from overhead observation. I wondered if the entire compound was covered because adapting to that level of concealment would take time. I wasn't used to hiding from the sun or the world.

It was a relief to feel the daylight's warmth when the trail ended. There were still trees, lush spruce and pine, but they did not overwhelm. They complimented the squat buildings and homes in Fort Vogel. The compound was organized yet at peace with the environment. Its architecture was softened by the boughs that brushed against it and the wildflowers that grew in garden plots.

General Stillwell led us to a stable, and we left our horses with a smiling man who wished us well. The end of our journey was completed on foot. Without instruction, we assumed a formation with the two leaders in the front and the rest of us in a horizontal line behind them. Our pace became an efficient cadence, *left, right, left, right.* Ten arms and legs marched in time, heading toward our new home.

We passed houses and a chow hall before we reached our destination. The barracks were painted the same tan and brown as the rest of the buildings, but their size stood out. The soldier's quarters dwarfed every other structure. There were also fewer windows dotting the walls. Inside, this was more obvious. After we entered the main building, it took a few moments for my eyes to adjust to the dimness. When they did, the emptiness in the room surprised me. Sergeant Roccio noticed my shock and spoke up. "It's not much to look at now, but we'll be bursting at the seams pretty soon."

The General agreed. "You three are some the first recruits we've brought to Fort Vogel. The village, Dorf, was built ten years ago, but we just finished this section."

A village? That was intriguing. From the men's descriptions of Starkesend, I had assumed it functioned solely as a military operation. When they used the word community, I'd pictured platoons of men working toward the same goals or bonding over shared experiences. It appeared that a broader definition of community was at play.

"Sir, will we visit the village?" I asked.

"The intent is to keep soldiers separate from breeders, but there might be changes to that policy in the future." He smiled. "But let's not worry about that now. Our first task is to get you situated."

The word breeders piqued my curiosity, but I knew better than to disobey. Staying on your commander's good side was the best way to gain trust and responsibility, two of my main goals. I followed the General down the middle of the barracks rather than ask questions. He went three-quarters of the way down the room before he stopped in front of a pair of bunks.

"Tanne, Miles, this is your spot. There are lockers on the back of the racks with your uniforms and PT gear. Everything should fit, but if not, let me know." He stretched out his arm, holding his hand flat. "I'll need your personal belongings now. When you entered Starkesend, you became part of something bigger, and you won't need mementos of your past life."

Tanne handed his bag over without hesitation. With slower movements, he unclasped the silver necklace he wore and gently placed it in the outstretched palm.

"Don't worry, son. We'll take good care of your property. If you ever want to leave, we give it right back." General Stillwell reassured him. He nodded at Miles. "Let's get on with it."

Miles' hands trembled as he removed the bag strap from his shoulder. He briefly squeezed his eyes shut before handing it over. The General peered at him warily. "Everything okay, recruit? You're not having second thoughts so soon, are you?"

"No, sir. I just…well, I've been writing a book and thought I'd have a chance to finish it here. My only copy of the manuscript is in that bag."

"A writer, eh? We need one of those around these parts. And like I said to Tanne, we'll take good care of your property." He tightened his grip on both men's possessions. "Welcome home, recruits. Get washed up and head to the mess hall. They're serving the midday meal now."

Reaching our destination had fired up my adrenaline as well as my appetite. I was a mix of excitement and hunger, although my craving for food dominated after hearing about the upcoming meal. If the mess hall here was anything like it was in the Army, the options would be bland and limited. Still, they would satisfy my appetite. I hurried after the General as he moved to the back of the barracks. He stopped in front of a single bed and turned to me.

"Congratulations, Private Cruse, you've received a promotion. I was impressed with you during our travels. You earned this rank by working hard and being observant, attributes we value here in Starkesend."

"Thank you, sir. This is a surprise."

"Keep it up, Cruse, and you'll be an officer in no time."

I handed him my belongings and gratefully accepted my dismissal. As I walked past Tanne and Miles on my way to the chow hall, they acknowledged my new rank.

"Congratulations, Cruse. You earned this." Tanne shook my hand.

Miles huffed and fixed me with a skeptical gaze. "Already brown-nosing? I'll be keeping an eye on you." He pushed past the two of us and walked out of the building alone.

Chapter 12 - Gunnar

Adjusting to life at Fort Vogel was painless. The years I'd spent in the Army equipped me for the early hours and physical regiment, and my time as an electrician prepared me for the menial tasks that filled the days. I was assigned to Bravo platoon along with seven other men. Our first duty was to complete finishing touches around base. Tanne and I worked well together. His skillset complemented mine, and we completed tasks swiftly. The only unpleasant part of this new routine was Miles. If his goal was to disrupt progress, he was exceeding expectations.

Miles tried to assert dominance while we toiled. Instead of helping install ovens or lay flooring, he shouted orders at the group. "That needs to be further to the right, Tanne. And Conroy, stop fraying those wires. You're going to get us electrocuted." His words were arrogant and ignorant, an infuriating combination,

We ignored him as best we could, but there were times when his voice bothered me. I wanted to hurt him, to force him to see the audacity of his actions. Or non-action. A group builds trust when people respect each other, when they see themselves as equals working toward the same purpose. Miles was disrupting this concept by neglecting his fair share of labor and subjecting us to his absurd attempts at superiority.

I waited two weeks before reporting him. It was sensible to give Miles enough time to make a choice. He would either correct his behavior or attach himself more fully to his unfit attitude. Unfortunately, he'd selected the latter. Sergeant Roccio was Bravo's leader, so I took my concerns to him. I knocked on his office door and waited for a response. Luckily, he was in. "Who's there?"

"It's Private Cruse. Do you have time to talk?"

"Cruse, come in. I'm just wrapping something up." I opened the door to a small, windowless room. It was austere. A desk, chair, and lamp were the only furnishings, and nothing personal adorned the walls or the meticulously clean desktop. Sergeant Roccio set down his pen and tucked away a file. As he slid it into a drawer, I noticed the words *Top Secret* stamped in thick black ink on its surface. He must have been finishing important business. "I'd say have a seat, but there's no chair. Sorry about that. We cut space from this area to make room for more bunks." He shrugged apologetically.

"No problem, Sergeant. This shouldn't take long."

He nodded. "What do you have for me?"

I let my curiosity lead. "Before I give you the bad news, Sergeant, you said something interesting. More room for bunks makes it sound like you anticipate a bigger group joining our forces. That will give us a tactical advantage if it's true."

"Indeed, it would, Cruse." He leaned back in his chair. "We've sent out recruiters and hope to double our troop count by the end of the year. That's why we have your team working on the homes and barracks. We need to be ready for a rush of people."

"What are our numbers now? I think I've met everyone on base, but it's hard to be certain." I thought about it for a moment. "If I had to guess, I'd say we have sixteen infantry, five NCOs, and three officers."

Sergeant Roccio was impressed. "Not bad, Cruse. If you don't include the men we sent out, you're exactly right. The recruiters, two corporals and two majors, will be making three trips from now until the last days of December. That gives them what's left of summer and the entire fall to grow our military."

"That's great news. We certainly have the space for them. The command team was right to prepare for an increase in patriots on base." It was time to bring up Miles. "Let me get back to business so I'm not wasting your time, Sergeant. The reason I asked to speak concerns a member of Bravo. He's causing disruptions to our work and morale."

"Now it's my turn to guess." Sergeant Roccio leaned onto his desk." I'd wager that you're talking about Miles. I've been observing him since I went through that book of his. He writes of things…how should I say this? Unbecoming a soldier." He grimaced. "What issues do you have with him?"

"You're right, Sergeant, Miles is the problem. He's put himself into a situation where it's him against the rest of us. He constantly critiques our work while doing none of his own. And his suggestions are complete bull. The man has no idea what he's talking about." I sighed. "I've tried reasoning with him, but it doesn't work. The rest of the team and I spoke this morning, and they agreed with my decision to bring this to your attention."

"What strong leadership skills, Cruse. You'll be going places around here." He let loose his own sigh. "Recruit Miles, on the other hand, only seems to be heading toward the exit. Let me counsel him. I'll give him a week to change his attitude, or he's gone." He shook his head and frowned. "We hate to lose numbers, but rotten apples need to be disposed of."

"Thank you for listening to me, Sergeant."

"It's my pleasure, Private." He stood and extended his hand. "Now, if you don't mind, I have a wayward soldier who needs a talking to, like a child."

We shook hands. "Some adults never learn to get right and get along. I'll see you at PT."

I left the cramped office, grateful that my complaint was taken seriously. It was unnerving to hear they'd rifled through our belongings. I'd suspected as much, but having it confirmed made it real. They were probably searching for weapons and other contraband. It was sensible to dispose of harmful items before they could be used. It appeared that less dangerous objects, like Miles' book, were also rifled through. Whatever he'd written must have been disturbing, judging by the Sergeant's sickened expression, but I'd leave worrying about it to the base's ranking members.

Time passed and Bravo team worked hard, finishing one house a day. Seven of us laid flooring, wired electrical outlets, and painted walls a cheery shade of yellow. The eighth member of our group sulked in the barracks, smarting from his discussion with our leader. Miles' presence had been a burden, and losing this weight made the team more efficient, more motivated. We completed tasks ahead of schedule and never complained when more was asked of us. It was invigorating to labor with such determined men. I felt driven and purposeful, a far cry from the restlessness that reigned during my last months in Casper.

A week after my meeting with Sergeant Roccio, Miles left Starkesend for good. It happened in the middle of the night. The evening of his departure, I'd seen the layabout in his bunk. His clothes were rumpled and stained, his complexion sallow. Miles was a man who had given up hope, but he hadn't given up his nastiness. He called out as I passed his bed. "Hey Cruse, what's it like being such a cad? I'm glad to be leaving you fools. I'd much rather be around people who matter."

I ignored him and left for the chow hall. When I returned, Miles' back was turned toward the wall, with a blanket tucked snugly over his head. I passed him unnoticed, grateful to avoid his insults. While his words had no impact on my mood, I preferred not to hear them.

Back in my rack, sleep came quickly, as did the next day. Our exercise regimen began early, 0500 hours, so I dressed and headed out of the barracks. I noted Miles' absence as I passed his bunk. His bed was neatly made, the corners pulled tight and angled sharply. His uniforms no longer hung next to Tanne's, and his helmet had been removed from its hook. He was gone. I whistled on the way to PT and the Bravo team celebrated at work that day, but that was the last impact he had on our group. We moved past Miles' dismissal and got on with life.

Despite his petulance, a small part of me harbored pity for the man who'd lost his footing in this new world. Some folks adjusted to circumstances better than others. They went along with change, correcting themselves when necessary. I was like this. My keen sense of observation, coupled with strong intuition, enabled me to adapt to any environment. I was someone who watched before acting, who thought before speaking. Stillness and silence could be powerful weapons in unfamiliar surroundings.

At the other end of the spectrum were people like Miles. You could sense their smugness, their ego, in every interaction. These characteristics were often shields for another emotion—worry. Miles was afraid of revealing his inadequacies, so he masked his anxiety with arrogance and loud assertions. In his eyes, silence indicated weakness, while volume implied power. His insults and commands were distractions from his inferiority. Men who were comfortable seldom shouted their way to the top. Men like Miles used their voice, rather than their value, to get places.

Unfortunately for him, the people of Starkesend hadn't fallen for his bluster. We'd lifted his cover and recognized smallness. When you're surrounded by those who are confident in themselves, concealment doesn't go too far. I pitied him because I knew he never had a chance. He was blinded by his pride, and it didn't alert him to the danger of failure. Still, I was happy to see him go. The fewer frauds we had around, the better.

Chapter 13 - Gunnar

After six months at Fort Vogel, General Stillwell promoted me to Corporal. He also assigned me to a new unit, Project Leer. When we discussed the operation, he noted that my electrical training would come in handy. He also mentioned human subjects.

"Cruse, you're logical, which makes you a good fit for Leer. We're still constructing electrical components down there, but with your knowledge, that will be finished in no time. The other part of your assignment will be much more important." He lowered his voice. "I should warn you about one thing. The test subjects' screams will make your blood run cold. We've tried reconfiguring the machine's settings multiple times, but nothing's worked. It's been hard keeping men in the lab with all the noise, so I'm hoping you'll have the stomach for it."

"Are the people…the subjects, in pain, sir? I know experiments can be necessary, as well as harm, but I want to know what I'm getting into. What exactly is going on?"

"It's smart to ask, Corporal. I appreciate your candor." General Stillwell leaned back and thought about my question. "Pain, huh? That's not quite right. I think I'd call it fear more than anything. You can see the horror in their eyes, hear it in their shrieks. It's quite haunting." He shuddered. "Dr. Brandt was surprised by the screams. The extractor is supposed to siphon fear away, but for some reason, it's creating it. That's why I'm asking you to join, Cruse. We need fresh eyes."

"Okay, sir. I'll give it my best. If you really think this will give us an advantage, I'll do whatever I can to help."

The General jumped out of his seat. "This is wonderful news. I'll let the doctor know, and you can start tomorrow. If we make this work, Cruse, Starkesend will be the apple of the Führer's eye." He gestured toward the door, and I left him to his excitement.

The next morning, I reported to Dr. Brandt. His laboratory was underground and connected by tunnels to Dame Hall and the armory. The ceiling was low. Anyone taller than average had to stoop to avoid injury, but this design flaw didn't appear to bother the Doctor. He greeted me with a smile.

"Good morning, Corporal Cruse. Welcome to Project Leer. I've heard excellent things about you." He stuck out a pale, thin hand, and we shook.

"Good morning, Dr. Brandt. I hope to prove those excellent things true. Please let me know how I can be of use."

"That's the right attitude, Cruse. Let's get to work. The wiring part of your job can wait until we finetune the extractor." Without warning, he handed me a key and strode off, shouting instructions as he walked. "I'll warm up the machinery while you grab Subject 004 from the cells on the left. Once you have him, come this way, then I'll teach you a thing or two."

I followed the doctor's directions and headed down a dimly lit hall. As I moved, a humming noise vibrated around me. It started at barely a whisper but picked up volume with each step. The longer I listened, the more the sound transformed, first filling my ears, then leaving them achingly empty. The further along I went, the closer I was driven to delirium by the crescendos and abatements. It took me too long to understand I was hearing sobs, not a morbid concerto. While the discord remained unsettling, I felt calmer knowing it came from human beings.

At the end of the passage, there were two barred rooms filled with unmoving shadows. When I approached, the shadows closest to me became people I recognized—they were the men and women banished from

Starkesend. General Stillwell kept their pictures in the war room, marking each of their photographs with the word *Traitor* in red ink. I'd memorized the faces in the photos and made it a goal to avoid their fate. Now, I knew their reality contained things worse than expulsion.

Males and females were housed in separate pens, six men on the left and four women on the right. Even with this division, everyone behaved the same. The subjects were seated bolt-upright on benches that lined the walls of their cells. Their jaws were stretched to the limit, and they cried together in a twisted harmony, a chorus of voices mingling sorrow and pain. The skin on their necks pulled taut as they stared at the ceiling with unblinking eyes. Because of this odd angle, I noticed the underside of their noses. Instead of two holes, each person had one nostril, a hollowed-out cavity where raw, swollen tissue was visible. *What had Dr. Brandt done?*

I breathed deeply, slowly gaining my composure. It wouldn't be wise to fail this mission. I needed to find Subject 004 and leave this area before I gave into the madness it inspired. I studied the caged group, hoping there would be a way to tell them apart without speaking to them. I imagined their words would be gargled, full of the blood dripping down their chins and onto the floor. Any speech from them would destroy my tenuous grip on sanity, and I would happily join in on their trance, wailing the hours away.

Luckily, each person wore a badge marked with their laboratory ID. The black number assigned to each person was easy to read from outside the cell, and I located 004 in a corner of the enclosure. The iron door creaked as I opened it, but the men inside the pen made no indication they'd heard it. I walked toward my target and grabbed his elbow.

"Okay, fellow, we're going to head out of here. Let's take it nice and easy, okay?" I spoke gently, reassuringly. 004 stopped sobbing and lowered his head. When we locked eyes, I recognized Ed Miles. He'd changed in the months since I'd seen him, and not just anatomically. His humanity had also departed. What I was staring at was no longer someone who experienced life's highs and lows, the joys and setbacks that meant you were living. Miles was now the embodiment of just a single emotion.

He was terrified and nothing else.

I stayed calm, not wanting to startle him or the others. "Are you ready, Miles? Let's take a quick trip up the hall. You can lean on me if you'd like." He was unresponsive to my voice. Whatever horrors captivated him weren't letting go of his attention. I gave up on coaxing him from the cell and escorted him out instead. We retraced my steps, then traveled in the direction Dr. Brandt had headed. The shadowy, narrow corridor led the way to a cavernous workspace. I no longer had to crouch or strain my eyes because the ceilings were vaulted, and light filled the space.

Miles kept up with my pace in the hallways, but when we stepped into the bright room, he slowed, pulling back the way we'd come. I whispered in his ear, hoping to encourage him. "We're almost there. You can do it." Instead of the soothing effect I hoped for, my words caused Miles to whimper and claw at my uniform.

A sharp voice brought my attention to the right. "Don't coddle him. He's a traitor who doesn't deserve your leniency, Cruse. Drag him over, and I'll strap him down." I followed the command and went to the doctor. He was waiting for us with a shackle in each hand. After I sat Miles down, Dr. Brandt enclosed his wrists with the thick metal, and a clanking sound echoed throughout the room.

That was when the screaming started.

Miles' high-pitched wails blasted through my skull and pierced my brain. The terror he'd shown in his cell was nothing compared to the fear filling his shrieks. They hit pitches a soprano would struggle with, and their volume belied the fact that they came from the throat of an emaciated person. Miles was petrified and fighting for his life. He strained against the cuffs, pulling his body into an arched position. He jerked his head back and forth, slinging blood from his open wound. Nothing he did was enough to escape, however. The iron on his wrists held tight against his struggles.

"Cruse!" The Doctor's voice barely cut through the racket. "We need to restrain his legs and head. Grab the straps by his feet and pull as hard as you can. Do it quickly too. He'll keep at it until we get him under control."

I buckled leather restraints around his ankles while Dr. Brandt fastened a cage-like box around his head. When we finished this process, Miles' screaming stopped as abruptly as it began. I shook my head to clear the remnants of the commotion, and then I addressed Dr. Brandt. "What the hell, Doctor? I don't think that's normal." I gestured around the room. "And what are we trying to accomplish here? I know the goal of Leer is to reduce fear in our men, but I don't think you're close to making that happen."

He surprised me with laughter. "I've been here a month, and you're the first person who's dared speak their mind to me, Cruse. The other men I was assigned were too scared or stupid to string together more than a few words. It's refreshing to hear some criticism. It doesn't happen often when you're at my level."

"I'm sorry to be blunt, Doctor, but it's shocking to hear a person make those noises. And the group of them, crying like that in their pens. I don't know what to make of it all."

"To tell you the truth, I don't know what to make of it either, but I only have another month to figure it out. That's when I leave Starkesend and head back to Germany." He placed a tube in Miles' nasal cavity trough the gaps in the cage, then walked to a control board. "I'm going to try something with 004 before we discuss things further. I set the extractor to one-third power today. Let's see if we get a good reaction from the subject. Step back, Cruse, and I'll start it up."

I edged away from the chair, and Dr. Brandt pressed a button that brought the machine to life. Miles immediately stiffened, his hands and jaw clenched, his eyes and tongue protruded. He used the small amount of strength left in his body to strain against the extractor. It tried to take from him, but Miles valiantly struggled against its probing.

The torment was brutal, but I forced myself to witness his pain since I was its enabler. I'd brought him to the current torture session. I was also the reason he was underground with Dr. Brandt in the first place. Reporting Miles to Sergeant Roccio felt right at the moment, but now I knew it was a mistake. His minor annoyances didn't equate to the amount of punishment he'd been given. Nothing equated to this. And I was seeing only a third of what Miles had faced. His other sessions, the ones at full power, must have been worse. I would bear witness to what I'd caused. It was the least I could do.

Seconds passed, then minutes, and Miles stayed locked in place. His fight against the extractor and the pain it was inflicting stretched on without signs of stopping. It seemed like the observation had gone on for an eternity. Since this was my first shift in the laboratory, I wasn't sure how long the experiments lasted. I looked at the Doctor, checking for signs of impatience, but his face was animated, and he observed our subject's movements closely. I shifted my viewpoint back to my old colleague, hoping his distress would end soon.

Without warning, his body unclenched, and Miles slumped as far as the restraints would allow. After his muscles stopped twitching and he was fully relaxed, thick, clear fluid flowed from his nose into the container Dr. Brandt had inserted. The liquid continued dripping after the tube filled, forming a puddle on the floor. I moved toward the spillage. The closer I got, the more disturbing it became. Tiny, reddish flecks dotted the collection of transparent runoff, and the specks grew more prominent the longer the flow continued.

I looked to the Doctor for guidance. His mouth was stretched into a smile that was a mismatch to the horror in front of us. He noticed my stare. "Cruse, you must be my lucky charm. This was the most progress I've made since I've been here." He came to where I was standing and bent toward the viscous liquid. "I finally made it to the brain. I knew I could reach it through the nasal passage, but I had the extractor level too high. Other things came out, not the cerebrospinal fluid I was searching for." He pointed, and somehow his grin widened. "But this is it."

"Why this stuff? I thought the purpose of Leer was to harvest fear, not deplete the subject's brain."

"My boy, this is the first step to gathering fear. We're doing things that no one has attempted. Plenty of lobotomies and shocks have been given to the human brain, but this…this is a whole new level. We're getting to the bottom of the mind-emotion connection." To my surprise, he reached out and stirred Miles' leavings with a finger. The red flecks swirled together, making a whorled pattern. "We still went a bit far. There shouldn't be this much blood." He shook his head. "I do suppose we need to consider how damaged 004 was. That may have contributed to the excess bleeding."

Apparently, it was Miles' fault he'd bled too much. Dr. Brandt blamed a mistreated man for failing to produce the proper fluids. The audacity floored me, but I couldn't shake the guilt over my role in this abuse. I'd placed Miles in the Doctor's hands. It was my fault he was strapped to a chair, having his essence drained away.

I turned from the Doctor and studied Miles. His face was peaceful, his limbs slack. It was a far cry from the terror he'd shown in his cell or his straining against the extractor. "Dr. Brandt, do we need the subject for anything else? I can take him back to his cell if not. It looks like he's ready to rest."

"Let me take his vitals before you move him." He grabbed a medical bag from the control table and walked to Miles. He waved me over. "Pay attention, Cruse. This will be one of your tasks."

I came closer while he placed a stethoscope on Miles' chest, then his back. The Doctor appeared bored as he took a small mirror from his bag and held it in front of Miles' mouth. He waited impassively for the second hand on his watch to complete two rotations. During those one hundred twenty seconds, not one breath fogged the glass. I knew what this meant, but I waited for confirmation.

Dr. Brandt's steady voice contrasted with my churning thoughts. "Time of death 0938." He wrote the information in a notebook. "We'll need to incinerate his body, Cruse. I'll show you where the oven is. Move him onto that stretcher and come with me."

I wheeled over the metal gurney and unstrapped Miles from the chair. After I detached the collection tube from his nose, I placed him on the cot, carefully avoiding the leakage on the ground. We rolled behind Dr. Brandt until we reached a brick wall with two rectangular doors on it. The Doctor opened the door on the right, and I lined up the table with the angled slot, lifting its end, so Miles slid into the chamber. And then he was gone, closed behind a metal door, never to be seen again.

"Would you like to say something, Cruse? I know he was your platoon mate before he ended up down here."

I shook my head.

"Very well." Dr. Brandt placed his finger on the oven's power button. "004 furthered our research. His noble death canceled out his transgressions against Starkesend. He shall be unburdened in the afterlife."

With those words, the Doctor turned on the heat, and Miles became just another memory.

Lizbeth, 1936

Chapter 14 - Lizbeth

I didn't trust the men in front of me. They spoke in terms befitting a lady, or in other words, they talked to me like my brain was full of fluff. Each man overplayed the benefits and underplayed the drawbacks of the procedure I would be undergoing. My parents taught me to be wary of this tactic because it was used by ill-intentioned people. That was the sense I got from our conversation—these two were not my friends.

"Hello there, you must be Lizbeth. I'm General Stillwell, and this is Dr. Brandt. Welcome to our laboratory."

I curtsied. "Good morning, sirs."

"So polite." The General glanced at Ms. Granth. "Still doing a fine job with the young ladies, I see. You continue to impress me, madam." His gaze returned to me. "Do you know why you're with us today?"

"No, sir, but I believe it has something to do with my birthday."

He nodded. "Right you are, Lizbeth. Starting at eighteen, each person on base begins contributing to Starkesend's medical knowledge. Our fine scientists take that knowledge and use it for good things here and overseas. It's quite a team effort, and we've already seen some real advantages from what we've learned." General Stillwell let out a shallow laugh and nudged his partner. "But I won't step on any toes by oversharing. Let me turn it over to Dr. Brandt."

"Thanks, General. Lizbeth, I'm sure you have questions, but I'm going to try and head them off by answering them now. First, let me say welcome to Fort Vogel. I know you arrived here a short while ago, and I hope you're adjusting well. It can be quite a change, coming from Dorf to the base." He smiled, but it didn't reach his eyes. "I know how you're feeling. I arrived yesterday, and I'm still adapting to the time change."

He took a few steps toward a hallway on the right and gestured for us to follow. When he saw that we were, he continued talking. "I'd like to show you our equipment, Lizbeth. I think you'll find it most impressive. Everything we have is top-of-the-line. Things were inferior when we started our work, but now that we've shown our worth, the Führer has rewarded us with everything we need."

Dr. Brandt must have come from Germany, which meant that whatever was happening at Starkesend was a priority to German leadership. Doctors and pricey equipment weren't sent to minor supporters. The laboratory must provide the Nazi party with valuable resources, and I would now be part of the yield.

We stopped in a bright room with vaulted ceilings. Spotless white paint showcased the cleanliness of the curved walls and the concrete floors. In the center of the domed space, gleaming machinery and a hospital bed rested, waiting for a controller and patient to fulfill their purpose. Lab tables and an observation deck finished off the décor.

"You're looking at my greatest achievement." Dr. Brandt gestured around the room, this time wearing a smile he meant. "To make this happen, I traveled across the ocean for almost three years, back and forth on dozens of trips. During each visit, I make progress." He laughed quietly and spoke in a voice almost too low to decipher. "It's quite remarkable, really. Just when you think you can't dig any deeper into the human anatomy, you find a way."

He shook his head and refocused on the group. "But that's not the information you're after, Lizbeth, so let me return to that. The people of Fort Vogel are superior human beings. The next time you walk around base, I challenge you to find one infirm or feeble person among your neighbors. Try it to satisfy your curiosity, but I'll tell you now, it will be an impossible task because no such person exists on these grounds." Pride filled the Doctor's eyes. "To maintain an exceptional level, we vet soldiers and wives for two purposes. First, we ensure they are suited for daily life since keeping the base running is tedious work. Of course, we only include those with clean pedigrees, but we also screen for work ethic and fitness. The fact that you're in this lab means you surpassed our entry requirements."

The words were meant as flattery, but I didn't appreciate the praise. For Dr. Brandt, people existed solely in terms of their biology. To him, I was an eighteen-year-old female of average height and weight, free of defects that would hinder a day's work. He didn't know about my love of reading or the pleasure I took in making others smile, nor did he care. These factors were unimportant in Starkesend, seen only as trivial hobbies suited to children. Reducing people to their observable features was a dangerous practice, a narrow worldview that acknowledged a single category and nothing else. Those who existed outside the accepted standard were excluded and made to feel inferior. Those fortunate enough to embody the ideal were pumped full of self-importance until they never questioned their inflated opinion of themselves.

I knew this was how my society operated. Intolerance for the weak was taught at school and home. I'd been shielded from this perspective by my parents. They told me stories of a grandfather who flourished after losing an arm and a deaf great-uncle who managed a successful bank. When I heard classroom lessons about the feebleminded and unfit, I remembered Papa Ira and Uncle Joseph, quietly, of course. Admitting a connection to someone with a disability was cause for immediate dismissal. I knew my parents opposed certain principles of our community, but I also understood that losing our home was not the outcome they sought.

As was expected, I graciously accepted the Doctor's compliment. "Thank you, sir. I'm happy to be of use to Starkesend."

"Young lady, besides Germany, there is no better place to be. I'm glad you appreciate your fortune." He walked toward the blinking machinery. "If you'll come this way, I'll explain the second reason we maintain such high standards."

The group followed, and the Doctor resumed speaking. "To the untrained eye, this appears overwhelming. I want to assure you that the man behind the controls is an expert who does everything he can to minimize the level of harm patients experience." He turned to me. "It is not my intent to frighten you with the word harm. I don't use it lightly. My desire is honesty. I want to prepare you for the discomfort that may come during and after your session. Over time, we've found that preparation speeds up the healing process, and that's our number one goal—to help you feel better faster."

General Stillwell chimed in. "What he says is true, Lizbeth. Your well-being is a priority. Without the men and women who serve Starkesend, there would be less information flowing to our leaders. We can only fulfill our duties because you're able to fulfill yours."

It pained me to hear another reminder of my insignificance, to know that I was interchangeable, a replaceable part of the community. Others had assigned each of my roles—first wife and worker, now laboratory subject. From morning until bedtime, I fulfilled these purposes, leaving no room to experience life on my terms. Lizbeth barely existed, and with each passing day, she faded more and more.

Thoughts of smallness or mortality weren't inherently wrong. They were a remedy to a swollen ego, a reality check to overflowing arrogance. Considering one's place in the country, the world, or the universe was humbling, and it was necessary to maintain a grounded perspective, but as with most practices, there was a line that could be crossed. If my existence was expendable, what reasons did I have to nourish the person inside? There was beauty in being a piece of the whole, but this beauty was dimmed when the piece's relevance was ignored. Overplaying someone's unimportance threatened the parts that made them an individual.

I knew not to take it personally, knew that the men in front of me treated everyone with the same disregard. Still, it was difficult to distance myself from their dehumanizing speech. I took a steadying breath before I responded.

"I'm grateful you've considered my health. Thank you both." I lowered my eyes and voice, portraying a shyness I knew they would respond to. "May I ask a question?"

General Stillwell replied. "Go ahead, Lizbeth. We'll answer if we can."

"I guess it's two questions, really." I kept my voice submissive and smiled demurely. "What type of harm will happen? I'm afraid of pain, so I was hoping you could calm my worries before we start."

"There's no simple answer, Lizbeth. Some subjects experience pressure during the extraction, and that's it. Other subjects feel off for longer periods. The effects are personal, and there's no way to know your reaction until you go through it." General Stillwell regarded Ms. Granth. "Emmeline, one of your pupils caused a disruption recently, is that right?"

"That's right, General. Marta Elridge had a bad spell after her first session and frightened some of the new brides, but now she's right as rain." Ms. Granth smiled reassuringly. "Dear, there's no need to worry about pain. These wonderful men have thought of everything and can fix you up if something happens."

The General patted her shoulder. "Thank you for the vote of confidence, Emmeline." He swung his gaze back to me. "Ms. Granth is right, Lizbeth. While you may experience discomfort, we can address it rather quickly."

I focused on my first morning at Fort Vogel, picturing the disruption they were referring to. My classmate's anguish and heart-wrenching sobs flooded my memory. I remembered the shock I'd felt. And the pity. Marta hadn't been allowed to keep her hurt private. Instead, it was played out in front of her peers in an uncomfortable public breakdown.

I'm sure Marta also went through this process, listening as the group tried to convince her of their goodwill, emphasizing the importance of output while minimizing the potential for distress. She might have agreed with this point and welcomed the opportunity to serve her community. If she and I were ever alone, I'd make it a point to ask—*Was the procedure worth the yield?*

Judging by Dr. Brandt's impatient movements, I would soon find out on my own. I hurriedly asked my second question, undeterred by the Doctor's darting eyes and jittery feet. I wanted to learn as much as possible before my session began, and I knew this would be my last chance to uncover information.

"I'm glad to hear Marta recovered so quickly, and I'm glad the same courtesy will be extended to me if needed." I forced extra cheeriness into my voice. "I hate to bother you with another question, but what is it that we're…producing? I'm sorry if that's not the proper word for it, but I was curious about what you take from us. It must be very valuable."

Dr. Brandt stopped tapping his toes and grew serious. "Lizbeth, you wouldn't understand the science behind our processes. No one in your position could. But I can tell you what the majority of our work involves." He paused. "Quite simply, what we do down here is harvest fear." He pulled his lips into a frightening grin. "Now, enough with the chit-chat. It's time for your procedure to begin."

He yelled out, "Colonel, commence extraction 316."

I turned in the direction he shouted and saw my husband approach. Although his presence was unexpected, it was a comfort after the unsettling conversation I'd had in the lab. Gunnar reached out his hand and spoke gently. "Come with me, Lizbeth. Don't worry. I'll make this as painless as possible."

Chapter 15 - Lizbeth

Gunnar was true to his word, and I made it through the extraction with minimal pain. After I took his offered hand, he led me to the padded gurney and tenderly maneuvered me into a facedown position. As I descended, I clasped my chest and positioned my scissors parallel with the table. The cold metal pressed against my skin, reassuring me. It wasn't the time to use the weapon—I was flanked by observers in an unfamiliar place—but its presence grounded me, as always. The secret knowledge let me maintain the smallest measure of control, something invaluable in my current plight.

I turned my head toward Gunnar, and he showed me each piece of equipment before connecting it. He attached gauges and patches to my left arm, plus a few lines of thin tubing. He rested the largest piece of equipment, two long needles attached to a pouch-shaped receptacle, just above my waist. Before he inserted the metal into my back, Gunnar offered some guidance.

"Lizbeth, I need to place these further under your skin. I've found it's helpful to take a deep breath before insertion and then a long release of that breath as I'm pressing the needles in. Can you do that for me? After I unbutton your dress, I'll count down from three. When I get to two, pull in your breath. When I reach one, slowly let it out."

I was afraid, but his reassuring instructions gave me something to focus on besides my terror. "I can do that. But Gunnar…."

His eyebrows drew together. "What is it, Lizbeth?"

"Will you please be gentle? I'm trying to be brave, but I'm barely holding on."

"I'll be as gentle as possible, I promise." He softly squeezed my shoulder before unfastening the buttons along my spine. A whisper of cool air brushed against my newly exposed skin. "Are you ready?" he asked.

"No." I smiled with trembling lips. "But I trust you. Let's start so that we can finish."

"You're braver than you think, Lizbeth." He grabbed the giant needles and pouch. "Okay, here we go."

"Three." I closed my eyes in anticipation.

"Two." I inhaled deeply.

"One." I released my breath.

It was easy to suppress the initial flash of sharp pain. It was much harder to ignore the seconds of scraping discomfort while Gunnar sought his target. The relief I felt when he reached this goal was immense.

Being pierced and probed was uncomfortably intimate, made more so by the audience in the room. I didn't want to show nervousness to the three onlookers, who sat directly in my line of sight, marking my movements with eager eyes. Remaining stoic was the best way to combat their unwelcome presence, and I projected this emotion while Gunnar finished his preparations. Avoiding Marta's fate was at the forefront of my mind. I wouldn't give them another story to tell future patients. I refused to become an example of what could happen in this laboratory.

After Gunnar completed my setup, he moved to the control panel behind me. Because of my position, I couldn't see what he was doing. He remedied this by talking through his actions. "Lizbeth, I'm reading your vitals and adjusting the machinery based on that information. Your heart rate is slightly elevated, but that's perfectly normal, considering the circumstances. Your blood pressure is well within the healthy range, so we won't need to compensate for it. I'll be turning some knobs now, and they may make noise."

I heard clicks as he rotated the dials into position. I could also make out a quiet melody. Gunner was humming a beautiful, haunting tune, one I'd never heard. The song's crescendos and dips captured my attention and put me at ease in the sterile surroundings. I blocked out the presence of the unwanted viewers, instead focusing on the music. And my husband. He had to know the effect of his song. The joy the notes inspired was exactly the antidote for my horrible situation. I closed my eyes and floated to an elevated place removed from bright lights and medical procedures.

"Okay, Lizbeth. I'm going to start the extractor now. Brace yourself for some pressure." The words barely registered. I remained in the space between awareness and sleep, with Gunnar's song playing in my head. The tugging force of the machine cut through my haze, but lightly, almost lazily. Eventually, I sensed the extractor's pushes and pulls matched the music's tempo. The realization lulled me further into the reverie. I felt at peace with the process and no longer worried about being hurt.

After some time, a shoulder tap roused me from my trance. "We're all finished, Lizbeth. It's time to disconnect. Just keep relaxing." Gunnar unhooked me from the equipment and taped soft gauze over my puncture site. He then rolled me onto my back.

"Going up." I heard the hum of machinery as the top half of my body rose into an almost-sitting position. Gunnar brought up the bedside rails, clicking them firmly into place. "Rest here while I clean up. It will give your body a chance to reacclimate to being upright."

I nodded and he began tidying his work area. Gunnar plucked vials of yellow, ruby, and white liquid from my bedside table. After he labeled the containers, he brought them to a large refrigerator lined with neat rows of similar ampules. Each vial was filled with colorful liquid, with shades ranging from flax to crimson to snow. I recognized the red substance, there was no mistaking blood, but the other contents remained a mystery. Gunnar added my contribution to the cooler and returned to my side. "I'm almost done here, and I've received permission to walk you home for lunch."

"I'd like that."

"Me too." He smiled before he turned back to the control station.

Gunnar wrote notes and sanitized surfaces. He was methodical in his movements, his tasks performed in a practiced way. I now had an answer to what he did at Fort Vogel—my husband ran this laboratory. While Dr. Brandt and General Stillwell claimed ownership of the underground lair, Gunnar seemed most confident down here.

During my procedure, the trio of observers had remained seated in the background, but the sharp clicking of dress shoes on concrete brought their presence back to the forefront. I turned to see them approaching, faces distorted with exaggerated grins.

The Doctor spoke first. "Well done, Lizbeth. An uneventful session is an excellent sign."

"You did beautifully, dear. You won't need to miss a single activity!" Ms. Granth chimed in.

General Stillwell added to the compliments, patting my arm as he spoke. "Way to be brave, young lady."

Rather than flinch from his touch like I wanted, I responded to their words, moderating my voice with the standard level of agreeableness. "Thank you all. I feel fine, really. I'm sure I'll be ready for nursery duty right after lunch."

Ms. Granth put a hand on her chest, practically swooning with glee. "I hear the strength in your voice already. That makes my heart sing!" She reached over and squeezed my hand. "I must be off, Lizbeth, as duty calls, but know that I'm very proud of how you performed." She acknowledged Gunnar. "And you too, Colonel. Congratulations on fine-tuning the process. Your bosses must be pleased with your work."

She turned and left the lab before Gunnar could reply. He laughed. "She's always a whirlwind."

"That she is, Colonel." Dr. Brandt agreed. He gestured at the tool Gunnar was cleaning. "Before you head off with your bride, show me the equipment you used for her retrieval. It's evolved since my last visit."

"Yes, Doctor. Let me open the receptacle so you can see the inner workings."

I tried to focus on their conversation but didn't recognize the technical terms they used. While I was strong enough for basic functioning, my energy was too sapped for deciphering a scientific exchange. I instead used the time to check on my needle-punctured skin. There was no bruising around the vein in the crook of my arm or the one on top of my hand, and neither spot was sensitive to the touch. The last location to inspect was just above my kidneys. I reached back and pressed the bandage covering my wound. A hot, prickling jolt caused me to wince. When I brought my hand forward, dots of red marked my fingertips.

"Lizbeth, are you okay?" Gunnar's concern took my focus off the blood.

I smiled through the pain. "Thank you for asking, but everything is fine. Don't let me interrupt your conversation, gentlemen."

Gunnar frowned, sensing my lie. "It's time to take our leave." He turned toward the Doctor. "Please forgive me for running off so soon, but my wife needs rest. Let's meet later in the afternoon, Dr. Brandt, and I can show you some of the other modifications I've made since we last spoke. I believe you'll appreciate their efficiency."

General Stillwell spoke up. "Take care of your business, Colonel. We'll reconvene at 1300. That gives us more than an hour."

"Yes, yes, we can discuss this later." Dr. Brandt made a shooing motion with his hands, then quickly returned his attention to the object he'd been examining.

"Thank you both. I'll return after lunch." Gunnar rebandaged my back, fastened my dress, and lowered the bed rails. "Your legs may be unsteady, Lizbeth, so don't be afraid to put your weight on me if you need to."

I tentatively placed my feet on the ground and put my right foot forward, followed by my left. "I can manage, but let's take it slow."

We shuffled unhurriedly out of the laboratory, up the steps into Dame Hall, and down the gravel path to our home. I sat at the dining table while Gunnar prepared our food, hearty plates of spaghetti.

"Something filling will help with your energy level. I always have pasta and bread after my extractions. Normally this much starch overwhelms me, but it's just what I need after losing so much of myself during the procedure."

"How many extractions have you been through?" I didn't know how often I'd be expected in the laboratory, but I was already dreading my next session.

"Let me think about that." He stirred the sauce as he pondered. "I was assigned to the lab six months after arriving at Starkesend, which means I've spent over two years there. I started experimenting on myself four weeks into the job and ran tests about once a week. That makes the extraction I'll receive tomorrow number 124 or so."

"Wow! I can barely move after my first one. How are you still standing?"

"I guess I got used to it." He shrugged. "You know, I've seen that number in logs and reports, but saying the total out loud feels strange. Like I'm admitting something absurd." His eyes glimmered as he grinned. "Bet you think I'm bananas now."

I pinched two fingers close, leaving a small space between them. "Maybe a little."

Gunnar threw his head back and laughing. "It's nice having you here."

"What was it like before, when you came home to an empty house?"

"I didn't come home." He cast his gaze down. "There's a closet in the lab. A tiny one with no windows. I put a cot inside and slept there most nights." Gunnar gestured around. "That's why it's so dull here. Klara and I had decorating plans…but we never got to complete them. After she died, I didn't care what this place looked like, especially since I was rarely here."

Hearing my sister's name stung, but I wouldn't let that discourage me from finding out more about her. "Did you two have any more plans?" I asked gently.

He was quiet for a moment before he answered. "I'm not ready to talk about that yet."

"I understand. I'm sorry for prying."

We stayed silent as he plated lunch and brought it to the table. During his first few bites, Gunnar stared at the wood grain, avoiding my eyes. When he finally glanced up, I noticed tears on his cheeks. The drops continued falling as he spoke in a hoarse voice.

"After Klara passed, it took me a while to wake up. I appeared normal from the outside, but on the inside, it felt like I was trapped in an endless nightmare. I completed my duties and ate enough to survive, but that was it. Promotions and advancements no longer mattered. Nothing did."

He paused to wipe his face. The liquid remnants of his grief disappeared, and a haunted expression took its place. "Life was covered by a cloud that made me feel…heavy. I dragged myself to work every day, forced myself to the chow hall, the shower, PT." His voice cracked. "I was the walking dead, Lizbeth, a broken man who didn't care what happened to him. If the General planned a dangerous mission, I volunteered for it. If one of my men needed a shift covered, I filled in. The less idle time I had, the better, because when I was alone, my thoughts turned dark. Like the idea I had for my extractions." He leaned forward and whispered. "I wanted to feel pain, to create a physical hurt that would overpower the void in my heart, so I siphoned more and more of my vitality during each session. It got bad, Lizbeth. but it was never enough to erase the memory of your sister's smile or the fact that I would never see it again."

His grief resonated with me. "I never hurt myself, Gunnar, but I can understand the desire. When you've experienced the highest highs, only the lowest lows provide any kind of counterbalance. I threw myself into raising my brother. Every ounce of energy went into making Ellis happy. Even then, I still thought about her. I still do. It catches me off guard sometimes."

Gunnar sighed deeply. Then surprisingly, he laughed. "I never wanted a wife, even made bachelorhood a goal of mine, but one day, a spark kindled inside, and there was nothing I could do to stop the pull I felt toward your sister." His face lit up. "I spent so long surrounded by men that I forgot the magnetism a woman can exude, and when I was suddenly in the presence of Klara's radiance, I wanted nothing more than to bask in the glow." His dreamy happiness took years off his face.

"Klara could charm anyone." I agreed.

"It was more than that, though." Gunnar thought for a moment. "You two are similar. Calm, mature, not impressed with my medals or rank, and smart. So, so smart." He grabbed my hand. "I know you try to hide it, Lizbeth, but I sense your intelligence." His voice took on a sorrowful note "You're right to keep it under wraps since we both know how females are viewed in Starkesend."

His grip tightened. "Never shine too bright, Lizbeth. It's a mistake your sister made, and it brought her the wrong kind of attention."

Gunnar, 1933

Chapter 16 - Gunnar

I got used to them dying. After Miles' passing, I learned to recognize the telltale signs of death. Relaxed limbs and a peaceful smile during a session meant I would be visiting the incinerator that day. The remaining men and women in our experimental group fell one by one, and four weeks after I joined Project Leer, the last of our subjects succumbed to their mortality.

The atmosphere in the laboratory became stifling as Dr. Brandt's departure date drew closer. The excitement of discovering Miles' cerebrospinal fluid waned, and his mood plummeted as the test group shrunk. When the Doctor flew into rages or retreated into sinister silence, I faded into the background, waiting for the tantrum to pass.

Three days before Dr. Brandt's return to Germany, I approached him with an idea. I waited until his temper was stable and his attention was focused on something other than the failure of Leer. The doctor was seated at a lab table proofreading paperwork when I offered my opinion. "Sir, I've been studying the books you lent me, and I came across some research that could be useful. What do you think about approaching our target from a different access point?"

He sneered at me over the records he was updating. "You're entering dangerous territory, Cruse. How would you, a mere electrician, know more about the human structure than me?"

I bowed my head, hoping to appear contrite. "There's no way I could, sir. You're right about that. I understand very little about anatomy or medicine or working in a lab, for that matter. I wasn't claiming proficiency, and I'm sorry if it appeared that way."

"I believe you, Cruse. You've more than shown your worth around here, and I don't take you for the kind of man to insult your leaders." His sneer turned into a sulk. He pushed the paperwork aside and paced. "I'm on edge because we've made no progress. I came here to provide value to our party, but there's only an oven full of ashes to show after two months of effort. What use will that be to the Fatherland?"

His callousness was shocking, but I controlled my reaction and commiserated with his frustration. "I'm feeling the pressure too, Doctor. Watching the experiments fail was disappointing, especially after the hours of labor and care we've put in."

"To tell you the truth, Corporal, this whole trip has been a disappointment. General Stillwell peddled Starkesend as the perfect location for Nazi headquarters in America." He scoffed. "But I've seen no proof to support that claim. You're the only man worth a damn around here, Cruse. The rest of the military, if you can even call it that, has room for growth, and not just in the numbers sense."

I nodded in agreement. While the Doctor's words were heavy with contempt, he was right about the size of our forces. The dream of adding more recruits to the barracks hadn't happened, and this failure had forced leadership to alter their outreach methods. I'd been included in several frantic meetings before they settled on a strategy. "Unfortunately, that's an accurate observation. The General wasn't pleased with last season's recruitment efforts, but he's developed a plan that should appeal to more people. He's going to use the Depression to our benefit. Promoting consistent meals and work will certainly grab folks' attention."

The Doctor stopped striding. "Does the General need a reminder of our ultimate mission? Yes, hordes will be lured by the promise of food and work, but I suspect the quality of this crowd will be lacking. Proper screening is a must." He smirked. "Starkesend doesn't have the space for more imbeciles."

I brushed past the insult. "Excellent point, sir. We certainly wouldn't want our purity diluted. General Stillwell shuffled men around to prevent that from happening. Lance Corporals Tanne and Conroy have been removed from the maintenance department and assigned to a new investigation unit. They'll check family lines, criminal histories, and service records to ensure no one defiled makes it through our doors."

"Now, that's a surprise, the General made a decision I agree with." He shook his head. "There's a first time for everything, I suppose." Dr. Brandt returned to his chair and gestured at the stack of paper in front of him. "Before I resume this drudgery, what was it that you wanted to share?"

"Thank you for remembering, sir. I don't want to disturb you more than necessary, so I'll make this quick." I took a steadying breath before outlining my thoughts. "Last night, I read about the adrenal gland and thought it would be a worthwhile area for us to explore. What they've already discovered about these tiny organs is intriguing. There are two of them, small triangles located above the kidneys, and when the adrenals were removed or damaged, humans and animals were sickened and died. So, they're quite important for survival, but the most relevant thing about them is what they produce."

I paused to gauge the Doctor's reaction. He seemed skeptical, but there was also a hint of curiosity in his expression. I continued talking, hoping this interest would grow. "In the beginning, no one knew the purpose of these glands. One researcher fed bovine adrenal to his son, but it provoked no response. Injecting adrenal extract into dogs *did* produce a noticeable effect, a huge increase in blood pressure, but they didn't know what caused it at first, until some chemists discovered the source of the increase and called it epinephrine or adrenaline." A note of excitement crept into my voice. "This chemical is closely related to what we're looking for, Doctor. At least, when it's combined with cortisol. Luckily, we can also find that in the adrenal gland. Together, these substances produce feelings of fear in the brain." I smiled. "If we can harvest epinephrine and cortisol, we'll be back in business."

Dr. Brandt leaned back in his seat. He was quiet, but I could tell he was considering my suggestion. After a while, he spoke up. "Bring me the book, Cruse. I want to read up on this farfetched idea of yours."

"I'll be right back, sir." I raced off before he could change his mind. My heart was pounding when I returned with the text, more from nerves than my sprint. I paged through the book until I found the section on hormones, then I handed it over and waited.

I stayed past the end of the workday, standing by as Dr. Brandt read and reread the adrenal gland articles. He skimmed the words with his fingers, occasionally making notes in the margin. As the hours ticked by, I responded to the Doctor's commands.

"Cruse, bring more coffee."

"I need a fresh ledger. Get it from the back."

"Grab all the volumes from the bottom row of my bookshelf, Cruse. I want to cross-reference some items."

Other than these demands, the Doctor kept to himself. He spoke out loud occasionally, but the scratching of pen on paper was the dominant sound throughout the afternoon and evening. Once he was done writing comments in each text, he switched to the ledger. He calculated figures and ran formulas at a steady speed, frowning from time to time as he filled in columns but mostly smiling and nodding.

Dr. Brandt finished his assessment just shy of midnight. He glanced up with wild, fervent eyes and waved me over. I sat in the chair next to him, ready to hear what he'd learned. "Corporal, I doubted you at first, but after digging deeper, I can confirm that you were on to something." He picked up a thick book from the stack in front of him. "What you found was rudimentary, but I was able to pick up the thread and configure a way to revive Project Leer."

He turned pages until he found the entry he was searching for. "This is the answer to our problems, Cruse." I skimmed the words while he explained his findings. "Are you familiar with Ivan Pavlov?"

I nodded. "If I remember correctly, he's known for his work on the digestive system, and he learned about it from dogs."

"At the very basic level, that's correct. Pavlov was one of the rare Russians with a brain, and he put it to good use. He was recognized for his physiology work, yes, but he had another endeavor that I think we can modify to our advantage." He turned a page in the book and read the next section's title, "Pavlov's Gastric Juice Factory." He tapped the words. "This is how we'll save Leer."

The page contained a sketch of the factory, a ghastly workshop where dogs were held in place to gather their intestinal fluids. Under the drawing, remarks from Pavlov's supporters claimed the canines were happy and that they willingly swallowed the food which fell from their throats through a hole, never making it to the stomach for digestion. Regardless of this cheerful reassurance, I can't imagine the dogs were content with their forced dissatisfaction. Continual craving without fulfillment sounded like torture to me. The collection and bartering of gastric juices couldn't have been beneficial for the dogs either, especially after reading information on their shortened lifespan. It was Pavlov who profited off the pooches, reaping the rewards created by their pain.

After I read the entire section, I was unsure of Dr. Brandt's plan. There were no dogs at Starkesend, and digestive fluids weren't our intended target. And if he wanted humans to fill his factory, we'd lost our last subject, and there was no sign of replenishing the holding cells before he left for

Germany. "Sir, I'm not grasping the brilliance of your proposal. Would you break it into plain terms for this simple electrician?"

"I forget that not everyone understands such high-minded concepts." He gave me a condescending stare. "Cruse, we'll have to raise your education to a more acceptable level. I don't have time to waste on explanations or lectures." He sighed. "But that's not the discussion we need to have right now. I will slowly walk you through my thought process, so we can move past this knowledge barrier and use the rest of my time here efficiently."

The Doctor pushed aside the book in front of us and replaced it with the one I'd brought from home. He paged through until he found an article titled *The Prolonged Existence of Adrenaline in the Blood.* He gave me time to read the short post before he flipped to another entry, *The Use of Adrenaline in Medical and Surgical Practice.* I studied the words, searching for a clear meaning, but Dr. Brandt's message remained unclear.

I glanced up when I finished reading. "I wish I could say that helped, Doctor, but I'm still struggling to connect everything."

"Let me spell it out more clearly, Cruse." Dr. Brandt grabbed the volume with Pavlov's diagram and placed it next to the book with the adrenaline articles. He moved his finger back and forth between the hardbacks, jabbing the pages with each word. "This is what we will be doing, Corporal. We will use the people of Fort Vogel to create an adrenaline assembly line. We will extract as much of this substance as we can and deliver it to Germany. There are men over there, doctors like me, who can put something like epinephrine to good use. Cortisol too. We'll harvest them both." He glared at me with contempt. "Do you have any more questions?"

"Just one, sir. How will you convince everyone to cooperate? I know we all came to Starkesend to fulfill a purpose, but medical experiments don't bode well with some folks."

He stretched his lips into a dreadful grin. "I won't be convincing a single soul, Cruse, because you will persuade them. Who better than the Fort Vogel golden boy to rally the troops?" Dr. Brandt laughed cruelly through his next words. "And what's more, you'll be our first test subject."

"I'm ready to begin the new and improved Project Leer." The doctor pushed back from the table. "Corporal, prepare for extraction 001."

Chapter 17 - Gunnar

Over the next 72 hours, Dr. Brandt worked at a frenzied pace. Obtaining access to my adrenals was his priority. The doctor's library contained few books that referenced the glands, and in this assortment, all entries detailed animal rather than human anatomy. This made the laboratory's x-ray machine a helpful tool for determining their proximity. Using it also cut down on the number of incisions I was subjected to. While I still underwent exploratory operations, the radiographs guided the Doctor's hand and allowed him to find my organs more efficiently.

After he located the adrenals, the next goal was to withdraw fluid from them. Dr. Brandt wanted a large quantity, enough to impress the Nazis and win their support, but my stingy glands gave up milliliters rather than the quart he sought. The doctor's desire for a prized rank in the German medical community would be stifled by my unwilling organs. At least that's what he muttered after he could harvest no more precious juice. I took secret pleasure in this knowledge, happy that my innards weren't doing him any favors.

I gave little thought to climbing the ranks while I was operated on. I merely strived for survival. As the Dr. Brandt used my body for his own ends, I maintained an even demeanor and focused on the clock in the lab. The seconds and minutes slowed to an almost unbearable speed, but the hour hand finally made it through six rotations, and I was freed from captivity. Of course, I wasn't released without a lecture. The doctor delivered it in a stern voice while he washed his hands post-procedure.

"If the Führer approves the continuation of Leer, which I'm confident he will, then I will return in February. That gives you two months to convince Stillwell of our plans." He looked up from the sink, fixing a steely gaze on me. "Cruse, I know the last few days have been hard on you, but I encourage you to overcome any reluctance or malcontent. What we're doing here is of great value to our people, and when we have an efficient factory running, there's no telling the rewards we will reap."

Dr. Brandt dried his hands and walked to my bedside. He checked my pulse, temperature, and blood pressure before he spoke again. "You're certainly healthy, Cruse. One more day of rest, and you'll be back on your feet."

I agreed with his assessment. "That was my thought too. I feel stronger than I did yesterday." The day before, blood had poured from my body, the world becoming hazy as a red puddle collected beneath the operating table. I remember Dr. Brandt's panic when he understood what was happening. His bulging eyes and frantic movements caused me to laugh until my breathing stopped, and I lost consciousness.

When I woke, the Doctor told me I'd needed several transfusions. He'd used the blood drawn from one of our first test subjects, Miles and I had the same type. I thought about that while I drifted in and out of fitful sleep. I'd sent Miles to his horror-filled final days, yet he saved me from a similar fate. I owed him my life, but there was nowhere to repay this debt, and I wrestled with restoring balance.

I decided what to do in a dream-like state. I'd work at bettering Leer to lessen the harm it caused participants. Miles wouldn't benefit from improvements or be aware of their existence, but other Fort Vogel residents would. A new process would impact a lot of people. It would make up for the path of pain I'd placed Miles on. I embraced the idea, and when I told the Doctor my plans, he approved them with gusto. This enthusiasm peppered his departing words.

Dr. Brandt opened my IV line and took a moment to watch the fluid drip in a steady stream. When his eyes met mine, they shined with ambition. "Heal up, Cruse, then get to work. I'm giving you a large amount of trust, which is a rarity for me. I usually hold my cards close and show them to few people." He sighed. "But in this instance, I cannot be in two places at once. This means you to be my proxy when I'm not in Starkesend."

The Doctor walked from my bedside to where his briefcase rested. He packed while he continued talking, loading papers and test tubes with efficiency. "When I'm not here, you will oversee this laboratory and the activities inside. Go about your business, and don't let the good General have a say. As much as he blusters, it's not him who has our leader's blessing. He needs me, Cruse." He smirked. "The man pines for my life in Germany. He wants to dine with the head of the Schutzstaffel or make decisions about our impure population, yet he is stuck here hoping that Starkesend will show promise. I regret that our work will satisfy his goals, but sometimes the bad gets fed along with the good." He closed his bag. "Do you have any questions before I leave?"

"I can't think of any right now, sir. Is there a way to reach you if something comes to me?"

"That *was* a question, Cruse." The Doctor held up a sheet of paper. "I'll leave this on my desk inside a file. On it, you will find addresses, one in Berchtesgaden and the other in Berlin. I expect weekly letters outlining your progress, and you can include any inquiries as well." He lowered his arm. "Telegrams would be too risky at this phase of our American operations since we can't chance detection. It would be a waste to expose this remote location, so I must accept that there will be a delay in communication."

Dr. Brandt grabbed his suitcase. "Inside the file, you'll also find information about the code you must use in our letters. It's a simple cipher code, but it has proven most effective when I've needed to transmit information in the past. General Stillwell will collect your mail, and have it brought to the post office at Clark's Hope, which is far enough away to prevent connection to Starkesend." He glanced at his watch. "That's it, Cruse. I must be off. Stay connected to the machines until tomorrow, then get to task." He gave a curt nod before leaving.

It was my first time alone in the lab, and although I could still feel the Doctor's presence, it faded as the seconds passed. Tomorrow I would make this space my own. I'd cover the picture of Dr. Brandt and his family. I'd play classical rather than patriotic music on the radio. I'd turn the lights to a lower level. Those small changes would alter the atmosphere of the lab and I'd be able to dive into the mysteries of the adrenal gland at my own pace. For now, rest was crucial. If I were going to be successful, I needed to be in better shape. After all, it was my organs that I would be exploring, at least until I found my first subject.

I closed my eyes and fell into a dreamless slumber.

∞∞∞∞

I recovered quickly, as the doctor and I had suspected. In two days, I was strong enough to emerge from my underground lair for a meal with my former platoon mates. Tanne and Conroy were thriving in their new investigation positions. They talked about the people they encountered over hamburger and vegetable hash.

"I have to tell you about my favorite group, Cruse." Conroy laughed at the memory. "It was this family of six, all short, dark, and ugly. I'm trying to remember their name, but it's not coming to me. It was Weinberg or Hoffman or something like that." He nudged Tanne. "Do you remember who I'm talking about?"

Tanne shrugged. "I don't know, man. It's hard to keep up."

"Eh, it's not important to the story. Just know that I could tell they were Jew scum right away. Their heritage was as obvious as I'd even seen it—their last name, their looks, the whole shebang. I knew Starkesend wouldn't welcome them, but figured I'd run them through the ringer to show them who's boss." Conroy smiled cruelly. "Plus, one of the girls was less ugly than the others. The crazy doctor you're working with, Cruse, is all about breeding the Jews out. He'd be proud of me for what I did."

Conroy's actions were disgusting, and I had no desire to hear the details of his assault. I jumped into the conversation, hoping to put a stop to his recounting. "It sounds like you've been busy. Any luck on increasing our numbers yet? I'm usually good at keeping track of new faces, but it's hard to do when I'm stuck in the lab."

Tanne made a so-so gesture. "There haven't been as many entrants as we hoped for. The promise of food has brought folks in, but of the three or four families a week I screen, only a small portion make it through to Dorf. The men who turn up alone have been more successful." He used his fingers to count. "I've granted entrance to eight recruits in the last two weeks. The barracks finally feel less empty." Tanne peered at Conroy. "You seeing about the same?"

"Yeah, it's been more of a trickle than a flood, but we have upped the number of soldiers pretty consistently. The new recruits are on the first phase of training, so we're not sure if they'll all make it to the ranks yet. I'm doubtful about it though." Conroy shook his head and grimaced. "You should see them. No strength, afraid of their own shadows. It's pathetic really, but the General told us to take on anyone who passes the background check, even if they don't look like a typical soldier." He lowered his voice. "I think we're watering down Starkesend's greatness in the search for numbers. Seriously Cruse, you should walk through the barracks with us after lunch.

Even someone as nice as you will have a hard time finding anything redeemable about these guys.”

“I don’t think they’re as bad as Conroy does, but they are somewhat…softer than anyone on Bravo team.” Tanne added.

I raised my eyebrows. “Soft, huh? Well now you’ve got my interest. I’d like to see these newbies myself.”

Tanne chuckled. “Too bad you’re not around for PT. I think they’d benefit from some Cruse cruising.”

“I haven’t run in weeks. I might be crawling instead of cruising right now.” I smiled. “Hopefully it won’t be too much longer before I can join you fellas again. I like helping the weaklings discover their muscles.” I flexed my arms. “My muscles might need some discovery too.”

We talked as we ate. It was nice to be with people again, even for a short while. I missed being involved in the daily ebbs and flows of Fort Vogel—the structured time, the physical exercise, the bland food. All of it was comforting, especially since Project Leer kept me isolated.

Emerging from the lab was a necessity because I sensed how quickly an aversion to others could form. Already I found myself recoiling from Conroy. While I’d always been closer to Tanne, I’d gotten along with the other soldier well enough. I overlooked his ignorance, and we cooperated on Bravo team, finishing tasks without strife. But now, it was different, I felt instant distaste at his words, his mannerisms, even his breathing. Everything about Corporal Dale Conroy pushed me toward a confrontation that would get ugly fast, and I didn’t want to ruin my career at Starkesend before I served my purpose.

We didn’t have to be friends, but coexistence was necessary because the constant suppression of rage would be exhausting. I had to reclaim the equilibrium that served me well, the observe-before-reacting attitude I’d embraced throughout life. I had enough foresight to sense that hiding in the lab would eventually inflame my anger. Although seeing less of Conroy was preferable, it only succeeded in the short term. Avoiding problems didn't make them disappear, they only remained out of view until you stumbled upon them days, weeks, or months later. The less I was around inescapable annoyances, the more they would anger me later. Building tolerance through exposure would prepare me for future meetings with Conroy or any other nuisance at Fort Vogel, and there was no better time to start than now.

I finished my last bite of food and leaned back from the table. "I'm ready to head to the barracks when you are." I gestured at my empty plate. "This stuff tastes better than I remember. Is my memory bad, or did they make some changes to the mess hall?"

"I forgot you weren't at the last company meeting. They did change some things, and they've been popular with the lads. Go drop off your dishes, and you'll see what I mean," Tanne suggested.

"You better hustle too, Cruse, because once everyone finishes eating, the wash window gets busy. No one wants to miss getting a peek at the lookers back there." Conroy moved his eyebrows up and down. "I'd sure as hell butter their muffins if I had the chance, especially the blonde, but the General says they're off limits." He winked. "What he doesn't know won't hurt him."

Although I sought patience with Conroy, I had to get away before I told him some hard truths. It would be tough for him to hear that no woman would bed a man with such a foul mouth and odor. I itched to yell the words, but I walked off instead, clutching my plate and utensils with a tense grip.

At the wash station, I mindlessly put my dishes atop a small pile. I was lost in my irritation until an unfamiliar voice interrupted my thoughts. "Sorry to be a bother, but silverware goes in this bin now. We found it much easier to sort when it's separated from the plates and bowls." I glanced up to see a woman with curly brown hair, hazel eyes, and a kind smile.

Her beauty stunned me into silence, but just for a moment. I quickly recovered my wits. "I'm sorry, miss. I haven't been to the cafeteria in a few days." I placed my knife and fork in the proper spot. "I'm happy to do whatever makes your job easier."

Her smile broadened. "Thank you, soldier."

"Welcome to Fort Vogel. I hope you find it pleasant here." I bowed slightly. "My name is Gunnar Cruse. I'm a Corporal in the army."

"Well, Gunnar, I don't have a rank, just the lowly title of kitchen assistant. I *do* have a name, though." She laughed before curtsying. "I'm Klara Dietrich, and it's lovely to meet you."

Lizbeth, 1936

Chapter 18 - Lizbeth

Gunnar's tear-filled revelations sparked my motivation. His knowledge was the key to understanding Klara's last moments, but he was genuinely upset, and pushing him too far wouldn't make sense. It would be cruel, plus he might retreat into silence, something I was loath to let happen. I kept this in mind when I continued our conversation about the painful subject.

We'd moved from the dining table to his cot, and I held his gaze while I spoke in a gentle but firm voice. "Thank you for giving me insight into my sister's life, Gunnar. When you imagine something, it's usually far worse than the reality, so I'm relieved to hear that you enjoyed each other's company." I paused, knowing my next words might cause him discomfort. "I'm about to be completely honest with you, and I don't want you to take it the wrong way. I'd like to tell you what I've thought of you for the last twelve months."

Gunnar had stopped crying, but his cheeks were still red with emotion. He nodded in assent. "You've listened to me, Lizbeth, and now I'll return the favor. Get your thoughts out." He tapped the braided silver rope on his collar. "Besides, I'm a colonel. I think I can handle whatever you have to tell me." His joking tone and smile lightened the heavy mood.

"My goodness, Gunnar. That didn't even cross my mind." I sighed dramatically and fluttered my eyelashes. "How could any words from little ol' me ever hurt a big, strong officer like you? The thought makes me faint." I flashed my own smile, letting the playfulness hang in the air for a few seconds. Then, I lowered my eyes and sank into the past. "When my parents and I were told what happened to Klara, my world shattered. I hadn't seen her since before the Frau Rennen, but I thought about her often. When she showed up in my mind, I pictured her happily married to a wonderful husband. She was supposed to be living the fairytale life society sells us from birth—the beautiful maiden with the dashing soldier. That's how I imagined Klara whenever I thought about her, but it was far from true." I peered into Gunnar's eyes again. "Thanks to you, I know she found moments of joy, but when we were told about her murder, I didn't have that information, and I'm afraid my thoughts went to a dark place." My voice trembled. Memories from that long-ago time were pulling me back.

I took a moment to calm down and force my way back to the present. "I mourned Klara hard. She was my big sister—a sweet, beautiful, light-filled person. You know that as well as I do." I steeled myself, knowing I was about to wound him. "There *was* one emotion that surpassed my grief, though. It was rage. I hated Starkesend. And I hated you."

Anger was alluring, and after Klara's murder, I'd been captivated under its spell. When sorrow overwhelmed me, I focused on fury, and because of this, I felt indebted to my fiery rage. The red, hot power carried me through the initial disbelief at Klara's death and the later sadness of missing her. I'd nurtured it over the last year, letting it grow to a dangerous level, the place where retaliation was the next step.

Unexpectedly, my ire fizzled when I was forced to confront one of its targets. Getting to know Gunnar, realizing he wasn't the monster I'd spun up in my mind, diminished the loathing aimed at him. In contrast, the hate I had for our society still bloomed. That's because anger was often kept alive by ignorance. When information was learned, rage either faded from exposure to reality or intensified despite, or perhaps because of, the new knowledge. The more I discovered about my husband, the less hate I felt, but the more I understood Starkesend, the greater my hostility grew.

After acknowledging the animosity for Gunnar, tiny tendrils of wrath sprang forth, ready to weave themselves back into my life. Talking about the dark emotions seemed to rekindle them. I'd have to maintain an even keel through the rest of our conversation, or I risked sinking back into the depths of outrage. A calming breath helped me recenter. After a few more, I felt my anger disappear, and I was able to focus. I studied Gunnar's face, searching for the shock and upset I expected. All I found was sympathy. "You don't look the least bit put out by my hate. That's surprising."

"Lizbeth, of course, you despised me. I can only imagine how much it hurt to learn about Klara's death." Tears welled in his eyes. "To be honest, I hated myself for a long time. It's my fault something happened to her. I should have been a better protector."

"But Gunnar, aren't *you* the something that happened to her?" I asked bluntly.

"That's partially true, but there were more factors involved than just me." He seemed puzzled. "What exactly were you told?"

"That you strangled Klara in her sleep. That she had a smile on her face when you did it." I blocked out the mental image my mind conjured. "Why would they tell me that? Did they think it was suitable to inform a sixteen-year-old about her dead sister's facial expression?" A sob punctuated the question.

Gunnar sprang to his feet. "I can't believe they told you that. It's not what happened at all." He paced back and forth, turning sharply every few steps. "Your sister did not die with a smile on her face. Klara died while she was trying to escape. I had no choice but to stop her." He let out a rueful laugh. "They certainly spread that to the people on base, but it looks like an entirely different story circulated around Dorf."

He stopped pacing. "Maybe they had a misguided sense of compassion and didn't want to tell your parents something to tarnish the memory of their daughter. That's the only explanation I can think of." His face filled with bitterness. "Of course, they chose me as the bad guy for their lie. No one would question my involvement. Not the man exposed to combat or the one who has apparently murdered scores of innocent people. That man *would* be the one to throttle his wife while she smiled up at him." He stopped moving and fixed me with a pained expression. "I've heard the songs they sing about me, Lizbeth. Gunnar the Great, Gunnar the Gory, and whatever other damn words are attached to my name. Kids sing about the death and destruction I've caused in their little high-pitched voices. They run around the playground, calling me a hero. Or a monster. There's not much difference between the two when you get down to it."

He flopped down on the cot and gripped my hands. "Do you know what the worst part is? None of it's true. I haven't killed scores of people or drank the blood of my enemies. I've had to harm people during combat, but I have always tried to minimize my impact, even during the Great War." His eyes lit up. "Let me show you something."

Gunnar stood up and pulled me to my feet. We walked to the back of the house, to the room he kept locked. He took a silver key from his pocket and opened the door to an office. The space was sparsely decorated, like the rest of the house. A desk, lamp, chair, and file cabinet were bland but neatly maintained, and they were arranged so the eye was drawn to the only colorful object in the room, a painting hanging on the rear wall.

The large, framed print showed Gunnar and Klara sitting under a tree, laughing at a shared joke. A blanket was underneath them, and half-eaten foods were spread out, hinting at an afternoon picnic. The beauty of the piece took my breath away. My sister's style was evident in the painting. I recognized the textures and lighting she used, although she had never painted so flawlessly. Klara had captured the couple's mood intimately—I could feel the love the two shared because it radiated from the canvas. As I took in the details of the work, it felt like intruding on a private moment not meant for my eyes, but I pushed through this feeling, using all my energy to immerse myself in my sister's last creation.

I stared at the artwork until Gunnar's voice brought me back to reality. "Lizbeth, it's almost time for me to head back to the lab." He walked to the file cabinet. "Let me show you why I brought you in here."

Gunnar opened the middle drawer. After thumbing past several files, he pulled out a thick envelope and brought it to the desk. He waved me over, and I came close. "These are the mementos from my time in the Army. I wanted you to see them."

He emptied the envelope onto the desk. A collection of newspaper clippings, letters, and photos fluttered out. As I sifted through the items, careful not to cause damage to his well-preserved history, a photograph caught my eye. I picked it up and studied the shot of four smiling, uniformed men sitting around a table. Each person held cards in their hands, and there were more cards and stacks of coins on the table in front of them.

I turned the picture over and saw a date scrawled in black ink: March 1919. I flipped it back to the front to examine the faces. Although the picture was almost two decades old, I recognized Gunnar. There were fewer lines on his face, but his smile was the same intelligent, happy one he flashed during the rare moments we joked with each other. His light brown eyes were distinct too. While they were crinkled with cheer, there was a shadow of sadness in them that matched the expression he wore daily.

I held out the image. "You were so young."

He laughed. "We were all so young." He gently took the photo. "We were eighteen when that picture was taken, and it was right before our last deployment together. We knew there was little to smile about in the trenches, so we used our final hours in the U.S. to play some hearts." He pointed to the dark-haired man sitting across from him. "That's Cohen. He was always my heart's partner, and when we were in the field, we covered each other's sixes. Cohen never let me down" He passed the photo back to me. "I'm sorry to see that we're letting people like him down now."

"What do you mean, Gunnar?" Thanks to school lessons, I knew scores of the most common Jewish last names, and Cohen was on the list. Our leaders felt that it was important for children to identify people from impure lineages. Looks could be telling of heritage at times, but family names often left little room for doubt. Before tests, I committed the lists to memory, angry that my learning was being used as a weapon rather than a tool.

Teachers encouraged their students to absorb as much information about the enemy as they could, including surnames but also subjects like common birthplaces, professions, and articles of clothing. Producing well-informed citizens increased the likelihood that these citizens would fulfill their purpose—succeeding at making the lives of American Jews a waking nightmare.

I hoped my husband was repelled by the hatred that defined our society. There was only a small chance Gunnar and I thought alike, since soldiers voluntarily entered Starkesend and pledged loyalty to its principles. Children, on the other hand, were brought inside by their parents, held hostage by ideas they may or may not embrace. But time and exposure were successful in eroding any resistance a young person may harbor. It was never long after arriving in Starkesend that conformity kicked in. If true belief wasn't a motivation for students in the beginning, going along to get along eventually blossomed into actual devotion. Blending in could be a dangerous activity, especially when the price of admission was bigotry.

My parents hadn't revealed a motive for entangling our family in this community, but they always provided a counterbalance to what I was taught in school. The instruction I received at home promoted a holistic lens rather than the narrow view I got from the classroom. Keeping this hidden was pivotal because the danger of discovery was real. Still, I held out hope that one day, a friend or neighbor would spill their secrets, and I would find an ally. And here I was, hoping again.

I waited anxiously for Gunnar to answer my question about his friend. He thought before he responded, studying the picture of his platoon mates while he spoke. "There are a lot of unfair things going on in the world right now, Lizbeth. Cohen and the rest of these guys aren't being shown the respect they deserve. I'm not saying that soldiers and veterans should be worshipped. I just think they should be able to live a life worth living after they finish their enlistment." Gloom filled his face. "A lot of them can't find work or get their benefits from the government, so they ramble from place to place looking for a home, but never quite settling down." Gunnar lowered his voice. "I think it's driving some of them to consider the Nazi way of life. Their own country doesn't appreciate them, and the people in the Friends of New Germany spin the sort of stories that fire up the GIs. They've been promising them things—jobs, land, women—the stuff these men are dreaming of, saying it'll be theirs if only they sign up to support Hitler's cause."

He pointed to a smiling, blond man in his picture. "That's Moore. Had a rough go of it in the war. Then, when he came home, he found out that his girl had left him and that his Ma and Pa had passed away within two weeks of each other. How hard do you think it was to sell the idea of Aryan dominance to someone so broken?" Gunnar asked with raised eyebrows. "Moore took the bait the Nazis were offering without looking back. He's in California now, helping Goebbels take control of Hollywood." He shook his head. "I told him about Starkesend, but he likes the action down there in Tinseltown. Guess it's too quiet up this way."

Disdain filled Gunnar's words. Or maybe I was projecting my own emotions onto him. It would be heartening to have a collaborator, and this conversation was the closest I'd come to hearing dislike for the German tyrants from anyone in the village or on base. Treading carefully was more important than ever, though. My husband worked with powerful men, and if my intuition about him was wrong, those in charge would cast me out quickly. Leaving society would likely be a positive event. I'd gain the freedom to express my true views, but shaming my family wasn't worth this benefit. They'd already lost one daughter. Losing a second one to treason would be too much to bear.

I asked Gunnar to clarify his thoughts in a roundabout way. "I wasn't aware of the terrible treatment our service members faced, but don't you think working toward a glorious purpose will help them? Completing tasks to support our Aryan birthright will surely make their lives more fulfilling."

Gunnar glanced at me sharply, scanning my face, before probing deep into my eyes. His voice was tight when he responded. "You sound just like Ms. Granth. You'll fit in well at Fort Vogel, Lizbeth." He grabbed the papers and pictures from his desk, tucking them back into the envelope with quick, mechanical movements. When he was done, he smiled ruefully. "It's time for me to return to the lab." He began to walk out of the room, surprising me with his abruptness.

"I thought there was something you needed to show me, Gunnar. I'd love to see it." I called out to his back.

He turned around, and I was startled by the hardness of his expression. "There's nothing in this room that you need to see, Lizbeth." He waved his hand impatiently. "Now, come along so I can lock up. You wouldn't want to keep your mentor waiting."

I bowed my head and hurried out of the room. The door closed loudly behind me, and I heard the lock engage. Gunnar sped up and reached the exit before me, nodding curtly as he passed. "Take it easy at the nursery. You may feel some weakness, but it should fade if you sit for a minute or two.

You'll probably feel like yourself by the end of your shift though." Compassion flashed in his eyes. "The first extraction is always the hardest." He walked onto the porch and started across the lawn before doing a sudden about-face. "Don't expect me home tonight. I have a feeling that they'll need me in the lab."

As Gunnar strode off, I regretted the way our conversation ended. Instead of finding an ally, I had pushed away the only person who could tell me the truth about my sister's last moments.

Chapter 19 - Lizbeth

The feeling of frailty came and went as I worked in the nursery. Picking up the older children was especially delicate. Every time I grabbed a toddler, waves of dizziness splashed around in my head. Luckily, a few moments of stillness calmed the spinning. I tried to hide these moments of rest from the little ones, but the more observant talkers gleefully called out my dazed spells.

"Mrs. Lizbeth is woooooozy!" They would giggle and run off, pleased to have learned a silly new word. I played along, of course, smiling through the gray seconds where I hovered between consciousness and oblivion. The children didn't know any better. How could they understand that I'd been strapped to a table while body fluids were suctioned out of me? Better to act pleasant, to reinforce to them that their teacher was still the same happy-go-lucky person they had fun with.

Ms. Granth was another story. She seemed displeased with my condition and found ways to bring it up. When I needed time to catch my breath before story circle, she tutted, "Being a bit dramatic, dear? You were right as rain when I left the lab, so there's no reason for this drastic change in your health." As we cleaned up, and I sat in a chair to organize the blocks, she hissed, "Lizbeth, just sit on the floor. Going all the way to the table wastes the precious seconds we get with these little angels." Her cutting words continued throughout my shift.

Like Gunnar had pointed out, the weakness eventually faded, but I didn't let Ms. Granth know. If there was an opportunity to sit, I took it and found delight in her annoyance. It was a small way to take back power, and I was amused that my child-like behavior bothered the coordinator, especially after I'd been accused of imitating her.

My husband was wrong in this allegation. If he could see me know, he'd know that a desire to be like Ms. Granth didn't exist. I'd have to wait until he returned from the lab to tell him about my minor rebellions. Then we could clear up our whole misunderstanding, and he would see that I wasn't the pushover he assumed I was. Until then, I'd do my best to undermine Ms. Granth's air of superiority.

I could tell I'd gotten under her skin when she gave me a lecture toward the end of the day. "Lizbeth, I expect you to be at one hundred percent tomorrow. No more of this delicate-flower routine. The wives of Fort Vogel appear ladylike and dainty, but underneath that exterior, we are hard as steel." Ms. Granth assessed me up and down. "You are young, strong, driven. There's no reason to act like you can't handle a minor medical procedure." She raised her chin and straightened her back, forcing her posture into a painfully rigid position. "I'm almost three times your age, yet I make it a point to volunteer for extra extractions because I know how valuable our participation is. Never once have I acted as injured as you did today. Your behavior was inexcusable, especially in front of the children." She fixed her steely eyes on mine. "No more skulking about, Lizbeth. I have great confidence in your abilities, but if you continue acting like an invalid, that confidence will vanish. Do you understand, dear?"

I forced extra cheeriness into my voice. "Of course, Ms. Granth. I'm sorry I was out of sorts today. I know that society depends on us having a can-do attitude, so I'll make certain not to leave mine at home again."

She studied me, probing my expression and demeanor, searching for hints of authenticity. I kept a smile plastered on my face until she was satisfied. Ms. Granth nodded. "I'm happy to hear that, Lizbeth. I'll see you at roll call in the morning. Don't be late."

Her stride was sure as she exited the building. I followed her compact form until she made a sharp left turn, heading toward the gardens, then the cafeteria, and finally the textile hall. Every day she repeated this pattern. Ms. Granth would work a shift, then make her way to each of the ladies' domains. She'd check on the workers, ensuring that everything was running up to standards. You could sense her enjoyment of the routine. The clockwork schedule met her needs for industry and efficiency, plus it allowed her to exercise a large amount of control over others. Some people needed to wield power to thrive, and Ms. Granth was the perfect example of this type of person.

An amused voice brought me out of my thoughts. "Thank heavens she's finally gone." I turned and found Maggie, an older Fort Vogel wife, staring in the direction Ms. Granth had gone. "I swear, she hangs around just to catch one of us doing something improper. The next shift you have with her, pay attention to how much work she gets done versus how much she struts around monitoring her charges." Maggie shrugged. "You'll be shocked at how little she actually does."

It was a relief to hear negativity in a place where unrelenting positivity was the norm. I flashed a grin. "Thanks for the tip. I'll keep an eye on her tomorrow. We're working textiles together."

"Oh, that's right. You and the Granthma were matched. How's that been going? The last girl she paired up with nearly lost her mind. There's something about our overlord that drives people cuckoo." She laughed and twirled a finger next to her head.

Maggie's merriment was appealing. I wanted badly to connect with someone, but I needed to move slowly, carefully. It wouldn't do to spill my guts to an undercover loyalist. I also didn't want to scare her away, like I'd done with Gunnar this afternoon. Acting too strait-laced could drive back such a bubbly person. I needed to pick a response between a snub and unconstrained joy.

A short laugh was the compromise I went with. "It's going as well as can be expected. Honestly, everything is still so new to me, I'm not sure what's normal or not." I lowered my voice. "I *can* tell you one thing. Ms. Granth sure is persistent. Everywhere I go, she's there. How does she know where to show up?"

"'Cause the bird's been here for years, and she's been studying us wives for a long time. She knows what we do, when we do it, sometimes before we even know. She acts like we're ducklings that she needs to herd into a line before we cross the street." Some of the amusement left her face. "I actually feel sorry for her. Can you imagine being so concerned with other people that you lose yourself in the process? I don't even know what Ms. Granth is really like, and I suspect that she doesn't know herself either."

Maggie laughed. "But we don't need to talk about how much pity I have for our overlord. What we really need to talk about is how to avoid Granthma. There are two places on base that the old lady won't set foot in. One's the traitor's cemetery, and the other is the mess hall." She tilted her head. "Charlie, my husband, is working late tonight. Want to meet up for supper? I mean, it's no home-cooked meal, but you'd be surprised by how much you learn to like the mess hall food."

This was the first invitation I'd received since coming to Fort Vogel, and the first offer of friendship I'd gotten in a while. I stifled the surge of joy I felt, not wanting to come across as over-eager. "You have great timing, Maggie. Gunnar is also working late, so it's the perfect night to meet up." I laughed. "And it's my birthday. Do they have any sweets?"

She shook her head. "They keep sugar locked up tighter than gold in a bank vault." A thoughtful expression crossed her face. "Let's meet at 7. Go inside the building and find the room with the pink door. Obviously, that's where the ladies eat. Us broads go gaga for pink." She rolled her eyes. "Grab a table and a plate of food. Then prepare to be wowed, not just by the culinary indulgences, but by the witty conversation and endless jokes I'll be serving up."

I could sense our meal would be filled with laughter, a thought that put a grin on my face. "Thanks for asking me, Maggie. I'll make sure to set my expectations sky high." Activity in the playroom caught my attention. "I think it's time to help wrangle the little ones. They can be a handful when it's this close to leaving."

Maggie put a finger to her lips. "I'm going to duck out early. Cover for me if anyone asks."

She was gone before I could respond. I shook my head as Maggie glided down the road. Her pace wasn't rushed like mine would have been. She took her time and kept her gaze level, nodding at the soldiers who passed. Anyone seeing her would assume she was on a leisurely stroll, not leaving work early without permission. Her boldness was enviable.

I tucked these thoughts away and returned to the playroom. Ten squirmy toddlers greeted me, and I entertained them until they were picked up. It was sweet to witness each child's excitement when it was their turn to leave. It didn't matter how shy the little one was during the day. When their name was called and they turned to find their mother, joy filled their face. Unfortunately, the elation was short-lived. Each child's expression returned to neutral after a gentle chiding from their mom. The lessons of society began at such a young age. Too young if you asked me.

After the last child left, the remaining wives split up the cleaning. We scrubbed, mopped, and tidied until the space was ready for the next day. I'd been assigned to the learning room, and I breathed deeply as I washed, enjoying the scents of lemon and vinegar as they mingled with the undertones of wax and chalk. There was something about the bouquet of a classroom that was comforting. A quick inhale of the fragrant air brought memories rushing back.

In Starkesend, laughter was rarely tolerated, but the schoolhouse was a place where this rule was bent. This didn't apply to lectures, of course. During these droning talks, we paid attention, sitting upright with both hands on our desks. No one wanted to be caught breaking form. The punishment for doing so was a rap on the knuckles. Or several raps if a student was considered extra obnoxious. Pain was a compelling motivator, and it only took two demonstrations of public discipline for my class to absorb this lesson. Compare this to the months it took for the entire class to memorize Hitler's twenty-five points, and it seemed that social behavior was learned more rapidly than the propaganda-heavy material we were continually force-fed.

In addition to lectures, recreation made up a large portion of our day. The Nazis were keen on physical fitness, and the Starkesend leaders followed this ideal rigidly. Schoolchildren were given ninety minutes each day to use their bodies. This included marching and hikes, where rows of children were corralled by red-faced, yelling teacher. It also involved free play, and it was during these unstructured hours that happiness dominated.

I played outside quite often, either rolling down grassy hills or jumping rope to catchy rhymes, but one indoor activity remained my favorite. I'd gather up the same four girls, and we'd use the classroom chalkboard as a canvas. The murals we created were simple at first, mostly made up of stick figures and uneven shapes. As we got older, the drawings became more sophisticated. Once, we crafted an undersea world complete with mermaids and a lobster orchestra. Another time, we'd imagined a planet different from our own, a lush eutopia covered with flowering trees and breathtaking views of its six moons.

We giggled while we sketched, glad for the opportunity to use our creativity, a trait we rarely wielded. Surprisingly, our teachers turned a blind eye to our art sessions, but we were required to erase each mural before the other students finished exercising. When we heard the first warning bell, our group of four would stand in front of the chalkboard, joining hands. We were calm and reflective, quietly proud of our efforts. The group stayed unmoving until the sounds of approaching footsteps prompted a sprint to the erasers and a speedy removal of our creation. Although we only drew five or six murals a year, the memory of those hours remained vivid, and I cherished them greatly.

I inhaled once more, smiling at the retained fragments of times passed. It was lucky that I had such recollections because many my age did not. If I could sneak imagination into the children's days, they would be better off and able to recall their own warm experiences later in life. Already, their lessons were dreary, and more focused on following the rules than exploring or playing make believe. I'd have to discuss the idea with Maggie. She'd know if it was worth the risk.

A scan the room assured me it was tidy. I tucked away the cleaning supplies and bid the remaining women good night on my way out. Excitement about dinner had taken hold, filling my steps with buoyancy. The walk home felt shorter than normal but more thrilling. Instead of taking it for granted, I marveled at the sun's rays peeking through the canopy of trees. The beams made the little things sparkle. Rather than blending into the background, everyday scenery stood out in newly discovered grandeur. The potential for friendship had lent a glow to my surroundings, and while a small voice advised caution, a larger part of me was ready to charge ahead recklessly.

My mood stayed bright until I got home and saw the darkened windows. I'd expected an empty house but encountering the lightless reminder of tension hit me hard. It wasn't unusual for Gunnar to work late. He'd been preparing for Dr. Brandt's arrival until yesterday, organizing perfection for the boss who only showed up thrice a year. Each evening, he'd come home after seven or eight, hungrier than I'd ever seen a person. We'd eat, then relax until bedtime. Judging by the lack of rattling noises and moans, Gunnar would sleep soundly until sunrise, when the pattern would begin again, with breakfast and coffee, followed by more than a full day's worth of work.

This evening was my first shadowy welcome. On the other nights, Gunnar turned the kitchen light on during his last break, a thoughtful gesture that caused a smile as I walked up the driveway. Encountering the opposite showed me how much I had enjoyed this small show of affection. It was one thing coming home to an empty house. It was quite another to arrive at a place that appeared cold and inhospitable. I much preferred the warmer greeting, which meant making up with Gunnar was a priority. At least it would be after I finished dinner with Maggie.

Now, preparing for my outing needed attention. I'd never eaten at the chow hall, and I wasn't sure of the dress code. Was wearing a work frock appropriate, or did I need to change into something less uniform? I scanned my memory, hoping to recall this bit of information. I also thought about my clothing options. The items in Klara's closet lacked frills or adornments. She'd worn plain dresses and aprons like the other wives. Fabrics at Starkesend were donned until they fell apart, which made my inherited wardrobe sensible. From an evening-out perspective, her clothes were more practical than stylish, and I wasn't sure if this was the norm where I was headed.

After a minute, I laughed out loud. I was wasting my time on foolish questions. No outfit would be considered too uniform here—I was on a military base where they were the norm. If anything, I'd stand out in flashy clothes. Wardrobes weren't usually a big worry of mine, so I must be lonelier than I thought. If tonight went well, I'd gain a friend who would help with that problem.

A glance at the clock showed it was 5:45, which left time to cook dinner for Gunnar, plus freshen up. I went into autopilot while I chopped, boiled, and simmered the ingredients for a simple stew, imagining the conversations Maggie and I would have in the chow hall.

Would I find out new information about Ms. Granth, or would Maggie spill about the other wives? How about the soldiers? I didn't know much about that group and learning more would be a benefit. She may be able to tell me more about Fort Vogel, too. Besides venturing into the traitor's cemetery and locating Klara's headstone, there hadn't been many opportunities to explore the grounds in my first eight days. There must be other areas I was unfamiliar with, and Maggie seemed like the type of person who would have the most interesting details about her surroundings.

After the vegetables cooked, I turned off the burner then carefully placed a lid over the meal. Chances were that Gunnar would stick to his word and stay in the lab overnight, but I wanted to leave a peace offering in case he had second thoughts about staying late. I grabbed a sheet of paper and penned a note explaining what was on my mind.

Gunnar,

I'm sorry for what unfolded between us today. We were both in an emotional place, and I think my extraction impacted me more than I realized. I would love to talk when you're done in the lab. I'll be home after dinner. Maggie Helmstedt invited me to the mess hall, so I don't need any food, but I made you a little something in case you're hungry.

Talk soon,

Lizbeth

I hoped my husband got a chance to read the words, and that he felt the same way. Being uprooted from home had been painful, but I'd found some comfort in my relationship with Gunnar. Although we were married, we interacted more like friends or siblings. Gunnar was a partner who provided a low-pressure way to adjust to our union and to life on a military base. Getting back to the easygoing companionship we shared was my goal. The note was my first attempt toward realizing it.

I placed the paper down in a noticeable place, then got ready for the evening. Washing up and ironing took a chunk of time, but I finished with five minutes to spare. After a quick peek in the mirror, I headed to the chow hall. There were still a few hours left of my eighteenth birthday, and I was eager to experience what the night had in store.

Chapter 20 - Lizbeth

Although I walked past the chow hall every day, I had never entered the squat structure. Even from the outside, I knew how busy the eatery became during mealtimes. Groups of men poured inside before morning PT, during lunch, and after dismissal. Whenever I passed soldiers on their way to the building, they seemed eager to eat, moving at a pace far quicker than the dawdle they used to reach the exercise fields.

The wives oversaw the cafeteria, three women per shift. It was this trio's job to cook and serve fresh food, morning until night. Although there was downtime built into the day, a stint in the chow hall demanded more time than any other wifely duty. I had yet to be assigned to one of the lengthy days. Since arriving on base, my volunteer hours had been split between the nursery and the textile mill. Because of this, I was only familiar with the cafeteria's brown exterior, not the happenings behind the scenes.

I imagined the interior would smell like other dining halls, where bland, heavy odors dominated. This prediction proved true. As I entered the building, the aroma of boiled potatoes and cabbage flooded my senses. Warm air carried the scent, thawing me after my walk in the cool evening. The heat would become stuffy after a while, but for now, I welcomed the toasty temperature.

A small wall separated the entrance from the main chamber, and deep voices slipped around the barrier. It sounded like a dozen or so soldiers were enjoying a meal. I listened to their muffled conversations for a moment, then stepped into the room where they sat. A brief silence told me I'd been noticed. Thankfully their discussion picked up again, and I did my best to appear composed as I searched for the lady's quarters.

At Dorf, being alone with a group of men was taboo. Starting in secondary school, boys and girls studied in separate classrooms, and also spent their free time apart. I studied, hopscotched, and jumped rope with other daughters, and we rarely had the opportunity or the desire to interact with males our age. My brother was an exception—our age gap meant Ellis was young enough to stay around when I had friends over. Unlike other young boys, he enjoyed being pampered by his sister and her mates. I considered his affable nature a win. He hadn't conformed to the angry masculinity that was the norm at Starkesend.

It was this personality trait girls were warned about. For as long as I could remember, we were told that boys were rough and wild. When we were older and became wives, we'd use our womanly essence to calm the savagery, but in childhood we should play separately to avoid any outbursts. Males would develop more control as they aged, and females would nurture their feminine spirt as they matured. In marriage, each spouse would complement the other, ensuring a relationship of balanced harmony.

Dorf marital pairings weren't as systematic as the marriages formed during the Frau Rennen, but there were criteria. Manhood began at age twenty, whereas womanhood started when a girl turned sixteen. The men who joined the military were the only ones entitled to a bride under eighteen. The men who chose roles outside of the armed forces were required to wait until a woman passed the age threshold for the Frau Rennen. After this, a man could coordinate a marital arrangement with the family of his chosen bride.

While soldier's matches were calculated formulaically, Dorf relationships conformed to a social hierarchy, where people married within their class. Certain factors were used to determine a family's ranking. This included length of time at Starkesend, number of children, importance of the patriarch's work role, and number of hours spent volunteering for Nazi sponsored programs. My family's rank was high because we'd lived in the community for over a decade and my father was the engineer who planned expansions for the village and base.

Looks also worked in some people's favor. Eligible men and women who closely matched the Aryan ideal were given preference in pairings. Ellis and Klara resembled my mother, who had curly brown hair and hazel eyes. In contrast, my honey-colored hair and blue eyes mirrored my father's features. If I would have aged out of the Frau Rennen, my hand would have been pursued by the highest-ranking men. Fair beauty was desirable and bestowing it upon the next generation was one of the greatest ways to advance civilization, at least, according to Starkesend doctrine. I wasn't pleased that youth or appearance were the two biggest drivers behind marriage, but women were given little choice in their fate.

I kept all of this in mind while I walked along the back of the cafeteria. While I didn't believe that all men were savages, the lessons from my youth left an impression and I was reluctant to test my ideas about the male personality. Hugging the wall helped me feel more secure, and the short glances I dared take of the soldiers confirmed they were more focused on eating and laughing than the scurrying figure behind them. My breathing became easier when I spotted the pink door Maggie told me about, and I picked up my pace, trying to reduce the time I was exposed to the uniformed men.

Mocking words stopped me ten feet short of my goal. "Well, well, well. Check out this tasty morsel, boys. She certainly looks more appetizing than anything they're serving us for supper."

I recognized the voice. It belonged to the crude guard who'd welcomed me to Fort Vogel. Conroy made me uneasy during our first meeting, and it was happening again now. Tendrils of disgust weaved together in my guts, forming a tight knot. I wanted nothing more than to run from the man behind me. Instead, I forced a tight-lipped smile on my face and turned to face the admirer who was sauntering my way. "Good evening, Conroy. I'll make sure to pass on your well wishes to Colonel Cruse."

A flicker of uncertainty flashed in his eyes before it was eclipsed by lust. "You can also tell him that he's one lucky man. If I was your husband, you'd never leave my sight. I'd just stay in bed with you, dipping my wick, from morning until night." Conroy licked his lips. "The Führer would have no problem getting his Aryan population from us. I'd pump you full of blond babies until you screamed." His nostrils flared, and he took a shuddering breath before he continued. "And then I'd pump some more, because hearing you scream puts a smile on my face."

Nausea turned my stomach. I pushed it away and stoked the rage that lurked behind it. Here was a man I barely knew, treating me like I only existed to satisfy an itch. Conroy was intimidating and he knew it. He spoke in a dangerous, gravelly tone as he towered over me, close enough to feel the heat from his body. His weaponized his presence, striking out at those he deemed weak or timid, and I'd landed right inside his sights.

If I bent to his harassment, I knew there would be more of it. Now was the time to stand firm. I steeled my nerves and responded. "Leave me alone, Conroy. There's no need for you to talk about the disgusting things you'd do to me." I took aim at his ego. "I bet I'm not the first girl you've made sick to her stomach, and I certainly won't be the last."

Conroy's face reddened. "No one talks to me like that, not even some floozy who's married to an officer." He leaned toward me. "Sounds like I need to teach you a lesson." He grinned cruelly. "I'm going to enjoy this."

I froze, afraid that any movement would further provoke his fury. The lessons I'd learned about a woman's place rushed to my brain. I'd made the mistake of stepping outside of my bounds, and now I would reap the consequences.

A booming voice rang out. "Conroy, get back here and leave the pretty lady alone."

We both turned to see who yelled. A mountain of a man, with kind eyes and a pleasant smile, was waving and pointing to the seat next to him. My harasser sighed and slumped his shoulders. "Tanne, you're always ruining my good time." Conroy gave me a hard stare before he rejoined the other soldiers.

My body wanted to tremble, but I had no interest in displaying fear to the bully who still stared. I stopped the external movement before it rippled through my limbs, but I couldn't halt the interior shiver. It traveled in waves from head to foot, coating my innards with revulsion and fear. The brief interaction shook me.

Awareness of my surroundings was crucial if I wanted to avoid getting caught off guard. Conroy had escaped my notice because I'd been afraid. Rather than evaluating the environment, I'd stayed close to the walls, making myself as small as possible. My attempt to blend in had failed, instead, I'd drawn the attention of a menace. A happier existence, a less fearful one, required the opposite of hiding. Confidence paired with vigilance would save me from future distress.

I put this thought into practice. During my final steps toward the pink-doored sanctuary, I kept my chin up and allowed my body to take up the space it deserved. No crouching, no quivering, no downcast gaze. I maintained poise until I was safely inside the room. After the door was closed, I released the breath I'd been holding and inspected the lady's quarters.

The space was small but pleasant. There was enough seating for eight women and framed floral paintings gave the beige walls a splash of color.

The most eye-catching feature was a pass-through window on the far wall. Delicious scents came from the opening, and I noticed activity on the other side of the glass. I walked closer to get a better view.

Dorothy, Anna, and Edith, three of my former classmates, worked together using dance-like movements. Anna and Edith floated from pots, pans, and ladles to the soldier's serving area, where they dished out hot food and removed older portions. Dorothy stayed in the kitchen, scrubbing incoming dishes with a cheery expression and lightly swaying hips. I was in awe of their harmony. It seemed as though they'd perfected their movements after years of practice. In reality, this was only their first or second shift in the cafeteria. After just over a week at Fort Vogel, they'd adapted seamlessly to their expected roles.

The ability to conform was a valuable trait. Life would be easier without constantly questioning the culture and morals of society. I'd made attempts to fit in, but the price of submission was always too high, and I gave up before fully submerging. It was crushing to feel alone in a world full of people. This was why the prospect of friendship excited me. Gaining an ally would reduce my loneliness and provide me with a small amount of acceptance.

I observed my classmates until the door opened behind me. As I turned, Maggie shot into the room with delight in her eyes and a plate of cookies in her hands. "You made it! I was half expecting you to skip out, but you actually showed up." She held out the dish. "Good thing you did because I was able to swipe some ingredients. Now, we can have a proper birthday celebration."

Her energy was contagious, and my words bubbled out. "What a surprise, Maggie, thank you. I wasn't expecting you to bring anything." I took the offered treats and set them down on a table. "You'll have to tell me your secrets. I have no idea how to swipe things or make delicious cookies."

She laughed. "Have a bite before you praise my baking skills. I could only grab half the sugar I needed, so they might taste funky." She squinted at the kitchen. "Can't tell who's working tonight. They look like newbies, though. You know anything about them?"

"You're right, they're newbies like me. I've been watching them, and I can't believe how fast they've adjusted to everything." I shook my head. "I certainly haven't. How long did it take you to feel like you belonged?"

"That's something I don't hear every day." Maggie tilted her head. "You really think I'm a true-blue, Starkesend-loving, happy-go-lucky wife?"

I thought before I responded, not sure how open to be. "I think you've got a lot of spunk. And you don't seem to have any fear. How is that possible?"

It was Maggie's turn to muse, and her eyes were serious when she answered. "Honestly, it's because I came here already grown. They never had the chance to teach me the proper way to be a lady." She paused, and there was an edge to her voice when she continued. "I've heard some of the lessons they teach the little girls, and I can barely keep my rage in check. Why are motherhood and husband-serving the only things we pass on to them? Sure, they're parts of being a woman, but damn it, Lizbeth, the wives here have forgotten the other pieces of themselves."

"I was a violinist." She glanced down at her hands, "Or at least I used to be. I was pretty good at it too. The local symphony invited me to play in some productions, just a few small plays and ballets you've probably never heard of. But you know what?" Maggie's eyes found mine, and she puffed up her chest. "Those sparsely attended shows meant the world to me. They may have been insignificant to the Broadway crowd, but they helped me find my confidence and my worth…and my husband." Her voice trailed off.

"Do you still play?" I asked gently, matching her soft tone.

Maggie smirked. "Lizbeth, you must be living in a fantasy world. Of course, I don't play. They'd never allow that sort of beauty around these parts." She sighed. "I just wish our little girls had a chance to experience the magic of doing something well. Something that was only for them, and not for their future children or spouse." She stopped abruptly, and shook her head, laughing. "Jeez, which one of us is living in a fantasy world? Once I start rambling, it's hard for me to stop. If I keep this up, the mess hall will close, and we'll never get a chance to eat."

I swung my eyes to the kitchen pass-through. "They're still moving around in there, which means there's still time for dinner." I raised my eyebrows. "To be fair, you did warn me about the captivating conversations we'd have, so, if I must miss a meal for their sake, I'd say it was time well spent."

"I knew we'd get along." Maggie's eyes sparkled. "Let's grab a plate, before the next chat begins. We need our strength to support the burden of such wit." She hesitated before we walked toward the kitchen. After a handful of seconds, she untied her apron and placed it on top of the cookies. "You can never be too safe."

"What do you mean?"

She cocked her thumb at Dorothy, Anna, and Edith. "I asked you about them for a reason. Filching sugar isn't the worst thing I can do, but it also isn't the best, and I like to avoid trouble if I can. When you told me those three were already perfect princesses, I knew they couldn't be trusted." She gestured to her apron. "Hence, the hidden dessert. Better to hide it, than to risk getting tattled on by a snitch."

Maggie's daring continued to surprise me. "You're right. It wouldn't be fun if your almost-sweet cookies got us in trouble." I grimaced. "They'd probably assign us extra extractions. No, thank you."

"You learn quick, Lizbeth. Those sessions are the worst." She shuddered. "They're especially bad when that jerk doctor is down there. He gives me the creeps. Yuck-o." She eyed the stacked dishes and cutlery next to the pass through. "Forget about him. Let's see what they're serving tonight. Nursery duty always makes me hungry."

Edith greeted us at the serving window. "Evening, ladies. What can I get for you? We have meatloaf or stew, with mashed potatoes, green beans, and cabbage. There's even a couple of rolls left if you want them."

Maggie spoke up first. "I'll take one of everything."

"One of everything?" Edith took a step back. "Are you sure? That's more than any of the men ate tonight." She gave Maggie a once over. "And you're a slip of a thing. Where would you even put all that food?"

"My husband and I are trying for a baby right now, so I need all the nutrition I can get." Maggie patted her flat stomach as she talked, then held out her empty dish.

"Well, in that case, let's see what I can rustle up for you." Edith took Maggie's plate to the serving trays. When she returned, it was loaded to capacity. "Nothing is too good for our little ones. Come back for seconds if you need it." She passed the meal to Maggie, then turned her attention on me. "What about you, Lizbeth? Are you and the Colonel trying to grow your family too?"

Color warmed my checks and neck. I knew Edith was being polite, but her question conjured thoughts about my tense standing with Gunnar, and the nights we spent sleeping apart. Our actions showed that parenting was the last thing on our minds—we lived like friends, not a romantic couple. Of course, no one on the outside knew this, including the curious girl in front of me. I decided a small misdirection was needed.

My blushing skin became an advantage. When I combined it with a modest smile and a downcast gaze, I transformed into a shy newlywed. "Oh, we're just enjoying each other's company for now. It's been quite the learning experience." I lowered my voice to a whisper. "I can't wait to see what he shows me tonight."

The words hit their mark. As I glanced up to pass Edith my plate, I noticed her reddened cheeks. She stuttered as she spoke. "Yes, I'm-I'm sure you've le-learned a lot." She grabbed my dish. "Le-let me get your dinner." Edith swiveled and hurried toward the food.

I felt an elbow in my side. "Holy moly, Lizbeth. She took off faster than a stampeding buffalo." Maggie laughed silently, and I joined her.

We barely got ourselves under control when Edith returned. Our neutral expressions appeared forced, but my old classmate kept any chiding thoughts to herself. She held out a plate that was as full as Maggie's. "I got you one of everything, too."

"Thank you, Edith. Everything looks tasty." I took the meal and offered an apology. "I'm sorry if I said anything unseemly. It's been a long day, which is no excuse, but I hope you'll forgive me."

Her embarrassment faded, and she beamed. "No worries, Lizbeth." She gestured to the kitchen. "Cafeteria duty is my favorite so far. Anna, Dorothy, and I usually sign up with each other, but maybe you can join me for a shift."

For some reason, the unexpected invitation caused a flare of annoyance. Instead of acting on it, I pushed the irritation down and grinned. "What a great idea. After Ms. Granth is done with me, I'll be ready to take you up on that offer. Let's talk about it more in a few weeks, at roll call."

Edith clapped her hands together. "Golly gee, that would be swell. It was nice talking to you, Lizbeth" Her eyes darted to Maggie. "And you, too. Enjoy your dinner, ladies." She waved, then rejoined the rest of her trio.

Maggie and I walked to our table in silence. When we sat, laughter exploded from us both. It was soundless, but the force of our merriment shook our bodies and forced us to lean against each other to stay upright. It was one of those contagious laughs, the kind that never seemed to end. When one of us settled down, we'd make the mistake of peeking at the other, and the fit would restart.

We went on like that for minutes—two quiet, quaking women, on the verge of tumbling to the floor. When the laughing stopped as suddenly as it started, we dug into the heaping plates in front of us, devouring the piles of food in record time, without a word. After we finished our dinner, plus a few cookies each, we were finally ready to talk.

"I haven't had that much fun in ages." I wrapped my hands around my abdomen. "And what a workout. I'll have sore muscles tomorrow, for sure."

Maggie's face glowed. "Let's do this again, Lizbeth. You're a riot."

"Well, Maggie, to borrow our dear friend Edith's words, I think that would be swell." We collapsed into each other again and stayed laughing until the chow hall closed for the night.

Gunnar, 1933

Chapter 21 - Gunnar

I toiled while Dr. Brandt was in Germany. He'd given me two months to produce results, so I dove right in, trying to progress from where he'd left off. Studying and experimentation filled the daylight hours, and I slept overnight in the lab. It wasn't a satisfying existence, but I settled into a routine as time raced by.

Conducting research at Fort Vogel was complicated. Resources on the adrenals were sparse, and the base's seclusion made gathering publications impossible. The lack of scientific literature forced me to use human testing as my primary information source. I remained alone in the beginning, using my own body to produce data. At the doctor's request, I filled logs with measurements and diagrams. For myself, I noted the sensations I experienced throughout the day. These observations would uncover my most painful or frightening moments, crucial information for pinpointing the worst parts of the extraction process. I'd vowed to improve our technique, and that included easing our participant's discomfort. If I could soothe people during the most distressing moments, I'd be well on my way to honoring that vow.

The lab's initial solitude was also ideal for perfecting my capabilities. After a week, I was able to locate my adrenal glands with precision and accuracy. This was far different than the inaccurate prods in the beginning. Those stabs left me in intense pain, and it was reassuring to feel the agony decrease as my skills enhanced.

After a month, I was ready to expand Project Leer. I drew up a plan and sent the petition to General Stillwell. We arranged a meeting in the laboratory where he'd hear out my request. When the scheduled day arrived, I was ready to argue my points, but it turned out I was over prepared.

I met the general at the armory entrance. "Good morning, sir. It's been some time since we've spoken. Thank you for agreeing to meet."

He brushed my greeting aside and headed down the stairs. "Cruse, there's no need to thank me. I've been chomping at the bit to see what you're doing down here. The good doctor told me to leave you alone until summoned, and the day's finally arrived." He threw a satisfied smile over his shoulder. "Let's get to it."

"Yes, sir." I hurried to keep up. "I've made a few modifications to the equipment that I'd like to show you. I think with those changes, Project Leer is ready for a fresh crop of subjects."

"Cruse, whatever you need, just ask." He waved his hand. "You can use the new recruits we've brought on. They're not quite suited to the soldier life, but they'd be perfect for the lab."

I was shocked at his quick acceptance. I'd expected pushback or questions, something to justify my need for more bodies, but nothing was required. It gave me insight into how disposable the general viewed his underlings, information I'd be sure to remember. For the time being, I'd take advantage of his indifferent attitude. "Thank you, sir. If you have a list of names, that would be helpful. I'd like to get started on the next phase of Leer as soon as possible."

General Stillwell nodded. "Conroy and Tanne keep track of arrivals. Get with them in the morning, and they'll get you the list you need." He stopped short as we reached the inner chamber. His head swiveled back and forth as he took it in. "Not much has changed since I was here last, but it feels different." He turned to me. "It's hard to explain, Cruse. Dr. Brandt has a way of making things colder than they are." He pondered the thought. "It's impressive really, how one person can suck the life out of every room he enters. That's probably why he's hobnobbing in Germany, and I'm here working myself to death." His gaze returned to me, and he laughed. "It pays to be scary as hell. Take note of that."

"Noted, sir." I took in our surroundings, trying to see them through the general's eyes. "I get what you're saying about the doctor. He's intense."

"That's one way of putting it. The polite way. I forget you're the one who's stuck with him." The general clapped my back. "Better to be respectful than to have the doctor find out you're bad mouthing him. Wouldn't want that intensity turned on you."

"Right you are, sir." I headed toward the center of the room, guiding the general toward the table I used as a desk. "Let me show you what I've been sending Dr. Brandt. It will sum up what I've completed so far."

I flipped through the papers containing my neat scrawl, explaining the findings as I went. General Stillwell was a man who preferred simple terms over scientific jargon, so I did my best to deliver the lecture in plain English. He feigned interest for a while, nodding occasionally, snapping his eyes back to the reports when they wandered, but the watered-down version still failed to engage him. The general gave into his inattention on the third page, when I was in the middle of explaining Leer's output. "This chart shows the yield for—"

"Cruse, I'm sorry to cut you off, but I don't understand 90% of what you're saying." He shrugged. "From the little I could grasp, it sounds like you're doing just fine, and I'm glad to hear it." He gestured at the equipment laid out, the needles, pliers, and vials I utilized daily, "But why don't we switch to something more physical. Tell me what these are for."

I explained each tool's purpose, then the steps of the extraction process. Our meeting concluded with a demonstration. I believed that operating on myself was the most efficient way to show General Stillwell the progress I'd made, but I knew it would be rough. Witnessing a person puncture their own flesh was off putting. While my hand was practiced, and I easily moved through the procedure, from the outside, my actions appeared coarse. I observed a green pall on the general's face halfway through the presentation, and he flinched when the first syringe pierced my skin.

General Stillwell was grateful when I concluded the procedure. "I like to think that I have a strong stomach, but every time I see blood or needles, I get as squeamish as a girl." He shuddered. "I'll leave you and the doctor to the gory details, and I'll provide above ground support. Then, when we deliver on our promises, we can all bask in the glory that will come our way." The general took a step back, narrowing his eyes. "I understood you correctly, Cruse? All those charts and graphs of yours meant that Project Leer is on the right track?"

"Sir, you have my word that things are moving forward. But I'll be honest," I lowered my head, "after the rough start we had, I wasn't too sure about the prospect of turning it around. Losing our initial participants was brutal, even if they were outcasts." I raised my eyes and found the general nodding.

"That's why you're the right man for the job, Corporal. You have the exact amount of kindness to balance out the doctor's shrewdness." He pointed at me. "You're human, and that's who's down here with you, fellow human beings. We'll be lucky if Dr. Brandt ever acknowledges the test subject's humanity, but I know damned well that you will." Seriousness filled his voice. "And that's the secret to getting what you want out of others—you treat them like people. The doctor could spend years down here trying to milk each person for all they're worth, but he'd always come up dry, because you can't get blood from a stone. You, on the other hand, will have no trouble getting what we're aiming for." The general glanced around the lab laughing. "But don't tell anyone I said that, especially not the doctor. If word got out, and people knew I was talking about goodwill and humanity, there'd be an uproar." The conversation abruptly changed directions. "I'm heading upstairs. I need to address some issues that have sprung up in the barracks." General Stillwell walked toward the exit, and I followed. "I'll let Tanne and Conroy know you'll be stopping by in the morning. They'll have that list ready to go."

"Yes, sir. I'll make that tomorrow's priority. When's the best time to gather men for lab duty?"

"Do it after PT. That way they'll be fed and exercised, and easier to handle. These fellas don't see the value in listening to commands yet, and if they don't learn it down here, they'll be hitting the road. Let's give them a week in the lab. After that, update me on their progress, although I'm not expecting much." He shook his head. "Lowering our entrance standards was a mistake, but the duds can contribute something of use before we send them packing."

We reached the stairwell, and the general climbed up. When he got to the landing, he called out, "Remember, Cruse, if you need anything let me know. Godspeed." He saluted with two fingers, before he turned and departed.

I retreated to the inner chamber, enjoying the silence as I strode. Tomorrow would be the end of my solitude, both an exciting and disappointing milestone. I was ready to progress, and expansion was the only way to move forward, but with expansion came attention and noise and dealing with others. And from what the general said, the soldiers I'd meet tomorrow would be a handful.

I'd dealt with rowdiness before. During the war, I'd overseen a ten-man squad who'd taken some time to adapt to military life. They'd come from farming families, like me, and I'd used this commonality to reach them. The soldiers underwent a transformation, from brutes responding in angry grunts and drinking on duty, to a group that outperformed the rest of our company. I'd related to them, proven myself worthy of their respect, and I sensed that was how I'd connect with my new patients. Finding a shared thread would be crucial, and I'd seek it out during the morning's interactions.

Ensuring comfort was another way to build a relationship with the test subjects. The observation that General Stillwell had made about output was correct—yields were larger when the person producing them felt safe. From my own experience under the knife, a calm session generated more fluid than a stressful one. There was also less pain involved.

∞∞∞∞

Two weeks ago, quite by accident, I'd discovered music's sedative effect. I was cleaning the lab after a long day, where nothing had gone right. Despite my newfound skills with a needle, I hadn't coaxed a single drop out of my body. I had welts to show—red, angry marks where I'd been too aggressive with my skin—but the vials I'd laid out in the morning remained empty.

Telling myself to relax didn't work. Even nibbling a piece of the doctor's left-behind chocolate did little good. The only thing that lifted my spirits was music. I didn't perceive it at the time, but notes flowed from my subconscious and spilled out my mouth. I hummed while I wiped down counters and put away equipment. I continued humming as I hurried out of the lab and across base to the mess hall before it closed. I even hummed the tune while I ate alone and kept at it when I placed my dirty dishes into the proper spot.

"What's that song?" The question brought me back to the present. I shook my head to clear it and saw Klara behind the wash window giving me a curious appraisal.

Since our first meeting, I'd made it a point to eat in the cafeteria during her shifts. They were right before closing, during the quietest hour. The two of us chatted every evening while Klara served food or I put away my dishes. We'd grown closer as the days passed, and I suspected she anticipated our conversations as much as I did, although neither of us had admitted it to the other.

I must have been deep in thought to have missed her back there. "Oh, hi, Klara. What song are you talking about?"

"You've been humming since you walked in the door, Gunnar. Luckily no one else is here or they'd think you were daft." She grinned. "I, on the other hand, know that you're batty." She reached through the window to grab my discarded dishes. "So, what was it? I've listened to plenty of music, but I've never heard that particular melody."

"I didn't realize I was making noise." I felt my cheeks heat up.

Klara tilted her head. "Really? That makes my daft comment even more accurate." She laughed, but stopped when I didn't join in. "Gunnar, you know I'm joking." She started scrubbing as she continued. "I do that sometimes, too. I'll get lost inside my head and come to after I've knit half a scarf or sketched something I saw that day. It's like my brain knows I need a break from the world, but my body must keep moving. Maybe the movement is hypnotic? There is something soothing about knitting or drawing…" She glanced up from the sink, "…or humming."

"That's the smartest thing I've ever heard you say." I quipped. Klara swatted at me with her wash rag, and I jumped back. "It's only fair if I can make fun of you too."

She let out a dramatic sigh. "I guess so, Corporal, if you must."

"I absolutely must. We need all the humor we can get." I winked, then grew serious. "But honestly, Klara, I think you're onto something. Music's always been a balm for me. The song I was just humming must have been one of my mother's. She played piano, and she'd come up with the most beautiful pieces." I smiled at the memory and noticed that Klara had stopped cleaning. She leaned forward, listening with her own small smile.

"Ma amazed me with her talent. She'd ask me to pick a key and would jump off from there, weaving notes together until something wonderful emerged." My eyes sparkled. "The songs were moving, even as a boy, I recognized it. Sometimes I'd feel sorrow deep in my chest. Other times my heart would flutter with happiness. And they were catchy. I could play each song over and over in my head and never get tired of hearing them." I pictured the carefree hours I'd spent with Ma, listening to her compose. When I was younger, she played often, sometimes four nights a week. During my adolescent years, when my father spent long period away at Friekorps, Saturday evenings became the only time she set aside for music. I was relieved Ma hadn't abandoned the baby grand when her farm duties expanded. Her musical ability was a gift I anticipated.

"Do you play?" Klara asked.

I shook my head. "Nah, I tried to learn but was never any good at it. When Ma sits at the piano, she comes alive. Music is a part of who she is, and she looks natural sitting on the bench. Me, on the other hand…let me think of how to put this." I paused to come up with the right words. "Well, if you combine the most rigid etiquette teacher with one of those stiff German soldiers from the videos they show us, you'd have me as a pianist. I could play the notes, but I looked like a piece of machinery while I doing it."

"I took lessons before we came to Starkesend." Klara offered shyly. "My parents forced me to practice in the beginning, but eventually I loved it—the feel of the keys under my fingers, the way I could press a pedal and the note would last and last." Her voice was soft, her thoughts a mile away. "Right after school, I'd run to the piano and play scales. Even that simple exercise captivated me. After I warmed up, my mom and sister would come in the room to be my audience. Lizbeth liked when I made up bouncy, fun tunes.

She'd get up and dance, clapping when I finished a song, begging me to play another."

The dreaminess left her eyes, and sadness replaced it. "We had to leave the upright behind when we moved. I probably cried an ocean's worth of tears, but it made no difference. Mom and Dad said to pack light and there was no room for arguing." She laughed bitterly. "How naïve I was, thinking I'd be able to play here. It was a child's fantasy because in Starkesend, musical talent would wither and die."

I held out my hand, and she reached to take it with a gentle grasp. "I'm sorry, Klara. It's hard to lose something you care about."

"Thank you, Gunnar. Luckily, I was able to find a substitute." She squeezed my fingers, before releasing them. She placed her hands on her hips and smiled broadly. "I'm an artist. Most of my subjects are people. I like to capture them while they do normal things around base or the village. Sounds boring when I say it, but there's something charming about the mundane." She tilted her head. "Maybe I can show you my paintings one day."

"I'd love that." I glanced at the kitchen clock behind her. "And I'd love to talk longer, but you should be getting home. You wouldn't want to worry your parents."

Klara sighed. "You're right. They're very protective of me." She raised her eyebrows up and down. "In fact, if they knew I was talking to a soldier, *alone*, with no one here to save me if something went wrong—" she touched the back of her hand to her forehead and raised her head in mock distress, "—I think they'd both have heart attacks."

"You're a firecracker, ma'am. Let them know that you'd be able to handle yourself around the likes of me." I chuckled before continuing. "I'm heading out. I'll be courteous and save your folks some cardiac trouble."

"See you, Gunnar." Her smile was brilliant, beautiful.

"See you, Klara." I tipped an imaginary hat. "And thanks for the insight. I'm going to use music on myself in the lab tomorrow. There might be something to that hypnotic quality you brought up. I'll let you know how it goes."

I walked away but glanced back when I reached the chow hall door. My eyes met Klara's, and she waved before returning to the dish pile. A swell of emotion surged, but I pushed it aside, knowing it wasn't the right moment to focus on feelings. For the next several months, the extraction process required my attention. After the procedure was refined, I'd be free to explore my friendship with Klara.

I just hoped it wasn't too late when that time arrived.

Chapter 22 - Gunnar

I turned into a terrible sleeper that night. Snippets of Klara appeared in my dreams, and I woke after each occurrence. Her laugh, her smile, her departing wave—my subconscious mind flashed through a dozen snapshots of the girl who'd become impossible to ignore. After each wakeup, I guided my thoughts in a different direction, but they always returned to her.

In the morning, I made a tortuous decision. Seeing Klara made me happy, but it also left me preoccupied. The workload of Project Leer was daunting, brutal, and it required maintaining an existence different than the rest of Starkesend's occupants. Lurking underground, trying to create a human assembly line—none of this was healthy, and I knew it. This damaging lifestyle left little space for casual relationships, let alone the deeper bond I sensed growing between Klara and me. But my primary loyalty was to the vows I'd made, and our friendship would sidetrack any progress. Plus, it wouldn't be fair to her. I couldn't give Klara the attention she deserved while I struggled to perfect Leer. With a heavy heart, I resolved to stay away from the cafeteria during her shifts.

Unfortunately, my insomnia didn't stop after cutting ties with her. The sleeplessness stayed with me like an unwanted companion, causing purple half-circles to form under my eyes and bone-tired weariness to become my default state. I pushed through the exhaustion for two weeks, maintaining a punishing schedule until I it was time for the new experimental group to show up.

The night before the test subjects arrived, dreams of Klara kept me restless. At 0330 I stopped trying to sleep and forced myself to rise and rustle through the clothes I stored in the lab. I pulled on my well-worn exercise shirt and shorts. Although it was early, I knew laps around the PT field would allow me to concentrate on something other than my Klara fixation. Physical exertion was a reliable distraction, and a diversion was what I needed to restore balance to my mind.

It was still dark when I reached the half-mile loop. The cool air felt refreshing on my cheeks as I set a pace just shy of sprinting. Oxygen poured into my lungs and powered my muscles along the dirt path. I pushed through four laps, then slowed to a jog for another four before walking a final circle. The run had replaced my exhaustion with an exhilaration that made me clear-eyed and revived, precisely the mood I was aiming for. I'd need to maintain this attitude during the intense work that lay ahead.

The lights were off in the barracks when I slipped in. Reveille was at 0500, which meant the showers would stay empty for another forty minutes. I took my time under the hot water, thinking through the day's schedule. My first to-do was obtaining a list of available men, but I couldn't visit the access booth to get it until Tanne and Conroy finished their morning routine and reported for duty. This was at 0600 for Tanne, who was punctual, and much later for Conroy, whose tardiness increased as he grew more comfortable at Starkesend.

This information was valuable because I planned to arrive early for a private conversation with Tanne. It would be best if our talk stayed between us, so it was crucial to reach him before anyone showed up, especially Conroy. If all went well, I'd avoid seeing the crass soldier altogether. He disgusted me, and if I could escape an uncomfortable run-in with him, I would.

I toweled off, dressed, and exited the building unnoticed. While the base began to stir as I walked to the armory, my descent into the lab went unseen. I settled into a chair and scooted under the table where a stack of paper rested. There was a choice I'd been hesitant to make, but now was the time to determine my direction since only hours remained before the lab would be swarming with outsiders.

Days ago, I decided to introduce music during future extractions. Klara had been right about the impact of a peaceful melody. Since our final conversation, I'd hummed through most of the day, giving life to my mother's concertos as I went about my tasks. Immediately, I experienced a drop in negative consequences, the decrease so sudden it astounded me. Worry was no longer my dominant emotion throughout extractions, it was replaced with acceptance. Feelings of pain also diminished, as pressure displaced my agony and created a much more tolerable sensation.

The effect of music was significant, and I wanted to finalize its place in my technique. Where to place the sound was the question that still lingered. I grabbed the papers in front of me, and once again, poured over the pages of my observation logs, searching for the highest points of pain or panic. I fixed my attention on the earlier weeks, the ones where I'd been silent, and humming hadn't neutralized my distress. These passages were filled with bleak words. My written reflections showed a perspective that was driven by distress—they were the ramblings of a person who'd made it through the days, but just barely.

In these entries two spikes stood out, the same two I'd identified each time I'd scanned the data. The first was during the beginning of the procedure. Multiple comments outlined the dread I endured during my initial contact with the operating table. Although I knew the ins and outs of the procedure, my words described feeling great anxiety about what was to come. The second peak came slightly later in the experiment, after I strapped on the collection equipment. During every extraction, I had braced myself for the agony I knew was inevitable.

The findings were surprising, but there was no mistaking their pattern—anticipation was the largest threat to our subject group. Actual pain wasn't the most devastating element, the *idea* of pain, had caused the most despair. When I knew it was coming, I braced for its impact, clenching my muscles in suspense until the needles had done their work. And what's more, awareness made my uneasiness grow. Each day, as I become more familiar with the extraction process, my overall anxiety level increased—the greater my insight into the agony I would experience, the greater my feelings of foreboding during the operations. It was interesting that repetition didn't calm my mood, but my entries outlined this truth. The last-minute data review convinced me that placing musical intervention at the onset of an extraction was the best decision. I'd head off stress before it began.

I'd decided on a song too, a haunting tune created by my mother on a bitterly cold night in 1914. I was a teenager, and it was during the bustling phase of Freikorps, when Pa preferred staying overnight in the bunker rather than at home with his family. Ma had called out to me while I was reading my lessons. "Gunnar, I need something to occupy my mind. How 'bout you give me a key, and I'll see what this lonely wench can spin up?"

"Oh Ma, you're far from a wench." I knew my father wasn't home, but I quieted my voice anyways. "And you're only lonely because Pa's out with his buddies instead of here, helping with the farm."

"Gunnar Cruse, do not speak ill of your father." She sighed, her chin sinking almost to her chest. "Although, after all these months, I have to agree. It's trying when it's just you and me, despite us being two of the hardest workers I know." Her head popped back up. "But you know what, son? We're not going to let our circumstances get us down." Ma strode to the piano. "You're going to listen to me play while you study…what subject was it again?"

"Trigonometry."

"While you study trigonometry." She pulled out the bench and sat. "Now give me a key and make it a good one."

I thought about the gusting wind, some of which was sneaking past the rags tucked into the crevices around the house. I also thought about my father and the mix of emotions his absence inspired. The evenings he was occupied with Freikorps had been some of the happiest nights of my childhood, although I'd never admit this to my mother. But the happiness was mixed with longing—a tiny part of me hoped to form a bond with my dad. The depths of my feelings inspired the choice of key.

"The weather and your loneliness make me think it's a D minor night, Ma." I grinned. "I bet you can make something nice out of all this negativity."

"Gunnar, that's a marvelous suggestion. I'll need a minute to come up with a melody." Her focus was far off, which meant she was working through the notes internally.

It was best to ignore Ma while she arranged her pieces. It gave her the space to create, to really dive deep into the measures that formed in her mind. I turned back to my primer, and angles kept me occupied as she developed music that only I would be lucky enough to hear. In the time it took for me to solve two problems, Ma played a few test bars, then jumped into the first notes of her intro.

I tried to continue my studies, but it was useless in the presence of such mastery. It was easier to give into the music, to lay down my pencil and listen while I closed my eyes to increase the potency of my hearing. The song captivated me completely, and I was pulled into the ballad, wrapped up in the layered story it told. There were somber parts, where the sound was filled with a sadness that contained both meaning and depth. Ethereal tones overlaid these sections. The airy notes balanced the melancholy, giving contrast to the darker textures by offering a delicate counterpoint.

When Ma finished, I asked for an encore, and she wound through her solo again. She obliged my second request as well. The third time I beseeched her, she laughed and pushed away from the piano. "Gunnar, I don't have another time in me." Ma came to where I was sitting, frowning when she saw my lack of progress. "Besides, you need to finish your homework. Bedtime is in less than an hour, and it looks like you have enough problems to fill three hours, maybe four."

I yearned to hear the music once more but knew better than to argue. "Yes, ma'am." I dared a comment before returning to my studies. "Ma, I will never hear anything more beautiful than what you just played. Thank you."

Years later, I felt the same way. We'd named the song *Silken Summit*, and it was the tune I chose for Project Leer. I hoped it impacted my test subjects the way it had impacted fourteen-year-old me.

∞∞∞∞

At 0550, I headed to the access booth. On the trek across base, soldiers milled about, and I received several nods and hellos, the rushed salutations of men on the way to an important destination. My assumption about Conroy's lateness was affirmed when Tanne greeted me alone. I entered the access booth, a wooden structure not much larger than a shack, after he swung open the door and waved me in. Tanne's gigantic frame filled a good deal of the booth's interior, but the tight fit didn't seem to bother him. He welcomed me with his standard smile and jolly tone. "Morning, Cruse. The General let me know you'd be stopping by." He picked up a thin packet of papers. "I have your list ready to go."

"You're damn reliable, Tanne." I scanned the workspace. "Unlike other soldiers we know."

He sighed. "I've tried talking to him, and it works for maybe a week." He shrugged his shoulders. "After that, he's back to his old ways."

"Sounds like you have some influence over him."

Tanne moved his hand in a so-so gesture. "Depends on the day, I reckon. But I think that's why Stillwell paired us up. Conroy's a wild one, and if there's any chance of reigning him in, the General will take it."

I shut the door behind me and lowered my voice. "I need to ask you a favor, Tanne, and I need you to be discreet about it."

Concern knotted his forehead. "Is everything alright, Cruse?"

"Everything is okay with me, but I think our friend Conroy might do some damage if we let him get out of hand."

"Did you hear something about him?"

"Not exactly. I'm only acting on a gut feeling," I admitted.

"There's nothing wrong with that, Cruse." Earnestness flooded his eyes. "If you're anything like me, I bet you acted on your gut during the war. And I'd wager that it saved you and your men a time or two."

"You're right, Tanne, and that's why I'm coming to you with my concern. I think we can prevent a good bit of harm, and maybe save some lives if we get ahead of it." I jumped into explaining the matter. "Remember about a month ago, when you, me, and Conroy had lunch together, and he was talking about that family he screened? It was six people, a mixture of adults and children."

Tanne nodded. "I think so. Was it the folks who were Jews?"

"Yep, those are the people." I looked around before I continued, verifying that we were alone. "He mentioned something that gave me pause, said he had done something to the youngest girl in the family. He talked about Dr. Brandt and breeding, and that led me to believe her hurt that girl, Tanne, hurt her in an unspeakable way." Disgust made me grimace while rage caused my hands to clench. I pushed forward and pitched my request.

"Do you think you can keep an eye on Conroy and intervene when it's needed? Someone has to monitor him so he doesn't have a chance to be stupid or cruel, and you're the one who's closest to him."

Tanne appeared solemn. "Some folks might take your ask the wrong way, Cruse. They'd hear a story about a Jewish girl getting hurt, and they'd cheer rather than become horrified." He thrust his chin at me. "And you *were* horrified. Your voice and body language gave you away." Tanne tilted his head, the shook it. "What he said *gave you pause*? Don't bullshit me. Tell me what you really thought, and then maybe I'll consider your request."

I measured Tanne with my eyes, taking in the massive man, considering how honest I should be. He and I joined Starkesend the same day, and we'd labored together during our first six months on base. He was a hard worker, a person quick to smile, and someone not afraid to speak their mind.

But Tanne was a hardliner, a true Nazi, and he'd report me in an instant if he felt I was sympathetic to the enemy. I had a long list of unfinished tasks and getting banished before they were accomplished would be a disaster. I'd also seen first-hand how exiled people were treated—once a person was deemed unfit for society, their personhood ceased to matter, and they were abused in unspeakable ways. I didn't want to end up like Miles or the rest of the deceased test group.

For those reasons, I chose my words carefully. "When Conroy says stuff like that, I imagine him taking his bad behavior and turning it on the women here." I shuffled my feet and grinned. "Mostly, I don't want him bothering the new girl in the chow hall, the one with the curly hair."

Tanne let out a laugh and clapped me on the back. "I see what's on your mind, Cruse—you're dizzy with the dame. I don't blame you 'cause she's a feisty one, always yakking about placing my dishes in the proper spot or stopping me from grabbing triple helpings." He patted his belly. "This man's got to eat, but that doesn't stop Miss Klara from yelling at me."

Hearing her name sent a jolt of longing to my heart. I stifled it and added a humble note to my words. "You've got me figured out, man. I'm just trying to protect her." I gave him a smile. "I wouldn't want anything happening to Klara before I've had a chance to be with her."

He held out his hand. "I'll keep an eye on Conroy and make sure he leaves the ladyfolk alone."

I accepted the offered palm. "Thanks, Tanne. I owe you." I took the list he'd prepared, and hurried out of the access booth, relieved there'd be someone observing one of the most dangerous men in Starkesend.

Lizbeth, 1936

Chapter 23 - Lizbeth

Maggie's house was on the way to mine. We traveled the short distance together, keeping our giggles quiet as we strolled home from the chow hall. I couldn't remember half of what we'd discussed at dinner, but it was a lovely, fulfilled forgetting. And while our evening was ending, we'd already made plans for two days in the future, this time for a walk to visit what Maggie called the "safe spaces" on base.

When we reached her house, Maggie walked backwards up the drive, talking as she moved. "Have fun with Granthma tomorrow."

"Thanks, Maggie." I rolled my eyes. "You have fun without her."

"Oh, I will. Every day I spend without Our Lady Scolds a Lot is a blessing." She reached the door and waved before she went inside.

There were limited moments of solitude in my life, so I relished the stillness while I finished my trip. The last time the base was this quiet was the evening I arrived from Dorf. That night I'd been afraid of the unknown but brave in my resolve to get to the bottom of my sister's demise. Over the past nine days, I'd learned details about her life at Fort Vogel, and I was grateful for the insight. It comforted me to discover her loving relationship with Gunnar.

The parts I'd yet to uncover would be less pleasant. If I trusted what my husband told me, Klara had been trying to escape when she was killed. I planned on asking Maggie about my sister during our next meetup, but my more immediate strategy was to make up with Gunnar and unearth his memories of Klara's last hours. I could begin tonight if he'd returned from work.

When I reached our house, the kitchen and porch lights were on, just the way I'd left them. The interior bulb shone through gauzy curtains, allowing me to see evidence of someone inside. Brightness outlined the shape of a body, and I recognized Gunnar's broad shoulders and confident gait. He was moving from the stove to the counter, holding a bowl of the food I'd prepared. My heart jumped, and I rushed inside.

My words bubbled out as soon as the door closed behind me. "Gunnar, you're home. I wasn't expecting you, but I'm happy you could break away from the lab." My eyes caught up with my jaws, and I noticed he'd paused with a spoonful of stew halfway to his mouth. "Oh, good heavens, I'm sorry. I came in here running my gums and look what I did—interrupted you midbite."

Gunnar lowered the spoon. "I should be apologizing to you, Lizbeth. There's no excuse for my earlier actions. I let my emotions take over and they spilled onto you." His voice hitched. "My father spent a lot of nights away from home, neglecting his family. I can't believe I threatened to do the same thing to you. It would be cruel to leave you here alone, when Fort Vogel is still new to you." He glanced down. "I'm ashamed, and I'm so sorry."

Our apologies summed up our relationship. Mine had been rushed and impromptu. Gunnar's was meaningful and weighty. That we had delivered them one after the other made the distinction more obvious, and my brain latched onto this discrepancy, twisting it into a joke. Dinner with Maggie must have primed my funny bone because laughter escaped my throat before I could stop it. Gunnar perked up, and gave me a puzzled stare, but after a moment, he threw his head back and joined the hilarity.

It was ludicrous that we were a married couple. We were two people who didn't really know each other, thrust together by circumstance, trying to make the best of it all. Our marriage distorted what was supposed to be a meaningful bond between two people and turned it into a caricature. Gunnar was like my awkward older brother, and I was his annoying younger sister, neither one of us spousal material. Being amused by our mispairing was the best reaction to have. It was better than focusing on our union's forced origin or the grief we shared over the loss of Klara. Humor provided an outlet that didn't hurt.

I made my way to the seat next to Gunnar and collapsed against his shoulder, shaking with merriment the whole time. It took us a while to get past our laughter, but when we did, I leaned back in my chair and spoke up. "Truce?"

"Truce." He wiped the tears from his eyes. "What were you laughing at?"

I gestured around the room. "The absurdity of this whole situation." A giggle burst out, but I pulled myself together and finished answering his question. "How whacky it is that last month I was enrolled in school, and this month I'm sharing a life with my dead sister's husband? It's quite baffling. And infuriating." I shrugged my shoulders. "But I'd rather focus on the first part and leave anger on the wayside because it's a lot easier to smile about our fortune than cry."

"That's the reason I was laughing too. We've found ourselves in quite a mess here, but we might as well use it to our advantage." Gunnar's brow furrowed. "It's probably a good thing we ended up together. We both loved your sister, and I think we can help each other make sense of what happened to her." He frowned. "Plus, there's some men around here you wouldn't want to be in a room with, let alone be married to."

"I'm pretty sure I had a run-in with one of them tonight," I admitted.

"Who are you talking about?"

"Conroy." I grimaced. "I assumed he was trouble the night we met at the gate, and he definitely proved that assumption in the mess hall today. He approached me like I was a piece of meat, Gunnar, talking about the things he wanted to do to me and how long we'd spend together in bed. And when I stood up for myself, he charged me. He had this awful look in his eye like he wanted to rip me apart." Shame reddened my cheeks." The worst part is, I just froze. My mind was busy regretting what I'd said instead of commanding my legs to get the heck out of there. Luckily, someone intervened, and Conroy backed off."

Gunnar shot up from his chair. "Sounds like Conroy needs a talking to. How dare he threaten you. How dare he even speak to you." He started toward the door. "I'll be back, Lizbeth."

I stood and grabbed his arm. "Don't! *Please*. He'll seek revenge, I know it." I tried to reason with Gunnar. "It's my fault I didn't notice him. I just need to pay more attention to my surroundings. If I would have, the entire run in could have been avoided."

"You're telling me it's your fault that Conroy was a jerk? I refuse to entertain the idea." He pulled away from me. "Some people only learn through pain, and I'll have no problem teaching him an agonizing lesson."

"No." I put force behind the word, and Gunnar gaped at me in surprise. "I asked you to please let the matter lie, and that's what I meant."

He stood quiet a moment before responding. "Letting Conroy get away with such despicable behavior makes my blood boil. I've known men like him my entire life. They poke and prod, seeing how far they can take something before they get called out." Gunnar stepped close and placed his hands around my upper arms. "When these vermin get no pushback, they attack and take whatever they can get their hands on, not caring who's harmed in the process." He gently squeezed my arms. "I don't want that to happen to you, Lizbeth. If I could force Conroy to stay away from you completely, I would, but that's not how it works around here. Folks have to cooperate and make every effort to advance our goals. So, even though

Conroy's lazy and wild, the scoundrel won't be banished because he's done a good job of showing his devotion to Starkesend, and that counts more than anything." He smiled cruelly. "I can still give him a good walloping, though. One that he'll never forget."

I stepped out of his grip and fixed my gaze on him. "I understand, Gunnar. You're trying to protect me, and I appreciate it deeply. I know my sister would be proud." I drew back my shoulders, standing as tall as possible. "But this time, let's move past what happened instead of piling onto it. I'm not saying we should forgive and forget. In fact, we shouldn't do either. We should remember what that wretch said and let it fuel our vigilance. I know I'll be keeping an eye out for Conroy. I plan to avoid him like my life depends on it." I lowered my voice to a whisper. "And I'll come straight to you if I see or hear anything unsafe. I promise."

Gunnar sighed. "If you insist, Lizbeth, I will honor your request. But remember, I'm doing this against my better judgment."

"Thank you for listening to me. It's a rarity in this world of ours." I motioned at his abandoned stew. "Why don't you finish your supper. Then we can talk some more or maybe tune into the Lone Ranger. There's a new episode on tonight."

He broke into a grin. "That's the best suggestion I've heard in a while. I could use the entertainment."

We spent the evening listening to the radio and each other, steering away from volatile topics. Gunnar told me about his electrical business, and I talked about my favorite books. It was nice to chat without encountering emotional landmines, to speak to someone without experiencing fury or sadness. What had begun as a lovely day, with Gunnar's pineapple upside-down cake, had ended the same way, with a relaxing conversation before bed. I'd even managed to make a friend. If I overlooked the extraction and the incident with Conroy, my eighteenth birthday was full of moments I would recall fondly.

At 10:00, we retired into our separate spaces. I could hear Gunnar in his office, going through files. Now that I knew what was in the room, I ached to see Klara's art again, but I would have to regain my husband's trust before he welcomed me back.

I made a mistake during our chat this afternoon. When Gunnar revealed details about his time in the service, I should have been straight with him, even at the risk of exposing my true loyalties. My gut told me that his allegiances were similar to mine, and instead of being honest, I'd coated my feelings in mockery, using words that smacked of Starkesend ideology.

Gunnar's actions tonight—coming home instead of staying in the lab, listening to me about Conroy—showed that he cared, and it was the start of rebuilding our fledgling relationship. Since he'd made the first move, I would have to make the next several. Throwing myself into the task was key to its success. I could no longer hold back like I was used to doing, especially if I trusted my instincts, and Gunnar and I could unite against society. Perhaps I would finally gain an ally.

I fell asleep thinking about the possibility.

∞∞∞∞

At breakfast, I mentioned the outing Maggie, and I had planned. "I'm not exactly sure where we'll be going, but we'll be together."

"I know Maggie's husband, Sergeant Helmstedt. We've been on some missions together." Gunnar sipped his coffee. "He's handy around an engine. General Stillwell has him assigned to the convoy, although two vehicles can hardly be called a convoy if you ask me." He shook his head. "But the man is pompous and fixated on Hitler. Hardly a sentence leaves his mouth without some mention of the Nazi. We can be talking about our work or the weather or food, and Helmstedt finds a way to insert him in our conversation."

I grimaced. "He sounds unbearable. I wonder how Maggie puts up with it because she's nothing like him at all."

"That's good. I'm glad you've found someone to spend time with." Gunnar leaned back in his chair. "It hasn't happened in about six months, but there are times when I may be absent. Missions have kept me away from base for weeks in the past, and I'd hate for you to face that alone. Having a friend is nice."

"I'm glad I found someone, too." I traced the rim of my coffee cup, knowing it was the right time for honesty. After a quick breath, I began the quest to earn Gunnar's confidence. "Don't think bad of me, but I find the girls my age incredibly boring. They've turned into brainwashed dishrags, and it's impossible to have a discussion with a classmate that doesn't include the word mother or wife or sacred duty." I sighed. "It used to be okay when we were younger. We didn't talk much during hopscotch or tag, so it was easy to bear their company, it was even fun most of the time. But interacting with them at the Frau Rennen forced me to see who they really were. I tried talking to the girls I'd been closest to, and it was like hearing a classroom lecture with giggles mixed in."

"That's why you and your sister are special. You both have opinions of your own." Gunnar paused. "Well, had in Klara's case." He locked his gaze onto mine. "And even though society may not value that quality, I certainly do."

"Thanks, Gunnar. It's something I admire too, although in Starkesend, it's rare to meet a person with any unique views." I beamed. "That's why Maggie is so great. She's funny, something else missing around here, and she isn't afraid to bend the rules."

"Humor is great." He finished the rest of his coffee and brought his cup to the sink. "Just be careful about sharing information until you're better acquainted. I know you said Maggie's not like her husband, but that man would report inappropriate behavior the moment it happened. If he even got a whiff of your thoughts about brainwashed classmates, he'd march to the general's office and make an official complaint." Gunnar's eyebrows drew together. "I'd hate for you to be harmed, Lizbeth, and even though you're tough and smart, things can still go wrong. I'll do my best to be there if you need me. I give you my word."

Gunnar glanced at the clock. "Time to head out. Dr. Brandt wants to review the updates I made while he was gone. I'm guessing he'll make me demonstrate them over and over again." He rolled his eyes. "It's always fun when he's around." Gunnar grabbed his hat and walked toward the entryway. He swung open the door before turning back to me. "See you later, Lizbeth. I think the Green Hornet is on tonight. Let's give it a listen." He waved as he closed the door and whistled a jaunty tune while he strolled down the drive.

I followed his lead, first to the sink, then out of the house. The day had started well, and I had high hopes it would continue that way. Not even the upcoming shift with Ms. Granth could dampen my sunny outlook. I whistled the tune I'd heard during my extraction and set off for roll call.

Gunnar, 1934

Chapter 24 - Gunnar

Before their arrival, I established a lab protocol, and the new group of men followed it without putting up a fight. When they learned that extractions would be their only work for the week, they listened to my instructions and got situated in the waiting area I'd set up. The empty cells in the far corner of the lab were perfect for this purpose. Stuffed burlap sacks, reading material, and lanterns made the stone-walled chambers hospitable, and the group of ten retreated to this domain while they waited for their turn on the operating table. I was the only one who knew about the anguish haunting the space, and no one else sensed the horrors that had happened in the rooms. For this, I was grateful. It would have been much more difficult to wrangle people who were afraid of their surroundings.

Music worked as Klara had predicted. It didn't matter who was undergoing the procedure, when I hummed *Silken Summit,* they entered a trance-like state, and I was able to complete incisions, insertions, and removals with ease. Logic told me the daze resulted from a combination of factors—my guess was that stressed-out patients heard the pleasing notes and fixated on them to diminish their pain. Regardless of the reasoning, music made the extraction process manageable for me and the patients.

After a week in the laboratory, I requested an extension from General Stillwell. He granted two more weeks with the men before the next progress report was due. I was thrilled by his response and resumed my work on Project Leer, hoping to have the procedure refined before Dr. Brandt's return. The test group remained happy over the next fourteen days, and I was confident the general would approve my request for a continuation. When I set up the meeting to discuss next steps, he asked to meet above ground in the war room.

I arrived at the appointed hour and found the general shuffling through papers at the front of the room. He peered up from the stack. "Cruse, are you early or is it already time for our meeting?" He glanced at his watch and shook his head. "I'd swear it was right after breakfast, but here it is almost noon."

"Looks like you're doing some paperwork, sir. It's real easy to get lost in the pages. I've had hours slip away too."

"That's exactly what happened, Cruse. I got caught up in planning this mission, and time just whizzed right past." He gestured to the chair across the table from him. "Have a seat. I'm always interested in hearing about what's going on in the lab. Anything new since the last time we spoke?"

"Nothing new, which is a good. Just more of the positivity I reported during our last check in." I counted points on my fingers. "The men have been cooperating, I'm able to locate their adrenals in record time, and I'm finally collecting fluid. It's small quantities for now, but I think it's only the beginning of what's possible."

"Hot damn, that's great news." The general grabbed the top sheet of paper from his pile and turned it around so I could see it. "And it certainly helps settle this matter."

I read the typed words.

Operation Mitternacht

Target - Temple Sinai

Team - Helmstedt, Tanne, Wallace, Cruse?

Dates - Departure: 6 February 1934,

Return: 15 March 1934

"February sixth? That's only two days away, sir. There's no way I can abandon the new group when I'm making such significant progress." I tried to control the panic in my voice, but it snuck in nonetheless "And Dr. Brandt. He won't return for another week. Deserting the lab is not possible."

"Cruse, hold your tongue." He leaned back in his chair. "I'm not a fool. I only considered you for this assignment because the doctor will be back early. He's due to arrive tomorrow."

I shook my head. "With all due respect, sir, the men won't trust the doctor right away. Plus, I need to show him the modifications I've made over the last two months. I need at least a week. Three or four would be even better."

General Stillwell fixed me with a stern glare. "The most I can offer is two days, Cruse. I know the doctor is your commander, but I still get a say about you too." He tapped a finger on the name of the mission. "This is an important one, and I don't want it screwed up. Last month, Dr. Brandt sent a letter with explicit instructions about Temple Sinai. Seems like someone high up in the Nazi party wants the little synagogue gone, so that's what we're going to do. We're going to set it ablaze and send a message to the Jew pigs living in this part of the U. S. of A." He raised his finger to point at me. "I want you on this assignment because you're a soldier I can count on. You're not going to screw it up like some of the lazy, morons around here." He lowered his hand and shook his head. "But instead of being honored, you're throwing a tantrum like a child." He gestured to a table further back in the room. "Take a seat over there. The rest of your team will be here at 1230 for a briefing. After that you can return to your precious lab." He stared down at his papers. "Get out of my face, Corporal."

"Yes, sir." I retreated as instructed and picked a chair with my back to the general. The clock on the wall showed fifteen minutes until the briefing meeting, giving me a short interval to determine the myriad changes I'd have to make. I ran through the items that required attention and made a mental checklist with a ninety-six-hour deadline. There was barely enough time to complete everything, but I would prevail. A great deal depended on my success, and letting people down was not an option.

A quarter of an hour flew, and before I knew it, Tanne was pulling out a chair next to me. I nodded my head in greeting.

"You know what this is all about?" He jerked a thumb over his shoulder.

"We're going on a mission," I answered.

Tanne's eyes lit up. "That's the best news I've heard all week." He clapped me on the back. "Look at us. We've been here less than a year, and the big boss already trusts us with a major job."

"We must know what we're doing." I was able to hide my disappointment, and Tanne continued celebrating.

"My ma will be tickled pink when I write her. She was doubtful about me coming here, but this should put her mind at ease." He grinned. "She'll be proud of her big galoot—he's making something out of himself."

Despite my frustration, Tanne's words made me chuckle. "I guess we never stop trying to make our mamas happy."

"You got that right. I'd never hear the end of it if I even thought about it." He studied me curiously. "How's that dame of yours feel about this? She okay with you being gone for a while?"

Klara. During my panicked planning, my brain hadn't flashed upon her. I conjured an image of her face, focusing on her eyes and smile. It had been weeks since I'd seen her, and the act of recalling her features left me desperate for more. The time away from Klara had only intensified my desire to be near her. To listen to her. To laugh with her. To watch her while she moved around the cafeteria.

There was a chance I wouldn't survive Operation Mitternacht. Emerging into the outside world carried risks, especially for the commission of a crime.

I'd completed offensive missions in the Army, but I'd operated under the protection of being on the good guy's side. While there were many Americans who embraced Starkesend ideals, there was a larger group of folks who did not. They presented a separate threat, one quite different than the menace brought forth by the Axis powers.

When I fought against a wartime enemy, I knew who opposed me and who to take out. Here, in my home country, the division was more challenging to discern. There was a wave of Americans sympathetic to the Nazi cause, but most hid in the shadows, afraid their allegiance would be used against them. Unlike the Schutzstaffel, these supporters did not wear a uniform that proudly declared their loyalty. In the United States, followers were everyday people who went about their lives carrying secret hatred in their hearts.

Instead of determining who was friend or foe, our four-man team would use covert tactics to remain out of view. In the barracks, I overheard seasoned Starkesend troops talking about their brushes with exposure. They were men who felt comfortable bragging about run-ins with the law or concerned citizens, not knowing that this made them appear incompetent. I wanted to avoid their careless mistakes, so during the briefing, I'd raise my concerns and hope they were considered valid. Either way, I'd stay concealed throughout the mission.

Regardless of caution, the chance of detection remained. Harm could befall me, and I may not return to Starkesend. I didn't want to abandon my post, but I would recover from that misfortune. Another consequence pained me more than expected—it hurt to think about losing my connection to Klara. In the short time I'd known her, she'd grown in importance. I'd reflect on this revelation later, but for now, I decided to break my resolution to avoid her. I answered Tanne's question nonchalantly, masking the excitement underlying my decision. "I haven't told her yet, but I will at dinner tonight."

"Maybe Miss Sweet Cheeks will give you a going away present." He batted his eyelashes. "I bet she will if tell her how purty she looks. Girls go loony over stuff like that."

"Thanks for the advice, Tanne. I'll make sure to follow it to a T."

"Just trying to help you out, man. I don't want my teammate feeling lonely while we're galivanting around. A little sugar might tide you over until we get back."

"I can make it a few weeks." I shook my head, waving my hand at him. "I've got some serious doubts about you, on the other hand."

His giant body shook with laughter. There were tears in his eyes when he finally stopped. "That sense of humor will come in handy when we're rucking in the wilderness. I haven't talked to Helmstedt or Wallace much, but I hope they're as entertaining as you are." He turned to a noise at the front of the room. "Looks like we can ask them about it."

I followed his gaze and saw the rest of our team enter the room. Helmstedt was thin, with dark hair and a scowl that gave the appearance of perpetual anger. Wallace was his opposite, a cornfed blond who never stopped grinning, despite his mouthful of yellowing teeth.

They joined our table as General Stillwell walked over. "Right on time, gentlemen. That means we can begin." He passed out paperwork to the group. "I asked you here today because I handpicked each of you for a special mission. I'll give you a few minutes to read over your packets, but overall, the tasks for Operation Mitternacht are quite simple. There's been a request to destroy a synagogue in Montana along with the rabbi and his family, who live on the back of the property in a separate house." He regarded the team. "Any questions so far?"

Helmstedt raised his hand, and General Stillwell nodded his way. "Sir, I appreciate you including me in this group. I'm happy to serve our Fatherland in whatever way I can." His scowl morphed into a smug smirk.

"That's not a question, Corporal." He considered at the rest of us. "Anyone else?" We all shook our heads. "Very well then. I want you to take some time to read the information I've provided. It details safe places to stop for supplies, information about your targets, and the route you will be traveling. You need to memorize this intelligence because the pages are not permitted to leave the war room. Having them fall into the wrong hands would be a disaster for Starkesend." He glanced at his watch. "Take five to study, then we'll talk about strategy."

I dove into the materials, trying to quickly absorb the information. The dates on the top page had been changed, the initial ones were marked out and moved two days later. Thankfully the general was true to his word, and he'd given me extra time to prepare for departure. It wasn't a lot, but I was sure it would be enough to accomplish my list of tasks before we left.

The second page of the document was where details about the synagogue were laid out. The location and dimensions were listed, and the layout drawn out roughly. Temple Sinai was in Rough Waters, Montana, and the building was 2,200 sq ft, a structure substantial enough for a small congregation. Details about the rabbi's homestead were on the following page. The two-storied house was a modest 1,400 sq ft, with three bedrooms and one bath. Parishioners had built both buildings five years ago, and the rabbi had been with the church since it was erected.

The next few pages contained the route we would take and safe houses along the way. I skimmed the information before turning to the final section, the one about our human target, Rabbi David Adler. He was young, just 26 when he began at Sinai, and he'd studied at Yeshiva University, where he'd earned his degree in Hebrew letters. He successfully ministered to his congregants, and the synagogue had grown in popularity with him at the helm.

After his biographical sketch, the reasoning behind our mission was laid out. Rabbi Adler was paying attention to Hitler's rise in Germany, like many in the Jewish community. What made him stand out was his pushback against the Nazi viewpoint. The rabbi had taken to interrupting Friends of New Germany meetings over the course of the last six months. He would blend into the crowd and wait until the perfect moment to sow chaos. His methods varied, but his tactics effectively ended each meeting he attended. After his interruption, Rabbi Adler fled home and never claimed responsibility for his deeds. His discretion was part of the reason he avoided recognition for half a year. The other part was the way he chose his encounters. The rabbi picked gatherings that were weeks apart and towns away, sometimes in different states. It had taken a while for the Nazis to connect the disruptions to Adler, but now that they'd pinned it on him, they wanted to teach his followers a lesson.

There was one more page in the packet, and I turned to it. A tiny picture was stapled to the top of the paper. Four people were in the photo—a man, woman, and two children—and they posed in front of a two-story brick house. The parents were beaming as they held their little girls, one who looked around four and the other just a few months old. The family wore matching clothes, navy slacks and a white shirt for the father, and navy smocks for the mother and her girls, each of their heads topped by a white lace bonnet.

A sense of dread settled over me as I grasped who was in the portrait. Text under the photograph confirmed my fears—Rabbi Adler's entire family was part of the assassination plan.

I closed my eyes and took a breath, fighting off an intense wave of nausea. When I reopened them, I glanced around the table, taking note of everyone's reaction. Their faces all showed the same combination of interest and eagerness, far different than the horror I felt. Once again, I was an outsider, a person with feelings deeper than anyone around.

Right now, thinking like this was a useless pursuit. Introspection would squander the last moments I had with the paperwork in front of me, and there was nothing more important than memorizing the details it contained. I spent the final sixty seconds of our study session cramming information into my brain, tucking it away for later use.

Chapter 25 - Gunnar

After the meeting, I began to prepare the laboratory for my departure. I put a pause on extractions and instead wrote extensive notes for the doctor. We'd have three days together, but several tasks outside of the lab required my attention, and I knew a subject or two might fall through the cracks. Documentation gave Dr. Brandt a point of reference, which was valuable when the original source of knowledge was unavailable. And I would be unreachable for a good chunk of time.

Writing kept me busy through the afternoon, but as the dinner hour drew near, anticipation slowed my progress. My thoughts kept returning to Klara and how our encounter would go. If my absence had angered or saddened her, I would apologize and await forgiveness. If she hadn't noticed the withdrawal of my presence, I wasn't sure how to react. Emotion signified meaning. When a friend realizes a companion isn't around, it suggests that their time together meant something. The opposite is implied when a person doesn't perceive a companion's disappearance at all.

My mind was a jumble, and I was carrying conflicting ideas in my head—I wanted Klara to feel, but I didn't want her to feel *bad*. I hoped she noticed my absence and that she'd fought through the confusing tangle of fury and yearning that emerges after losing an important person. At the same time, I regretted any anguish my actions may have caused.

In the past, I avoided these dilemmas by maintaining shallow relationships. I was upfront with my intentions, and it kept people at a distance. The few acquaintances I had knew not to pry into my personal life. The rare woman who kept my company understood my disavowal of marriage from the get-go. My mates in the Army were the closest I'd ever come to true friendship, but our bonds had been forged by shared danger, an element that demanded mutual trust. In the outside world, I had the freedom to select the recipients of my confidence, and thus far, Klara was the only person to inspire a reconsideration of my antisocial ways.

The decision to cut off contact with her had been painful, but it only hurt because she was special. I knew I would miss her, and I did, more than was warranted after such a brief connection. Tonight, I'd have to face the consequences of my absence, but whatever Klara threw my way, I'd accept in a heartbeat if it meant I got to see her again.

Making it to 1900 was tough. When the clock finally struck the hour, I ran to the chow hall, not caring who saw me along the way. It was quiet, though, and no one stopped me as I rushed across base. I arrived at the cafeteria out of breath and excited, but my elation dimmed when I tried the doors and found them locked. Last call for food was at 1930, thirty minutes from now, and there were usually two or three late eaters who stopped in for to-go portions near that time. The doors remained open until the last man scurried away, carrying a brown bag with them to the barracks.

During my initial months at Starkesend, the dining hall often closed early. This was because of a rule that prevented intermingling between village members and soldiers. At Fort Vogel, the number of available workers varied by day. Men were assigned to the chow hall, if possible, but recruiting or day labor was far more important than cooking or dishes, and kitchen duty became a low priority. If there weren't enough men to staff the cafeteria, the building would shutter, and rations would be handed out. Luckily, a vote among the founders revised the strict separation rule, and volunteers from Dorf took over the operation of meal management. With their help, the dining hall was open for breakfast, lunch, and dinner, and early closures no longer occurred. Until tonight, that is.

I peered into a side window, searching for clues that would explain the unexpected shutdown. The lights were off in the main dining room, but beams of illumination shined through the open kitchen door. The glow was enough to show the signs of evening clean-up—chairs rested on top of tables, and the floor sparkled underneath. The light also created shadows inside the cookhouse. I could make out the outline of a person carrying items from the dishwashing area to the storage cabinets and back again. I tracked the black shape as it glided across the floor, momentarily hypnotized by the repetitive motion. The trance was broken when Klara moved into the main room, carrying a stack of plates to the buffet.

My breath caught, and I took a step back. The lighting in the cafeteria infused Klara's features with a radiance so brilliant I almost had to turn away. Never had I seen such beauty, and her allure was enhanced by the confident grace of her movements. Klara made the mundane appear lyrical. Even the way she stacked dishes was captivating. She was a woman who knew her place in the world and who drew satisfaction from this knowledge. It translated to everything she did, but not in a brazen manner. Her entire being exuded quiet sureness, and Klara's calm certainty reassured those around her. You got the sense that everything would be okay when you were in her presence.

I basked in these feelings until she put the last plate away. Then I announced myself. My light taps on the window caused Klara to turn sharply toward me. She walked closer until recognition lit her features, then she turned and headed back to the kitchen, closing the door behind her.

Disappointment rushed over me as I stared into the deserted room. The still darkness in the cafeteria mirrored my mood. I felt empty and alone, but I'd earned this shunning, which was the most agonizing part of the situation. I'd anticipated several reactions to my appearance—anger, sadness, confusion. I hadn't considered complete disregard, the fallout I now faced.

There was only one response to rejection, and that was acceptance. As much as I wanted to lurk around, waiting for Klara to finish her duties inside, I knew it would be disrespectful of her wishes. It was time to own up to the consequences of my neglect. It was time for me to return to the lab. I stepped off the stoop and trekked across base, upset I hadn't spoken to Klara, yet glad I had tried.

A quiet rustling cut through my thoughts. I stopped walking and held my breath, listening for a repeat of the noise. When I heard it again, I turned toward the sound, barely believing what I saw. The door to the mess hall was open, and Klara stood in the entry, calling softly into the night. "Gunnar. Gunnar, come back."

My heart thudded as I ran to where she waited. "Klara, I'm—"

She cut me off and put a finger to her lips. "Come inside. We don't want anyone overhearing us."

I brushed against her on the way in, and she moved to let me pass. After I cleared the threshold, Klara closed the door behind us. She bowed her head before speaking, her back still facing me. "I shouldn't be talking to you, but here I am, already breaking that vow. Watching you walk away was too much, Gunnar. I couldn't stand seeing your dejection." She sighed. "It was your eyes. Your sad, pathetic eyes pushed me over the edge." Her voice got louder. "Why did you disappear? I waited for you, and you never came back." She let out a hitched sob. "When you first stopped showing up, I became something I never wanted to be. I wasn't Klara anymore, I was the silly fool who pinned her hopes and dreams on some man, only to discover my dreams didn't matter and that the man was an unreliable jerk. Just thinking about it makes me angry." She took a few deep breaths before continuing. "It's been weeks since I've seen you, and you have the audacity to traipse over here, tapping on the window like you're on a romantic liaison. What makes you think I want you around?"

I wasn't sure of what to say, so I kept it simple. "I'm sorry, Klara. There's no excuse for how I treated you. I know it's not a good answer, but it's the truth."

She slowly turned around and locked her gaze onto mine. "What happened, Gunnar? If you want me to forgive you, you need to tell me what's going on."

"I made a vow too, Klara. It was a promise to focus on work and not relationships. Whenever I wanted to see you, which was every day, I'd remind myself that a lot was depending on me, and I couldn't afford distractions." I moved a step toward her. "And that's what you are, Klara. You're a distraction. A beautiful, smart, funny distraction." I swallowed the knot in my throat. "But today, I realized that I was wrong, and what I really need is you back in my life." I brought my head down. "If you'll have me, of course."

Klara moved close and put her hand under my chin. She gently lifted until our eyes met. "Gunnar, those are the words I've been waiting to hear." She leaned forward, and our lips met for the briefest moment. "That's all I'm ready to give right now. I hope it's enough."

I closed my eyes, savoring the feel of her mouth on mine. The surrounding world moved in slow motion, but my body responded with lightning speed. Blood pounded in my veins, my breath came in short gasps. I'd been given the gift of her affection, and the bliss flooded my being, igniting sensations as it zipped around.

When I was ready, I returned to reality. "Klara, you've given me more than enough."

She laughed. "Who knew that such a tough soldier was such a softie? Don't worry, I'll keep it to myself."

I bowed. "Thank you, m'lady. I owe you a debt of gratitude. Can you imagine how the other men would react if they knew how sweet I was? I'd never live it down."

Klara gave me a nudge, and I straightened up. "I wouldn't go that far, Corporal. A sweet man would never have left his lady wondering where he was." She grinned. "Good thing I'm so forgiving."

"See? I already owe you my endless thanks. I'll never overcome that big of a burden." I reached out and tucked her hand into mine. "Since we just rekindled our friendship, I want to start off on the right foot and be completely honest with you. There's a reason for my visit tonight."

She pulled away from my grip. "Of course, there is. And I'm guessing I won't like it."

"No, you won't like it at all, but I'm hoping you'll understand." I grabbed two chairs from the nearest table and placed them side by side. "It might be better if we sit."

"Are you in trouble? Is everything okay?"

"Everything's as okay as it can be." I sat, and Klara followed suit. "General Stillwell pulled me from the lab and put me on a mission that leaves in three days. I'll be gone for the next five weeks."

"I have the barest understanding of what our military does, Gunnar. What does going on a mission mean? Will you have to hurt people?" Concern filled her eyes. "Will you be in danger?"

I shook my head. "Part of what makes this so difficult is that I can't give you any details, I can only tell you when it's happening." I paused before continuing, knowing I was about to entrust Klara with a part of myself I'd never exposed. "There's a small chance something could go wrong when we're out in the public. I'll do my best to ensure nothing bad takes place, but there are a lot of variables outside of my control." My voice became thick with emotion. "Although the chance of not returning is small, I couldn't bear the thought of never seeing you again. That's why I came here—I couldn't leave without seeing your face. The memory of tonight will keep me going when I'm far away from home."

"Gunnar, I'll be waiting for you when you return." She grabbed both of my hands. "And you *will* come back. I know it."

"That's my only goal, Klara. To make it home to you."

Chapter 26 - Gunnar

Dr. Brandt was impressed with the progress I'd made. He requested a walkthrough of my day-to-day tasks, and I brought him along as I bantered with the test group before selecting two participants for the afternoon session. After I instructed them to meet in the main chamber at half past the hour, the doctor retreated with me to the laboratory.

"You're quite chummy with those fellows, Cruse, but it appears to be effective. They listen to you without batting an eye." He stopped at my makeshift desk and leaned against it. "I'm an adherent to discipline, structure, and fear, and it's what I use when working with the German troops." Dr. Brandt acknowledged my accomplishment with a slight nod. "But I do appreciate seeing alternative tactics. It's a major enticement in our field. As they say, there's more than one way to skin a cat, or in this case, there are many techniques for extracting adrenaline."

"Thank you, sir. I thought back to my time in the Army and remembered the impact of cooperation. Back then, having a good relationship with my troops helped with task completion, and I've done my best to replicate that environment here. The men want to participate, and as you can see, it's been very successful." I walked to the cooler. "Although the success has led to one problem" —I lifted the ice box lid— "we need a bigger cold storage area, Doctor. This one is at capacity."

Dr. Brandt joined me and leaned over to peer inside the cooler. A grin spread across his face as he scanned the neatly labeled rows of fluid inside. "You've been productive in my absence, Corporal. I hope to be just as prolific while you're gone." He straightened back up. "I have some news that should solve your storage issue. If you're not aware, I am quite close to the Führer. There's been talk that I may become his escort physician. As you can imagine, I would be honored to assume this coveted position." The doctor began to pace. "Regardless of any promotion, I have received approval for Project Leer's continuation. The Führer was intrigued by our endeavor and has demanded priority be placed on getting the adrenaline assembly line up and running. He would also like us to 'milk', which is how he phrased it, our subjects for cortisol. Our Leader sees promise for these products, and he believes we can use them to our advantage during the upcoming ascent of our Fatherland." He stopped pacing and turned sharply toward me. "Cruse, I will need you to pledge your cooperation and dedication to the work we are doing. Together we can ensure that Leer is a victory for our people. And for ourselves, of course."

"That's excellent news, sir. I'm at your service." I closed the ice box lid before carrying on the conversation. "Will we receive funding? If there were upgrades in the lab, I think we could increase our productivity tenfold."

"I was told that money is no object." The doctor replied.

"Outstanding, sir." I sat at my desk and pulled out paper and a pen. "I'll get started on a list right away. If the supplies are delivered by the time I return from Mitternacht, I could implement them into our routine within a week."

"Cruse, aren't you forgetting something?" He demanded.

I scanned the room, making sure everything was in its place. "I don't believe so, sir. Everything is organized and ready to go."

"Not according to my watch. We have two men arriving in fifteen minutes. Don't you think we should begin preparations?" The doctor sneered. "I shouldn't be reminding you of these things at this point in your training."

"With all due respect, sir, the modifications I've made to the process have eliminated the necessity of lead time. We no longer need to strap anyone down or prepare extra setups." I gestured to the extraction area. "The equipment we need is waiting. I've pared it down to three needles, two collection pouches, and an IV. It's enough gear to gather the adrenaline and cortisol, plus provide the patient with a saline solution while we're working on them. The only task remaining is ensuring the subject's comfort." I countered Dr. Brandt's sneer with a reassuring smile. "After that, I'm able to begin their procedure and everything is complete after half an hour."

I got up and went to the metal cart stationed near the operating table. Its three shelves were full. The top two levels held medical devices, and a portable gramophone rested on the bottom. I bent to pick up the music player, marveling at its novelty. It was thrilling that such an invention existed. It was incredible to have possession of one.

I carefully set the machine on a table, then explained its role in the lab. "About a month ago, I discovered an interesting approach to extractions. I was going to show you during the first procedure, sir, but it's probably better to demonstrate beforehand, that way, you'll have an idea of what's going to happen."

Dr. Brandt waved an impatient hand. "Get on with it, Cruse."

"Yes, sir. As you know, extractions can be difficult for test subjects, me included." Memories of earlier sessions with Dr. Brandt flashed through my head. His cold bedside manner, combined with the rough exploratory hacking, would forever occupy a space in the dark parts of my mind. I pushed past the recollections and continued my explanation. "Luckily, I stumbled upon an item that neutralizes fear, and that's music. I couldn't believe the immediate impact humming had on our patients. I've tested it on myself and the men in the holding cells, and the results speak for themselves.

There was an immense reduction in anxiety and pain during the extractions I hummed through."

I opened the gramophone and took out the record inside. "When I heard I was leaving, I knew I'd have to adapt the technique I was using. There isn't enough time to teach you the music I hum, plus I wasn't sure if you'd be comfortable making the sound yourself. That got me thinking about a substitute for the days I'll be away—I needed to get ahold of something you'd be able to use on short notice." I passed the record to Dr. Brandt. "The gramophone was General Stillwell's idea. I spoke with him this morning, before your scheduled arrival. When I approached him with the issue, he asked me if a recording would suffice. I wasn't sure at first, but I completed two extractions using that record, and the impact was only slightly lower than my live performances."

Dr. Brandt read the label on the disc. "Lascia ch'io pianga, a superb choice." He placed the record in the player and wound the machine's crank. When he lowered the needle to the shellac surface, haunting notes filled the space.

"I found that once through the record is enough, so you won't have to worry about resetting it." I paused to absorb the soprano's voice. Her vocals were captivating, and it was no surprise the aria induced a trance-like state. "Once your subject is seated, play the song, and begin the procedure, and that's it." I smiled. "It's amazing what a few minutes of music can do, sir."

The doctor turned his head toward the entry hallway. "I hear the subjects approaching, Cruse." He gestured to the gramophone. "You've certainly presented a compelling case for your technique, but let's see it in action."

"Yes, sir." I called out to the approaching recruits. "Hello, gentlemen. Thank you for arriving on time." I waved them over. "Billings, we'll have you go first today. Go ahead and lay down on the table, and I'll be right with you."

As Billings got settled, I wound up the gramophone and placed the needle in the record's outermost groove. When the first notes of Lascia ch'io pianga flowed into the air, I began extraction 027.

∞∞∞

I did my best to showcase viable techniques for the doctor, but time constraints made it impossible to demonstrate everything. Unfortunately, the brief instructional period would have to suffice because February 8 approached with startling speed. I was somewhat confident that Dr. Brandt would run the lab with a more restrained hand. What I was able to show him got through his hard exterior. The extractions he observed convinced him of music's benefits, and the positive interactions I had with the test group had shown him an alternative to cruel indifference.

The day before Operation Mitternacht commenced, Dr. Brandt dismissed me at 1500. "Cruse, take the rest of the day for yourself. I can manage without you."

"Thank you, sir." I wiped down the operating table. "There are some things I need to wrap up, and this will give me the chance to finish them before I leave."

"Get going, Corporal. Don't worry about the mess." He scoffed at my questioning expression. "Why must you be so impertinent? I'll clean after I finish the daily report. The lab will not sink into disrepair by then." He shooed me with his hands. "Hurry, or I'll find something else for you to do."

I dropped the rag and left before the doctor changed his mind, rushing down corridors and up the stairs. Above the surface, the sun remained high over the horizon, and I squinted at the brightness, grateful for the radiant glow. The extra daylight would be helpful for one of my tasks.

After a stop at the barracks, I hiked to the outskirts of base and found an isolated area where the forest was dense, and the trees created natural cover. I pushed through branches until I found the perfect spot to complete my duty. It was a small clearing encircled by waist-high ferns. The deep green fronds concealed my whereabouts from any passersby but also formed an opening overhead. Sunlight broke through the taller trees and beamed into the center of my hideaway. I settled on the ground and took out writing materials from the knapsack I'd gotten from my bunk. It took thirty minutes to translate information into the proper code, a tedious but necessary undertaking. I read over the two letters I'd written, making sure they would be indecipherable to anyone without the decryption key. The handwriting was legible, but the words would resemble nonsense to anyone but the intended recipient, exactly the result I wanted. I folded the rough papers in half and stuffed them into the waiting envelopes.

Only one message needed addressing, and I scrawled the location details reflexively.

JO CRUSE
30 MILL ROAD
TAVERN CITY, WY

Both pieces of correspondence went into my rucksack, and I sprinted to the edge of Dorf, careful to stay hidden among the firs and pines. Because I'd left work early, plenty of time remained before my meeting, so I brought out the last piece of paper in my pack and penned a letter to Klara.

Klara,

I wanted to leave you a token of my affection, a keepsake that you could hold in your hands if you're ever forlorn. I find that physical connection provides the best relief from sadness. There's something reassuring about the space an object takes up. You're certain of its existence, because you can feel its weight in your palm, unlike more abstract things like friendship or happiness.

Often, moments of hurt untether us from the world. We float in dark streams of pain, waiting for a glimpse of the shore so we can pull ourselves out of the torrent. This memento will provide you with a point of focus to prevent the aimless drift of distress. I've clutched it during my own bouts of grief and poured sorrow and loss into the cherished pages. After it all, I've emerged a stronger person, forever grateful for my grounding item.

While I'm leaving you something tangible, I'm also entrusting you with a piece of my heart. Guard both, Klara, and think fondly of me while I'm gone. I know you'll never be far from my mind.

Yours,
Gunnar

The letter rested on my lap while I searched the knapsack for Klara's keepsake. It was secured in a small cedar box, which had made its way to the bottom of the bag. I pulled out the slim wooden rectangle and clutched it to my chest. There were a lot of memories inside the container, memories I'd never displayed to another soul. I unlatched the box's lock and removed the ten sheets of paper inside.

I unfolded the sheet music slowly. Twenty years had passed since *Silken Summit* was composed, and age had taken a toll on the document. The pages were discolored by dull, yellow spots, and the black ink Ma had used to notate the piece had faded. It took a good deal of concentration to distinguish the details among the staffs, measures, and notes. My mother wasn't one to notate her compositions, but I'd begged her to write my favorite down. The pages in my hand were the only copy of the music, and they had traveled with me overseas and across the country. I folded the letter to Klara on top of the older paper, then placed my most treasured item back inside its holder.

A noise caught my attention, a drawn-out whistle followed by two shorter blasts. The sound combination was repeated twice more. I pursed my lips and emitted a pattern of my own—three short whistles, a pause, then three more—in response. After about a minute, my contact Etta made her way to the prearranged spot. "Gunnar, it won't be too long before I'm missed." She held out her hand. "Let's take a look at the intelligence you gathered."

I set the wooden box on the ground and grabbed the two envelopes from my knapsack. "These parcels contain the same information, but one goes to an outside contact and the other stays here. We need the mailed letter sent off as soon as possible." I passed over the package addressed to my mom. "The recipient will acquire materials that will make the mission appear successful. She knows what it will take to convince Stillwell and Brandt, but she'll need to coordinate with some folks, and the longer she has to make arrangements, the better." I gave Etta a worried stare. "Timewise, we'll be cutting it close because the recipient lives days away. I'll do my best to slow the Starkesend team down, but you'll need to get this delivered without delay."

Etta nodded and took the offered letter. "I'll take the second parcel as well. Leon has been waiting on it all day."

"Of course." I handed her the other envelope, then picked up the cedar box. "Will you deliver one last thing, Etta? I don't know where the recipient lives, but I'm sure it won't be too hard to establish." I gave the wood one last squeeze before holding out the container. "This goes to Klara Dietrich. She's a volunteer at the mess hall on base, and lives with her parents in the village."

Etta tilted her head. "Gunnar, are you sure Klara Dietrich is her name?"

"Of course. I've known her for months now," I replied.

"Gunnar"—she spoke cautiously—"our main Starkesend contact, the man you know only as Leon, has the surname Dietrich. He also happens to have a daughter named Klara."

"That can't be true," I said, forcing down the lump in my throat "Before I went undercover, I learned about Leon and his family from a briefing report. The record mentioned small children, two if I remember correctly, and it said the little ones made it easier for him and his wife to blend in." I shook my head. "She's much younger than me, but Klara is not a small child. She also has a younger sister *and* brother, making it a family of five not four." I smiled at Etta. "There must be a misunderstanding. The Klara I know can't be the Klara you're talking about."

"Gunnar, I assure you that it's true. Klara Dietrich *was* a child when her family infiltrated Starkesend, and at that point, her parents only had two daughters. It's been several years now, and a lot has changed, so it's hard to associate her with the out-of-date intelligence you read." She placed a hand on my shoulder and squeezed. "I'm sorry that you're finding out this way. Never truly knowing a person is a pitfall of the life we've chosen." Etta smiled. "I can still drop off whatever it is you have for Klara. I'll leave it with her father, and he'll make sure she receives it."

I pulled the box back and placed it safety inside my bag. "It's okay. I'll give it to her when I get home."

"Sounds good, Gunnar." Etta glanced at her watch. "I have to get going." She threw a quick salute. "Be careful out there. You're very valuable to the cause."

I returned the salute. "Don't worry, Etta. I'll make our people proud."

"May only good line your path," she said before fading into the trees.

I counted to sixty, then headed to the barracks. Men were shouting as they changed into PT gear, but I ignored them and packed for the weeks I'd be gone.

There was a lot riding on the success of Operation Mitternatch. My career as an agent. And more importantly, the fate of the four people listed as targets.

Lizbeth, 1936

Chapter 27 - Lizbeth

Walking to roll call was pleasant. The sun warmed my cheeks, and a light breeze cooled the air. It seemed everyone on base was enjoying the balmy weather too—each person I passed gave wider smiles and cheerier greetings than usual. I couldn't blame them. It appeared as though the world was flaunting her grandeur, and ignoring the beauty was impossible.

I did my best to savor the outdoors while I could. Soon I'd be stuck inside the mill, roasting away in dusty humidity. It was absurd that textiles were Ms. Granth's favorite activity. To me, the oppressive atmosphere offset any positive qualities the work produced, but the lady's coordinator chirped the shifts away, oblivious to the heat. Ms. Granth was my guide through the next week, and I assumed most of our upcoming days would be spent mending clothes and dying wool, the last things I wanted to do. The upcoming confinement give me more reason to bask in the sunshine, not that I needed much convincing.

Because I lingered outside, Dame Hall was almost full when I arrived. There were only six seats available, all near the stage. It wasn't my seating preference—I'd rather be further from Ms. Granth—but I could make it through one meeting. From the entrance, I scanned the wives up front, searching for someone I knew. The most senior women occupied the first half of the row, a group Maggie called the Granthma Gang. This bunch showed up to roll call early, pointedly choosing seats near their leader. Throughout the gathering, each woman aimed an unwavering stare at the speaking podium, desperate for acknowledgement from Ms. Granth, and never receiving it. There was no way I wanted to sit near them.

I continued my search and was relieved to see a familiar petite frame topped by blonde curls. Marta Elridge was sitting beside one of the empty seats and didn't appear to be saving the open chair. I headed to the spot next to hers, and while she looked my way as I sat, my former classmate immediately turned away without a word or hint of recognition.

In the village, Marta had always been talkative. She was the first to welcome Starkesend newcomers during school and spent all her free time giggling with friends. As young girls, we'd played together, and while I'd never been as bubbly as Marta, I appreciated her social energy, in small doses, of course. She didn't let awkward silences hang in the air, unlike me, and her presence was useful for fending off unwanted attention at gatherings. People were drawn to her vivacity, which helped conceal my detachment.

The details of Marta's background made her quiet restraint a cause for concern. My worry grew when I considered her breakdown last week. Prior to being escorted out, Marta's face had been pinched in fear, her cries full of agony. While I'd seen her around base since the episode occurred, it had been from afar, never close enough for true contact. An opportunity to chat hadn't popped up until now, and I decided to break out of my comfort zone and speak with Marta in the minutes before the meeting was called to order.

Despite the differences between us, I wished no harm on my former classmates. Like me, they were removed from the outside world as children, then forced to grow up in a dreadful environment. They'd adapted to their surroundings, while I had refused the indoctrination. Even still, I recognized how easy it was to fall prey to years of brainwashing. I may not sympathize with them, but I did feel great empathy, and in this moment, a conversation with Marta was the humane thing to do. It would give me a chance to determine how my old friend was doing, offering help if it was needed.

I leaned over to tap Marta's shoulder. The movement was gentle, but at my touch she stiffened and let loose a short, guttural cry. My apology rushed out as she turned my way. "I'm so sorry, Marta. I didn't mean to startle you."

"Can I help you?" Her face was blank when our eyes met, her tone of voice odd. She sounded muffled and confused, almost like she just awoken from a deep sleep.

My instinct was to recoil. Instead., I forced a smile. "Marta, how are you? I was hoping we could catch up before roll call." I scanned the room. "Ms. Granth isn't here yet, so I think we have a little time."

She answered in the same flat tone. "Hi there, it's nice to meet you. I'm Marta Elridge. What's your name?"

Marta held out her hand, then jerked it back robotically. She repeated the movement twice more before she was able to keep her arm straight. I placed my palm next to hers and gripped her hand, but Marta didn't return the squeeze. She kept her had flat during the shake, then preformed the same machine-like retraction of her arm.

This time there was no stopping my reaction. I shrunk back, eyeing my schoolmate warily. "Have you been to the doctor lately, Marta? We should go there right now." I scrambled out of my seat, ready to run to the infirmary if Marta agreed to be seen.

"No." She shook her head back and forth, growing rougher with each pass. "No, no, no, no."

I sat back down. "Shhhhhh, shhh, it's okay. We don't have to go anywhere." I plastered on cheery grin. "Why don't we sit right here and wait for Ms. Granth to arrive. I bet she can help us figure out what's going on."

A childlike smiled filled Marta's face. "I like Ms. Granth. She always has sweeties for me." Her voice had changed. It no longer sounded dull and tired, it had become high-pitched with excitement.

We waited for our leader to show up, each teeming with our own type of anticipation. Marta was eager, anticipating the treats dancing around in her head. My eagerness manifested in a different form. I looked forward to Ms. Granth's appearance because it meant I could pass my classmate off to one of my elders. It would be a relief when someone took over the reins of this troublesome scenario. What had begun as an attempt to help had turned in to a situation that was way over my head. I realized now that Marta needed major assistance, and I wasn't the person to give it to her. I was dubious of Ms. Granth's abilities, but she would be aware of Starkesend resources, and connecting my classmate with the proper support was the most immediate undertaking.

We both perked up when we noticed Ms. Granth's arrival. She had entered the hall from the rear entrance, the one that led directly to the stage. She strolled across the pine planks, vibrantly dressed in a turquoise dress with red accessories. Ms. Granth was the picture of health and happiness— her cheeks were flushed, her eyes shone. Everything about the older woman was in stark contrast to the unwell girl on my right.

I waved and caught the coordinator's eye. Her smile transformed into a frown when she saw that I was pointing to my seatmate. Ms. Granth gave her head a slight, almost imperceptible shake, then continued to the speaker's podium, ignoring my ongoing gestures. When she reached the stand, she gave the call to order, then began the morning announcements, pointedly excluding the front row from her sweeping gaze. I had the option of interrupting the meeting but decided against this action. Ms. Granth was my guide, and I would have her full attention as soon as our head count was complete. Disturbing the prickly woman might produce an effect that hindered my efforts, making relief for Marta tougher to attain.

Mercifully, the assembly proceeded without hitches. As soon as the wives were dismissed, I rushed to the front of the stage and pleaded for assistance. "Ms. Granth, I could really use your help. I think Marta's in a lot of trouble, and I'm not sure what to do. Can you please come talk to her?"

"Silly girl, there's nothing wrong with Mrs. Elridge." She gestured behind me. "Turn around and see for yourself."

I spun on my heel and searched for Marta among the departing wives. She was easy to spot. Her jerky movements stood out in the sea of otherwise graceful women and girls. I monitored my classmate as she met up with her guide, and the two traveled together on their way out the building. Marta leaned against the older woman, who braced her with an arm across the small of her back. Their progress was halting, but the pair eventually made it through the front door and headed off to complete their assigned duty.

"See dear?" Ms. Granth's voice rang out. "Your friend is doing just fine."

Her false narrative destroyed the prospect of receiving assistance, so I decided to mention Marta's strange behavior to Gunnar later in the day. I took a calming breath before facing my guide, and when our eyes met, mine were full of agreeance instead of the anger I felt boiling inside. "You're completely right, Ms. Granth. I guess I saw something that wasn't there."

She smiled in response, and the sickly-sweet expression seemed to mock me. "I'm sure you had good intentions, Lizbeth, but let this be a lesson in restraint. There's no need to get upset about something you aren't sure of." She scanned the room. "It looks like everyone has cleared out. Are you ready for a busy day? I got word that a uniform order came in from our sister facility. They're expecting a group of ten recruits next month, and they need assistance in their preparations. Lucky for them, our wives can take on the extra burden. I know they've only been operational for a year, but the people running Murphy Ranch really need to get organized." She tsked. "Depending on others will only get you so far."

"You have such breathtaking insight, ma'am."

Ms. Granth was pleased. "I appreciate that, dear. Young people have so much to learn, and I'm always happy to pass on my wisdom." She checked her watch. "We best be off. I'll meet you in front of the building." She took a few steps toward the stage exit, then turned back. "Be a good girl and dim the lights on your way out."

Before I could reply, she whirled around in a blur of turquoise fabric. I seethed while she strode away, fighting the urge to scream at the unfairness of it all. Wives at Fort Vogel knew that flattering Ms. Granth was a necessity, at least for those who wanted to climb the social hierarchy. Our leader thrived on the praise, and she clearly favored those who words were the most honeyed. I had no intention of ascending the ranks, but still, I had reason to compliment the despicable woman. Blending in depended on being overlooked, and the less real attention I was given, the better. When I fawned over Ms. Granth, she viewed me differently. It was as if a haze clouded her eyes and she saw me through a filter, one that worked in my favor.

There was a cost though. Each pretty word chipped away at my capacity to form the next false phrase. The longer I traveled down the path of appeasement, the less willing I became to continue the entire façade. It was maddening to withhold my true thoughts. It was even more infuriating to participate in the horror. But I had to persevere and maintain the illusion a bit longer. After I found an ally, I would be able to relax, but until then, I'd wear the mask of my enemy.

I sighed, then walked to the light switch and out the hall's door, practicing my smile the whole way. I'd be using it a lot today. Ms. Granth would expect it.

∞∞∞

It was close to 6:00 when I finished my shift. The sun had already set, and I welcomed the dark sky. After hours spent under an artificial glow, the shadows were a soothing balm for my tired eyes. The quiet was also blissful. While there were still people walking around base, the noise from their travel was minuscule compared to the discord in the textile mill. All day, I'd heard the grating combination whirring sewing machines and sloshing wash water. The other wives seemed to adjust easily to the clamor, but for me, adapting was close to impossible.

I wasn't a person who dreaded silence, or one who felt the need to create constant sound. In fact, I found a quiet room alluring. Unlike noisy environments, hushed quarters gave space for the mind to get loud, rather than the voice. The absence of racket prompted my brain to manifest pictures or ideas or solutions. I could read a book and imagine the scenes taking place, sit in a sunbeam to contemplate what life outside Starkesend was like, or work through a problem on a sheet of paper—there were too many possibilities to list. Once the volume in my surroundings increased, my comfort diminished, and while I remined efficient, overcoming the noise required extra energy.

Aside from concentrating on spools of thread and fabric swatches, I'd spent the day consciously muting the mill's incessant background racket. It was a relief to escape into the quiet night air and revel in the simplicity of my walk. I nodded when I passed others, but the actions were automatic and not meant to promote interaction.

Although the path home was short, the trip gave me enough time to reset my mind and prepare for the conversation I planned to have with Gunnar. I'd come up with a list of questions to ask about Marta, and while I hoped his answers were encouraging, chances were, the information would be grim. But communication with my husband was vital, and I wouldn't let fear of his replies prevent our discussion. If there were important details, I wanted to hear them in case I could use the knowledge Gunnar shared to prevent future harm. What if Marta's affliction had something to do with our environment? What if was caused by a certain food from the mess hall or by some other hazard on base? I needed to get to the bottom of her ailment, not just for my classmate's sake, but for everyone else's as well.

I was relaxed yet motivated when I got home, and ready to dive into the truth about Marta. Light shone through the rear window, letting me know Gunnar had arrived earlier than normal. His timing was unexpected but splendid. It would allow us to get a potentially negative talk out of the way earlier than I had figured. I headed up the walk, opened the front door, and stepped inside.

Immediately, thoughts of the inquiry were brushed aside by what was happening in the house. My senses were awakened by the lively tones of swing music combined with the heady aroma of cooking food. The fusion filled the room with a warmth I hadn't felt since leaving the joyful confines of my childhood home.

Gunnar's thoughtfulness put a smile on my face. In a society dominated by men, coming home to a cooked meal was a rarity, and this was the second time my husband treated me to the extravagance. He was skilled in the kitchen, I knew that from yesterday's pineapple upside-down cake. Whatever was baking in the oven smelled like it would taste just as good.

A door closed, and Gunnar emerged from the back of the house. Surprise filled his face when he noticed me. "You're home, Klara." He checked his watch. "I wasn't expecting you for another few hours, since those chow hall shifts usually keep you out late." A grin replaced his surprise. "But I'm happy you were able to cut out early. That'll give us some extra time together."

I froze, not knowing how to respond to Gunnar's mistake. He looked so vibrant and elated, like he'd fully surrendered to the mirage in front of him. It was a shame that I would have to shatter the illusion, but I had no choice. Eventually I found the courage to speak. "Hi Gunnar, it's me, Lizbeth." I pointed to the kitchen. "Something smells good in there. I can't wait to see what you whipped up for dinner."

Realization dawned on his face, followed by sadness. "Hey Lizbeth. I'm sorry about that." Gunnar took a moment to breath. "Sometimes my mind wanders, and I see what I want to see, which is always your sister. I don't think it's happened in a while, but you did the right thing by snapping me out of it." His shoulders slumped in defeat. "I sure miss her. I know you do too."

I walked over and wrapped him in my arms. Gunnar melted into my grip. "It's okay. I understand how you're feeling." I paused. "Well, maybe not exactly, since you and Klara had a different sort of bond, but I can imagine how deep the ache goes." I gave him one last squeeze before stepping back. "You've only mistaken me for Klara once before. It was the night of our Joining, when you took me to my parent's house one last time." Shame flooded Gunnar's face, so I quickly reassured him. "Don't feel bad about it. I bet the ceremony, plus the trip to my home, triggered something inside of you. Why wouldn't you associate both things with my sister?"

Gunnar nodded slowly. "I think you're right, Lizbeth. This is also a trigger," He gestured to the kitchen and radio. "When Klara had a mess hall shift, I'd get home before her and start dinner." He smiled, but it was filled with a deep sadness. "Smelling the food, hearing the music, then seeing you standing there…well, I was transported back in time, and it became two years ago, when I was the happiest I'd ever been." He reached out and grabbed my hand. "I'm happy to see you too, Lizbeth, so please don't feel bad. But I will always miss your sister."

He sighed heavily. "She's the love of my life, and I don't think I'll ever recover from losing her."

Chapter 28 - Lizbeth

We moved past the memory glitch and settled down to dinner. Gunnar served up potato and ham casserole, a concoction that lived up to its delicious smell. Lunch had been only a small sandwich, so I made up for it with the evening meal, by eating ravenously and downing two helpings in no time. When I finished the second plateful, I complimented the chef.

"I can't eat another bite, Gunnar. Thank you, that was just what I needed after a long day at the mill." I pointed to the empty dish. "Was that another one of your mother's recipes?"

He nodded. "It sure was. The woman can cook, and she'd be pleased to know I was making my favorites from way back when."

"Well, I'm pleased to be the recipient of such a tasty concoction. The next time you write your ma, give her my thanks. She's a gem for passing down such superb culinary skills."

He laughed. "I sure will. She'd like you, Lizbeth. You're smart with a sense of humor, and that's exactly the type of girl she wanted me to end up with."

"Maybe I'll be able to meet her one day." I said wistfully.

"Do you mean leave Starkesend?" He gave me an inquisitive look, one that leaned toward curiosity rather than interrogation.

I considered hiding the truth but decided to stick with my vow of honesty. "I do. I don't think this community is the place for me." I lowered my head "I know Klara ran into trouble when she tried to leave, but I still want to go." It felt good to reveal my inner thoughts, yet I was still fearful of my husband's response.

Gunnar placed his hand under my chin and lifted until our eyes met. His face had a serious expression. "Have you shared this with anyone else?"

I whispered my reply. "No, only you."

He let out a huge breath. "Thank God, Lizbeth. You'd have been in real danger if you spilled anti-Starkesend views to the wrong person. And the wrong person just happens to be all the people who live around us."

"Are you one of the wrong people too?" My voice cracked. "Will you turn me in, Gunnar?"

Fire filled his eyes. "Never. You're Klara's sister, and I will support you until my heart stops beating." He raised his eyebrows. "But maybe keep your thoughts to yourself, Lizbeth. I'd hate to see what would happen if the General got a whiff of your rebellion."

"Mum's the word." I pretended to zip my lips closed.

Gunnar shook his head. "Until you do silly things like that, I forget that you just turned eighteen." He leaned back in his chair. "We ask a lot of our women and girls, and I'd guess it's easy to become overwhelmed with the rules and regulations restricting everything that you do. I can see why you'd want to shake off the heavy burden you've been given, Lizbeth. You're yoked with all these constraints simply because you're not a man—it doesn't seem fair."

"It isn't fair, but that's not the only reason I'm keen on leaving Starkesend." I gave him a searching stare. "Maybe I'll trust you with all my secrets soon. It sure would be nice to have someone to confess them to."

"I'd be honored to hear your deepest, truest thoughts, Lizbeth"—he glanced at his watch—"but can they wait until the Green Hornet is over?"

Laughter burst out of me. "Of course, Gunnar." I leaned close. "Who do you think he's going to catch tonight?"

"Hmmmmm, last week it was a gas racket." He grinned. "Tonight, I say he'll stop the leader of a diamond smuggling ring."

"That's a good guess." I tilted my head in thought. "I'll go with a bank robbing syndicate. He'll obviously nab all the members and force them to denounce their lives of crime."

"One of us will be right." He picked up our plates and stood. "How 'bout I wash the dishes, while you change the station?"

"You won't catch me arguing when I'm getting the better end of the deal. Thank you for picking up the slack, sir." I walked to the radio and turned the dial to the right frequency. Dolly Dawn's voice floated out of the speakers, melodically crooning about her heart. I sang along with her as I waltzed to the kitchen and grabbed a rag. Despite Gunnar's protests, I got to work on the plates waiting to be dried. "Come on, it'll go faster this way. There's only five minutes before the show starts and I don't want you to miss anything."

We finished the chore in silence, each of us lost in our own heads. When the last dish was put away, we hurried to the living room and sat side-by-side on the floor. For the next half hour, far away voices regaled us with the thrilling adventures of Hornet and Kato. They zoomed across town, outsmarting bad guys, always making sure the story got published in the news. The main characters were on the side of good and right. They knew evil thrived in the shadows, so they intervened by shining a light on the underbelly of humanity.

It hurt that I couldn't follow suit. I was protecting the dark side of Starkesend by accepting what went on around me. If ever there was a chance to increase the goodness in the world, it was now, but I remained muzzled by fear. As much as I disagreed with the hate underpinning society, my family had brought me here, and because of that, we'd further advanced the notion of racial purity that defined our community. We weren't the most active members, but it didn't matter. Places like Starkesend thrived with the help of zealots, yes, but they were kept afloat by the masses who went along in silent approval.

After the show, I asked Gunnar his thoughts. "Do you ever feel like we're on the wrong side of history?" I stretched my legs and leaned back on my palms. "When I listen to how courageous Hornet, Kato, and Case are, I want to do something just as brave. All we do around here is promote hateful ideas, but we've never done anything positive for the world."

"That's a deep question, Lizbeth." He followed my example and eased his weight onto his hands. "I think that in the moment, choosing the right or wrong side of history can be tough. A lot of the time, what's taught as history is narrated by the winners, and unfortunately good doesn't always triumph." He furrowed his brow. "In the Army, we were told who to attack, and there was little choice in the matter. Luckily, we *were* on the right side, but authority can mess with people's heads and cause them do things they normally wouldn't."

"What do you mean?" I asked.

Gunnar gazed straight ahead and considered the issue. His words were deliberate when he answered. "Many people have an aversion to making a fuss. They live quietly, plodding through life without giving much thought to their surroundings. They'll go to the same shop to get their bread, attend the same church every week, and cook the same meal every Tuesday night. They establish a routine and get comfortable with it. Everything stays ho-hum as long as their way of living isn't disturbed, but once their comfort is impacted, things get a little messy." He turned to face me. "My dad started a militia when he thought our town was getting overrun with outsiders, which to him was anyone who didn't look like him. Pa was never the best farmer, but he stuck to the farm until his lifestyle was threatened. After that he ranted and raved, and a bunch of other men joined him. They never did any true harm, mostly target practice and handing out pamphlets, but if the right leader would have come along, their hate could have been whipped up into a frenzy."

I was still unsure of his meaning. "You said authority can mess with people, but to me, it sounds like the initial threat pushed your Pa and the people he rallied into action. He didn't need a head honcho to kick start his militia, and even though you said they didn't cause any true harm, I think forming the group itself created some level of damage. How did the outsiders feel when they learned a posse of militiamen hated their existence?"

Gunnar responded in an impassioned voice. "But Lizbeth, imagine how much worse it could have been if someone like Hitler was telling them what to do. Energizing hate is when the real damage begins."

I sat in stunned silence while digesting his words. To me, it sounded like my husband was critical of the Nazi regime, that he knew the devastating harm a charismatic leader could inspire in an angry population. If this were the case, why was he here? Why did he back the goal of bringing fascism to America?

Before I could ask my questions, Gunnar spoke up. "Don't attach too much weight to what I said, Lizbeth. I don't want you poking around in something that might get you hurt." He bowed his head. "I'm sorry for getting out of line. I should know when to keep my mouth shut by now."

I sat up, folded my legs on top of each other, and turned to face him. "Don't apologize. From the ideas I've shared with you tonight, I think you've gotten a hint of where I stand on the matter." I lowered my voice. "Don't be afraid of me, Gunnar. I can help if you need it."

He smiled wryly. "You don't know what you're offering. It's best to stay out of it."

"I hope you'll trust me soon. Remember my offer when you do. It's sincere." I suddenly remembered what happened this morning and bolted upright in excitement. "Gunnar, maybe there's something *you* can help me with. Do you know Marta? She's one of the new brides from Dorf."

He nodded. "She was the first in your group to turn eighteen, right on the day of her Joining."

"Wait, I thought girls became ineligible for the Frau Rennen on their eighteenth birthday. Am I misunderstanding?"

"Since we started the marathons, we've had three races, and this year was the only time we ran into the birthday issue. General Stillwell told the Makers to present Marta with a choice—did she want to stay in Dorf, or did she want to marry a soldier and move to Fort Vogel? You can see she went with the second option." He shrugged. "I'm not saying it was the best decision, but I'm glad she was given the opportunity to have some say in her fate."

I shook my head. "That's not true at all. What she was given was the illusion of choice." Gunnar appeared puzzled, so I explained my reasoning. "For most of her life, really, for most of every girl's life, we're pushed toward a particular type of happy ending. The overall theme is that we'll marry, have children, and run a household. The most splendid and coveted role is to be the wife of a soldier. Nothing shows your support for Starkesend more than being married to the men who fight for our rightful place in the world." I raised my eyebrows up and down. "And young ladies find military men quite attractive, so it's no surprise that Marta agreed to live on base. I bet she panicked the closer it got to her birthday, probably thinking she'd be stuck in Dorf with a dull fellow who had an unimportant job." I smiled sardonically. "Lucky for her she was given a"—I made quotation marks in the air—"choice."

"Okay, okay, I see your point. Marta had less say in the matter than I thought." He thrust his chin at me. "Why'd you bring her up?"

"Have you seen her lately? She's an entirely different person." I thought back to the vivacious girl she'd been in school. "In Dorf, she was outgoing and happy-go-lucky, but here..." I searched for the words to describe Marta's abrupt change in behavior. Not only had she lost her shine, but she'd regressed in other ways. While she was a woman, she now acted like a young child. It was like parts of her were missing, and she'd become half the girl she was prior to her Joining. "The best way to describe her is empty. It's like someone drained her essence, then filled her with a portion of who she was not even two weeks ago. Her speech, her memories, her gestures, they're not hers at all." I pictured her awkward attempt at a handshake. "Everything she does is infantile yet robotic, if that makes it any clearer."

Gunnar lowered his head for a moment. When he brought it back up, his eyes blazed with anger. "This is why I insisted on conducting your extraction, Lizbeth. That man has no idea what he's doing."

"What does this have to do with extractions?"

"Well, Marta turned eighteen the day she arrived on base, so that made her eligible for an extraction. And of course, the good doctor wouldn't let me complete her session because he thinks I take it easy on our patients, or as he still calls them, our test subjects." Gunnar banged a fist on the floor. "Your classmate was eager to help the General and followed him to the lab without protest. She never had a chance to settle into her home or get acquainted with her husband. Dr. Brandt ruined her because he took her operation too far and didn't listen to me when I begged him to stop."

"An extraction caused Marta's changes? And what does ruined mean?" I looked him square in the eyes. "Gunnar, you have to tell me everything you know. It's not right that you're withholding information."

"Part of being a soldier's wife is staying out of your husband's business. There are a lot of things done on base that aren't fit for the mind of a young bride. The perfect action to take is none—just pretend like nothing happened." He shook his head disgustedly. "At least, that's what I'm supposed to tell you." He reached out with an open hand. I placed my palm in his, and he closed his grip. "When I was assigned to the lab, Dr. Brandt did horrible things to the men and women who ended up in his clutches. The initial test group was made up of ten people, and all of them died under his care. You should have seen him, Lizbeth. He was drilling into people's brains through their noses, thinking he would somehow gain access to the source of their fear."

Gunnar shuddered at the memory. "I took it upon myself to find an alternative to the doctor's methods. I did some research and discovered the adrenal glands, and the epinephrine they produce. These powerful little organs seem to be responsible for a lot, and they're located above the kidneys, far away from the brain. I was able to convince the doctor of their value, but he did his own research and came up with the idea of creating a human assembly line." He laughed derisively. "That man has lost touch with humanity. It's insane to treat people like machines, expecting them to produce an item you seek while offering them no reward for their servitude." Gunnar shrugged his shoulders. "But that was our plan, and we went about making it work until your sister inspired a positive change."

Learning of Klara's involvement was bittersweet. I was delighted to hear more about her life, and each tidbit I learned added color to the grayed image I had of her last months. Still, every reminder forced me to acknowledge that she was no longer alive. The hurt of this reality had dulled over the past year, but even a diminished ache left its mark. It would be wonderful when I'd captured enough memories to become immune to the punch of new information, when I felt confident that I knew who Klara was during her time in Fort Vogel. But was that level of knowledge even possible? Could you ever dive into the remnants of a person to discover who they really were? I was doubtful, but I would persist.

"How did Klara help?" I asked, hopeful to gain new insight into my older sister's life.

"I'm not sure if you knew this, but I met Klara before we were Joined." I shook my head at this revelation. Gunnar nodded in response. "She was a volunteer at the chow hall when the base opened. There were no women at Fort Vogel in the early days, and leadership had the idea of bringing them from Dorf to assist." He smiled. "As soon as I met Klara, I could tell she was special. She didn't take crap from the soldiers and had a sense of humor that made following her orders a pleasure rather than a chore. We got to know each other as the weeks went on, and one night, she brought the power of music to my attention."

I recalled my sister's rich alto voice. "Klara loved music as much as she loved painting. On leisure nights, she'd find a big band on the radio and sing along while we worked on whatever project our parents had given us."

"She was always singing around here too. It was like living with a cheery little bird." Gunnar chuckled. "But the night she talked about music, I was the one acting like a bird. Klara heard me humming, and she noticed that I was almost in a trance. Apparently, she watched me the entire time I was in the mess hall. She saw me get my food, eat it, and return my dishes, all while I was oblivious to the noise coming from my mouth." His eyes widened in amusement. "I was embarrassed when she pointed it out, but that didn't last long. As we talked, Klara suggested certain activities, like humming or knitting or sketching might cause the brain to partially fall asleep." He frowned. "That's not quite right. What she meant is that people lose themselves when they experience certain things. For me, that certain thing is music."

Gunnar began to hum low notes, and without realizing it, I joined him, and we harmonized for a few bars. "My mother composed that piece. It's the most beautiful song I know."

"I remember it from my extraction. You two were right about its mesmerizing quality." I hugged myself as I recalled the song's comforting effect. "When you started humming, I was put at ease and able to forget that you were performing an operation on my body."

"Incredible right? I put it to use in the lab the day after Klara and I talked, and there was an immediate reduction in fear and anxiety throughout my patients." He sighed. "The practice lasted a few weeks before Dr. Brandt ditched it. I'd begun humming while he was in Germany, and when he returned, I showed him how to recreate the effect with a gramophone. Unfortunately, I deployed for a mission, and by the time it was over, the doctor had gone back to his old ways."

"Did he hurt the group you left in his care?" I braced myself for the answer.

"He did." Gunnar lowered his eyes in shame. "I had to convince Dr. Brandt to treat them better or we'd lose the productivity aspect of our assembly line."

"Why didn't he use the music? It seems like such an obvious way to get what he wanted."

"The problem was the per-session output. When music was used, fear was reduced, which meant epinephrine and cortisol were produced in lower quantities. It was all worth it though, because it was sustainable, and a person was much more likely to withstand multiple extractions. But that was long-term thinking, and the doctor is not a long-term type of man." Gunnar tapped his watch. "Dr. Brandt wanted everything as quickly as possible, and that meant doing what we could to elevate our patient's discomfort, since more pain equaled more fluid."

Gunnar continued in a pained voice. "Since we're not making holes in heads anymore, most people can withstand the occasional extraction. That's why you're only required in the lab once a month, starting on your eighteenth birthday." He lowered his voice. "But, some people, people like your friend

Marta, can't handle a single extraction, and they become permanently damaged."

He gave my hands a squeeze. "She'll never regain her vitality, and it's all Dr. Brandt's fault."

Gunnar, 1934

Chapter 29 - Gunnar

Operation Mitternatch lasted for the entire span it was allotted. I did my best to slow the group on the way to Temple Sinai and found great success in these efforts. Early in the trip, I'd emphasized the importance of remaining undetected, and the three men with me had absorbed the lesson. This groundwork allowed my delays to proceed without distrust. Each time I expressed alarm about discovery, my team took the matter seriously and waited until the manufactured threat had passed.

Overall, I was able to give my mother an extra two days to prepare for our arrival. She worked within her network of morticians and grave diggers to procure bodies resembling the members of the targeted family. The four Adlers were secreted away to a safe location a day before Mitternatch's violent acts. They'd taken possessions with them, but not enough to rouse the suspicions of the men I was with or the community who would discover their tragedy.

True to the mission's name, we chose midnight as the action hour. Two of us burned the synagogue, while the other two attacked the rabbi's home. We stuffed petrol-soaked rags into the crevices of each structure and when enough accelerant had been placed, we lit them unceremoniously. The four of us watched the blaze from the woods. A firefighting crew eventually showed up, but by the time they pumped water onto the buildings, it was far too late to save them.

Amongst the trees, the three men surrounding me thrummed with excitement. Like the fire, their energy grew as they consumed more fuel. For the flames, the more oxygen and wood devoured, the more they expanded.

For Helmstedt, Tanne, and Wallace, the greater the devastation in front of them, the larger their thrill. The fever pitch came when four bodies, pulled out one by one, were laid on the charred ground around the smoldering house. I felt the aroused tension of the men around me, and heard their panting breaths, as they took in the scene. Helmstedt, Tanne, and Wallace were in their glory, viewing the aftermath of the destruction they had set in motion.

It was difficult to pretend, but I forced my body to match the manifestations of their voyeurism. I feigned pleasure and enjoyment, which on some level I felt because my work had saved lives. The most complicated part of blending in was the knowledge that I was syncing with the physical expression of such sick motivation. As much as I assured myself that my satisfaction was separate from theirs, my mind still rebelled at sullying my good deeds with their perverseness.

Human actions are dictated by intent, and while the purpose of my behaviors was to promote kindness and light, the objectives of the men huddled around me were quite different. The thing about intent, is that it only exists in the thoughts of the actor. People who observe the outcome of an action see only the consequences in front of them. If I were to stab a person on accident or on purpose, the outcome remains the same—someone is bleeding from a puncture wound.

Right now, the results of Operation Mitternatch were playing out. While three-quarters of the group had acted with hate, I had been guided by fairness, and the overall damage was reduced by my principles. Still, I acknowledged the power of their hostility. No lives had been lost, which was an important victory, but hate had destroyed a place of worship and a home, plus caused several people to organize panicked counteractions to undermine the mission's goals. Combined, the intent of all involved parties had resulted in property damage rather than human harm. I knew this, knew that decency had triumphed and reduced the level of evil in the world, but nevertheless, I was angry.

I was incensed about Operation Mitternatch's existence, and the knowledge that people could be responsible for such bigotry and violence. I was furious that outsiders would never know the intentions of the virtuous actors who worked behind the scenes. People would only see the outcome of hatred rather than the relief delivered by love—they'd notice a destroyed parish, and evidence of the Adler family massacre, but not the network of do-gooders who prevented a greater tragedy from occurring. But I was most irate with the men next to me, the trio hunched over in pleasure, smug in the satisfaction that their views had dominated, and an inferior group had been punished.

Secrecy was the most vital feature of the work I did. It enabled the transfer of information and provided cover for those who operated under its shroud. The current mission would not have been possible without stealth and fast response because access to my shadow network had prevented four murders from occurring. But secrecy also had a downside, and I was witnessing it firsthand. Helmstedt, Tanne, and Wallace didn't know they'd lost. They'd go back to Starkesend, drunk with importance, spouting tales of bravery to anyone who would listen.

Retribution was a dark desire, but I wanted it so badly, I ached. I wanted to rub failure in their faces, to shout about their incompetence to the entire world, yet I refrained. One day, after people like me were no longer needed, perhaps Helmstedt, Tanne, and Wallace would learn of the trickery used against them. They might be elderly by then, but shame would still carry weight, and I hoped it dragged them to the depths of regret, not that remorse changed their despicable actions. Until then, I'd remain silent and keep my vengeful thoughts buried deep.

We stayed watching until the last firefighter left, after the aroma of wet ash had replaced the suffocating smell of smoke. As we walked from Temple Sinai, the silent gawking of my team turned into giddy chattiness. Each man fantasized about the attention we'd be paid once we returned to base.

Tanne stuck his elbow in Wallace's ribs. "When General Stillwell gets word of this, boys, we'll be sitting pretty. Maybe we'll get one of them houses we put together during our early days, Cruse. They're just sitting there waiting for occupants, and there's no one better than us right now."

Helmstedt jumped in. "My wife won't move to Starkesend until we get our own place, so I sure hope that's true." He chuckled. "Imagine how proud the Führer would be. This is something right out of his playbook, and we performed our duty without hesitation." Helmstedt raised his eyebrows. "Maybe Dr. Brandt will share our information with him. It sure would be nice to get a letter or something from the big man."

"You sure are living in fantasy land, Helmstedt. Hitler doesn't have time to pay attention to such a small mission. He's got bigger fish to fry then sending fan mail to America." Tanne's booming laugh rang out. "But we may get a promotion or two out of the situation. I'd be happy having my own platoon, even if it's just four or five guys."

"Some extra stripes would be okay with me." I added, making sure I contributed enough to the conversation to prevent suspicion.

Wallace nodded. "That's what I think will happen. We'll pick up some rank, and maybe get one of those houses you mentioned." He smiled, flashing his yellowed teeth. "There was a rumor floating around about a special event they're cooking up for the senior soldiers, which we'll be when we return. We have to complete some task, it was a marathon last I heard, and then we get a wife." He surveyed the group. "There might be more to it than that, but as far as I'm concerned, I'll run a few marathons to get a woman of my own."

"Hot damn, I hope you're right. It's been far too long since I've enjoyed the company of the fairer sex." Tanne said. "I'm basically a heathen at this point."

"There's no basically about it, big man." Helmstedt chimed in. "But that sure is an interesting rumor, Wallace. When we get back to base, I'll ask around, see if I can figure out the details." Wallace gave him an odd look, so he kept talking. "Not for this happily married man, of course, but there are some fellas back home who are this close"—he pinched two fingers together—"to joining us, and a guaranteed wife would sure sweeten up the deal."

Tanne slapped me on the back. "I bet Romeo here will sign up for the marathon, lickety-split. He might be able to rope that pretty gal at the mess hall into some marital bliss, if you know what I'm saying."

"Klara and I are just friends, Tanne." I glanced to the right and met his eyes. "Besides, I don't have too much interest in getting married. My Ma and Pa didn't give me a very good example to follow, and I wouldn't want to end up like them."

He held up his palms. "Okay, okay, I'm just messing with you, Cruse." He winked. "If she's still up for grabs, maybe I'll make a play for her."

White rage blinded me, and I blinked until my eyes cleared. I choked out a reply. "That's enough, Tanne."

He laughed. "You make it easy for me, Cruse." He raised his eyes to the sky and thankfully changed the subject. "Thank God it's a full moon tonight. These woods would be impossible to navigate if it was pitch black."

I agreed. "You're right. We've got about two miles to go before we reach the first safe house. If we pick up the pace, we can be there in less than half an hour."

"Let's get at it. I can't wait to climb into bed." Wallace stifled a yawn. "It's been a long night."

∞∞∞

Detours were no longer necessary, so the trip home was quicker than the one on the way out. Most of the journey was spent in relative quiet, but when we hit the final miles, excitement took hold of the group. Each man spun tales of the welcome we'd received, and by the time we made it to the boundary tree, expectations were incredibly high.

Tanne called out to the sentries. "Come out, come out, wherever you are."

Leaves rustled until Conroy emerged from the dense brush. "Hey there, fellas. You sure are a sight for sore eyes." He laughed and came around to all of us, shaking hands as he went. "I had a feeling you'd be back today, and it looks like I was right on the money." Conroy's lips stretched into a cruel smile. "Can't wait to hear how everything went. I bet you made those Jews scream."

"Same ol' Conroy." Tanne clapped him on the back. "Don't worry, we'll spill the gory details soon, after we debrief with the general." His stomach rumbled. "And maybe get some real food. If I never see another ration pack, I'll die a happy man."

Wallace approved of the sentiment. "Here, here. If I see another C-rat I'm likely to have a fit. It's time for an actual meal."

Helmstedt waved us forward. "Let's get to that debriefing, so we can get fed."

"See ya'll later," Conroy said with a twang that came out on occasion. "Good luck with the general." Conroy found my gaze and squinted at me. "And Cruse, keep an eye out for the doctor. He's been pretty high strung since you've been gone. I've heard tell the men down in the lab are dropping like flies."

A flash of anger flared, but I tamped it down. "Appreciate the heads-up."

Conroy faded back into the trees, and I began the walk toward base, calling over my shoulder. "I'm ready for dinner too. Let's get a move on."

We hiked under tree branches until we reached the main drag. It was 1600, and most people were still completing their work hours. The streets were quiet, thankfully, and there were no interruptions to our progress. Under these conditions, the trip to General Stillwell's office took just over a minute.

He called out when we knocked. "Who is it?"

Tanne answered in his deep voice. "It's us, sir. The Mitternatch men."

"I'll be right out, boys." We heard his chair scrape against the floor, followed by heavy footsteps. Our commanding officer swung open the door and greeted us with his customary animation. "Welcome back, gentlemen." He shook each of our hands, flashing a toothy grin as he walked between us. "I made sure to get the big Montana papers sent over, and the Temple Sinai fire was front page news. From what I read, it sounds like you boys did a bang-up job, and while that's enough to celebrate in itself, you'll have plenty of other things to be happy about after our debrief." He closed his office door. "Let's use the war room. This damn closet won't fit more than two people comfortably."

We followed him and made small talk until we reached the table that had launched our mission and would now close it out. Unlike before, General Stillwell sat with us. "Okay gentlemen, tell me what happened, and be as detailed as you can." He pointed to Wallace. "You kick it off soldier."

Each of us spoke in turn, and the general peppered us with questions as we talked. When he was satisfied with our responses, he leaned back in his chair. "I think your first mission was about as successful as it could be. You did a good thing out there. It's not every day you get to put an entire family of uppity Jews in their place. Congratulations on furthering the Starkesend cause."

Helmstedt said as he saluted the Nazi flag in the corner of the office.

"We thank *you*, Corporal." The general paused. "Or should I say, Sergeant…" He waved a hand at the group. "…to all of you." He let the words settle in for a moment before continuing. "We're also moving you men to base housing. We just wrapped up construction on four bungalows that have your names on them."

Helmstedt replied enthusiastically. "You couldn't have given me better news, sir. I'll get a letter out to Maggie first thing in the morning, and she'll be here before I know it."

"Excellent. We're always happy to increase our population." The general peered at the rest of us. "Speaking of increasing the population, there's some additional news that applies to the bachelors in the room." He continued in a quick tone, the one he used when giving orders. "We have a new resident, Ms. Emmeline Granth, who comes to us from California, the Sonoma State Home specifically. She oversaw the sterilization program there, and her diligence prevented hundreds of unfit children from being born." He chuckled. "We're not trying to prevent any births here, since we screen members for genetic defects prior to admission, but she'll be using her organizational skills to manage the group of ladies that we'll soon have on base."

He paused and Wallace filled the silence with a delighted cackle. "It sure would be nice to have some womenfolk in these parts," he said.

General Stillwell nodded. "With Ms. Granth's help, I've come up with a plan that will put Starkesend on the map." He stood and walked toward the front of the room where he removed a thin file from the top drawer of a battered cabinet. He returned to our table and placed the file's contents in front of his seat. "These papers outline an event called the Frau Rennen, which we intend to host after each successful military mission." When he sat, he resumed talking. "The point of the event is to join villagers and infantrymen in fruitful unions. We want to fill the base with happy families, to have passels of pureblooded children running around, carrying forward the legacy of our Fatherland."

"There is one catch." He raised a finger. "To claim a prize at the Frau Rennen, you not only have to participate in a mission, but you must also complete a marathon that cuts across base, into some of our more adventurous territory."

"Sir, even with those conditions, I don't think you'll have trouble finding participants." Wallace volunteered. "I know I'll be signing up as soon as you allow it."

"That's good to know, Sergeant. I hope the other men share your enthusiasm." The general frowned. "Unfortunately, our first group of maidens will be small, since only eight Dorf girls meet the eligibility requirements. This means there aren't enough brides for every man who runs." His frown changed to a beaming grin. "But we anticipate a surge in population when word of the Frau Rennen makes it through our outside network. As we welcome new people to Starkesend, the difference in numbers should correct itself over time."

General Stillwell considered Wallace, Tanne, and me in turn. "You three will have a couple of weeks to enroll in the race." He shuffled through his papers until he found the sheet he was searching for. "One of the most alluring features of the bridal pool is their age. All eligible girls are sixteen or seventeen, the point in a maiden's life where she sheds her childhood and is ripe for the phase of motherhood." He rotated the paper he held and laid it down so we could read the text it contained. "These are the eight brides you will be competing for."

Although I had no intention of participating, I scanned the list of names, curious about its contents. My heart stopped when my eyes reached the fifth entry. I had to read the neatly typed letters twice. There was no mistaking what it said, though. The black ink forming Klara's name stood out against the white paper it was printed on.

I knew Klara was young, but I had no idea just how young until this moment. She was still a girl, and in less than fourteen days she would be offered to a group of men who didn't deserve her radiance. I needed to find out more about this race, so I could pass on the details when we next spoke. The more she knew, the better prepared she could be for the cruel twist of fate.

Keeping this in mind, I filled my voice with conviction and fished for more information. "Sir, do the winners of the race get to pick their wives?"

General Stillwell shook his head and chuckled. "No, we decided against it. Ms. Granth, wise woman that she is, thought such freedom of choice would be disruptive, and I happen to agree. You fellas can get mighty competitive, and we don't want any fights breaking out at the finish line."

I echoed his cheerfulness with a laugh of my own. "We definitely have some driven soldiers. I could see them getting upset if they didn't get their first choice."

"Precisely, Cruse. If everyone wants the belle of the ball, there would be a lot of friction at what's supposed to be a joyous event."

"How exactly do you pick the couples then?" I asked.

General Stillwell puffed up with pride. "It took us a while to come up with an answer to that question, but I am quite satisfied with our solution. To make everything even, we eliminated human interference and created an easy-to-use formula. All we do is insert several figures into an equation, and it determines a compatible match for the race winners." He grinned knowingly. "Of course, we consider what each of you wants, but we also factor in pedigree, social standing, and Aryan appearance for both the bride and the groom." The general shuffled through his papers again and pulled out another sheet. He slid it across the table, and I read it while he continued talking. "We've also created a new occupation that hand-picked Dorf residents will step into. Ms. Granth titled them Pair Makers, which is an apt name since they'll be responsible for gathering the matchmaking information we'll need for our calculations at the end of the race."

The page contained four names, and while I didn't recognize the first three, the fourth listing was my contact in the village, Etta. There had to be some way to use her position to Klara's advantage. Maybe Etta could rig the formula in her favor, and we could get her paired with the best possible participant rather than leaving it up to the general's equation. I wasn't sure of the most beneficial tactic yet, but the days before the event gave me much-needed time to devise a solution.

No matter what, I had to come up with something. Klara's livelihood depended on it.

Chapter 30 - Gunnar

After the briefing ended, we were dismissed with two instructions. The first was to resume our usual duties the following day. The second was to consider the Frau Rennen and decide if it was something we wanted to participate in. Helmstedt was married, but I knew Tanne and Wallace would enroll in the race. I wasn't one hundred percent sure of my response.

The general had taken marriage, a practice that already made me wary, and added coercion to its formation. Although arranged relationships had existed for millennia, they were fading from favor in more recent times. Thirty-five years ago, when my parents wed, family negotiations had still been common, especially among first-generation Americans. Ma and Pa, the daughter and son of immigrants, had been pushed together by economics. My mother's kin thought a career in music would leave her destitute, so they selected a land-owning farmer as her partner—problem solved, poverty prevented. Except their union had resolved only a singular issue, and created many others, like loneliness, anger, and regret.

Before I joined Starkesend, I'd attended a few weddings, and I could tell love was the gathering's focus. During the ceremony and reception, happiness radiated from both the bride and the groom, and guests knew they enjoyed each other's company. This contrasted with photos from my parent's wedding. Ma and Pa were grim in the images, like they sensed the miserable future that awaited them. Based on these observations, I leaned toward the promise of love rather than the negotiation of a business transaction like my parent's arrangement.

Pairings from the Frau Rennen were worse than arranged marriages. Here, village girls were forced to partner with unknown men, and there was no safe haven if things went south. While resources for women and children were rare in the outside world, they didn't exist at all inside Starkesend. Divorce was off the table, as was aid for marital abuse and neglect. Family support was another missing refuge. The bride's parents fully backed our community's ideals, and there were no grandparents, aunts, uncles, or cousins to consult for help. A bride was stuck.

We were hidden away for a reason. Our founders knew that isolation made people more susceptible to a leader's whims. They designed society so an implication of danger was ever-present, and members were afraid to step out of line. So, if General Stillwell wanted child brides, they were handed over without a fight.

The wife race excited Tanne and Wallace, and they talked about it nonstop on the way to the mess hall. I mumbled one-worded replies but focused my energy on the fast-approaching crisis, searching for a way to reduce the harm it would cause. I did the same throughout lunch and only broke my concentration to speak with Klara.

She smiled as I approached the dishwashing window and greeted me when I got close. "Hi there, stranger. I heard that you were home but didn't believe it until just now. You look well." She reached out to take my plate and utensils, leaning forward as she moved. Klara whispered urgently. "When can I see you again? We need to talk."

I whispered back. "Tonight. I'll come by before closing."

Her volume returned to normal. "I hope you enjoyed your meal, Gunnar. Thanks for returning your dishes."

"My pleasure, ma'am." I saluted her with two fingers, then headed out of the chow hall, heart pounding the entire way.

It wasn't until I reached the barracks that my pulse slowed, and I was able to focus on something other than Klara. I packed my sparse belongings into my rucksack, tidied up my bunk, then walked down the squadbay to Sergeant Roccio's office.

He responded to my knock immediately. "Come in, come in." He was standing when I opened the door, holding out a hand with a smile on his face. "Congrats on a successful mission, Cruse."

After we shook hands, he sat back down. "You should be proud of what you've accomplished. Your actions will give nightmares to Jews across the country." He let out a barking laugh. "That is, *if* they can fall asleep. The scum might develop insomnia, instead." Cruelty twisted his features. "I bet they see flames whenever they close their eyes."

I jumped in before he could continue his rant. "Thank you for the encouragement, Sergeant. I agree with you—I think a lot of people will feel the repercussions of my actions."

"That's the spirit, Cruse." He reached into his desk and pulled out a file with my name on it. "I'm guessing you're here about your relocation."

I nodded. "You guessed right."

"Well, Sergeant, it looks like you'll be moving into house 12. There isn't a lot of square footage, but it does have two bedrooms if you plan on growing your family." He tilted his head. "Speaking of families, are you signing up for that race we're having? If I was a single man, I'd be the first in line, but my Linda would pitch a fit. You know how women are."

His grin stretched, and I had to resist the urge to recoil from the clownish expression. Instead, I responded in a pleasant tone. "I haven't made up my mind yet."

"Well, with your running ability, I think you'd have a real shot at a win." Roccio moved his eyebrows up and down. "And from what I've heard, the dames up for grabs are mighty fine. The fellas who snag them will be lucky, indeed."

"That's certainly something to consider." I switched my pack to the other shoulder and edged closer to the door. "I have to head out. Do I get my key from you?"

"You do." He opened the file and took out an envelope that he handed over. "Enjoy the new place. It takes a few days, but after you adjust to the quiet, you'll appreciate how nice it can be."

I thanked him, then made my way out of the barracks to the house that was less than a minute away. Number 12 was tan and shaded by the elms and spruces that covered the entire base. I opened the door to a spotless interior. The layout was identical to the homes Bravo Team had worked on during my earliest days in Starkesend—half of the house was a living room-kitchen combination, and the other half consisted of two bedrooms and a shared bath. It was small as Roccio had noted, but I would have plenty of space to spread out and make the place my own. For now, I needed to unpack and get ready for tonight's conversation with Klara. I'd meet her in the dining hall, but we'd make our way here, to talk in private.

∞∞∞

I waited until 2130 to leave the house. It had been dark for some time, and I sensed how deep the night had settled onto the base. I was the only human outside, but plenty of critters were undeterred by my presence as they roamed the darkened lanes or flew overhead. There was a chill to the air, a crisp wind that convinced me to button up my coat and pick up my step until I reached my destination.

The lights were off inside the chow hall, but the door was unlocked, so I made my way inside, leaving the cold behind. The sound of clanking dishes drew me to the kitchen where I found Klara singing while she scrubbed. Her crooning voice filled the room with ethereal notes, and I didn't step into view until she finished her song. When she heard my soft clapping, Klara swung my way and rushed into my arms. "You're here!" She moved her lips against the skin between my neck and shoulder.

I pulled her in tight, then released her. "I am. And we have a lot to talk about." I gestured at the sink. "Are you done here? I'm out of the barracks, and I was thinking it would be safer to discuss everything at my home." I peered around the room, searching for observers, but thankfully saw none. "Just in case."

"I'm almost finished." Klara threw me a rag. "Why don't you start drying that pile over there, and I'll keep scrubbing."

Despite the glances we kept taking of one another, we worked through the dishes efficiently. We were quiet as we locked up the mess hall and moved across base to house number 12. When we got inside, I left the lights off and we sat on the living room floor, shoulder to shoulder. Klara reached over and found my hand, lacing her fingers through mine. We stayed this way for minutes, enjoying the weight of our bodies pressed against each other. Eventually our breathing synced up, and we inhaled-exhaled as one. In those moments, nothing else in the world mattered except the simple joy of being near one another.

I was reluctant to break the spell, but it was necessary. I shifted my weight and turned to face Klara, and she followed suit. When she got settled, I began speaking. "How long have you known about me?"

She inhaled sharply before she replied. "Since before you got to Starkesend. My father told me that we had recruited another agent, one who would live on base." My eyes had adjusted to the darkness, and I could make out a smile as it formed on her face. "Dad was very excited about you. So many veterans had been lured by Hitler's propaganda, and he was sure we'd never get someone who could blend into the military ranks." She snapped her fingers. "Then you fell into our laps. Not only are you a veteran, but you're a highly regarded one who was also happened to be a successful business owner. Dad thought he'd hit the jackpot when he got word of your pledge."

"As soon as the Starkesend recruiters showed up on my doorstep, I knew I had to step up." I stared at the floor in shame. "I wish I would have done something sooner. My mom had been keeping an eye on the Nazi party for years, and she was terrified as they gained power. When Hitler became Chancellor, I was surprised, but Ma wasn't. She sensed the evil brewing in Germany long before I did."

Klara gently squeezed my hand. "Gunnar, there's no sense in beating yourself up. Everything you're doing now helps diminish the advancing evil. That's what you need to focus on—the here and the now. Regretting the past is a dangerous game."

I met her gaze. "You're right. What we're doing now is the only thing that matters."

"I also have a regret." She admitted.

"What is it, Klara?"

"I'm sorry I didn't tell you who I was when we first met. I kept thinking you would find a way to speak to me about our work, but I had no idea you were in the dark about our connection."

I reached out and laid a hand on her cheek. "Let me tell you what a wise friend once told me—regretting the past is a dangerous game." She laughed. "But seriously Klara, in our line of work you can never be too careful. It was smart to wait."

She placed her hand on top of mine. "Luckily, we found other things to talk about." She sighed contentedly. "I feel like I can talk to you forever, if I'm being honest."

"I feel the same way, Klara." I pulled my arm back. "But that's as far as our relationship can go—we can only talk to each other as friends. I'll admit I let my imagination run wild after getting to know you. I've never been one for romance, but I wanted to explore that side of myself with you." I shook my head. "I had to cancel those thoughts when I learned that you were young enough for the Frau Rennen. Eighteen was already pushing it, but sixteen or seventeen means you're closer to childhood than you are to becoming an adult."

Her smile widened. "What if I told you I was closer to twenty than seventeen?"

"I'd ask you to tell me more."

"Eight years ago, when my parents joined the fight against Nazism, they started looking for a way to make the biggest impact. Starkesend was just forming at that time, and little was known about the community, but from what my parents did learn, it appeared as though they were angling to become Hitler's springboard into the United States. Mom and Dad decided to relocate here and monitor any progress toward this goal, but first we had to be accepted as members." Klara put her elbows on her knees and rested her chin in her hands. "Mom's Jewish, so we needed to create a whole new family background for her, but my parents thought making me appear younger would work to our benefit."

I raised my eyebrows. "Why'd they think that?"

"Because Starkesend is all about brainwashing their population, and the younger a child is, the more moldable they are. My parents figured we'd have a better chance of admittance if they had daughters who were six and eight instead of six and eleven. I looked like a baby too, so it was an easy adjustment." She giggled. "They even changed my name. I'm really Clara with a C, not a K." She grinned and shook her head. "My parents are smart people. They knew that Hitler's mother spelled her name K-l-a-r-a, so they thought it was another way for us to seem like real Nazi lovers."

"So, you're telling me, Clara with a C, that you're almost twenty years old?"

"I am." She gave me a searching stare. "Does my age change your mind about our relationship?"

I nodded. "It does."

"Well in that case, I'll give you the kiss I've been holding back." Clara put her palms on the ground and stretched up until her lips met mine. Her kiss was timid at first, but it quickly became heated. When our tongues met, a zap of excitement caught me off guard, and I almost surrendered to desire. It took most of my strength to regain focus, then the rest of it to back out of the fiery embrace.

I took a few seconds to calm down, and after my breathing returned to normal, I tried to get back on track. "Clara, please, let's finish talking first. We need to make plans for the Frau Rennen. I don't want you married to some man against your will."

"You sweet, sweet, man." She untied the ribbon holding her hair and chestnut curls bounced to her shoulders. "Gunnar, I've already got it figured out." She stood and held out her hand. "We're going to have Etta rig the formula, so you and I will be paired off." I placed my palm in hers, and she pulled me to my feet. Clara stood on her tiptoes to plant another kiss. "Now, come with me. Curfew is soon, but there's still ten minutes before I need to leave."

I followed her to the bedroom, and we used the last of our alone time getting to know each other better.

∞∞∞

Four days passed before we spoke again. During that time, Clara and her father worked with Etta. The trio ran tests on the matchmaking formula, trying to manipulate the results in our favor. I returned to the lab as instructed and tried to come to terms with the fiasco I found down there. Conroy's warning about Dr. Brandt had been an understatement. During my first shift, I was berated for my ignorance and blamed for the failed state of our test group. I kept quiet about the fact that I hadn't been around for over a month, and instead waited through the doctor's tirades.

By the second shift, Dr. Brandt had calmed enough to tell me what had transpired while I was away. "Everything was going well, Cruse, until about two weeks after you left. That's when the first man had a fit. I was performing a perfectly normal extraction, but it quickly turned into an emergency when he seized for minutes at a time. I stopped the operation, but it didn't help. On the way to the holding pens, another seizure caused his breathing to stop, and he never recovered from it."

"Is that what happened to the other men?" I asked.

"More or less." He moved his hand in a so-so gesture. "Once Hines was gone, it was like a domino effect. A day or two would pass without a death, but then I'd find a body in the cells, or someone would stop breathing while they were on the operating table." Dr. Brandt grimaced. "They were weak stock, so it shouldn't be a surprise. General Stillwell informed me that this bunch of men were well on their way to being rejected from Starkesend before you brought them down here." He fixed me with a withering glare. "In essence, their demise was your problem, and I expect you to clean it up."

"Sir, with all due respect, I reject the blame you're assigning to me. The lab was at its most productive before I left for Wyoming. The group of men you had so much trouble with, was the same one I used in an effective and humane way."

He snarled. "You are impertinent, Cruse. How dare you speak to your superior in such a way."

"I apologize if my words were too harsh, but I'm trying to set the record straight." I waved my arm around the room. "What happened, Dr. Brandt? How did the lab go from productive to completely broken?"

Dr. Brandt started to reply but thought better of it. He clenched and unclenched his fists a few times, then found his voice. "I didn't use the music, Cruse. During the first day I gave it a try, but after that I just performed the extractions like a proper medical procedure." His voice got louder. "I hated that you were coddling those worthless men. Why did they deserve to listen to Lascia ch'io pianga when the soldiers I work with in Germany get no such treatment?" He shook his head vehemently. "They don't deserve it, which is why I stopped playing that blasted gramophone."

The doctor stood up and walked to the record cabinet. He reached in the second drawer and brought out a handful of files. When he came back to the table, he slapped the top folder in front of me. "Edwin Hines, death by asphyxiation." He laid down the next one. "Robert Cummings, death by aneurism." He slammed the next eight folders down in one swoop. "The rest of them passed in similar ways." He sat back in his chair. "And now, we're without a test group."

"There has to be some sort of compromise we can reach sir, where you're satisfied that the patients aren't being coddled, but we're not overextending their capabilities until they die." I mulled it over for a moment then asked for more details. "How long were the sessions you preformed? How often was each man put under the knife?"

The doctor gestured to the pile of folders. "You can read detailed observations in each man's notes, but I suppose I can give you a quick summary." His voice adopted the cadence of an arrogant professor. "During the first week of analysis, I subjected our test group to extractions every other day. In this phase, they produced acceptable levels of fluid, but I'm not here to obtain acceptable results, I'm here for greatness." A hint of bitterness slipped into his voice. "Obviously, upping the lab's output was the only way to achieve this goal, so from the second week forward, I employed daily extractions." The doctor's chin lowered slightly. "Initially, the levels of adrenaline and cortisol I collected were remarkable. Admittedly, the men were hesitant before their sessions, then quite lethargic afterward, but I was excited by the full vials I was gathering." His eyes met mine. "Then they started dying. After one week of daily extractions, Hines fell out, followed by the rest of the group."

To me, the answer was obvious, but it seemed that the doctor was missing the point—he blamed the lab's failure on the men who had died rather than his aggressive techniques. I made a suggestion I hoped he would accept. "What if everyone on base was part of our test group? I think if we had a larger participant pool, we'd could space extractions further apart, and cause less damage to each person." I smiled. "Plus, you wouldn't have to use music or pamper them in any way. I think the break between sessions would give everyone enough time to recover between procedures."

Dr. Brandt considered my proposal. "Your idea has promise, Cruse." He pointed to the supply cabinet. "Bring me a ledger, and I'll conduct some calculations. We want to make sure this scheme is worth it before we present it to the general." He sighed. "Even though the man is an idiot, he still oversees the base. The more figures we present him with, the more likely his eyes will glaze over, and he'll give in to whatever we want."

∞∞∞

Clara came to my house a week and a half before the Frau Rennen. We sat on the living room floor holding hands while she assured me that she'd cracked the matchmaking formula, and it would place us together at the end of the race. All I had to do was finish in eighth place or better. At least, that's all Clara thought I needed to do.

"I can't believe you haven't signed up yet, Gunnar." Her face was a mask of disbelief and hurt.

"Clara, I've told you about my parents, and about my vow against marriage. I'm still coming to terms with the idea of rushing into a relationship because we've been forced into a corner." A tear slipped down her cheek, and I brushed it away. "I don't mean to upset you. I'm just wrestling with my inner demons." An idea came to me. "Wait right there."

I ran to my bedroom and retrieved the gift I'd never given Clara. I brought out the precious possession and placed the wooden box in her hands. "When you get home tonight, read the letter inside. I mean every word." I hung my head. "Give me a few more days, Clara. That's all I'm asking."

She set the box down and pulled me close. "Don't forget, Gunnar, a few days are all I have left."

Lizbeth, 1936

Chapter 31 - Lizbeth

I tossed and turned all night, floating in and out of nightmares about botched extractions. Some dreams featured Marta, while in others I pictured my sister at the mercy of Dr. Brandt. I'm not sure why I associated Klara with my former classmate, but my unconscious mind blended them together and assigned them the same horrific fate. It was a relief to wake up and smell the familiar aroma of coffee. I threw back the covers and got ready quickly, throwing on a tan dress, braiding my hair, and splashing my face with cool water. The specific twists and turns of my nightmares had faded, but the overall feeling of unease clung to me as I made my way into the kitchen.

Gunnar noticed my arrival and set a steaming mug of joe on the counter in front of me. "Morning, Lizbeth." He glanced at his watch. "I was about to wake you. Did you get a good night of sleep?"

I grimaced. "Not exactly. I kept thinking about what happened to Marta, and my brain whipped up a bunch of dreadful dreams when I was finally able to close my eyes." I grabbed my braid and ran my fingers along the loose hair at the bottom. "For some reason, I dreamt about Klara too. I imagined her as one of Dr. Brandt's victims, and that scared me more than anything."

Gunnar's face paled. "Well, she did have a run in with the doctor."

"What did that man do to her?" I cried, horrified to hear there was some truth behind my nightmares.

"He got to her when I wasn't there to protect her." Gunnar blinked back tears. "Klara was looking for me in the lab, and when she couldn't find me, she started talking to Dr. Brandt." Color flooded his cheeks. "The swindler forced her to get an extraction. He told her that I was intimately familiar with the procedure, and that it was harmless. He said it would benefit my career if she participated." Gunnar lowered his head and shook it slowly. "She was never the same." He glanced up and quickly added. "But she was nowhere near as bad as Marta. Klara was much more herself than your poor friend."

It took time to absorb his words because they were tough to process. It pained me to learn that my sister had fallen prey to a deranged, power-hungry man, and that his intrusion had impacted the remaining months of her life. I felt both guilty and grateful for Gunnar's presence during my extraction. It was unfair that Klara had missed out on this protection, and that she had suffered as the result of a chance encounter with evil.

I finished my coffee in silence, lost deep in unpleasant thoughts. Gunnar respected my reverie, and sat next to me, quietly sipping his drink. Eventually, he stood to plant a kiss on the top of my head, saying goodbye before heading out the door. "Be well, Lizbeth. I'll see you after work." I acknowledged him with a brief smile, then continued deliberating until it was time to leave for Dame Hall.

I remained detached during roll call and was thrilled when the morning ritual passed without incident. My enjoyment increased when I noticed I had nursery duty that day. The children's vibrancy would be the perfect antidote for my negative emotions, and I jumped into activities as soon as I stepped into the building. My group had fun during story time and lettering, although most of the three-year-olds scribbled rather than printed, but the greatest joy came when I convinced Ms. Granth to let us play hopscotch outside. Over the next two hours, the children and I laughed in the sunshine, and I was able to release the anxiety that had dominated my early hours.

Maggie was in the nursery too, and she helped me wrangle the toddlers when it was time for lunch. When we had them settled at their table, she looked over and smiled. "Good lord, they are a handful."

I shrugged. "I needed this kind of chaos today."

"Everything okay, Lizbeth?" She asked on her way to the food cart.

"Miss Lizbeth, are you sad?" Chimed in a tow-headed boy. The thread was picked up by the other children, and twelve high-pitched voices began to chatter about their teacher.

"Shhhh, little ones. Miss Lizbeth is fine. Don't you remember her laughing with you outside?" My reassurance seemed to satisfy them, and Maggie and I handed out their trays to further distract them.

When the entire class was preoccupied with eating, Maggie leaned over. Her voice was a whisper this time. "Are you ready for our outing tonight?"

I had forgotten our plans but didn't admit the omission. "I can't wait. When and where should I meet you?"

"I was thinking the graveyard." She crinkled her nose. "Not the fancy pants Mother's Glen, but the other one. The one where your sister is buried." She peered at me then darted her eyes away. "Don't worry, I won't judge you for your sibling's sins."

"Thank heavens," I said through gritted teeth. Anger threatened to spill out, but I restrained the emotion, instead recalling the laughter we'd shared in the chow hall, and how much I'd enjoyed her company there. With this memory, I convinced myself that her forwardness wasn't personal. Maggie was just a bold person and having her as a friend meant I should anticipate brazen behavior.

Keeping this in mind, allowed me to continue in a warm tone. "I can show up any time after dinner, which is usually around 7, 7:30."

"Be there at 8:30. It will be quiet on base by then, and even quieter back there in the woods." Her eyes glinted mischievously. "My husband got his hands on some German lager. I'll bring a bottle for each of us."

We were interrupted by giggles and turned to see the youngest child in the group on top of the table. At the same time, Ms. Granth entered the toddler room, mouth agape at the scene. "Girls, what is going on?"

Maggie ran to the table and grabbed the offending tyke. She spun around to place him on the ground, then turned toward Ms. Granth. "Whatever do you mean?"

"Maggie Helmstedt, your smart mouth will get you in trouble one of these days." She swung her gaze to me. "And don't think you're immune, missy. A lady's worth is determined by the company she keeps." She eyed me up and down. "You already have a strike against you, dear. I suggest you don't earn another by slumming with the likes of Mrs. Helmstedt."

Ms. Granth gave us a scathing look, then marched out the door she'd come in. The children had quieted at the interruption, but now they danced around the room, yelling the word *missy* over and over again. I rolled my eyes, griping to Maggie in a hushed voice. "For someone so concerned about impressions, she sure doesn't hold her tongue when it matters."

"She's a witch, and I hate her. But the best thing we can do, is let it roll off our backs. She only wins if she gets to you."

I nodded. "That's true." I tilted my head. "But I did have a question— what did she mean about having a strike against me?"

"I bet she's talking about your sister. Unlike me, Granthma *does* judge you for your sibling's sins." Maggie grabbed my arm. "Come on, let's get these kiddos back under control." She pulled me to the center of the room and touched her toes. I followed suit, and soon the children were reaching for their own feet. We had them settled in under a minute and tucked into their cots for naps shortly after.

The rest of the day passed easily. There were no more outbursts from the kids or disappointed visit from our coordinator. Pickup also went smoothly, with everyone's mother arriving before 6:00. The five of us on duty began cleaning right after the last child left, and before I knew it, I was out the door on the way home.

The sun had already dropped below the horizon, but the star's lingering rays created purple, orange, and red patterns among the clouds. I took in the spectacle and inhaled the perfume from the reemerging flowers. Spring had barely started, but nature was bursting with life everywhere I turned. Jackrabbits nibbled on blades of grass in the twilight. Bats flitted from bug to bug, making zig zags in the darkening sky.

It was a shame that Starkesend's corruption was masked by such beauty. Or perhaps the bigger disgrace was allowing the community's vileness to mar the splendor of the surrounding environment. Either way, it was paradoxical to witness the coexistence of these contrasting entities, one built on erasing certain life forms, the other on supporting rebirth each year.

These notions followed me home, and I mulled over them while sipping a cup of coffee. I liked to think I was on the good side of the Starkesend-Mother Nature relationship, but the more I explored this idea, the more I saw the flaws in my logic. I'd lived here for more than a decade, spending my youth bending to the will of others. I had taken orders from Nazi supporters, memorized hate-filled propaganda, and endured endless pushes toward marriage and motherhood. And worst yet, I was still putting up with those situations in the prime of my life. How had I arrived at this point?

As the warm liquid rolled down my throat, I pinpointed my weaknesses and the roles they'd played in my current circumstances. For years, I'd accepted fate through quiet acceptance. There'd been no searching for solutions or ways to fight back—passivity was the only form of resistance I'd employed. But it wasn't enough to disagree. To truly make a difference, you had to shine a light on the dark side of humanity by standing firm and creating noise.

I wasn't like the trees or the jackrabbits. These beings remained true to their form despite the humans who'd intruded into their world. I was the opposite. When a dark adversity had stepped in my path, I'd cowered and altered who I was as a person. Admitting it pained me, but honesty demanded that I come clean.

Another realization was of equal importance—the time to step up was now. If I did nothing, I was allowing the negativity to win, and I'd already given the enemy too much support. Physically resisting would do no good, since a single person would be no match against 200 residents who would lay their lives on the line for Starkesend. And while using arson or weaponry would make mass destruction possible, there was no way I wanted to murder or maim others.

Escaping was the best bet, but I was hesitant to leave my family, especially Ellis. Was it honorable to secure my own freedom while my brother remained trapped in this loathsome place? Definitely not, but if I left Starkesend, I could report their wrongdoings to the outside authorities. I wasn't sure where the closest police station or newspaper was, but maybe I could fish around for that knowledge. If I learned who the right people were, I could share my story with them. Then, I'd be able to rescue my family, and fully sever out connection to this awful place.

These thoughts buoyed me while I chopped vegetables, formed a meatloaf, and tucked the food in the oven. They carried me through sweeping and dusting, and accompanied me to the bedroom, where I decided to conduct an inspection. So far, the time I'd spent in the room had been practical—I washed up, got dressed, and slept in the space—but now that I was actively planning an escape, every location held potential sources of aid.

My first stop was the pine box at the end of my bed. Gunnar had given me three dresses and a nightgown, and I kept these items inside the trunk, alongside my marital robe. During my time at Fort Vogel, I'd worn two of the frocks, modest things with low hems and high necks, identical except for their color. The navy and brown garments held no secrets. I knew as much because I'd gone through their pockets and seams, hunting for forgotten detritus before plunging them into the wash each Sunday night. It was different with the third dress, though, and I was less familiar with its olive fabric.

The unworn gown was more faded than the others, but I hadn't neglected the garment because of this flaw. The reason it was buried under the rest of my clothes was a personal one—I wanted to preserve its connection to Klara. When I first held the rough green dress, the ghost of a fragrance had risen from its folds. A wave of nostalgia washed over me as I pressed the material to my face, inhaling the quiet echo of lavender coming from the fabric. In some way or another, the faintest scent of my sister's soap lived on, and I clutched the dress for minutes, happy to possess a small piece of the person who'd worn it last. After weeping an ocean's worth of tears, I refolded the garment, tucking it underneath everything else, hoping this position would prevent the fragrance from disappearing.

It had remained there until today, when I needed the dress for more than just a trip down memory lane. I placed my other clothing on the bed, then gently grabbed the olive frock from the bottom of the trunk. Before further disturbing the faded A-line, I took a moment to savor its lavender scent, breathing deeply of the fragrance, this time without the tears. After a few inhales, I brought my arms down, knowing it was time to investigate the well-worn dress for anything that would aid my escape.

I unfurled the fabric and shook it vigorously, all the while scanning the ground for falling objects. Nothing tumbled free, so I flipped it over and ran my hands along the inside of the skirt. When that produced no findings, I righted the garment, then turned out each of its pockets. There were two on the hips and one on the blouse, and I groaned in frustration at the three empty compartments, hating the fact that nothing was revealed. Although it was my first search attempt, my expectations were high, and I was sorely disappointed at the lack of progress. Like a child, I took my disappointment out on the dress. Instead of folding it, I wadded it up and threw it toward the other clothes, turning away as it landed on the bed. After my pivot, the sink and towel rack were in my sights, so I walked their way, planning to investigate that corner of the room next. But something told me to stop. I changed direction and stared at the green heap on my bed, squinting my eyes to focus on the dress' one piece of adornment—a white peter pan collar that had flipped up during its tumble through the air. An object was attached to where the collar and neckline met, a thin, tube-shaped item I had missed during my inspection. I hurried to the bed and bent closer to the thing, looking before I touched, barely believing it was real.

But it *was* real, and it appeared to be a tightly rolled piece of paper, almost hidden by the slim swatch of fabric holding it in place. I plucked the sheet from its holster, pinching it between two fingers as I brought it closer. My breathing stopped as I unwound the scroll, but I let out a gasp when I saw what was on the page.

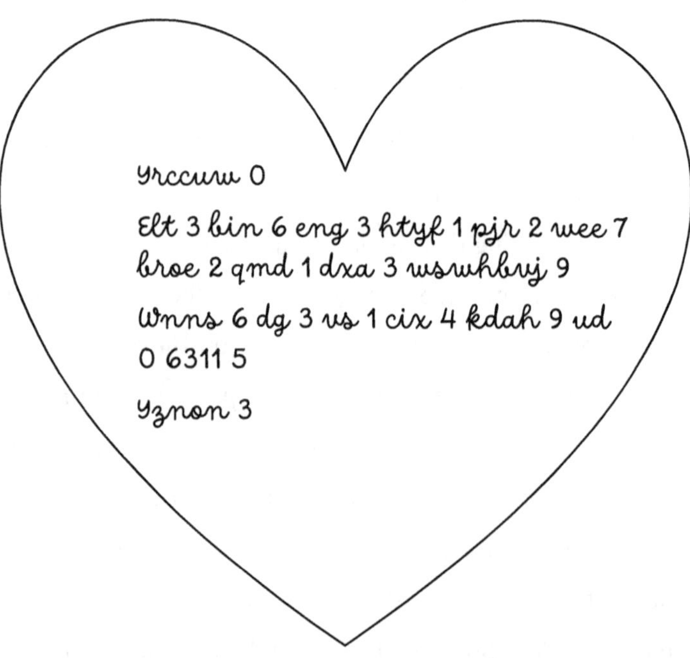

The paper contained a note scrawled in the middle of a heart. To another person, the message would appear bizarre and unreadable, but I recognized the text immediately despite not having seen it in years. It was strange that my sister would write in this made-up language, but there was no denying the proof in my hand.

Klara invented Encatian when we were young, and we used it in a silly game that went on for months. After school, we'd write notes, and stash them around the house, waiting for the other sister to find them. I left letters in what I thought were good hideaways, like under pillows or between the pages of a book, but Klara uncovered them easily. Her hiding places were much better than mine, and it took me longer to discover her messages. Once, after two days of searching, Klara led me to the kitchen to reveal her spot. She'd hollowed out the handle of a pot and placed her paper in the crevice, something eight-year-old Lizbeth never would have found. I was impressed. My parents were too. Their positivity came as a surprise because I'd expected a lecture on respecting belongings, the usual consequence for breaking something. Instead, they'd laughed at their eldest daughter's cleverness, amused by her concealment skills and the contents of the note she'd written.

We always said cheeky things in our shared language. I was fond of short rhyming poems, using them to make fun of Klara the way a younger sibling does. The words smelly and stupid often made it into my verses, and I'd laugh myself silly while I waited for her to translate them. My sister was more creative with her output. She wrote a series of stories featuring me as the main character, where I was called Beth the Brat and the plot followed my never-ending mishaps. One time, Beth broke into a bakery and ate all the cookies, a nod to my sweet tooth. On another adventure, the Brat was caught after she played outside instead of doing her homework. Of course, Beth blamed a roaming wolf for scarfing up the math equations she'd worked so hard on, a fib I'd told the previous year.

Neither of us was mad at the teasing. In fact, we loved the notes, and would run off to write more the instant a hidden letter was uncovered. When Klara moved from primary to secondary school, we stopped our game. My sister spent more time on her studies, which meant I needed to find activities to fill my new alone time. I settled on reading and needlepoint, but neither matched the fun of exchanging notes with my sister.

Seeing the language again made me smile. It also left me unsettled. Klara and I had joked around in Encatian, and I had fond memories from that period of my life, but other than providing amusement to children, I wasn't sure of this imaginary language's purpose. Maybe once I translated the message, I'd understand what she'd been saying.

Offhand, the only phrase that looked familiar was Yznon 3. This word used the third Encatian alphabet to form the letters of Klara's name, although it was spelled incorrectly, starting with some other letter than K. Since this word was at the bottom, I assumed the letter was signed by my sister, but that was as much as I could decipher. I'd need to focus on the text to figure out the rest. Maybe some time spent with the words would trigger my memory.

"Lizbeth, are you back there?"

Gunnar's voice startled me, and the paper nearly slipped from my grip. I tucked the precious item into my pocket before answering my husband. "Yes. I'm in my room." I glanced at the disheveled clothes on my bed. "I'll be out in a moment." The dresses went back into the trunk, and I walked out to the living room, beaming with excitement. Soon, I'd understand the hidden message left behind by my sister.

Chapter 32 - Lizbeth

"Did your day get any better?" Gunnar asked from across the table.

It took a few moments to realize that he was referring to my extraction-filled nightmares from last night. I nodded in response. "Thankfully, it did. Being around the little ones always puts me in a good mood." I took a bite, thinking while I chewed. "What's funny is that I'm not certain I want children of my own. Is it weird to like kids so much, yet not be sure about motherhood?"

"The thought itself isn't strange, but it's odd that someone from Starkesend is having it." Gunnar kept talking while he scooped another helping onto his plate. "Around here, everyone is baby crazy. I know you get an earful of it in school, and they certainly push it onto the soldiers." His gaze flicked to my hair, then back to my eyes. "You're the kind of woman Nazis dream about, and usually, a person with your coloring tries their hardest to have a large family. Everything to help the Fatherland, and all that" He offered a smile. "It's brave to dissect what's been pushed at you. Most people don't."

"Thanks, Gunnar. Lately, I've felt the need to consider things more deeply than I used to." I laughed. "Guess that means I'm growing up. My parents would be proud."

"They really would. I appreciate them, and the fine job they did raising you and your sister. I'm sure they're doing the same with your little brother too."

"They're great parents." My shoulders sank. "I just wish they'd picked somewhere else to raise us."

Gunnar smiled in understanding. "Your heart still longs for a life outside Starkesend, doesn't it?"

"It's true."

"It's not fair when the heart wants something unobtainable." He whispered his next words. "But Lizbeth, I've been thinking about leaving too. Today, I learned something that made me question everything I've done here. It might be time to move on." His posture folded inward.

While Gunnar appeared defeated, his words had the opposite on me. Excitement rocketed through my body, and when I whispered back, my reply was quick paced and upbeat. "Do you really mean it? I would go with you in an instant."

He raised his head, and I saw the torment on his face. "I need to consider every option. Rushing into a decision would be a mistake"—he pinched the skin between his eyes and sighed—"but waiting too long creates its own set of complications. Can you give me a day? There are some people I need to talk to, and they'll advise me on the right move."

In light of his unease, I spoke with seriousness, masking the joy rocketing through my body. "Yes, of course, take a day. And Gunnar?" He met my eyes. "If I can do anything to help with your decision, please ask. I know I'm young, but I can provide insight about Dorf, and how that side of Starkesend operates. The knowledge that I have is yours. All you have to do is ask."

"I value your insight quite a bit, Lizbeth. Thanks for the offer." He pushed back from the table. "But right now, I know you have somewhere to be, so why don't you take off, and I'll clean up." Gunnar stacked our plates and brought them to the sink. "Don't worry, I'll quiz you about Dorf when you get back."

"I hope it's not a tough quiz. You haven't given me any time to study." I was happy to hear his chuckle. Perhaps he wasn't as upset as he appeared. Or maybe he was good at hiding his emotions. Either way, the laugh was a welcome sound. "I'll be back before curfew."

"See you then. Have fun and—"

"Be safe?" I cut him off. Gunnar nodded, and I waved as I headed out of the house. "I'll do my best to avoid any danger, sir. See you later."

After the door closed behind me, I allowed my delight to surface. Today's good fortune put me in a tizzy. Uncovering Klara's note had been remarkable. Adding Gunnar's revelation on top of this was almost more than I could handle. For the first time, my wish of leaving Starkesend was less of a fantasy and more of a probable outcome. And it was something that might happen soon. This notion gave me a jolt of energy that quickened my pace and put a bounce in my step.

Maggie had been right about the hour. Not a single soul was out, and even the animals were more subdued than normal. The quiet didn't bother me though. I was happy to revel in my newfound joy without an audience or distraction. Light from the halfmoon accompanied me until the cemetery's entrance. Once I passed into the graveyard, moon beams had to fight through the brambles to be seen. Still, there was enough illumination to get a general sense of my surroundings, so I was able to find my way to the spot where Klara rested. I spoke to her in a hushed tone, trying to get everything off my chest before Maggie arrived.

"Hi, sis. I've been thinking about you a lot lately. The unfairness of this whole situation has really done a number on my mind. I can't stand that you ended up in this wretched place"—I gestured to the dilapidated grave markers and the overgrown weeds—"especially because you never had the chance to truly live. They take that away from us here. Since childhood, we've been pushed into a parody of what life's supposed to be like." I paused, struggling with my emotions as they plummeted from the euphoria I felt on the way here, to fresh pangs of sorrow. When I regained enough control, I went on. "Sometimes, I pretend that you're still alive and that we're just regular people. We go on dates and try on pretty clothes and eat dinner with Mom, Dad, and Ellis every Sunday night. It's simple, but it's perfect because it doesn't involve oppression or hate."

A branch cracked behind me and I whirled around, holding my breath while I waited for Maggie to emerge from the bushes. I counted to thirty, then sixty, and no one appeared. After running through the numbers again, I turned back to my sister's grave and picked up my thread, this time decreasing my volume below a whisper.

"I know you found love with Gunnar, and I'm grateful you had the chance to experience it even for a short while. He's been kind to me, Klara. I feel like you had something to do with our matchup, but that's impossible, since you were gone before it happened." I smiled. If Klara were here, she'd laugh at my foolishness, and lecture me on the impossibility of my thoughts. I rolled my eyes at our imagined argument. "You're right, of course, dead people can't be matchmakers, but it's a feeling I can't shake."

I crouched and placed my palm on the earth. "Love for you, and for the rest of our family, is what's kept me going. Through it, I found the strength to shake off my indifference, the factor that's chained me here for far too long." Tears slipped down my cheeks. "I've been a coward, Klara. I wasted years waiting for someone to save me from this place, when all this time, I should have been the one blazing my own path." The tears rolled off my face, crashing into my hand below. The water trailed down a path of skin until it reached the dirt. I watched a few drops turn into mud before continuing my confession. "I'm going to leave Starkesend, Klara, and when I do, I'm going to scream about its secrets until I go hoarse. And after I lose my voice, I'll find another way to get my point across, because what I have to say is important. There are lives at stake." I traced a heart on the ground, copying the shape from the letter that rested in my pocket. Klara's essence was mixed with the black soil. She was forever intertwined with this place, a fact I couldn't change.

What I *could* alter was the future. I brushed the dirt off my finger, returning it to its rightful spot, then finished making my promise—I was ready to destroy the only home I'd ever known. "There are good people out there, Klara, and I'm going to show them the evil flourishing right under their noses. It's time to go to war against Starkesend."

I stopped speaking when another branch cracked. This time the sound was accompanied by rustling leaves. I snapped my head toward the movement, and Conroy came into view. My eyes had adjusted to the dimness, so I could make out his grin. And his tongue. He swiped the pink muscle back and forth across his lips as he advanced.

"Ain' this…a lucky find…came to piss and there's a…a stuck-up broad sittin' in the ground…dirt." His words were halting, his gait unsteady. Conroy seemed like he had a few drinks in him, a frightening addition to an already dangerous man. He kept talking as he got closer. "Lookslike yer waitin' for ol'Conroy to show you…a thing or two. Don' worry…I will." He reached for his belt buckle, struggling to unhook it while stumbling forward.

I stood to face him, planting my feet on the ground and my hands on my hips. Strength was my only weapon, and I tried to convey it with an unafraid presence. "Leave. Me. Alone. Don't take another step, Conroy, or there will be trouble." I scanned the area, hoping to see Maggie or anyone who could help. "My husband will arrive at any moment, and if you don't back off, he'll have no choice but to hurt you."

A lecherous laugh rang out. "Always hiding behind tha'husband of yers…an lyin' about him comin' here." He shook his head. "Naughty naughty girl…I need to show you…teach you a lesson."

Out of nowhere, Conroy lunged forward and closed the distance between us. I reached into my slip, bringing out the scissors I'd hidden for so long.

But I moved too slowly. A rough hand closed around my ankle, and I crashed to the ground on top of my sister's grave, spilling the weapon from my grasp. Conroy's breath was hot on my leg as he pulled me closer. Its whisky-soaked fog assaulted my nose and caused water to well in my eyes. The putrid scent let me know that Conroy was more than a few drinks in—it smelled like he'd consumed an entire barrel. I flailed my arms, and a swipe caught his cheek with my nails. Blood poured from the wound, but alcohol had dulled his senses, and the injury didn't slow him at all. I kept struggling, though. There's no way I'd let this monster win without putting up a fight.

A *thwack* brought everything to a halt. After the dull, heavy noise, my assailant dropped on top of me, crushing me with his dead weight. I wiggled around, straining my neck, searching for the source of Conroy's unconsciousness. To my delight, I saw Maggie over his shoulder. She was beaming from ear to ear, holding an object high above her head.

"Maggie, you saved me." I closed my eyes and took a few breaths, basking in my gratitude.

"Let's move this lunk off you." She grabbed his arms and tried pulling, but he didn't budge. "Maybe it'll be easier if I push his weight up, and you can slide out from under him." She laid next to me, putting her feet and hands on Conroy's shoulder. "I'll count to three, then lift. See if you can get out from under him before I let him fall."

"Okay, I'm ready." I agreed.

Maggie adjusted her position. "Here we go. One, two, three." She grunted and strained, and after a moment I felt an easing of the burden on top of me. I rolled away, and after I cleared the body, Maggie let it drop back to the ground. Her breathing was heavy, but she managed to speak through the gasps. "Good lord, he's heavy. And he stinks worse than a hobo." She laughed. "If his actions didn't kill you, his stench certainly would have."

I joined in the laughter, not out of humor but out of relief for my safety. We stayed on the ground until we quieted, then Maggie popped to her feet. She stretched out an arm. "Time to get up." I took the offered hand, and she pulled me upright in a single motion. When I lifted my head, a wave of dizziness washed over me, and the world went black.

Maggie recognized what was happening. "It's okay, Lizbeth. Just lean against me and it'll pass."

I did as I was told and put my weight on my friend's left side. After a few moments the fog lifted, and I could see again. "I hate those spells."

"Me too." She grimaced. "Glad you didn't have one while the jerk was on top of you." She nudged his stomach with her foot. "Think I knocked him out cold."

"What'd you use?" I replayed the thud noise in my head. "The sound it made was brutal."

"Just some good ol' German lager. The bottles make a good bat. I swung it like I was hitting a home run." She reached down to pick up the closest beer. "We more than deserve a drink after dealing with Mr. Grabby." Maggie pulled out an opener and popped off the lid. She held it out to me. "First sip is yours, Lizbeth. Don't be shy."

Alcohol wasn't forbidden in Starkesend, but drinking was an uncommon practice. I knew that soldiers imbibed, and even the men in Dorf partook on occasion, but I'd never heard of a woman drinking. I tried to hide my shock, but Maggie picked up on it.

"Fine, I'll take the first pull. This is how it's done." She put the bottle to her lips, then tilted her head back for a deep swallow. She smiled when she righted herself. "See? Nothing to be afraid of." She pressed the amber glass into my hand, and I reluctantly closed my fingers around it. "Go on. I bet you'll like it."

I took a taste of the foamy liquid and swished it around. It was interesting, not bad, so I took a bigger sip before passing it back to Maggie. She raised the bottle again, and we passed it back and forth until it was drained. "Shall we open the other one?" She asked.

"Probably not." I stared down at Conroy. "I can't believe he hasn't woken up. Do you think he'll be okay?"

"Seriously, Lizbeth? Why do you care if this pig wakes up?" She gave him a kick. "It would serve him right if he never came to. The world would be a better place if there were less Conroys in it." She took out the opener and pulled the cap off the second bottle. "Now that's something we should drink to. There's less evil out there now because we took this piece of trash out of commission." Maggie took a long swallow before handing me the beer.

I drank, then asked a question. "Do you ever think about doing more to fight evil?"

She tilted her head. "What do you mean?"

"What if you had the opportunity to do something big?" I took another swig. "Like, what if you could make a difference in the lives of a lot of people?"

"I have no idea what you're talking about, Lizbeth." She reached over, taking back the bottle.

Before I realized what I was doing, my mouth opened, and a secret spilled out. "I'm talking about this place, Maggie, where we're standing now. Not the cemetery, but Starkesend, our entire society." I searched for the right words. "It's bad here. Really bad. There's so much hate and control, and that's the way it will always be…unless someone does something about it."

Maggie's eyes raked across my face, appraising me in a calculated way. She was silent, pensive, and I waited for her response in panic, regretting the mistake that might ruin everything. When she finally spoke, it was in a cool manner far removed from the friendliness that usually filled her voice. "I think you've had too much excitement tonight. Conroy's attack, followed by what I'm guessing was your first beer, was just too much for you to handle." Maggie abruptly raised the lager to her lips, draining the contents in a single gulp. After she finished drinking, she threw the glass and observed its arc as it flew into the moonlit woods. While it crashed into the underbrush, she reached down to pick up the second bottle, disposing of it in the same way. After the trees stopped rustling and the night returned to a quieter state, she turned her attention back to me. "Get some sleep, Lizbeth. A good night of rest should put you back to rights." She began walking away but faced me one last time. "I can give you until morning. After that, I'll have to report you."

Chapter 33 - Lizbeth

I burst through the front door and slammed it behind me. "Gunnar, we have to leave tonight."

Footsteps approached from the rear of the house, and my husband shot out from the hall, red-faced and worried. "Lizbeth, what's going on? Did something happen?"

When I tried to talk, sobs burst out instead of words, and I collapsed to the floor, useless for the time being. Gunnar came to me with open arms, staying silent while I worked through my anguish. Precious minutes wasted away as he held me. Whenever I opened my mouth, moans and sniffles emerged rather than the warning I wanted to shout. My fragility was disappointing, but I would have to wait it out.

It was 10:26 when I settled enough to check the clock. Almost half an hour had been lost to my emotions, but I felt better now, stronger, and prepared for what had to be done. Gunnar must have sensed the change in my demeanor because he spoke up gently. "Are you ready to talk now?"

I pushed back and sat on my own, no longer needing to rely on his shoulder for support. "I am." I wiped the lingering tears from my face. "But I have to warn you—you might not like what I'm about to say."

"Lizbeth, just tell me what happened. I'm here for you no matter what," he said.

"Thanks for the support, Gunnar. It means a lot." I steadied myself with a deep breath, then began talking. "Let me start with something good, something from earlier today, right after I got home from the nursery." I reached into my pocket and retrieved Klara's note, passing it to Gunnar before I went on. "I found this in my room, hidden under a dress collar, rolled up tight in a little tube. I was excited when I saw it, and even more so when I unrolled the paper and recognized Encatian right away. So far, the only word I managed to translate was my sister's name, —" I frowned, "—or at least I think it's her name since the first letter looks wrong. But it has been almost ten years since I've seen the language, and the alphabets are long gone from my memory."

Gunnar beamed. "Let me show you something. Follow me." He jumped up and rushed toward his office, leaving me to trail behind. By the time I reached the room, he'd spread the contents of a folder across his desk. He waved me over, then pointed to the papers. "Klara and I sent these to each other. Let me translate the note you found." He glanced back and forth between the decryption key and the paper, then told me what the words meant. "Gunnar, you are the best and I love you for eternity. Meet me at our spot at 2100 - Clara." He shook his head. "The message never made it to me."

I scanned the papers he'd set out, recognizing my sister's handwriting on about half the sheets—it was the same swirling script that was on the letter in Gunnar's hand. The language also matched. "These are all in Encatian." I picked up the closest note and saw Klara's misspelled name at the top, meaning I was holding a message from Gunnar. "I have a question."

"Ask away."

"Why did you write in this nonsense language?" I gestured to the collection of letters. "Klara and I used Encatian to joke with each other when we were kids, but that's all I thought it was, just the short-lived whim of two little girls. I never expected adults to use it."

His leaned toward me, answering in a serious tone. "This nonsense language is actually a sophisticated cypher. Your sister and I used it to communicate important information to each other."

The words caught me off guard. "Are you saying…why did you need—"

"We were agents." He sighed. "Well, Klara was. I still am."

My voice was wobbly when I found it again. "I had no idea."

"That's the way it's supposed to be. The fewer people who knew about us, the easier it was for us to do our jobs." He studied the letter I'd given him. "Klara told me all about your game. She loved writing those Beth the Brat stories, and the poems you wrote tickled her pink. But it was all practice, Lizbeth. Even back then, Klara was training to become more involved in the movement."

"It's hard for me to wrap my mind around an eleven-year-old training to become a spy." I fixed him with a questioning gaze. "And why are you telling me this? Why reveal your hand now?"

"I'll answer your second question first." He smiled wryly. "If you'll recall our conversation over dinner, I made a revelation. I said that I'd learned something today, something that shook me to my very core."

"You never told me what it was." I reminded him.

"Yes, I needed more time to think about it, and to plan out my next move. I was able to do that while you were with Maggie tonight."

Hearing her name reminded me of the danger we were in. My next words were loud and filled with panic. "Gunnar, I forgot to tell you. I blabbed to Maggie, and I think she might report me."

He tensed up. "What did you say. Tell me the exact words."

"My memory is a little blurry, I'm guessing that's from the beer, but I know it had something to with leaving Starkesend."

"Lizbeth, this is bad." He scoffed. "I wonder if the conniving witch was using alcohol to get to you. I wouldn't put it past a Helmstedt."

I lowered my head and spoke in a whisper. "She saved me too."

Gunnar titled his head, thrown off by what I'd said. "Tell me," He responded in a gentler tone, and I told him what happened.

"I got to the cemetery before Maggie, and instead of sitting around, I went to Klara's grave to work through a thing or two. That part of the evening was really nice. I hadn't visited her in a few days, and a lot has changed since then, so that meant I had plenty to tell my big sister. I keep an ear out for Maggie the whole time, but it wasn't until I'm finished talking to Klara that someone showed up—", I shuddered, "—but it was the last person I wanted to see." A wave of terror rolled up my spine as I recounted the next part. "Conroy was there, and he was drunk out of his mind, intent on having his way with me. He could barely speak or walk, but he cut across the graveyard faster than I thought possible." A whimper came out of my throat. "He was right there, Gunnar. The monster had hold of my ankle, and I could smell his rancid breath while he panted in lust" I closed my eyes, and images from the assault came rushing back. Conroy had been so close to getting what he'd wanted, but fate had intervened by sending a red-headed bottle-wielding savior to my rescue. Regardless of her reaction to my thoughts about Starkesend, I was grateful for her intervention. "That's when Maggie knocked him out cold." I stretched my lips into a vicious grin. "He might still be there, for all I know."

Gunnar sat silently as I recounted the details, his face cycling from curious to enraged to thrilled by the end. He closed the distance between us and pulled me into a hug. His lips moved against my hair while he spoke. "I'm sorry, Lizbeth. That's nothing that you or any other person should have to endure. Conroy is scum, the lowest of the low, and he deserves to be locked up as far away as possible." He paused. "I'm happy that Maggie was there to help you. If she wouldn't have pummeled him, you can bet that I'd be out there teaching him a lesson he'd might never recover from." He loosened his grip and found my eyes with his. "I hate to rush you, Lizbeth, because I know you've had a traumatic evening, but after you talked about leaving Starkesend, did Maggie say anything I should be aware of?"

I nodded. "She said she was going to give me tonight, for what I'm not sure, but that she would report me in the morning." Panic once again surged through my body. "That's why I ran into the house the way I did. We need to leave now, so they won't have the chance to capture us."

"I think you're right to worry." He picked up the papers on his desk and placed them back in their file. "Let's grab what we can, and then head to the lab."

"The lab?" I asked, not sure I'd heard him right.

"Yes." He'd turned to his cabinet and pulled out the contents, stacking the folders on the desktop. "There's something I need to do there before we take off. It's important. Vital really."

"Can I request a stop too?" He turned his attention from his task. "I want to get Ellis."

Gunnar shook his head. "Lizbeth, that's very honorable of you, but I have to protest." He returned to his sorting. "Ellis is six, and a child that age will slow us down. I'm not sure if you remember the journey here, since you were young when you made it, but it's long and arduous. Taking your brother with us would put us at a disadvantage."

"Gunnar, I refuse to leave with you unless Ellis comes along." I crossed my arms. "Come to think of it, if you say no, I'll go to my parent's house and do my best to convince everyone to leave with me. I bet we can find a safe haven on our own."

"Leon, your father, is my main contact in the village, Lizbeth. I met with him tonight, and he helped me decide on a course of action." He raised his eyebrows. "My guess is he wouldn't be too keen on us taking your brother."

"My parents knew about Klara? And you?" It was almost too much to believe.

"They were the ones who encouraged your sister to join the resistance." He waved me over. "Help me pack, and I'll tell you what I know."

This time, it was my turn to listen in silence. Gunnar told me about Clara's real name and age, and how hard my family had worked to prevent Ellis or me from learning about their shadow lives. Although my parents kept their true purpose in Starkesend obscured, they couldn't stand by and let their youngest children become products of their toxic environment. Mom and Dad did everything in their power to prevent this from happening. They used various resources to open our hearts and minds to a kinder way of life. The operas, books, and laughter I'd grown up with had been tools to counteract the propaganda Ellis and I were forced to consume. Luckily, their plan had succeeded. I hated to consider the alternative.

Gunnar informed me about his position in the movement. He'd joined three years ago, after Hitler became Chancellor of Germany. "I had to do something, Lizbeth. Doing nothing was never an option. That's not the kind of man I am." His mother had helped him secure a place in the resistance, and he'd worked to foil Starkesend since the day he'd stepped foot inside its boundaries. He and my father collected information about their respective areas—Gunnar reported on Project Leer and my dad provided details on the infrastructure and scope of Dorf. "When we talked tonight, I let Leon know what I'd found out, and he was just as horrified as I was. We agreed about moving on, that it was time for both of us to find another way to help." He glanced at me. "Although I should warn you, moving on won't be a simple task. Once you've been undercover, emerging becomes a hassle."

"I'm up for the challenge. I'll do anything to shake off the remnants of this place." He handed me the last file, and I tucked it into the rucksack he'd brought into the room. "What did you find out, Gunnar? Can you tell me?"

"I can, but it's not the easiest piece of information to digest. Are you sure you want to hear it?" He asked in concern.

"I do, Gunnar," I assured him. "Honestly, I want to hate this place as much as I possibly can. The more I learn about society, the more I despise it, and in the end, the sordid details will make it easier to break free." I gave him a piercing stare. "It's better to hear the particulars now. I'd rather get it over with then read about them in the news months or years later."

He chuckled. "If you ever decide to join the cause, I have a feeling that you'll be a valuable agent, ma'am." He tipped an imaginary hat. "Let's move to the kitchen. We can take as many supplies as we can. And while we're topping off our packs, I'll give you the gruesome details you asked for."

I glanced at the clock when we emerged from the office: 11:16. "Can we move faster, Gunnar? I'm worried Maggie won't stick to her word, and that she'll rat me out sooner than she said." I shivered. "It's just a feeling I have."

"We'll trust your gut, Lizbeth. Let's gather what we can from the cabinets, then get the hell out of here." He tossed his open rucksack on the counter and shoved cans inside. He talked as he loaded. "Since I started working in the lab, I've been on damage control. Dr. Brandt is the most depraved person I've ever encountered, and if he had been left to his own devices, Project Leer would have turned into a never-ending slaughterhouse. As it was, he killed two groups of patients—twenty men and women met their demise under his care. Luckily, I was able to talk some sense into him, and there haven't had any more deaths." He paused and closed his eyes for a moment. "Not to say there wasn't harm going on. As you know, the doctor still went overboard at times. Like he did with Marta. And Clara."

I touched Gunnar's hand, and he smiled in thanks. He shook off his remorse, then returned to his explanation. "The doctor stays in Germany most of the year. While he's gone, I keep things running smoothly by collecting a steady supply of adrenaline and cortisol, both substances that interest the Nazis. I balance their wants with what's good for my patients, and so far, there haven't been any complaints about the amount of fluid I send overseas." He maneuvered the contents of his bag, making room for more canned food. "When Dr. Brant is in Starkesend, he takes over the lab.

I've been able to contain his crueler urges…most of the time. This week, during his visit, Dr. Brandt was more insufferable than normal. He's been moody and impatient, and those are the attributes that make him more dangerous to his patients." He looked my way. "As soon as he arrived on base, I brought you up. It took hours to talk him out of performing your extraction, but that was something I stood firm on, and he finally bent to my will. After I won the argument, he got even worse" He sighed. "The man's like a child. He threw tantrums every day and broke several pieces of equipment when he flew into a rage. Today, just before he left for Germany, he confessed the reason behind his poor attitude."

"What was it Gunnar?" I asked, dreading his response.

His face was pinched as he brought the top of his rucksack down, snapping it in place. He stayed silent while he slung the pack over his shoulders, and while he walked to the nightstand next to his cot. Gunnar opened the bottom drawer to verify its contents. "Good. It's still here. Let's put this in your bag, Lizbeth. I'm out of room." I made my way over and held out my bag. He placed rags, kerosine, and matches inside the pouch, then stepped back so I could put it over my shoulders.

After I settled, he finally spoke. "Dr. Brandt is a climber—he does everything to gain rank and power, not caring who he steps on as he moves up the ladder. Lucky for him, Project Leer is a favorite of the Führer, which means he's a star at Nazi headquarters. Over the past two and a half years, the good doctor has taken the adrenaline and cortisol we harvest and given injections to Germany militiamen. He records their reaction to the chemicals and reports it to Hitler, who rains praise on physician." He shook his head. "But that glory wasn't enough for him. Dr. Brandt was jealous this week because another member of the Schutzstaffel, a woman no less, proposed an idea that intrigued Nazi leadership."

Gunnar stopped talking to scan the house. "I'm ready to leave. How about you, Lizbeth? Are you ready to head to the lab so I can destroy what I helped create?"

I nodded. "I'm ready. Let's do it."

"Okay. Stay low and hang to the walls of the house. We'll go around back and run to the edge of the woods. From that point, we'll head to Dame Hall and breach the lab through there." Gunnar headed for the front door, then paused. "I'll tell you more when we get to the trees. We need to stay quiet until we're more isolated."

"Sounds good."

He finished the trek to the entry and twisted the handle. Gunnar smiled before sending us off. "On your mark, get set, let's go." He opened the door and we raced away, careful to stay close to the building.

The cool air felt good on my cheeks as I ran faster than ever before. Girls were discouraged from sprinting in Starkesend, but I broke the rule with my brother often. We'd play tag, and he'd chase me around the field where the Frau Rennen ended, giggling in pure delight. I was happy that this joyful activity had prepared me for tonight's dash to the forest. It was fitting that defying society's expectations set me on the path for a successful escape.

Gunnar and I reached the edge of the woods and darted between the trees on the perimeter. When we got far enough into the forest, my husband slowed his pace to a jog. I followed suit and stepped beside him, only slightly out of breath. Gunnar gave me an appreciative nod. "You've got some speed!" He flashed a toothy grin. "You could definitely hold your own at PT."

I laughed. "You're darn tootin'." It had been a while since I used my muscles, and it felt good to move through the darkness. "Girls are forbidden to have fun here. I bet a lot of my classmates would have been good runners if they had the opportunity to try."

"You'll have a lot more freedom when we're far from Starkesend, Lizbeth." He eased his pace to a quick walk. "Let's slow down some. It won't take much longer to get to the lab, and I want to finish telling you about Dr. Brandt. I think I was explaining how he used the adrenaline and cortisol we harvested." He considered for a second, then nodded. "Yes, that's where I left off."

Gunnar lowered his voice, then resumed his account. "When the doctor was using the chemicals on the soldiers, I wasn't bothered one bit. These were the men who signed up to support Hitler and his campaign of hate, so it served them right to suffer through a shot or two." He hesitated for a moment, wanting to hold back but knowing that he had to finish. His whisper was filled with revulsion when he went on. "I got sick to my stomach when the doctor told me what they wanted to do next. One of the Nazis wants to use adrenaline on children—children, Lizbeth—and there's no way I can be part of something like that," he said with a catch in his throat. "They want to put it in their eyes, for God's sake. They think adrenaline can cure heterochromia, and they're going to inject it into little kids to see what happens." Gunnar's pace increased slightly, an unintentional response to the horror he felt. "I know that curing heterochromia isn't what's driving this sick venture. Having different colored eyes isn't a pressing medical issue, they're just using it for power. With them, it's always about power."

He scoffed. "The woman who suggested this research is treating it as a pet project. She read a study that used rabbits, and now she wants to inflict torture on children she's deemed disposable, just because she can." He almost choked on his anger. "Every person involved in the Nazi regime is a heartless coward. I hope the damage we're about to do sets them back a few years." He glanced my way and nodded. "Let's get to the lab and turn the doctor's playground into a pile of ashes."

Right as we resumed running, a shout rang out. "Stop. Traitors! Stop now." I recognized General Stillwell's voice. He was in a field outside the forest, surround by four others in a tight formation. They rushed toward us, moving through the grass in a coordinated attack.

Gunnar was calm, but firm. "Lizbeth, we have to split up. If we become two targets, they'll have to separate, and it will weaken the group." He arms and legs moved smoothly, his breaths came in an even cycle. I could tell my husband was used to acting under pressure. "I'll take care of the lab. All you need to worry about is reuniting with your family."

The voices pursuing us faded as we sprinted ahead. Unexpectedly, we passed into the traitor's cemetery, and a quick scan of the ground told me Conroy was no longer there. A flicker of terror threatened to overwhelm me, but I focused on Gunnar's words instead of folding under my fear. "I can't leave you. Don't you think we'll be better off together?" Gunnar took a sharp left, and I followed. Dame Hall was in front of us, but instead of heading to the building, we retreated deeper into the brush. I felt a stich forming in my side, and I hoped we would have the chance to slow soon.

"Clara's last request was about you, Lizbeth. She wanted me to watch over you, since she couldn't do it anymore. And that's what I'm doing here. I'm trying to do what's best for you." He darted under a tree branch, then turned right. I followed, barely keeping up. "I love you, Lizbeth. You remind me so much of Clara, and I'm happy we got to know each other better. But now, it's time to separate, and we can meet again on the other side." He took one last right turn, then slowed to a jog, and finally a stop. "We have to be quick." He took off his rucksack. "We need to trade bags."

"Why?"

"One, because I packed the kindling in your pack. Two, there are more supplies in my bag because they were heavier, but now it's more important for you to have them."

I lowered my backpack to the ground. "Okay. But I'm doing this under protest. I want to stay and help you."

Gunnar smiled. "I appreciate it, Lizbeth, but I still refuse the offer." He grabbed a stick and wrote in the dirt. "Memorize these details, then destroy the evidence before you depart." He pointed at his scrawl. "This is where you must travel. It's where your parents and brother will be waiting. It'll take about three days to reach on foot, but I have confidence that you'll make it with no issues." He wrote a few more words, then gave me a tender look.

"You're stronger than you think, Lizbeth. You'll be with your family in no time." He stood. "I have to go. You should be safe here for a few more minutes, but don't stay any longer than that." Gunnar held out his hand, and I gripped his palm with all my might. He beamed as he pulled me into a short embrace. "I'll meet you at the farm, Lizbeth. That's a promise." He released me, and I saw the tears on his cheeks. They matched the ones rolling down mine.

My husband gave me a salute, then took off running back toward Starkesend.

Clara, 1934

Chapter 34 - Clara

I liked to think I was tough. Afterall, I'd become a spy at the age of thirteen and had evaded detection or even suspicion for over seven years. Not many teenagers could pull this off, but I was lucky to have my mother's charm and wit, plus my father's calm in the face of danger. These attributes prepared me for living under the radar, and it was a place I thrived.

But nothing could have readied me for a confrontation with pure evil. Sure, I'd rubbed elbows with Nazis, or whatever the people of Starkesend fancied themselves, but I'd never encountered someone who took the worst characteristics a human can possess and proudly wore them on their sleeve. That is, until I ran into Dr. Brandt on a sunny Tuesday afternoon.

Who thinks one of the more boring days of the week can be the setting for a life-altering experience? I certainly didn't believe it before I ventured in search of my husband, bursting with joyous news, only to find tragedy instead. But I suppose that's one of the most devastating parts of misfortune—it can take even the most mundane circumstances and turn them into terrifying experiences you never recover from. At least that's what happened to me on that lovely Tuesday in May.

The day started out normal enough. First roll call, then duty stations, but right before lunch, I changed the direction of the afternoon. After a fake bout of nausea, Ms. Granth granted me an extended break. "Go rest for a spell, Clara. Quiet time in bed will be just the thing you need." She glanced at the toddlers, a rambunctious group who made me smile, but her grimace. "I can handle the little ones for a couple of hours. Thank goodness there are only four." She hastened to add, "Of course, the precious babes aren't a burden. They've just got more energy than me, and I'm feeling my age today."

"You can't be a day over twenty-five, Ms. Granth." I added a sickly-sweet smile, knowing she was a glutton for praise.

She blushed at the compliment. "My dear, I haven't seen my twenties in…well, let's just say it's been a very long time." She waved her hands at the me. "Off with you, now. Come back when you're feeling better."

"Thank you, Ms. Granth," I replied. But she had already moved on, heading toward the children who were growing impatient for their midday meal. I did my own retreating before she could change her mind, cutting a path to the door, then out into the sunshine.

The sun beams felt delicious, but I held tight to my bliss, knowing Mrs. Granth would be peering through the window. I had her trust, but one mishap could ruin the fragile faith that had taken weeks to cultivate. Having the coordinator in my corner was vital to my work. Plus, I liked lying to the witch. It gave me one of those dark jolts of satisfaction, the kind that thrummed through your body, leaving shivers on the inside. If Ms. Granth no longer trusted me, I wouldn't secretly break her confidence with every fib. That would make the lies less satisfying, and I'd hate to lose the guilty pleasure. So, I plodded for a good distance, hand on belly, wincing in pain, to cement the image of a sickly Clara in her mind.

Half-way to Dame Hall, I dropped the charade, and walked the way my mood demanded. The remaining distance was traveled with a light bounce, a nimble step, and a smile that matched the radiance of the day. The buoyancy stuck around as I entered the building and climbed onto the stage. It lasted as I descended into the lab and ambled down the main hall toward the inner chamber, and continued when I stepped into the main area, squinting my eyes at the room's bright austerity. The white walls and harsh lighting were a contrast to the dim corridor that led to the room, but my vision quickly adjusted to the change. After it did, I swept the perimeter, searching for signs of my husband.

The chamber lacked personality, which matched the work conducted within. Cold and sterile were adjectives that corresponded with both my surroundings and the procedures performed inside. And I couldn't forget the doctor in this comparison, for he was a mirror to his environment. From what Gunnar relayed to me, Dr. Brandt was a man more comfortable dissecting humans than having discussions with them. The two months I'd spent in Fort Vogel had been free of the doctor's presence, and it was my intent to avoid him for as long as I could. And as far as I remembered, he was in Germany, mingling with other snooty Nazis.

I took a final scan of the room, hoping to see my husband, but resigning myself to the fact that he wasn't around. When the empty space confirmed his absence, my mood dipped slightly, from euphoric to gleeful. I grabbed hold of the remaining happiness and encouraged the merrier parts of my body to rally in support. Thankfully my inner cheerleaders perked up, and I felt a boost of delight as I determined the next place to search for Gunnar. Home was the most logical location, so I began my trek there, ponytail swinging with every step.

"Can I help you?" a voice blared across the lab. I was near the hallway, so I ignored the question and pushed harder to reach the exit. The person, who I assumed was Dr. Brandt, didn't give up and lobbed a second and third inquiry my way. "You're not supposed to be here, you know? But since you are, why don't you stay for a while?"

I turned to face the doctor, whose waxy features and slicked back brown hair were exactly as I'd imagined. He was halfway across the room and decreasing the distance between us at a pace just shy of a jog. I addressed him before he got too close. "Hello, sir. Unfortunately, I must decline the invitation. I only came to find my husband, but he's not here, so I must be off." I whirled back around, trying to escape while I still had the chance.

"Nonsense, Clara." His voice was closer. "I've been looking forward to meeting the wife of my right-hand man. Sergeant Cruse has told me a lot about you, all of it wonderful," the last word was spoken right behind me.

I closed my eyes in resignation, then pivoted to confront the brute I wanted nothing to do with. "Oh, has he? I'm happy to hear it." I curtsied in greeting. "You must be the world-renowned Dr. Brandt. A pleasure to meet you." I was proud of myself for not choking on the words.

"Ah, my dear. The pleasure is all mine." He scanned me from the ground up. "You have beautiful hair, Clara. Do brown curls run in your family?"

His compliment was cloaked in suspicion. I answered with caution, knowing that he was fishing for hints of my background. "Just me and my mother. My sister and brother were lucky enough to take after my father. They have beautiful blond tresses." I grinned. "The sergeant and I hope our children take after my dad, too. And him of course. Gunnar's as blond as they come."

"It would be an honor to pass on the Aryan traits that our Führer is so fond of. I wish you luck as you expand your family." He cocked his head. "Have you and Sergeant Cruse discussed his job? He performs essential duties that help the Fatherland, here and overseas."

Gunnar and I spent many evenings speaking about that very thing, but I knew the doctor didn't want the truth. He wanted a vessel he could fill with his accomplishments. I went ahead and played the expected role. "Oh, golly no. My husband keeps to himself about work. He knows I wouldn't understand it, so he tries not to burden me with a lot of heavy information." I ended with a giggle and a grin.

"Young lady, you're in luck. I arrived on base this morning, and I'm eager to get my hands dirty." The doctor moved his eyelid in a grotesque attempt at a wink. "I mean that in a respectable way, of course."

I placed a hand on my chest, feigning astonishment. "Dr. Brandt, I would never assume you had anything but honorable intentions. A man of your status is always on the right path."

"You assume true, Mrs. Cruse." He swept a hand toward the middle of the room. "Please, join me. I have time for a quick extraction, and I know it would please your husband if he knew how much his wife supported his work."

"I wish I could accept, doctor, I really do, but duty calls. Ms. Granth is expecting me back any minute now, and I'd hate to leave her waiting."

"She'll understand." He came close and placed a palm under my elbow. "Let's see if we can encourage an ounce or two out of you, Clara dear. Sergeant Cruse will be delighted at your contribution." His grasp tightened, and he led me to the empty hospital bed in the center of the chamber.

Gunnar had told me about extractions. They sounded brutal, and entirely too intimate of an experience to share with Dr. Brandt. An image of him exploring my innards flashed in my mind, and the earlier lie about nausea almost became a reality. I tried again to get out of the situation. "Sir, I must leave. I'm expected elsewhere, and punctuality is one of Ms. Granth's sticking points."

"Clara, I see how this may appear abrupt and frightening, but just pretend that it's your husband performing the operation, and it will be over before you know it." His eerie grin stretched from ear to ear. "It's been months since I've done an extraction, and I've never performed one on someone as lovely as you."

The excitement in his voice repelled me, but his grip drew me closer and into the waiting chair. He forced me to lay face down, and as my vision was obstructed by crisp white sheets, my trickle of panic turned into a river. Two clanks rang out as the doctor closed the thick leather arm restraints. The disturbance bounced around the room like a frightened rabbit, eventually fading from earshot, but embedding itself into memory. I braced myself for pain by squeezing my eyes shut and digging my nails into the arm rests. I wasn't prepared for his touch, though. My nerves revolted while he cut a hole in my dress, then placed two fingers on the skin in the middle of my back. He pushed on the area, testing it for firmness, and horror gnawed a path up from my stomach to my heart and brain.

"You'll feel some pressure." Dr. Brandt remarked nonchalantly. As he said the warning, something hard and cold pierced under my ribs. My body screamed as the rigid spike penetrated, but I refused to give voice to the terror. Even in a haze, I sensed that displays of discomfort would please the doctor, and providing any sort of benefit to the beastly man was the last thing I wanted to do.

Clenching my teeth provided only slight relief, so instead, I retreated into my mind, seeking comfort in the confines of the known. I recalled happy snatches—glimpses of my family and husband, small wins against society, hikes inside the forest—but it wasn't enough. I had to dig further, past the memories of people and actions, to find what I needed. I stumbled upon it when I recalled a small cedar box. Inside, was the music my husband cherished, faded notes penned on yellowing pages. He'd given me the gift before our Joining, and it was the most precious keepsake I owned. In my free time, I'd rewritten the composition, hoping to play the piece when Gunnar and I finished our business in Starkesend.

The music called to me, then lulled me into a twilight state. Notes played in my head, and I focused on the melody and the mood of the song, a dark yet uplifting cloak of sound. I looped through *Silken Summit* while the doctor hacked away. The trauma happening to my body was still there, but it had dulled to a bearable level.

"What's going on here?" The words were muffled, like they were traveling through water. "Oh my God, what have you done?" The voice was closer, almost recognizable. "Clara, come back to me." I felt a gentle back and forth motion on my shoulder, but I remained in the dream realm. "Clara, sweetheart, it's time to wake up." The shaking became more persistent. I was annoyed at first, but when I perceived who was doing the jostling, I quickly came to.

"Gunnar! You're here." The pain hit after the words came out. I held my stomach with my newly freed hands, afraid of what the stabbing cramps meant. "We have to go home," I stammered.

He nodded and picked me up, cradling me against his chest. Gunnar turned to the doctor. "We'll talk when I get back. This is unforgiveable."

I saw the doctor's face glowing with perverse satisfaction right before the world went black.

∞∞∞

By the time I opened my eyes, Tuesday afternoon had turned into Tuesday evening. The warm aroma of dinner slipped through the open bedroom door and welcomed me from my slumber. A rumpled divot at the foot of the bed told me that Gunnar had only recently ventured into the kitchen. I smiled at his vigilance. He was a good man. Unlike the one who'd put his hands on me today.

I lifted the blanket to examine the lower half of my body. Layers of white towels rested underneath me, and the ruby stains atop them stood out against the bright canvas. I stared at the blotches, letting tears spill over my lashes and down my cheeks. This was the conformation I'd been dreading. In the lab, I'd known something was wrong, but seeing the evidence of this insight was crushing.

"Hey there. I just took dinner off the stove. How are you feeling?" Gunnar asked gently. I turned my head toward the doorway, unashamed to show my devastation to the man I loved. When he saw my tears, he frowned. "Oh, Clara." He rushed to my side, sweeping me into his arms as he lowered himself to the bed. He smoothed my hair, and rubbed my back, careful to avoid the wound from my extraction.

We stayed that way for a while. I gathered strength as he held me, preparing myself for the words I'd soon have to form. Eventually I was ready. Or as close to ready as I would get. I untangled my limbs from his and leaned back against the pillows. "There was a reason I tried to find you today." My voice trembled, but I continued through the quivers. "Before meeting you, work was the only thing I looked forward to, besides my family. I loved the challenge of infiltrating and destroying Starkesend. It kept me going in this godforsaken place, where there's so little joy. After we met, and then Joined, I was as happy as I'd ever been. At least until this morning." I held out my hand, and Gunnar took it in his. "I was ecstatic today because of something that didn't happen." He raised his eyebrows. "My monthlies have been due for seven weeks now, and when they didn't show up today, I knew it was time to share the news. I didn't want to say anything before, because it was too early to be sure, but Gunnar, I'm pregnant." A howling cry burst from my throat, containing bits of the anguish that flowed through my entire body. I waited until I calmed to continue. "Or I was pregnant, before the extraction." I spit out the last word, hating the feel of it on my lips.

Gunnar pulled me in tight, and we stayed as one for as long as he needed. I felt his shudders, heard his sobs, and sensed the weight of his sadness. When his words finally came, they were heavy with remorse. "If I'm in this much pain, I can only imagine how much you're hurting right now. I'm sorry, Clara." He hung his head. "I know you'll tell me it wasn't my fault, but I failed in my duty as your husband—I wasn't around when you needed me the most." He glanced up, smiling sweetly. "You are the last person on this earth who needs protecting. You're my spirited, smart, sensational wife, who can do damn well what she pleases, thank you very much." His smile faded. "But still, I failed to be there when my presence would have been the biggest deterrent of all."

This time, it was me who pulled him close. We sat together in our grief, silent except for the occasional sob. Sometime before sunrise we fell asleep, each of us emotionally spent.

∞∞∞

It took time, but I healed, physically and mentally. And what's more, I became pregnant again. Gunnar and I delighted at the news but kept it to ourselves. Fortunately, I was very good at hiding things, and this secret was no different. The biggest help was my wardrobe. I altered frocks to hide my growing belly, and no one seemed to be the wiser. It was one of the benefits of being a woman in Starkesend—no one really paid me much attention as long as I did my work and kept my husband happy.

I'd been able to convince Gunnar not to assault Dr. Brandt after the forced extraction. I appealed to his sense of compassion, not for the doctor, but for the mission we were undertaking. I reminded him of the people who depended on us, and he reluctantly agreed with my reasoning. He did have a talk with the creep but kept it to words and didn't escalate to violence.

Life continued without issue. Gunnar gathered intelligence on the lab, and I collected info about the lady's portion of society. We reported to my dad and Etta, and they passed it up the chain, to the important decision makers. I kept my eyes and ears pealed for anything exciting, but Starkesend was very ho hum throughout my pregnancy, a fact I was grateful for.

As I entered the last trimester, I began scaling back effort. It wasn't enough to attract the attention of Ms. Granth or any of the other wives, but it allowed me a small bit of breathing room, and I didn't come home exhausted every evening. Like the gem that he was, Gunnar took over the cooking and cleaning chores, and my only responsibility was the wee one inside me.

In the middle of my seventh month, I decided to plan a picnic for Gunnar, on our first anniversary. We'd soon welcome a third member to our family, and even though I was excited about the addition, it would still alter the dynamic I currently shared with my husband. A moonlit meal was a way to celebrate our marriage and spend time together before we became Mom and Dad, in addition to Clara and Gunnar.

I was able to gather materials on the sly, with help from the gals in the dining hall. They were delighted when I told them about preparing my husband's favorite meal, although I left the picnic part out. I stored the supplies in the mess hall until a night Gunnar worked longer than normal. He let me know he'd be late over breakfast, and I set my scheme in motion after my shift. I snuck the ingredients home and prepared the pot pie, grinning with excitement while I cooked.

Everything was ready and waiting when I heard a knock on the door. A glance at the clock told me it was 1922, an odd time for visitors, so I was curious as I approached the entry and swung open the door. Ms. Granth was waiting on the stoop, and when she stepped to the left, I saw that she'd brought Dr. Brandt with her. Both had eerie smiles plastered on their faces. "Hello dear. We're sorry to bother you at this hour, but there's been an emergency in the lab, and we need your help to sort it out."

I felt the blood drain from my face. "Did something happen to Gunnar?"

The doctor shook his head. "No, no, he's perfectly fine. In fact, I sent him to town this morning for bandages and vials." He checked his watch. "He should be back in an hour or so. Which leaves us plenty of time to address the emergency Ms. Granth is referring to."

There was no way I was heading off with the pair, but I needed to put space between us before I was able to escape. "Can you give me a few moments? I was just finishing dinner preparations when you knocked. Let me turn off the stove and grab my coat." I rubbed my hands up and down my arms. "It's chillier out here than I expected."

Ms. Granth smiled. "Hurry up, dear. We'll wait for you on the porch."

I calmly closed the door until just a crack remained. The gap would be enough to convince my visitors I had nothing to hide, but it would also cover me as I made my next move. A window in the baby's room faced the forest, and I headed there, low and fast. It was open—I'd been hot when I'd gotten home for the day—which meant the creaking frame wouldn't draw attention to my whereabouts. There was a chest near the crib, and I pushed it under the window, grateful the container was only half-full. As soon as the trunk was in place, I climbed on top and shimmied into the outside air. My belly rubbed against the frame as I exited, but there was no time to assess the damage. I was fleeing for my life.

My training had prepared me for emergencies, and I worked out my plan as I ran among the trees. There was a place that Gunnar and I used for our meetings with Etta, a clearing just outside Starkesend's boundary. I headed there and waited for my husband. Although there hadn't been time to place my note on the counter, I knew he'd travel to the glen when he found the house empty and an abandoned picnic basket on the table. For now, I'd lie down and try to calm myself. The evening's excitement was agitating the baby—they kicked and turned ceaselessly as I'd sprinted through the woods—and I wanted to reduce any stress the little one might be feeling. I closed my eyes, and drifted into the zone between sleep and awareness, keeping my ears open for rustling, while shielding my mind from the chaos.

It worked. By the time Gunnar arrived, eyes wide with terror, the baby had quieted, and I had come up with a plan. He rushed to where I was sprawled and crushed me against his chest. "I was so worried about you, Clara. What happened?"

"There's no time to explain. What we need to talk about is getting me out of here."

"What do you mean?"

"Gunnar, my love, I'm in danger, and the only thing that will stop that danger from destroying me, is to get out of Starkesend."

He gripped me harder. "What needs to happen?"

I outlined my idea. He would report me missing, and a search would ensue. While the search went on, he'd work with his mother to obtain a body that was close to my size. He'd plant it in the woods, and would stumble upon the corpse days later, when the features were unrecognizable, and easier to pass off as mine. Gunnar would suggest a story to General Stillwell and Ms. Granth, one that they would eat up. He'd proclaim his unyielding support for society and offer to take credit for my slaying. The tale could serve as a warning for future escapees, and he would gain the image of a man who was not to be messed with.

My "death" would make him a Starkesend hero, the perfect cover.

There were tears streaming down his cheeks by the time I finished. "And where will you go?" he asked, his voice contained the aching pieces of his heart.

"To Ma Josephine's house, of course." I grabbed his hand and squeezed with all my might. "I know you don't want me to leave Gunnar, but this is for the best. The baby and I will be better off at the farm, and you can continue doing important work until we decide to pull you from the mission."

I raised his hand to my lips, gently kissing the knuckles between words. "You'll be with me before you know it. And then we can bring our little family to the piece of land you have out in the country."

I fixed him with a serious glare. "But for now, you have to fight against the evil that's growing, for my mother and her kin, and for the rest of the people who have no idea what's coming for them." I smiled while warm tears rolled down my cheeks. "And protect my sister too. You know what to do if there's another Frau Rennen. Don't worry, I won't be mad if you take another wife."

"You're the best thing in my life, Clara." He brought me in for one last kiss, and I cherished the remaining seconds I had in his arms. After we separated, he took a deep breath, steeling himself for what needed to happen. "Let's get you to the closest path out of here, and then I'll head back to base. It's time to get this charade started."

Lizbeth, 1936

Chapter 35 – Lizbeth: The Farm

The weeks of travel were rough, but bearable, and I was happy to be surrounded by family during the journey. My parents dropped all pretenses on the trek, and they answered questions without hesitation. They were relieved to be rid of their secrets, and I was relieved to understand the truth. When they told me Clara was alive, I cycled through disbelief at the news, devastation at the secret, and finally elation at the reality. I would see my sister again, in a matter of days.

Ellis was a bright spot on the trip. He'd taken the news of leaving Starkesend without complaint, and he chattered and laughed as we walked down roads, across fields, and around rougher terrain. Dad knew the way to Tavern City, and he guided us without hesitation. After fifty-three days, we reached our destination—a well-maintained clapboard home nestled in a sun-drenched valley. Despite my family's weariness, we all picked up speed when we saw the house and hustled until we made it to the front porch.

It's difficult to describe the joy I felt when we reached the farm. This place marked the beginning of my new life, one free from hate and oppression. I couldn't wait to reconnect with Clara and then get out into the world, experiencing it for the first time in more than a decade. The possibilities were almost endless.

Dad knocked on the door, then stepped back to wait for a response. The sound of giggling came from inside, high-pitched squeals of delight that made the four of us smile. A little one was in the house, and from the patter of their footsteps, it sounded like they were running to greet us. Muffled words rang out. "Sophie, wait for Mommy."

My breath caught in my throat. It was Clara's voice, but she wasn't a mother. I snapped my head to see my parent's reaction, and I could tell they were having the same thought. The voice called out a second time, again full of the exasperation and love that defines parenthood. "Okay, little miss. Let's see who's visiting." The door swung open, and Clara emerged with a chubby-cheeked toddler on her hip.

The joy of arriving at the farm was eclipsed by the bliss of seeing my sister again. We all rushed to her, shedding tears and shouting greetings. When the initial burst of excitement was over, Clara introduced us to her daughter, Sophie Jo. Fresh tears poured out as we took turns cuddling the sweet girl. Eventually, she got tired of being held, and her and Ellis chased each other across the front yard.

Gunnar's mom, Jo, joined us after a bit. She brought lemonade and sandwiches, and we ate while the children ran on the grass. Clara talked about the year she'd been gone and apologized for keeping us in the dark. She grinned when I told her about Gunnar. "He'll be here soon, I just know it." Clara laughed. "And don't worry Lizbeth, you don't have to stay married to him."

"Thank goodness. Not that he was a terrible husband, I just want to find someone on my own." I glanced at my parents. "I plan on taking my time, though."

When night fell, we retreated inside, and I helped Jo prepare dinner while the other adults stayed with the children. As we chopped and baked, I learned a lot about Gunnar's mom. She regaled me with stories from her youth and about her activities within the Resistance. She also asked about my time in Starkesend. Jo shook her head when I finished explaining. "You, your family, my boy—you all did important work in that horrid place. I know it doesn't feel like it now, but one day, you'll wake up and understand just how brave you were, and how much good you accomplished during your years there. I'm proud of you, Lizbeth."

Later, the seven of us sat around the table, eating roast and potatoes while we talked and laughed. We savored the meal and each other's company. Food tasted extra delicious after a long journey, especially when you were surrounded by wonderful people. Mom, Dad, and Clara cleaned up, and Jo put the two little ones to bed. I walked around the parlor, exploring the space where Gunnar had grown up.

"It's beautiful here, right?"

I turned to my sister. "It really is." I gestured to the piano. "Have you taken it up again? I vaguely remember you playing, but it was so long ago."

Clara nodded. "I have. Mama Jo is a wonderful teacher." She walked to the instrument and pulled out the bench. "Would you like me to play something?"

"I would love that."

"Okay. This is a piece you'll recognize." Clara smiled. "I think it helped us both at different times." She sat, and after getting situated, dove into the music.

Clara was right. After a few bars, I recognized the tune as the one Gunnar had hummed in the lab. The beautiful notes filled my senses with an aching beauty, as they'd done before. Surprisingly, I didn't associate pain or hate with the concerto, only strength and love. It was just like the place I was standing in now—there was so much warmth and happiness between the walls. I perused the room, taking in my sister and the portraits of Gunnar as a child, and I felt peace settle over my body. After only a few hours, the farm felt like home. It was nice, comforting, and unlike anything I'd experienced in Starkesend.

I gave into the feeling, and made my way to the sofa, letting the music wash over me as I sat. Thoughts flooded my brain as I listened to the melody.

I was proud of my sister, my parents, and Gunnar. They'd selected a difficult path, one that required great sacrifice and discipline, but they'd come out on top. Instead of doing nothing about the problems they saw in the world, they'd strapped on armor and charged directly into the fray. Maybe I would join them in the quest against evil. One day.

For now, I had simpler things to do. I leaned my head back and gave into the piano's allure. The tap, tap, tap of the keys would certainly change my life for the better.

Instead of Doing Nothing, 2025

Thank you, readers!

Instead of Doing Nothing had a few sources of inspiration. The first happened many years ago, during an NYC Midnight writing contest. I was given three prompts:

Genre – Drama
Item - A box of chocolate
Location – The finish line of a marathon

With these prompts I had to write a 1,000-word story in two or three days—I can't recall the exact timeframe. It was short, that's all I remember. From this challenge, came what would turn into the opening two chapters of this novel. If you go back and reread, you'll see the box of chocolates and marathon finish line right away.

Over time, those 1,000 words stuck in my head, and I knew I wanted to expand on them. I've always loved dystopian novels, and since my short story fit into that genre, I decided to go with it.

When I learned about the legend of Murphy Ranch in Los Angeles, California, I knew I had the perfect location for my book. According to rumors, Murphy Ranch was supposed to be the Nazi launchpad in the United States, and when it was raided by the FBI in 1941, 50 Nazi collaborators were arrested. There is no proof of raid, and relatives have spoken out against this urban legend.

Regardless, the rumors were darkly fascinating, and I wondered *what if?* The idea of a Nazi stronghold in the U.S. was horrifying and I wanted to write a story as if it had taken place.

Enter Starkesend, the setting for *Instead of Doing Nothing*. This isolated community, which I imagine to be in the Pacific Northwest near the Canadian border, tries to be what the legend of Murphy Ranch aspired to—a village that fostered hatred, and did its darndest to spread it.

Now for the bright side of this story. During my research, I came across Leon Lewis, a Jewish lawyer who fought against Naziism by running a spy ring in Los Angeles. Lewis was a hero, and he inspired several characters in this book, mainly Gunnar and Clara. The courage Lewis had was mind-blowing. I'm in awe that he risked his life to combat the rising tide of hatred.

And that's the main inspiration for this book. When we are confronted with the bad and the unjust, there's no excuse for letting it go unchecked. You should do something, anything, instead of doing nothing. The world would be a better place if we all acted this way.

Thank you for reading. It really means a lot :)
-Leigh

Check out *Tour Wives,*

Leigh's rock and roll mystery thriller with a twist!

https://www.leigh-foley.com/